Acclaim for the
Psychic Eye Mystery Series

"A great new series . . . plenty of action!"
—*Midwest Book Review*

"An invigorating entry into the cozy mystery realm. . . . I cannot wait for the next book."
—Roundtable Reviews

"Well written and unpredictable. Everything about this book is highly original . . . a fun protagonist with just enough bravado to keep her going."
—*Romantic Times*

"The characters are all realistically drawn and the situations go from interesting, to amusing, to laugh-out-loud funny. The best thing a person can do to while away the cold winter is to cuddle up in front of a fire with this wonderful book."
—The Best Reviews

"A fresh, exciting addition to the amateur sleuth genre." —J. A. Konrath, author of *Dirty Martini*

"A fun, light read, and a promising beginning to an original series."
—The Romance Readers Connection

"Victoria Laurie has crafted a fantastic tale in this latest Psychic Eye Mystery. There are few things in life that upset Abby Cooper, but ghosts and her parents feature high on her list. . . . [A] few real frights and a lot of laughs." —Fresh Fiction

Also by Victoria Laurie

Psychic Eye Mysteries

Ghost Hunter Mysteries

DEATH
PERCEPTION

A Psychic Eye Mystery

Victoria Laurie

AN OBSIDIAN MYSTERY

OBSIDIAN
Published by New American Library, a division of
Penguin Group (USA) Inc., 375 Hudson Street,
New York, New York 10014, USA
Penguin Group (Canada), 90 Eglinton Avenue East, Suite 700, Toronto,
Ontario M4P 2Y3, Canada (a division of Pearson Penguin Canada Inc.)
Penguin Books Ltd., 80 Strand, London WC2R 0RL, England
Penguin Ireland, 25 St. Stephen's Green, Dublin 2,
Ireland (a division of Penguin Books Ltd.)
Penguin Group (Australia), 250 Camberwell Road, Camberwell, Victoria 3124,
Australia (a division of Pearson Australia Group Pty. Ltd.)
Penguin Books India Pvt. Ltd., 11 Community Centre, Panchsheel Park,
New Delhi - 110 017, India
Penguin Group (NZ), 67 Apollo Drive, Rosedale, North Shore 0632,
New Zealand (a division of Pearson New Zealand Ltd.)
Penguin Books (South Africa) (Pty.) Ltd., 24 Sturdee Avenue,
Rosebank, Johannesburg 2196, South Africa

Penguin Books Ltd., Registered Offices:
80 Strand, London WC2R 0RL, England

First published by Obsidian, an imprint of New American Library,
a division of Penguin Group (USA) Inc.

First Printing, September 2008
10 9 8 7 6 5 4 3 2

*For Nora Brosseau,
the most hilarious woman I know
and a dear, dear friend* ☺

Acknowledgments

For my fortieth birthday, I was invited out to party it up in Las Vegas. And going was an absolute no-brainer—I mean, what better way to ring in the big *four-ohmigod!* than Vegas?

So I went, I saw, and I came home *completely* inspired to write the next Abby adventure set in Vegas. Therefore, if you read this book and enjoy it, toss a hand wave out to my dear friend Jim, who talked a grumpy 39.99999-year-old into taking on Sin City. I'd divulge more about that trip but, folks, what happens there stays there for a reason! ☺

Special thanks go out to Kristen Weber, editor extraordinaire, and Michele Alpern, copy editor extraordinaire, along with the world's best literary agent, Jim McCarthy, who keeps me laughing and fully employed, and of course my dear friends Karen Ditmars, Leanne Tierney, Maureen Febo, Suzanne Parsons, Debbie Huntley; my amazing Web master, Jaa Nawtaisong; Laurie Proux, Janice Murray, Pippa Terry and her delightful mumsy, Betty Stocking; Ellen George (who has *always* been kind to me); Silas and Nicole Hudson; my writing buddy, Catherine Morris; Rebecca and Brian Rosen,

Molly Boyle—and her mom!—and, of course, the woman responsible for opening the door in the first place—Martha Bushko.

Additional thanks and love go out to my family, John and Naoko Upham, Mary Jane Humphreys, and Elizabeth Laurie. Hugs and kisses to all of you!

Finally, very special thanks are in order for Nora and Bob Brosseau and their wonderful brood, who have provided such fabulous inspiration. Thank you, Nora, Bob, Liz, Katie, Michael, and Nicky; the world would be a better place if everyone's family were as terrific as yours.

Chapter One

Death has an energy.

It is thick as sludge, heavy as iron, and pulls you down into yourself like an imploding building. And as I sat across from the concerned mother of a very sick young woman, it was the last thing I wanted to feel. "Please tell me my daughter will make it through this," she whispered, her voice filled with fear. She'd obviously read the look on my face after she'd asked about her daughter.

I had two choices here. I could tell her the truth or I could avoid telling her that her daughter had no hope— no chance at all. I looked up, prepared to meet those pleading eyes and be straight with her, but when I did . . .

I.

Just.

Couldn't.

"Marion," I said gently, "the energy I'm feeling here isn't good." A tear slid down Marion's cheek, yet her eyes remained fixed on mine, unblinking and welling with moisture. "I believe you and the doctors are doing absolutely everything you can to save her," I added. "And I don't think there is one thing more you can do to change the outcome. I believe you have done everything humanly possible to help your daughter fight for her life, and if she survives, it will be because of all the efforts you've already offered her. The rest is up to her and God."

Marion made a soft sound as she swallowed a sob, and I fought to hold my own emotions in check. "I can't lose her," she said. "She's my only daughter, Abby. How can I go on without her?"

I swallowed hard and took a breath. Breaking down in front of this woman would not help her. In fact, it would only add to her fear. "I know you're scared out of your mind right now, but your daughter needs you to be okay with whatever her outcome is. She needs to know that if she loses the battle against her cancer, you'll be able to go on. That's the one gift you have left to give her, Marion. The one thing you can still do is reassure her that you're strong enough to live your life to the fullest—even if she's not around."

Marion buried her face in her hands, and I reached forward to rub her shoulder. "It's my fault," she sobbed. "It's all my fault!"

"How could this possibly be your fault?" I asked.

Marion's body shuddered while she tried to pull herself together. "April called me from college. She said she found a lump on the side of her neck. She said it was about the size of a bean. I told her that it was probably a cyst. I had them when I was her age and didn't think anything of it. I told her that if the lump was still there when the semester ended, we'd get it checked out. The cancer had eight weeks to spread to the rest of her lymph nodes."

I bit my lip. Oh, man, that was rough. "Marion," I whispered, "my crew is saying there was no way you could have known. You *didn't* cause this, and even if you'd rushed her to a doctor right away, the end results would likely have been the same." I had no idea if this was actually true, but at this point the only thing I could do for this woman was allow her the chance to forgive herself. Marion lifted her chin and stared me in the eyes, and I willed myself to look back without blinking. "It wasn't your fault, sweetheart," I said firmly. "You *couldn't* have known."

She nodded, and that's when the bell that was my appointment timer gave a small *ting!* We were out of time. Marion stood, and I handed her several tissues to go with the one in her hand. "You're very kind," she said as she took the tissues.

"And you're very brave," I replied, leaning in to give her a long, hard hug. "Now go and be with your daughter," I said, stepping back. "I'll keep April in my thoughts and prayers, and you call me anytime you need someone to talk to, okay?"

Marion sniffled and handed me some bills. "I will," she said hoarsely.

After she'd gone, I went into my office, which was adjacent to my reading room, and sat down heavily. Turning my chair to the window, I put my feet up on the sill, leaned my head back, and let the tears flow.

Sometimes my job sucked.

"Hey," said a voice behind me.

I wiped my eyes before swiveling my chair around, and looked up at my suitemate and friend, Candice Fusco, standing just outside the door. "Hey," I replied, my voice shaky.

"You okay?"

I inhaled deeply and again wiped at my cheeks. "Tough session."

Candice came into the room and sat down on the other side of my desk. "Feel like sharing?"

I attempted a smile. "Just the psychic blues. I'll be okay."

Candice gave me a sympathetic look. "Must be hard to see what you see sometimes, huh?"

I cleared my throat. "Can be. Is that a file you need me to look at?" I asked, changing the subject and pointing at the folder in her lap. Candice and I had formed a partnership around her private-investigation business, combining her highly honed investigative skills with my natural intuitive talents. The results had been fantastic, and Candice's business was now booming.

She nodded. "It's our latest assignment. Family of a missing person wants to see if we can hunt down their father. He's in his seventies with severe Alzheimer's and he wandered away from his nursing home a month ago. No one has seen him since."

I frowned at the immediate sinking feeling I got as I gazed at the folder in Candice's hand, and I knew I didn't want to look into it right now. I'd seen enough tragedy for one day, and I didn't think I could tune in on another family about to be torn apart by the worst-case scenario. "Any chance it can wait?"

Candice smiled. "Of course. I told the family we were pretty stacked with cases right now, and I'm not supposed to get back to them until late next week, so whenever you feel up to it is cool. Anyway, you look like shit—why don't you go home to that hunka-hunka-burnin' love and have him take your mind off things?"

That got a genuine smile out of me. "Thanks for understanding," I said, standing up. "I'll see you at the gym bright and early, okay?" Candice and I were also workout buddies.

"Sounds good. You hang in there, Abs."

I left my office, which sits in an old but charming building in the heart of downtown Royal Oak, Michigan, and stopped at the liquor store, where I picked up a bottle of wine—okay, two bottles of wine—and hurried home.

Dutch and I had taken a big step in our relationship

when we'd moved in together a few months earlier. The transition had gone surprisingly well, and we'd settled into a nice, comfortable rhythm together.

With relief I noticed Dutch's SUV parked in the driveway, but then I noticed the beat-up blue pickup parked at the curb. My handyman and other business partner, Dave McKenzie, was also in attendance. *Damn*, I thought. I was really hoping it would be just my honey and me.

As I breezed through the door, I was greeted by the smell of fresh-baking bread and a roast in the oven. My boyfriend can *hang* in the kitchen—hence, the reason Dave was taking so long to finish the addition he'd started three months ago: He kept getting invited to dinner. "Abs?" Dutch called when he heard the door open.

"Hey, babe," I said as I flopped wearily on the couch, where I was immediately pounced on by my dog, Eggy, and Dutch's new puppy, Tuttle, who kissed and wriggled and fought each other for my attention.

Dutch poked his head out of the doorway of the kitchen and took one look at my face. "You okay?"

I nodded. "Yeah. Just a really long day."

Dutch brightened. "Your practice is back up and kickin', huh?" My professional-psychic practice had suffered greatly when I'd had to take a three-month hiatus to recover from a bullet wound I'd gotten earlier that year.

I nodded again. "It's good to be earning my own keep again."

"Dinner will be on the table in two minutes. Can you let Dave know?"

I gave him a level look. "Ah, yes, our foster child. I'll let him know."

Dutch grinned. "He's bound to be done sometime, Edgar," he said, using his nickname for me, after the famed psychic Edgar Cayce.

"Oh, trust me, if anyone can milk the clock, it's Dave." I pushed up off the couch and trudged to the stairwell.

"Be nice," Dutch called after me.

I headed up to the bedroom and found Dave on a ladder with the world's smallest paintbrush. I rolled my eyes again and cleared my throat to get his attention.

"Hey, Abby," he said as he swiveled around. "How was your day?"

"Productive," I said to him. "I got *so* much done!"

"Good for you," he said, turning back to paint the wall with itty-bitty strokes.

I scowled. He'd missed the hint. "Wouldn't that go on better with a roller?"

Dave swiveled back to me again. "Yeah, but you don't get the great texture results that you get with a brush. Trust me, when this is finished, you'll appreciate the attention to detail."

"*When* being the operative word here," I said with a grin.

"True craftsmanship takes time," Dave said, and took a whiff. "Dinner smells like it's about ready."

"You mean you can smell something other than paint fumes?"

Dave smiled. "This snout smells all," he said, pointing to his slightly oversized nose.

"Yes, Dave, dinner is ready. Put the paintbrush down and come to the table."

Dave nodded and I headed back downstairs. As I walked into the kitchen, Dutch handed me a glass of the wine I'd brought home, "Here," he said. "It'll take that edge off."

I smiled happily and leaned in to wrap my arms around him. "You're a really great boyfriend, you know?"

"So you need to keep telling me."

I laughed and sat down at the table. A moment later

Dave joined us, and Dutch handed out plates of food piled high with roast beef, mashed potatoes, green beans, and fresh bread. "Man!" Dave said as he ogled his plate. "All my old lady ever serves up are TV dinners!"

I gave Dutch a pointed look that said, "See? *This* is why he won't go home!"

Dutch hid a smile and pulled out from under his chair something wrapped in plain pink paper with a matching bow. "Here," he said, passing it to me.

"What's this?" I asked, my mood lifting.

"For you," he said. "Open it."

"Is it your birthday?" Dave said with a note of panic and a mouth stuffed with food. " 'Cuz no one told me!"

"It's not my birthday," I said to him, eyeing Dutch quizzically. "And it's not our anniversary. . . ."

"It's a 'just because' present," Dutch said. "Now open it."

I ripped off the paper and realized it was a book. Turning it over, I read the title. *"Cooking for Dummies,"* I said, all the joy leaving me.

"Yeah!" Dutch said with enthusiasm. "You know how you're always telling me you wish you could cook?"

I scowled at him, because—for the record—I was *not* always telling him I wished I could cook. This was Dutch's not-so-subtle attempt to domesticate me, something I fought him on tooth and nail. "Ah," I said, a flicker of anger in my voice. "So, all the copies of *Cooking for Absolute Idiots* were sold out?"

Dutch sighed. "Edgar," he began.

I flipped open the book and pretended to read. "Oh! Here's something I can handle! Quick dinner suggestions: First, remove outer plastic wrapping from popcorn package. . . ."

"Opened up a can of worms there, buddy," Dave mumbled to Dutch.

"Abby," Dutch tried again. "I didn't mean—"

I flipped a few more pages dramatically. "Oooo! A recipe for pizza! First, look up local delivery options in your neighborhood. Next, pick up phone and dial number. . . ."

Dave looked sympathetically at Dutch. "If you need a place to crash tonight, you can bunk in my spare bedroom."

Just then the phone rang, and my head snapped up, my radar on high alert as warning bells shot off loudly in my head. "You have to get that," I said in all seriousness to Dutch. He gave me a quizzical look and the phone rang again. "Now!" I said, closing the book and setting it on the kitchen table.

Dutch stood and walked over to the phone on the counter. "It's my mom," he announced, looking at the caller ID. My stomach bunched when he picked up the line. I didn't know what had happened, but something awful was about to unfold here.

My assumptions were confirmed when we heard Dutch say, "Mom . . . Mom, it's okay, don't cry. I'm here. Just tell me what's wrong."

Dave and I exchanged a look as Dutch walked out to the living room to sit down on the couch and talk to his mother. "What's your radar telling you?" Dave whispered to me.

"It's bad," I said. "I don't know what it is, but it's bad."

Dave ate the rest of his meal in silence and I pushed the food around on my plate while we both strained to hear snatches of conversation from the living room. Finally, Dutch came back, his face pale and his features tight. "It's Chase," he said.

"Your cousin?" I asked.

He nodded. "He's been kidnapped."

I gasped. "Oh, my God!" I hurried over to him. "What happened?"

"He was working security for some wealthy businessman in Vegas, and the last anyone saw of them was when they headed out of a strip joint on the south end of town. Mom said they found the car—it was pumped full of bullets—but there's no sign of Chase or the guy he was guarding."

I squeezed my arms around Dutch. "When do we leave?" I asked him.

He hugged me back. "I'm going to catch the first flight I can. You should stay here."

"Not a chance in hell, cowboy," I said sternly. "You'll need my radar now more than ever."

There was a long pause and finally I felt Dutch kiss the top of my head and whisper, "Okay, Edgar. You're right—I could use you along. Now go upstairs and pack us a suitcase while I book our flight."

"What can I do?" Dave asked as he got up from the table.

"Could you look after the dogs and the house while we're gone?" Dutch said.

"You got it, partner," Dave said, and gave him a pat on the arm.

I left them to hurry up the stairs and pack. My radar had hinted earlier that today was going to bring something terrible. I figured it was my reading session with Marion, but now I realized it was that awful phone call. As I pulled a large suitcase from the closet, I had no real appreciation for the fact that our nightmare was only just beginning.

Several hours later, Dutch and I were standing in the security line at Detroit Metropolitan Airport. Worried, I kept glancing up at Dutch, who was as pale as when he'd gotten off the phone with his mom, only now his brow was slick with perspiration. "You okay?" I finally asked him.

"Fine," he said, wrapping an arm around my shoulders and looking anxiously at the line in front of us.

"We've got plenty of time to make the flight," I said. Dutch had booked us on the red-eye to Vegas.

"I know, but I was thinking maybe I should flash my badge and get us through here quicker."

"We're fine," I said, my radar telling me there was no need to rush.

Dutch swayed a little and I glanced at him in alarm. "Hey," I said, forcing him to look at me. "You don't look good."

Dutch mopped his brow. "I haven't felt well since I got that phone call. I'll be okay once we get on the plane."

"I have a good feeling that we'll find Chase," I said, trying to reassure him.

Dutch pulled me against him. "Thanks, Edgar," he whispered, and I could detect the worry in his voice.

I'd never met Dutch's cousin, but I knew that my boyfriend's mom and her best friend, Dutch's aunt, had been best friends since grammar school and had ironically grown up to marry twin brothers. Dutch's father, Bruce Rivers and his identical twin, Bill. The foursome had remained close and had lived just down the street from each other while they raised their families. Dutch and Chase were only a year apart in age and the two had also been tight growing up. They'd even had similar career paths in the navy and working security gigs through college. Dutch still had a small security consulting practice on the side with his best friend and Royal Oak detective Milo Johnson, and Chase seemed to have a similar setup in Vegas.

"How's Laney holding up?" I asked, referring to the short conversation Dutch had had with Chase's wife before we left for the airport.

"She's holding her own," Dutch said with a hint of pride. "Best thing my cousin ever did was marry that girl."

"I'd be out of my mind," I said honestly. "Especially

if I had an eight-month-old to worry about too." Chase and Laney had a bouncing baby girl.

"You'd be okay," he said, looking down at me with a smile. "But the kid might be the deal breaker."

"What do you mean?" I asked.

"Well, if I weren't around, the baby might starve to death."

"Ha-ha," I said woodenly, giving him an elbow. Dutch immediately doubled over and turned a pale shade of green. "Ohmigod!" I said. "What's wrong?"

"Is there a problem here?" one of the security guards asked, seeing Dutch doubled over and holding his stomach.

"I just gave him a little jab in the side," I said, trying to guide Dutch out of line.

"I'm fine," he said, waving me off.

At that moment the security guard caught sight of Dutch's gun, which was showing clearly now that he was doubled over. "Sir!" the security guard said in alarm. "Are you carrying a concealed weapon?" At that moment Dutch bolted from the line, leaving me and his carry-on luggage.

"Sir!" the security guard yelled. But Dutch was running as if his life depended on it. The security guard spoke rapidly into his walkie-talkie and took me firmly by the arm.

"But you don't understand!" I insisted as I was pulled away while watching three men run after Dutch. "He's FBI!"

"Come with me *now*!" the guard said, and there was nothing more I could do. I couldn't even grab our luggage because yet another guard had come up next to me and was picking up Dutch's carry-on along with my backpack.

"Dutch!" I yelled as I was hauled away, but he'd just ducked into the men's room.

Twenty minutes later Dutch and I were sitting in a closed-off room with six beefy-looking airport-security guys in uniform, and even though my boyfriend had flashed his magic badge, no one was willing to take our word for it until a call came back from the bureau to confirm he wasn't a terrorist. "How much longer is this gonna take?" I whined.

"Should be any time now," Dutch said, still looking pale and shaky. "They'll hold the plane for us just in case our story checks out."

"Are you sure you still want to fly?" I asked, looking at him skeptically.

"I'll be fine," he said for the umpteenth time. "Just something I ate didn't agree with me."

I rubbed Dutch's back and looked around at the beefy squad. "Can one of you get him some water at least?" I barked. I'd had it with these unsympathetic bozos. It was clear Dutch had dashed out of line because he'd needed to give up his dinner, and the fact that we were still being treated like terrorists was pissing me off.

"Agent Rivers?" said a man on the phone across the room.

"Here," Dutch said.

"We have an Agent Robillard on the line for you."

I tensed. Raymond Robillard was Dutch's boss and former CIA, now the ASAC, or assistant special agent in charge, for the Michigan Federal Bureau of Investigation. He was also a man I'd had a vision of murdering a fellow CIA agent named Cynthia Frost some years earlier. Dutch knew of my vision, and he'd been quietly investigating his boss ever since. "Be right back," Dutch said, with a pat to my knee.

I glared at the beefy bozos while Dutch walked stiffly to the phone. None of them seemed offended. They just continued to stare at me silently, probably hoping that I'd crack and reveal some plot to take over the world.

I don't much cotton to intimidation tactics. Gets my dander up, so after trying to ignore them for a few minutes, I got mighty irritated and switched on the old radar to see about having some fun. "So!" I snapped at the guard nearest me. "How's school going for you?" The guy blinked, but he didn't respond, so I kept going. "Must be hard to take classes with a full-time job," I said. "Still, I think it's interesting that you've chosen . . . cooking to study?" I ended with a question, but his reaction was all the validation I needed.

"How'd you know that?" he demanded.

I gave him a winning smile and turned to the next target, the guy to his left. "And you," I said. "That engagement ring burning a hole in your pocket?" Beefy bozo number two's jaw dropped. "Well, you'd better get cracking, honey. If you're waiting for the right time, I'm thinking it was yesterday."

"Cut that out," said bozo number one.

"Or what?" I said, feeling ballsy. "You'll cook me a soufflé?"

That stopped him. He just looked at me dumbly while his buddies ogled me, rather stupefied about how I knew such personal information.

"And you," I said, pivoting to the last guy on my right.

"Me?" he asked with big round eyes.

"Yes, you," I said. "Your shoulder needs surgery, and the longer you put it off, the more painful your recovery is going to be. And call your mother in Phoenix," I added. "She's lonely and you're a poor excuse for a son for not calling her sooner."

Last bozo turned a shade of fuchsia that wasn't his color. "Oh, man!" he said.

"Edgar," I heard Dutch say behind one of the bozos. "Let's go."

I got up and waved to the guards as I passed by them. "Ta-ta, boys!" I said.

"How did she . . . ?"

"What the hell was . . . ?"

"Is this some kind of a joke?"

I left Bozo the Clowns and followed my boyfriend triumphantly. "You just can't resist toying with the innocent, can you?" Dutch said.

"They asked for it," I said defensively. "Maybe next time they'll think about picking on some poor innocent law-abiding citizen like me."

"And which part would you say best describes you," Dutch said, the corner of his mouth lifting into a smirk, "the innocent or the law-abiding?"

He had a solid point. My personal history was a little less than squeaky clean. "*They* don't know about any of that stuff," I insisted. "As far as they're concerned, I *am* innocent and law-abiding."

"Come on, Edgar, we've got to hustle to catch this plane."

As we settled into our seats, I gave Dutch an apprising look. "You still don't look so good."

He leaned back in his seat and closed his eyes. "What gave it away? The bolt to the bathroom or the cold sweat I'm feeling right now?"

"The pasty complexion," I said. "You look white as a sheet."

"Must have been something I ate," he said, opening one eye to look at me.

"Don't look at me!" I said. "*You* made dinner."

"I didn't eat dinner, remember? I was on the phone the whole time."

"Oh," I said. "Well, when was the last time you ate?"

"Today at lunch," he said, his other eye opening.

"Uh-oh," I said. I'd made his lunch.

"What was in that sandwich you made me?"

"Chicken salad," I said. "Wasn't it good?"

"Apparently not," Dutch said, wrapping his arms around his stomach. "Did you eat any of it?"

"No," I admitted. "Candice sprung for pizza this afternoon. The sandwich took a deep six in favor of something better."

"Lucky you," he said grimly.

"Sorry," I said weakly. Dutch grunted and closed his eyes again and we waited in silence for takeoff.

When we were in the air, I got him a pillow and blanket and made sure he was as comfortable as possible. His brow was wet with sweat, but he shivered slightly under the blanket and the more he suffered, the worse I felt. Finally, when we were over the Rockies, he seemed to settle down and fall asleep.

I wasn't so lucky. Worried I'd poisoned my boyfriend, I continued to check him for any signs that he might be getting worse. But by the time we landed, Dutch and I had swapped complexions. I was pasty faced with bloodshot eyes, and his color had returned and he seemed to be back to normal.

"Morning," he said as the flight attendant announced we were coming in for landing.

"Hey there," I said. "You look better."

"I feel better," he said, pulling one hand out from under his blanket to feel my forehead. "But I think I might've passed this on to you. You feeling okay?"

"Just tired," I said. "No beauty sleep last night."

Dutch glanced at his watch and yawned. "The hotel's on the Strip," he said. "It shouldn't be long before we can get you settled into the room and you can take a nap."

"And what're you going to do while I'm napping?"

"I'm going to head over to the police department and talk to the detective on the case and have him take me over to the crime scene."

"Where you go I go, cowboy," I said.

"You sure you don't want to rest?"

"I'm fine," I said. "Besides, I might be able to pick something up at the scene." Dutch gave me a worried look that suggested he was wavering about letting me come along, so I added, "Really. I'm fine. I'll sleep later this afternoon, 'kay?"

"Okay," he said, stroking my cheek. "Thanks for being a trouper, Abs."

"Oh, I'll expect to be wined and dined for my services," I said with a grin. "And when we crack this case, I'll also insist on a show."

He grinned. "A show, huh?"

"Yep. I hear Cirque du Soleil gives one hell of a performance."

"That they do, babycakes," Dutch said. "Okay, you help me find Chase and I'll take you to any show you want."

"Deal!" I said, and stuck my hand out for him to shake on it.

Just then someone behind us said, "Oh, look at that!" and our attention was diverted to the window, where the dark landscape was unexpectedly lit by the glow of a bazillion lights.

"Whoa," I said, leaning across Dutch to get a better view. "That's awesome!"

"Are you a Vegas virgin?" he asked me.

I giggled. "If by that you're inquiring if this is my first time to Vegas, then yes."

"Under different circumstances I'd show you the town, Edgar," he said, his expression pinched.

I rubbed his shoulder. "We'll find him really soon, babe."

"Is that what your radar's saying?" he asked hopefully.

My right side suddenly felt light and airy. "You know," I said, giving him an encouraging smile, "it is actually saying just that."

Dutch breathed a small sigh of relief. "Thank God." And he turned back to the window. Looking at him staring out at the landscape with lines of worry around his eyes, I wanted to give him more. I wanted to tell him that I felt everything was going to turn out just ducky. But when I focused my radar on the ending of this ordeal, all I felt was a sense of unease, and that sent a shiver and feelings of dread up and down my spine.

Chapter Two

We landed about ten minutes later and deplaned. I followed wearily behind Dutch as we made our way to the rental-car counter and a short time later loaded our luggage into a snappy-looking Lexus. "This must not be an economy trip," I said, sliding into the front seat.

"I'm thinking about buying one of these," Dutch explained as he turned the key and pulled out of the lot. "Thought I might as well test-drive it while I had the chance."

"Where are we staying?" I asked as Dutch made his way into traffic.

"The Wynn."

"Is it nice?"

Dutch grinned. "No, it's a dump."

I gave him a quizzical look, unsure if he was poking fun or not. I found out a few minutes later when we pulled up to a huge green glass tower, oozing with opulence. Dutch drove up to the entrance, and the area around us was bustling with traffic and pedestrians. He got out and handed the keys to the valet, who unloaded our trunk for us and directed us inside to the reservation counter. As we entered, my jaw dropped. The lobby was rich and extravagant, with beautiful marble tiles, gold leafing, and designer labels everywhere.

Dutch was watching me with a knowing look on his face. I closed my jaw and regarded him coolly. "What? The Holiday Inn was booked?"

He laughed. "Come on, Edgar, let's get our room."

As dawn broke over the distant hills, Dutch and I were in the room unpacking when his cell went off. He looked at the caller ID and answered with, "Hey, Laney." Chase's wife said something and Dutch replied, "Yeah, we just got in. I'm headed over to the police department right after we unpack. What's that? Sure, honey, we can stop by. How're you holding up?"

I paused as I was unpacking and regarded my boyfriend.

Dutch is a bit of an enigma, even to someone as intuitive as me. On the surface he's a guy's guy. Roguishly handsome with square features, he's got a body that Adonis would envy and a demeanor that is reserved but watchful and always alert. Over the year and a half that we've been together, I've noticed that he often has a hard time dropping the cop face and just being an average Joe.

Until I came along, he didn't believe in a sixth sense. He was a "the evidence points to . . ." man. And he hadn't been swayed to think that psychic intuition was a real, honest-to-goodness ability even after we'd been dating a while. It wasn't until I'd worked a few cases with him that he began to come around. And just like he'd accepted the fly-by-the-seat-of-my-pants, throw-caution-to-the-wind-as-long-as-the-old-radar-says-it's-okay side of me, so too had I come to accept the unflinching, focused, cool-as-a-cucumber, and overly cautious side of him.

Trust me, we're really fun at parties.

Still, in those moments when the cop face came off,

and Dutch showed his soft underbelly—like now when he was on the phone with his cousin's wife—I realized how madly, deeply crazy, head-over-heels in love with the guy I was. And just then I felt a cold tickle of fear and remembered a moment that was more dream than reality, and it made me shiver.

Last February I had been shot in the chest and for about two minutes, I'd actually died. During that time I'd had a near-death experience that still haunted me.

I vaguely remember my deceased grandmother taking me on a kind of art tour where I glimpsed beautifully painted portraits of the people in my life. One of those portraits was of Dutch, and my grandmother said to me that if I didn't return to my body, his life would be cut short. Only I could stop his premature death, but I had to return.

That had been the deciding factor in bringing me back. Well, that and the paramedic performing CPR, but still, you get the picture. I'd come back, and I hadn't forgotten my grandmother's message. Why I was recalling it now only made me shiver more.

"You cold?" Dutch asked, pulling me from my thoughts.

"Huh?"

"You're shivering," he said, sliding his cell phone back onto the clip at his waist.

"Oh," I said, turning to put the last of my clothing from my suitcase into the bureau. "I'm fine. Are we going to stop by and see Laney?"

Dutch came over and wrapped me in his arms. His skin felt hot. "Yeah," he said. "She's a wreck. It might do her good to talk to you, if that's okay."

"You mean you want me to let her know that my radar says that Chase is still alive?"

"If you're cool with that."

I glanced up at him and noticed that his coloring was

pale again. Reaching up to touch his brow, I said, "It's fine. How are you feeling?"

"Still a little queasy," he said, arching one eyebrow. "You know, that cookbook I gave you probably has a good recipe for chicken salad."

"Yeah, yeah," I laughed, and pulled away from him to grab my purse. "Save it for when we get back, cowboy. We've got a bad guy to catch and a cousin to bring home."

We left the Wynn and headed out into the thick Las Vegas traffic. The morning rush hour had just started and it took us a while to get off the Strip and make headway out into the surrounding suburbs. We eventually pulled up in front of a small ranch with mud brown stucco, a terra-cotta clay roof, and a bright orange door. "We're here," Dutch said, parking in the driveway behind a Toyota Corolla.

The door to the house opened as Dutch and I were getting out, and in the doorway stood a stick-thin redhead with freckles and a pointy chin holding a baby tightly to her hip. Dutch waved and waited for me to join him before we headed up the walkway. "Hey, girl," he said as we got close.

"Man, am I glad to see you!" she said, her voice smoky and cool.

"Hi," I said, sticking out my hand. "I'm Abby."

"I've heard a lot about you," Laney said, taking my hand. I noticed there were dark circles under her eyes. "Most of it was even good," she added with a grin.

"I'm sure," I said, breaking into a smile myself.

Laney turned away from me and gave Dutch an awkward one-handed hug. "Is this Hanna?" he asked as he let her go and looked closely at the baby on her hip.

"It is," Laney said. "She's grown some since the last photo we sent you."

"I'll say," said Dutch. "But big babies run in our family."

"Come on in, you two," she said, stepping back from the door.

Dutch and I entered and glanced around. The house seemed sparse for furnishings. A green sectional couch dominated the living room, along with some TV trays for side tables and a small television on some milk crates. The only other large object in the room was a play yard, and while Dutch and I took a seat on the couch, Laney placed Hanna carefully in the play yard, shaking a small silver rattle for her to play with while we talked.

"Did you get any sleep at all?" Dutch asked.

Laney glanced up at him as she stepped away from the pen and over to a folding chair leaning against the wall. As she unfolded it and sat down, she said, "Not a wink. The call from the police came in late yesterday morning. Chase wasn't even due back from his job until tomorrow."

"When was the last time you spoke to him?" Dutch asked, taking out a small pad of paper and a pen from his jacket pocket.

"Right before he left for his assignment, so last Wednesday."

"Did he talk to you about the job?"

Laney sat back in her chair and rubbed her bloodshot eyes. "He's been working with this Delgado guy for a couple of months now. From what Chase says, the guy's a player. He burns through cash like water, has an eye for strippers, and likes to travel out of the country on occasion. My understanding was that he liked to have Chase along whenever he felt he needed to be flashy, which lately was more and more often."

"Do you remember any details about Delgado's plans? Where he and Chase might have been before the kidnapping?"

Laney sighed and rubbed her forehead. "He said

something about a short business trip with Delgado that required him to use his passport."

"Do you know where they went?" Dutch asked, and his body language revealed that he was really interested in the trip.

Laney shook her head. "Delgado's got a private plane that he uses to travel all over the country. That's why he likes Chase, in fact—he can use him for double duty."

"Double duty?" I asked.

"Chase has a pilot's license," Laney explained. "He's certified to fly small aircraft."

"Do you know when they were supposed to leave or when they might have gotten back?" Dutch asked.

"No," Laney said. "Chase was pretty mum on the details, but I assumed they would be out of town until tomorrow, when Chase said he'd be home. That's why I was so surprised when the police called me to say that Chase and Delgado had been abducted from that strip club in town. I'd really thought they'd both been out of town."

"Did Chase say anything specifically about maybe someone following Delgado around, or that he was nervous about the assignment?"

Laney shook her head. "No."

"Did Chase call you while he was on duty at any point during the week?"

"No, but that's not unusual. He knows I'm writing my thesis and that any free time away from Hanna has been spent at the computer. He wouldn't have wanted to disturb me."

"Laney's working toward her PhD," Dutch explained to me.

"Impressive," I said.

"Not really," she replied. "It's more expensive than anything else. I should have gone for my doctorate ten years ago—it would have saved me a butt load of money."

"You two doing all right?" Dutch asked, his voice concerned.

"We're fine," she said. "Just the stress of being new parents with too much debt and not enough money coming in, but we've got each other and I'm as crazy about your cousin as I've ever been."

"I can help, you know," Dutch offered.

"We're fine," Laney insisted again. "I took advantage of another student loan. It's helping out a lot, and Chase has been doing well with the number of jobs he's been getting. I mean, Delgado paid really well and on time." And then Laney's faint smile seemed to fade and I watched a small tremor go through her slight frame. "You have to find him, Dutch," she whispered as her eyes drifted to her daughter in the playpen. "I can't do this without him."

"You have my word," he said. "I won't stop until I find him."

She took a deep breath, and it was obvious she was trying to collect herself. "Laney," I said softly. "Is it possible for you to lend me a picture of Chase?"

She looked at me curiously. "Uh, I guess. Why?"

Dutch glanced at me, and his look said not to tell her the truth. The truth was that from a photograph I could tell if a person was alive or dead, so I planned to use his photo to tune in on his mortality. "Sometimes I can get a pretty good bead on someone from their photo," I offered. "It helps me to focus on their energy and what's happening around them."

Laney got up and walked into the kitchen, which was right behind the living room, returning a moment later to hand me a photo taken sometime shortly after Hanna's birth. In the picture, Laney was in a hospital bed looking exhausted and holding a pink and pruney baby while Chase grinned proudly to one side.

I breathed a sigh of relief as I looked at his image. Chase was still alive.

Glancing up at Dutch, who was watching me intently, I allowed the smallest of reassuring smiles. His face remained cool and composed, but I noticed his shoulders relax and he turned his attention back to Laney. "Thanks for the picture, Laney. We'll take good care of it."

"I'd rather you just bring my husband back," Laney said, and for the first time since we'd entered her home, I could see the intense fear in her eyes.

Dutch got up from the couch and walked forward to her, where he wrapped his arms around her and hugged her. "We'll bring him back, honey, I promise," he said after a few moments. He kissed the top of her head and stepped back. Laney wiped at her eyes and took a few deep breaths before she said, "Can I offer you two some coffee?"

Dutch grimaced and I knew his stomach was still bothering him. "Thanks, but we really should get over to the police station as soon as possible. Can I call anyone for you? Maybe a family member to come stay with you while we look for Chase?"

Laney shook her head and wrapped her arms around herself tightly as if she was cold. "My mom is my only family. She lives in Phoenix and her diabetes is bad enough to prevent her from traveling."

"You have my side of the family too, ya know," Dutch said kindly. "I'm sure Aunt Beth would fly out here in a heartbeat. And for that matter, so would my mom."

Laney attempted a smile. "They've all offered, Dutch," she said wearily. "But if they were here, I'd feel like I had to be strong, and I just can't put up that kind of bravado right now."

"Friends?" Dutch pressed. He was clearly worried about Laney and wanted her to have someone around for support.

"We're new in town," Laney said, and I could tell her tone meant he should drop it. "I'll be fine."

Dutch pressed his lips together and gave her a nod. He'd let it go and then he turned toward the door. I stood to leave and Laney walked us to the car. Before we left, I gave her shoulder a squeeze and said, "He's still alive, Laney. I can feel it."

Laney looked at me in all seriousness and said, "So can I."

It took us another twenty minutes to backtrack and make our way to the Las Vegas Police Department on Ninth Street. The department building wasn't much to look at. In fact, if you weren't looking for it, you might miss it altogether. Sandstone covered the exterior with a salmon-color trim, and the rather small building seemed to meld into the desert landscape. Palm trees lined the driveway and parking lot, but other than that, there was no landscaping to speak of.

Dutch parked and got out of the car. I followed close behind him as we walked to the entrance and stepped into the cool interior with its parquet flooring, plastic seats, and imitation-wood counter. "Charming," I whispered as we headed toward the dispatch desk.

"Your basic PD interior," Dutch said. "No frills. They have better things to do with taxpayer money."

"Like buy doughnuts," I muttered.

"Edgar," Dutch warned. "I'm here unofficially. Try to keep from offending anyone while I milk them for information—'kay?"

"Oh, if I must," I said dramatically.

"And if you get any hits from your radar, just keep them to yourself until we're alone. I don't want to scare these guys off with a bunch of psychic shtick."

I rolled my eyes but shut my trap and allowed Dutch to do the talking. Dutch gave his name at the dispatch desk and requested to speak to a Detective Brosseau. We were told to wait in the lobby and the dispatch clerk would check to see if the detective was available. I noticed that in the course of the exchange Dutch didn't identify himself as "Agent" Rivers.

"How come you didn't flash your badge?" I asked when we were out of earshot of the dispatch clerk.

Dutch grimaced. "I don't want people to think this is official FBI business," he said. "Local PDs tend to clam up when they feel their jurisdiction's being trampled on, and I really want to get a look at the crime scene, the limo, and dig into any leads these guys might have without them feeling threatened by an FBI badge."

"And you think this detective will fill you in on all those details just 'cuz you have a cute smile?" I asked.

Dutch grinned. "I have a cute smile, huh?"

"On occasion," I said coyly.

"Good. I'll flash it for the detective and see if it gets me anywhere."

A door opened off to the side of the dispatch clerk and out stepped a very tall man with gray hair, a square face, and glasses. He lumbered over to us and I was impressed—he was at least a few inches taller than Dutch, who's around six-two. "Good morning," he said warmly, extending his hand out to Dutch. "I'm Detective Bob Brosseau."

Dutch and I introduced ourselves, and the detective motioned us back through the door and up a short flight of stairs. We arrived in a large open room with lots of cubicles and white fluorescent lighting that gave everyone a sickly green cast. "Over here," he said, and we followed him into a small office off to the side.

The detective motioned to two chairs in front of his hugely overcrowded desk and we all took our seats. "I understand, Mr. Rivers, that you are the bodyguard's cousin?"

"Yes, sir," Dutch said, flashing the detective his pearly whites. "Chase is more like a brother, though. We grew up together."

"I see. Have you been in contact with him recently?"

the detective asked, pulling out a legal pad to take some notes.

"Yes," Dutch said. "I talked to Chase about two weeks ago."

"Did he happen to talk to you about Ricardo Delgado?"

"Who?" Dutch asked as my radar kicked in.

"The man Chase had contracted to bodyguard for."

"No," Dutch said. "He didn't mention him."

In my head I heard, *Liar, liar . . . pants on fire . . .* and I knew that Dutch was purposely withholding information. I cut my eyes to him, but he was ignoring me.

"Did he mention anything unusual happening recently? Perhaps he might have suggested that while he was guarding Mr. Delgado, he'd noticed someone following them?"

Dutch shook his head and looked for all the world like he was telling the detective the truth. "He didn't mention anything at all like that," he said.

"What did you two talk about during the course of your conversation, then?" the detective asked.

"Mostly sports," Dutch said. "We're both Yankees fans."

I squirmed in my chair. For the record, it is really difficult to sit by and listen to someone lie so outrageously to the police, even when it's your boyfriend and you trust his judgment. "I'm a Red Sox fan myself," said the detective. "We're originally from Boston," he added, indicating a family picture with the wife and four kids.

My attention went to the photo and as my radar was already in high gear, I said, "Congratulations to your daughter and her scholarship. She'll be very happy back East. And how fabulous that she got into the Ivy League—she must be very smart."

Dutch's gaze darted to me and I realized what I'd just said out loud. Detective Brosseau smiled proudly. "Thanks!" he said. "We just got the news yesterday.

Katie's got a full scholarship to Brown University. . . ." His voice drifted off as his brain caught up with the fact that there was no way I could possibly have known that.

"Getting back to my cousin," Dutch said, sending me a warning look as he tried to redirect the course of the conversation.

The detective wasn't falling for it. "Hold on," he said, putting up his hand in a stopping motion and turning to give me his undivided attention. "How the hell did you *know* that?"

My eyes cut to Dutch for a cue. His face had gone flat, which meant he was furious. "Er . . . ," I said. "Um . . ."

"What's going on here?" he said, turning back to Dutch, his tone icy cold.

Dutch rolled his eyes and wiped his face with his hand. "You might as well share with the detective how you know that, Edgar."

"Who's Edgar?" the detective said, looking first at Dutch, then to me.

I raised my hand. "That would be me, Detective."

"You're a *guy*?" he said.

Dutch snorted, hiding a grin with his hand. "*No,*" I said, feeling my cheeks flush with heat. "I'm definitely not a guy. I'm a psychic."

The detective blinked once, twice, then broke out into hysterics. He laughed so hard that it was impossible not to join in. He slapped his knee and wiped his eyes and had himself one heck of a good time before sputtering, "Okay, okay. You got me!"

"I do?"

"Who put you up to this? Was it Malcolm? Wyatt? Tombrewski?"

"Er . . . no," I said. "Detective Brosseau, I really am a psychic."

"Yeah, sure you are," he said, continuing to humor me.

I looked back to Dutch, who only shrugged his shoulders. "Can we get back to my cousin now?" he asked.

The detective didn't seem to know how to react. He was caught between the thought that our entire conversation was some kind of joke put together by one of his comrades and the possibility that the relative of a missing person had come into his office dragging his crazy girlfriend with him. He kept looking back and forth at us, waiting to see who would crack first.

Finally I said, "Detective, I really am a psychic. For instance, I can tell that you have a serious condition in your lower back. I'm guessing that it goes out on you a lot and that you've been ignoring it for years. I can tell that your wife is, at this moment, sending out résumés, hoping to find a little part-time job—which she will find, I might add, very soon. Tell her to look at something involving a bookstore or the library—I keep seeing shelves loaded with books. A job posting will open up soon that she'll be perfect for. I can also tell that this little guy," I said, pointing to the picture of one of the blond-headed boys, "is enamored with space and rocket ships. If you're considering a camp for him in the summer, you'll make all his dreams come true if you send him to space camp in Florida . . . which is where your mom lives, right?"

To his credit, it took Brosseau a very short time to absorb that I was the real deal. After only a few rapid blinks, and a jaw drop or two, he finally spoke. "Whoa," he said. "That was cool!"

I grinned and noticed that Dutch seemed to be letting out the breath he'd apparently been holding. "Thanks. It's a gift," I said, tongue firmly in cheek.

Swiveling back to Dutch, he said, "Did you bring her along to help you find your cousin?"

Dutch glanced my way. "In a manner of speaking," he said. "She's here to help look for clues we might miss. I should tell you, Detective, that I myself am a former detective with the Royal Oak PD, and Abby here has helped out on a few of the cases I've worked."

"No kidding!" Brosseau said, looking at Dutch with newfound respect. "How long were you in law enforcement?"

Dutch smiled wryly. "Since college, so about fourteen years." I noticed that he was careful to leave out the fact that he was still in law enforcement, albeit a different branch now.

"Why'd you leave?" Brosseau wanted to know.

"Burnout," Dutch said, and Brosseau nodded like that one word said it all. Then he turned his attention to me. "What's your success rate?" he wanted to know.

"Not bad," I said, feeling pressured.

"Don't let her fool you, Detective. She's terrific."

"Call me Bob," he said, and right before our eyes he seemed to warm up to both of us. "Now, getting back to your cousin, Mr. Rivers. I'm assuming you'll want to see the crime scene?"

"That would be great," Dutch said. "And if you could keep me in the loop with any witness testimony or lab evidence you come across, I'd really appreciate it."

"We're a little short on both, I'm afraid," Bob said with a sigh. "Nobody saw anything, nobody heard anything. Typical reaction considering where the car was found."

"Where was the car found?" I asked. I hate being out of the loop.

"The Pussy Palace," Bob said. "It's a seedy strip club on the edge of town."

"Cute name," I said, making a face.

"Pretty much sums up the type of establishment," Dutch said reasonably. "Detective, my cousin's wife told me that a call came in from the manager around five a.m. yesterday. As I recall, one of the busboys was taking the trash out when he saw the limo Chase was driving parked in the alley behind the club with the lights on and some blood on the pavement?"

"Yep," said Bob. "The Dumpster's down the alley, about fifty yards from the club, and to their credit, the joint was cited for excessive noise a few years back and since then they've improved their soundproofing to the point where it wouldn't be unusual for them not to hear a commotion—or gunshots—from fifty yards outside the club."

"Whose blood was on the pavement?" I asked.

"The sample was sent to the lab for DNA analysis. Your cousin's wife provided Chase's comb for us, and we collected Delgado's toothbrush from his wife, but I can tell you that the preliminary blood test identifies the blood as AB positive."

I saw Dutch go very still and his face became even whiter under the fluorescent lights. "What?" I asked him.

"That's Chase's blood type," he whispered.

Brosseau nodded. "Mr. Delgado is type O positive."

"So they found a little blood," I said reasonably. "Chase could have been nicked, or shot in the toe."

Bob looked down at his desk and shuffled papers around. "Yeah, about that," he said.

"Let me see the crime-scene photos," Dutch said quietly.

Brosseau glanced up at him and my heart gave a pang. By the look on his face, the photos were bad. Reluctantly, Brosseau handed them over and Dutch pulled them out of the large manila envelope and began sorting through them. I inched my chair over to him and put a hand on his arm while looking over his shoulder.

The first few pictures were of the front of the limo parked near a Dumpster in the back of an alley. In the photo the car's lights were still on and two of the doors—the driver's side and the passenger side—were open.

Another series of photos showed bullet holes riddling the car doors and the windshield. As Dutch flipped to the next series, I felt him tense. The interior of the car on the driver's side was pooled with blood, so much so that I was amazed Chase could still be alive, yet my radar insisted that he was.

"He's not dead," I whispered to Dutch, looking at him. His face was set, firm, and only the thin line of his lips and the haunted look in his eyes hinted that he was moved by the photos. "We'll find him, Dutch," I insisted. "We will."

He inhaled deeply and gave me a little nudge with his shoulder. Then he flipped through the rest of the photos and handed them to Brosseau. "I'd like to see the car if I can," he said to Brosseau.

"Of course," Bob said easily. "The CSI guys should be done with their evidence collection in the next twenty-four to forty-eight hours. I'll get you in to see it as soon as it's clear."

"Thanks, Bob, I appreciate it," Dutch said warmly. "In the meantime, can you take us to the alley?" he asked.

"Sure," Brosseau said, putting the photos away and standing up. "It's not far from here."

We took the detective's car and drove the few miles to the seedier side of town, parking next to an adult bookstore and a gun shop. "Nice," I said, taking in the neighborhood.

"The strip joint's across the street," Brosseau said. "Come on, I'll take you round back."

We got out of the car and waited for a car to pass before we walked across the street. The Pussy Palace was an odd rendering of purple-coated chrome and black-tinted glass. A bright neon yellow castle with a green neon cat sitting demurely on one turret hovered over the entrance. From inside, the thump, thump, thump of a bass oozed through the soundproofing.

"Around here," Brosseau said as he motioned us away from the front of the strip joint into a back alley. Yellow crime-scene tape ran between a Dumpster at the far end and a telephone pole to the side of the building. A third strip connected the triangle from the pole to a hook on the far wall of the building.

While Brosseau stood to one side, Dutch approached the tape warily, his eyes darting around the scene looking at the stains on the dirty cracked concrete and small piles of broken windshield that dotted the area within the tape.

I moved a few steps behind him, my eyes darting too. I wasn't sure what to look for, but maybe a gum wrapper or a missed shell casing would reveal a big clue. "You said your CSI team is processing the car?" Dutch asked, making sure.

"They're on it, Mr. Rivers," Brosseau said.

"Have you identified the weapon yet?" Dutch asked, glancing away from the scene to Brosseau.

"Based on the shell casings, two firearms were used. A Glock and a semiautomatic."

"There were *two* shooters?" Dutch asked.

"As far as our investigation can tell, yes."

"What model Glock?"

"Nine-mil."

Dutch squatted and poked at the small piles of glass on the ground. "Where were the casings found for the Glock?"

"Both inside and outside the car," Brosseau said. "We're still piecing the sequence of events together."

The scowl on Dutch's face deepened. "What?" I asked.

"Chase carried a Glock," he said. "So either he got

off a few rounds, or his gun was taken from him and he was shot with it."

"He's still alive, Dutch," I repeated, and I realized this had become a little mantra for us.

Dutch nodded and stood up. Looking at me, he pointed to my head and said, "That thing on?"

I smiled. "It is now." Moving closer to the crime-scene tape, I closed my eyes and focused. Bringing in my crew for some support, I began to feel out the energy surrounding us and noticed right away that the scene felt heavily imprinted.

When events that have monumental importance take place, they can leave a sort of imprint or stain on their surroundings that is detectable only with the right equipment—like a psychic's radar. It's almost as if we're able to detect the nature of the event—a violent act like murder feels chaotic and heavy and confusing, whereas say, a coronation for a king would feel stately and formal and orderly.

What I was feeling now was definitely on the chaotic side. "Blach," I said as I felt the energy up and down the alley. "A lot of stuff happened here."

"Can you be more specific?" Dutch asked gently.

Keeping my eyes closed, I raised my arms and literally felt the energy out with my fingertips. "It started over there," I said, pointing in what I knew was the direction of the door leading from the strip club. "I have a sense of shouting, and chaos, and something familiar."

"What's familiar?" Dutch said.

I didn't answer him right away—something in my head was trying to clear itself into a coherent thought and my crew was trying to help me get there. *Start with family* finally swirled around in my head and my eyes opened. "We need to look at Delgado's family," I said. "My crew said to start with them."

Dutch looked to Brosseau. "Have you been in contact with Delgado's family?" he asked.

The detective blanched and his own lips pulled down in a deep scowl. "Yeah," he said. "They were all broken up over it."

"It can be hard to hear that your loved one is missing," I said, "especially under these circumstances."

"No," Brosseau said, shaking his head. "You don't understand. I was being sarcastic. The only question Delgado's wife asked me was if he was dead. When I said I didn't know, she said I shouldn't call back until I did."

"Sounds like trouble in paradise," Dutch said.

"I found a separation agreement filed last week on the happy couple. We're keeping a file on her as a person of interest."

"I heard from my cousin's wife that he'd mentioned a trip out of country. Have you guys tracked Delgado's whereabouts from last week?"

"Yeah, Mrs. Rivers mentioned that to me on the phone when I talked with her yesterday, and to answer your question, no, we've looked into Delgado's flight plans and nothing comes up for out of the U.S."

I closed my eyes again and trained my radar on the alley. It was rife with violence and I squirmed against that negative energy. The ether was so thick with chaos that I stepped back a few paces to gain a better perspective. It was then that I turned a bit to my right, which faced farther down the alley, and I noticed the violence seemed to permeate down there too.

I opened my eyes and continued to hold my hands out in front of me as I walked down the alley. For a very long stretch past where the limo was parked, I was still sensing that awful energy, and I couldn't figure out why.

I closed my eyes again and called out mentally to my crew. *What's going on here?* I asked. *Why am I picking up so much violence?*

Their answer surprised me. My mind's eye filled with the scene of an endless desert and a name drifted into my mind. *Death Valley.*

I opened my eyes and squinted down the length of the alley. I now realized that what I was picking up wasn't just the one incident involving Dutch's cousin, but layers of different events that took place here, and I knew, without a doubt, that this alley had seen its fair share of dead bodies.

"Abs?" Dutch said, and I realized he was standing right behind me.

"They're calling this Death Valley," I said, waving my hand up and down the length of the street. "My radar is saying it's claimed a lot of lives."

There was an audible gasp off to my left, and I noticed that Brosseau had come up to me with Dutch. "Whoa," he said. "Man, you're good!"

"We're in Death Valley?" I asked. "I thought that was west of here."

"It is, but around here we call this Death *Alley*. The Pussy Palace has been around for a long time. It was once owned by one of the more famous mob bosses to run most of Vegas in the seventies. Back then, this alley was used to dump the mob's garbage, or anyone who stepped out of line or didn't pay up."

I took in a deep breath and turned to my boyfriend. "In that case, sweetie, I don't think I can get a clear picture of what happened. There are way too many layers here, and the closer I get to the limo, the more chaotic it is."

"Lots of people were dumped in that Dumpster," Brosseau said. "It doesn't surprise me that's where you're getting the strongest energy."

I noticed that Dutch had gone quite pale and clammy again, and one of his arms was wrapped around his stomach protectively. "Okay," he said, blinking his eyes as if he was struggling to focus.

"You okay?" I asked, stepping toward him and reaching for his arm.

"Nauseous," he said. "I think I need to sit down."

"Is he sick?" Brosseau asked.

"He's had a touch of food poisoning," I said, putting Dutch's free arm over my shoulders and guiding him toward the car. "I think we need to get him back to the hotel for a rest."

"I'll be fine," Dutch said, but I could tell he was struggling to walk.

"You need to lie down, my friend. We'll get back to work on this when you've had a chance to get some sleep and maybe something to settle your stomach," I said.

Brosseau drove us back to our car at the police station and we took our leave. "We'll be in touch," I said as I helped Dutch over to our car.

"I'll be working here until five," he said. "Unless we find something, and I'll call you if we do."

I drove Dutch back to the hotel using the car's navigation system. Even with the electronic voice telling me where to go, it was a stressful ride because of how bad Dutch looked. A few times he even groaned as if he was in pain.

"Should I take you to the hospital?" I asked. He shook his head no. "Sweetie, you look bad," I said gently. "Maybe you should see the doctor."

"I'll be fine," he said, and I could tell it took effort for him to talk.

I debated for a bit about what to do. My radar suggested a doctor was just the ticket, but ultimately I gave in and drove back to the hotel because I knew that Dutch really wanted to focus on finding his cousin and I didn't want to further upset him by taking a detour for several hours in the emergency room.

And it was that small decision to route us to the hotel instead of the hospital or a clinic that ultimately was our entire undoing.

Chapter Three

Dutch got straight under the covers the moment we were back in our room. I ran water on a washcloth and made him a compress, which brought him only the barest of relief. He complained of a vicious headache and by the feel of his forehead I knew he was running a fever. "Are you sure I can't call a doctor?"

"I'll be fine, Abs," he said, and I knew he was tired of me asking him questions. "I just need some sleep."

Thankfully, he nodded off a little later, but his body continued to sweat and battle the bacteria that must have entered his system. Twice he woke up and bolted for the bathroom. All I could do was sit on the king-sized bed and stress about how bad he looked and feel guilty about not sniffing the chicken before I mixed up the salad.

I dozed most of the afternoon myself, as I really hadn't slept at all in well over twenty-four hours. Around three p.m. Vegas time, I rubbed my scratchy, tired eyes and got out of bed. Dutch was sleeping and when I checked his forehead, I was relieved to see that his fever had broken.

I got him a large glass of water and put it on his nightstand along with some crackers I got from the vending machine around the corner from our room. I didn't know if he'd have an appetite when he woke up, but I knew he'd have to put a little something in his system eventually.

After making sure he was taken care of, I headed out of the bedroom in our suite and into the sitting room, carrying my backpack. Sitting down at the table, I checked my watch: quarter after three, which made it quarter after six Eastern time. I pulled out my appointment calendar and flipped to the current date. I'd been able to reschedule all my clients for the rest of the week save three that I had penciled in for this evening. I trailed my finger down the list of the three names and phone numbers before I wrote them down on separate three-by-five cards. Then I laid my hands over them and closed my eyes.

Although I'm used to flipping my radar on and off like a switch, to do a proper reading, I find that some meditation and protection exercises are a must. The meditation connects me to my crew—those spirit guides assigned to yours truly to help me make sense of the unknown—and protection energy so that no nastiness either attaches itself to me or manages to get through while I'm delivering my messages.

At exactly three thirty, I opened my eyes again, took a deep breath, and dialed the number of my first client.

"Hi, Melody, it's Abby Cooper calling," I said when she answered the phone.

"Hi!" she said, her voice squeaky and excited. "I'm so excited about this," she added. "And a bit nervous."

I smiled. "No worries," I said. "Most people are nervous before a session. Your job is to sit back and let me do most of the talking for the first half of the reading. After I'm done, I'll turn it over to you, and you can ask me questions if you have them. But if you could remember to keep them as specific as possible, that would be fantastic."

"Sure, sure," she said, and after I focused on her energy for a bit, I began the session.

"Okay, Melody, to start with, they're showing me some paperwork, and they're saying there is something legal and binding about this paperwork. I feel like you're heavily involved with this, almost like you're surrounded by legal paperwork. Does this make sense to you?"

Melody giggled. "I'm a legal secretary."

"Great, I'm on the right track. Regarding this paperwork, they are making me feel like it's coming from two different sources."

"I report to two partners," she said.

"Perfect. Is one of those partners getting ready to retire?"

Melody gasped. "He is!"

"Super, and there's a young man taking his place. I believe he has brown hair and he's got this flashy energy about him. They keep saying he's a prince trying to fill the king's shoes."

More laughter wafted through the phone line. "The man retiring is a named partner. There have been rumors that he plans to leave his son a seat on the board, and most of us don't think he's up for the job. His dad is a great attorney. The son is just so-so."

"I would agree," I said. "I don't think the son is up for it. Give it six months and this kid will be asked to leave. After he's gone, I feel like a woman with black hair will come into the picture, and she's like lightning in a bottle, Melody. Whatever you do, you absolutely *must* get on her team."

Melody paused before speaking. "I don't know who that could be," she finally said.

"This woman has a connection to Chicago. I feel she is either from there or coming from there."

"No one at our firm fits that description, Abby."

"That's fine, Melody. As I said, we're about six months out and a lot can happen in that time period. Just remember that I said this woman would be amazing to work for, and if and when she shows up, you've got to angle yourself to work for her. It would really benefit you in a lot of ways—more money, higher profile, nicer boss, et cetera."

"Great! I'll look out for her."

"Now they're showing me boxes, but it's odd. I don't feel like these are your boxes. I feel like they belong to an older male. And I don't feel like he's moving—I feel like he's storing these boxes somewhere."

Again, Melody chuckled. "That's my dad!" she said. "He's living in this really cramped condo and I offered to take some of the clutter off his hands. I'm going there this weekend to pick up the excess and store it in my garage."

"Awesome, now . . ." I paused for a moment as a few more thoughts came into my head along with an all-too-familiar energy that made my shoulders sag. "Melody?" I asked.

"Yes?"

"How's your dad's health been lately?"

"That's one of the things I wanted to ask you about, Abby. My dad's been complaining that he's had some trouble breathing, but he won't go to the doctor. I think he's scared of what they'll find."

In my head I saw the unmistakable symbol that meant dear old Dad was running out of time. An hourglass appeared in my mind's eye, the sand seeping through the little hole at a rapid rate, and a sense that Melody's father had something truly serious going on in those lungs. "Is there any way you can convince him to go to the doctor?"

"I've tried," she said. "He won't go."

My radar said that it wouldn't do any good anyway. What he had wasn't curable. "Okay," I said, working to keep my voice light. "If your dad wants to take responsibility for his health, then there's not much you can do about it. Just make sure you spend some really good quality time with him so that you can keep tabs on him, okay?"

"Absolutely," she said. "I love my pop."

Now, I'm sure you're wondering why I didn't divulge what I believed was Dad's demise. The simple fact is that sometimes the truth does hurt. Melody hadn't asked me the question, "Do you think my dad will die?" so I *technically* didn't have to tell her what I felt. This way, she and her father could enjoy life without some horrible doomsday hanging over their heads. I figured he had about three to six months left, and they'd find out soon enough as his health continued to deteriorate, so why give her the death sentence now? It wouldn't do anyone any good.

So we went on with our reading and I filled her with high hopes for her future, which wasn't a lie. I just glazed over the energy in March, when I felt her father would cross over and she'd be sad, because I could see that by June she'd be right as rain again.

After I hung up with her, I had a few minutes before my next appointment, so I headed in to check on Dutch. He was propped up on some pillows and had the television on mute. He still looked pale, but I could tell his fever hadn't come back and he did look better. "Hey," he said when I appeared in the doorway.

"Hey, yourself," I said, easing over to his bedside. "How're you feeling?"

Dutch held up the small package of crackers; two were missing. "And that's my second glass of water," he said, motioning to the side table where I'd set his glass. As I reflexively looked over to the glass, my breath caught. For just the briefest moment, I thought I'd seen an hourglass instead of a drinking glass on the table. "What?" he asked, noticing my quick intake of breath.

"Nothing," I said quickly, shaking my head a little. "I'm just tired and my readings have been plagued with bad news lately."

"It's tough being you, isn't it, Edgar?" he asked, and I noticed the little smirk on his face that suggested he was humoring me.

"Only when I have to play nursemaid to a certain someone," I said.

Dutch scoffed. "Better nursemaid than cook."

I rolled my eyes and glanced at the digital clock on the nightstand. "I gotta get to my next appointment. You eat another cracker and drink a little more water, okay?"

Dutch saluted me and I knew that he was starting to really feel better. He was playful only when he felt well.

I finished up with my other two readings about an hour and a half later and as I got up to go back to the bedroom, I felt really light-headed and dizzy myself. "How *you* doin'?" Dutch asked when he saw me.

"I need to eat," I said. "I think the last time I had anything was last night, and that wasn't much."

"Cracker?" he asked, extending the last cracker in the package out to me.

I smiled. "Naw. That's all you, cowboy. I think I'll call up some room service."

Dutch handed me the menu and I looked through it, trying to decide what I was hungry for. As I was bouncing back and forth between a club sandwich and a Reuben, Dutch's cell went off. I heard him answer with his usual curt, "Rivers," and pause while the caller talked. I couldn't really follow the conversation as the caller seemed to be doing all the talking, but it was clear it was about Chase and the case we were working.

While Dutch was still on the phone, I quietly placed my order using the hotel phone in the sitting room. Then I came back into the bedroom, where Dutch was just sliding his cell back onto the nightstand. "Did they find Chase?" I asked hopefully.

Dutch shook his head. "No. But Delgado's wife called Brosseau. She said a note arrived about an hour ago suggesting that her husband was alive and that ransom instructions would be arriving soon. Brosseau and another detective are headed over there now to wait with her."

"Oh, God," I said, sitting heavily on the bed. "Was there any mention of Chase?"

"No."

Dutch's face was back to resembling a granite sculpture, which meant he was really worried. I crossed over to my purse on the dresser and pulled out the picture Laney had given me. With my back to Dutch, it was a moment before I could bring myself to look at the picture, but taking a deep breath, I focused on Chase's image and felt my shoulders relax.

"Is he still alive?" Dutch asked from the bed.

I turned and gave Dutch a hopeful smile. "Yes. He's still clearly present in this photo, Dutch. He's alive."

"Do you have any idea where he might be?" My stomach gave a growl and I walked weakly over to a chair in the corner of the room. "That's okay," he said, watching me sit down. "We'll wait until after you've eaten."

"Thanks, cowboy," I said gratefully. "I really do work better on a full stomach."

We watched the television in silence until the room service arrived. Dutch paid and tipped the waiter and inspected my meal. "You're having soup and a salad?" he said, looking skeptically at me. "I thought you were thinking of a sandwich. Aren't you afraid all that healthy food will go right to your hips?"

I laughed. I'd been working out with Candice for the past several months, and all of my clothes were loose, even given my insatiable appetite for fast and greasy food. "I know, I know, not my usual fare. And I couldn't decide on which sandwich to go with, so I figured I'd order this instead. The soup is actually for you, and if I'm hungry later, I'll order a pizza or something."

Dutch sat down at the table where the waiter had set the tray. "Not sure I can handle the beef barley," he said.

"Don't go for the whole thing," I said, lifting the bowl off the tray and setting it down in front of him. "Just sip a little of the broth. We need you at full strength as soon as we can get you there," I said. "And putting a few calories and liquid into your system will help."

Dutch continued to gaze skeptically at the broth, swirling it around with his spoon. I shoved some crackers his way too. He took the hint and tried a tiny sip of the broth. "Not bad," he said after tasting it.

I relaxed in my seat and dived into my salad and we ate in silence for a bit. "Did Brosseau let on if he knew who might have kidnapped Chase and Delgado?"

"No," Dutch said. "And right now he's debating about calling in the local FBI to handle it."

"That would be a good thing, right? They'd let you assist with the case out here, wouldn't they?"

"Trust me, Abs. It would not be a good thing."

I cocked my head at him when he didn't explain, but just then there was a chirp on Dutch's cell phone and he had to answer the call. This time Dutch did a lot more talking, so I was able to follow along. "How long ago?" he said, glancing at his watch. "And the delivery boy couldn't give you a description?" There was a pause while Dutch listened; then he grabbed a pen and paper off the side table and began to scribble on it. "We'll meet you there, Detective. Thanks a lot."

Dutch hung up and I polished off the last bite of my salad. "I take it we're heading out?"

"You can stay here, doll," he said kindly. "You look beat."

"I'm fine," I said, feeling better than I apparently looked. "Trust me, if there's an opportunity to home in on Chase's kidnappers, I'm up for it."

Dutch gazed at me for a long moment, and when he spoke, his voice was soft and endearing. "I am really glad you're my gal, Abs."

"Buying me a pair of those Jimmy Choo sandals we saw downstairs would go a long way toward making me feel appreciated," I said with a grin.

"Sweethot," he said, giving me his best Humphrey Bogart, "you find my cousin, and I will buy you a pair for every day of the week."

"Deal," I said, and we were off to Delgado's.

Traffic was beginning to pick up on the Strip, so it took us some time before we were able to make it to the highway and head out to the burbs. Half an hour after we left the Wynn, we came to a stop in front of a gigantic Spanish-style mansion; copper gates barred our entry but allowed our eyes to gaze at the house beyond. "Delgado's got dough," I said.

"Oh, yeah," Dutch replied. Rolling down the window, he stuck his head out and hit the intercom button located on a box outside the gate. "Yes, hello?" said a thickly accented woman's voice.

"Dutch Rivers here to see Detective Brosseau," Dutch said.

There was a long pause followed by a beeping sound and then the gates began to move apart and we were allowed to enter. Dutch parked us between a Buick minivan and a Mercedes S-Class. "I'm guessing the Mercedes isn't the detective's car," I said as we got out.

That won me a smirk as we moved to the huge, intricately carved wooden door, where I punched the doorbell. There was a chorus of barking and yipping from within the mansion, and a woman speaking rapid Spanish above the noise opened the door while holding back a small brown and white Pekingese with her foot. *"Sí?"* she said.

"I just called on the speaker," Dutch said. "We're here to see the detective."

"Ah, *sí, sí,*" she said, bending over to pick up the dog. The moment the dog was lifted, another took its place, trying to make a run for it. I bent down and caught the little bugger in the nick of time. "Tank you, tank you," she said, waving us in. "They are loco, no?"

I smiled and walked inside, where we were greeted by a whole pack of small, furry, yipping dogs. "It's like *Animal Farm*," Dutch muttered out of the side of his mouth as I handed my dog to the woman.

"Are you Mrs. Delgado?" I asked.

The woman laughed. "Oh, no!" she said. "No, the senora is this way."

We followed her through the front hallway with the dogs in tow, arriving in an enormous sitting room, twenty feet by twenty feet, with travertine floors, creamy walls, and a marble fireplace. "Senora?" the woman who'd opened the door to us said to a small, very thin woman with taut skin, unnaturally thick lips, and a perfectly thin nose.

"Yes, Rosa?" she said without looking at her housekeeper.

"These people are here to see the police."

The woman I took to be Mrs. Delgado turned steely gray eyes on me and Dutch, and I realized as she seemed to take stock of our tired and slightly ruffled appearance that she immediately dismissed us as people of no interest to her. "They're on the other side of the room, Rosa," Mrs. Delgado snapped.

"*Sí,*" Rosa said, completely unperturbed by the tone her employer had taken with her. "They are over there," she repeated, pointing to the opposite corner of the room.

Dutch and I swiveled around and saw Detective Brosseau already walking toward us. "Did you find it okay?" he asked.

"Just fine," Dutch said.

Brosseau looked past us to Mrs. Delgado and he

seemed to flinch. I could only imagine she'd turned the dagger eyes on him too. "Over here," he said, motioning us over to join the two other detectives in the opposite corner of the room with a large seating area.

"Jason, Colby, this is the guy I was telling you about, the bodyguard's cousin, and this is his . . . er . . . girlfriend?"

"Dutch Rivers," my boyfriend said. "And yes, Detective, this is Abby Cooper, my girlfriend."

We all shook hands and took our seats. Brosseau seemed anxious to fill us in, and Dutch gave him a small hand gesture that indicated he was ready to listen. In a hushed tone, Brosseau brought us up to speed. "According to Mrs. Delgado, a deliveryman from FedEx arrived here at approximately five ten p.m. The housekeeper, Rosa, signed for the package"—Brosseau paused as he pointed to a FedEx envelope sealed in a plastic bag marked EVIDENCE—"and then he left. Rosa took the envelope directly to Mrs. Delgado, who opened it at approximately five thirty p.m.

"Inside was a single sheet of paper." Again Delgado paused as he reached over and picked up another plastic bag, containing a white sheet of paper with a short typewritten note. "And this," he added, setting down the envelope and picking up another Baggie, containing a bloodstained watch that looked heavy and expensive.

"Is that Delgado's Rolex?" Dutch asked.

Brosseau nodded. "The wife confirmed it. Says she gave it to him on their twentieth wedding anniversary."

"Romantic," I said, and got a warning look from Dutch.

Brosseau smiled. "Hardly. When she handed it over to us, she asked when she could have it back. She knows a good pawnshop downtown that pays top dollar."

The corner of Dutch's mouth turned up slightly, and I knew he had a good one-liner, but he held his tongue and let the detective continue. "The note's not very helpful," he said. "Only three lines: 'We have your husband. We will kill him unless you hand over the money. Instructions to follow.' "

"I'm assuming you've been in touch with FedEx?" Dutch asked.

One of the other detectives, Colby, spoke up. "I interviewed the route supervisor fifteen minutes ago. The package was dropped in one of the bins collected on the early-morning shift on the north side of the city. We've dispatched a patrolman out there to secure the bin until we can haul it into the lab for fingerprint collection and analysis."

Dutch reached forward and picked up the evidence bag with the letter in it, squinting at the type and holding it up to the light. "No watermark," he said. "Just generic white print paper."

"We're sending it to our lab for analysis," Brosseau said.

Dutch set the paper down and peeked over his shoulder. "How cooperative is the wife being?"

Brosseau shrugged. "She answers every question directly. Doesn't elaborate but doesn't appear to be hiding anything either."

"But she benefits if Delgado dies, right?" I asked, and everyone looked at me. "I mean, if her soon-to-be exhusband dies before they file for divorce, she gets everything without the pain of attorney fees."

"What are you getting at?" Dutch asked me.

"Well," I said, "if she had anything to do with this, wouldn't she play up the concern? I mean, I could see her killing him, then inventing some kidnapping scenario to cover it up, but wouldn't she play it up as the grieving, distraught wife?"

"She's right," Dutch said. "She wouldn't be this blatantly indifferent."

"But I thought you were the one that said look at the family," Brosseau said, and I could tell from the look of interest from both of the other detectives that he'd already clued them in on my little area of expertise.

"Yes," I said, immediately switching my radar to ON. "But it might be a different family member." I closed my eyes for a moment and felt the energy surrounding Delgado's abduction. "The energy is distinctly male," I said. "And younger than Delgado. Does he have any brothers or sons or cousins of his own?"

The detectives all looked at one another, then over to Mrs. Delgado, who was flipping through a magazine as if she didn't have a care in the world. "Mrs. Delgado?" Brosseau said sweetly.

The pages of the magazine paused ever so slightly before flipping again. "What, Detective?" she said with a voice that sounded like extra-gritty sandpaper.

"Can you come over here, please?"

The sigh Her Royal Highness emitted was loud enough for us to hear and we watched with mild shock as she slapped the magazine down and got up off the couch in a huff.

As she walked brusquely over to us, I noticed how tiny she was, yet protruding from her torso like two large battleships were two mounds that had to be mostly silicone. She halted when she reached Dutch's chair, placed one hand on her hip, and examined the long, well-manicured nails on the other. "What is it?" she snapped.

No one spoke for a moment as I noticed Dutch pass a look to Brosseau that looked like a request to do the talking. Brosseau shrugged his shoulders slightly and nodded.

"Regarding the members of your family," Dutch said in his best silky tone.

Delgado cut her eyes to him and cocked an eyebrow. "Yes?" she said.

"Do you and your husband have children?"

"Yes."

"How many?"

"Two."

"Sons? Daughters?"

"One of each."

"Their names?"

"Ricky and Bethany Delgado."

"How old are they?"

"Twenty-eight and twenty-two."

I noticed that Brosseau was jotting down Mrs. Delgado's answers. The rest of us were cutting our eyes back and forth as though we were at a tennis match, watching Dutch ask questions and Delgado give curt, monosyllabic answers. "Who's oldest?" Dutch asked.

"My son."

"Do either of your children live here with you?"

"No."

"Where does your daughter live?"

"In our house on Lake Mead."

I could tell Dutch was growing impatient even though his tone never changed. "And your son? Where does he live?"

"In a condo off the Strip."

"May we have his phone number? We'd like to talk with him."

Mrs. Delgado gave Dutch the number and said, "Is that all?"

"What about extended family?" Dutch asked. "Does Mr. Delgado have any brothers or cousins or relatives living nearby?"

"No."

"No, he doesn't have them, or no, they don't live nearby?"

"He has two sisters. They both live in Spain."

Just then my radar gave a small blip and I felt another clue bubble up to my brain. Quickly I reached into my purse and pulled out a pen and an old receipt I'd stuffed in there. On the back of the receipt I wrote, *Ask her about the girlfriend!* and handed it to Dutch.

Dutch read the receipt, cut a quick glance at me, then said casually, "Do you know if Mr. Delgado was seeing anyone after you two separated?"

Mrs. Delgado's cheeks and neck became flushed. She stopped inspecting her nails and gave Dutch the full venom of her dagger eyes. "I don't pay attention to my husband's extracurricular activities," she snarled.

Liar, liar . . . pants on fire . . . swirled into my head. I gave Dutch a look that suggested she'd stopped being truthful.

"I see," he said smoothly. "I apologize for asking, ma'am. But we want to explore every avenue to bring your husband home safely."

Mrs. Delgado pursed her lips distastefully. "Are we finished?" she said.

"For now, but I'd appreciate it if you could put together a list of people that might want to see your husband out of the picture. Maybe some former staff or business acquaintances or people your husband might not have gotten along with who could be capable of this type of thing."

Mrs. Delgado gave him a sardonic look before walking over to a side table where a white telephone sat. She opened the drawer and pulled out the telephone book, which she brought back and handed to Dutch. "Here's your list," she said flippantly, then turned on her heel and marched back to her couch. When she was out of earshot again, all four men let out a collective sigh. "Can you imagine cuddling up to that thing every night?" Brosseau said.

The other two detectives shook their heads. "Still," Dutch said, "I think Abby's right. She's too direct. I don't think she had anything to do with this. We'll need to talk to the kid Ricky and track down Delgado's girlfriend. Abs, is that what your radar said? Delgado's girlfriend is somehow involved?"

I nodded. "When you were talking with her, I felt like

one of the players was the girlfriend, but to be honest, I'm not really sure if it's Delgado's girlfriend or the girlfriend of whoever is involved."

Brosseau turned to Jason, the other detective, and said, "Jay, I'll need you to pull Delgado's phone records. Let's see who's on his most frequently called list and try and track his girlfriend down that way. Also, call the family accountant. I want to know Delgado's net worth—and I also want to know who might have known his net worth. Look through the records and see who he dealt with on a daily basis."

"On it," Jason said, and he got up to leave.

Brosseau next turned to Colby. "Buddy, sorry to do this to you, but someone's got to stay here and wait for the instructions."

Colby eyed Mrs. Delgado across the room warily. "Why do I always get the short straw?"

We all smiled. "Call me the moment you hear anything," Brosseau said, getting to his feet. "If this gets too sticky, I'm gonna have to pull in the FBI."

Dutch and I got up too and Brosseau waved to us to follow him. We headed out of the sitting room and back through to the front hallway. Before opening the door, Brosseau turned to Dutch and said, "You know that part of the reason I haven't called the local FBI bureau is because I've got an out-of-towner on loan right here."

Dutch broke into a grin. "Checking up on me?" he asked.

"Part of the job," Brosseau said. "I appreciate that you didn't want to throw your badge around and step on my toes, Agent Rivers."

"And I appreciate that you've been so willing to include me in the investigation, Detective Brosseau."

Bob nodded, then pulled open the door, and we walked outside. "How about you follow me back to town and we'll see if we can find this Ricky Delgado?"

"That works," Dutch said, and we headed to our cars.

*   *   *

We followed Brosseau back into town and the nearer we got, the more congested it became. "Man," I said. "This is worse than I-Seventy-five in the mornings."

Dutch cut me a look. "Your morning commute is six minutes and you don't go anywhere near I-Seventy-five."

"Yes, but on my six-minute commute I listen to traffic and weather, and I-Seventy-five sounds *baaaad* in the morning."

Dutch smirked and focused on following Brosseau. We arrived on the north end of the Strip not far from our hotel and took a right, winding through some side streets until we stopped in front of a ten-story building with gold-tinted glass, large balconies, and an expensive-looking lobby. "Nice place," I said, getting out of the car.

"The address dispatch had for Ricky is on the top floor," Brosseau said. "I tried the number his mother gave me. It goes straight to voice mail."

"Worth knocking on his door," Dutch said, and we headed inside. We were stopped by a security guard as we entered the lobby. "May I help you?" he asked.

Brosseau flashed his badge and said, "We're here to talk with Mr. Delgado."

"Which one?" the guard asked, his eyes cutting to his computer screen.

The three of us hesitated and looked at one another for a moment, confused by the question. "You have two Mr. Delgados here?" Dutch finally asked.

"Yes. Father and son, both named Ricardo."

"Which floor does the father live on?" I asked.

"Top floor, down the hall from his son, in unit P-twenty-six."

"And son is in . . . ?" Brosseau asked.

"P-twenty-two."

"We'll look in on both, thank you," Brosseau said.

"The elevators to the penthouse suites are around this corner," the guard said. "Your guest-pass code is four-eight-four."

"Thank you," we said in unison, and walked over to the designated elevators.

"I didn't know they both had condos," I said.

"Now we know where Delgado's been hiding to get away from the wife."

"You'd think he'd try and move a little farther away . . . like Canada, or Mars," I said.

Brosseau snickered and Dutch shook his head. "Let's hit the son's place first. After all, we know Pop's not going to be home."

At that moment the elevator doors opened and we trooped inside. Brosseau hit the P button and the electronic display asked him to enter a code, which he did. The doors closed and we were headed up. "Wonder what a place like this runs for," I said quietly.

"A penthouse this close to the Strip would run you a million to a million five," Brosseau said. "Easy."

Dutch whistled. "Pricey."

"Welcome to Vegas," Brosseau replied.

The doors opened and we stepped out, making our way to the double doors of unit P-22. Brosseau pressed the doorbell and we waited. Seconds ticked by and the detective knocked loudly on the door, calling out, "Mr. Delgado? It's the Las Vegas Police. We need to talk to you about your father."

After a few more seconds, Brosseau turned to us. "Looks like no one's home." Taking his business card out of his wallet, he wrote something down on the back and wedged it into the doorjamb. "Let's go knock on Ricardo's door and see what happens," he said.

We followed after him down the hall just past the elevators to another set of double doors marked P-26. From inside we could clearly hear music playing and something else a little more carnal. "Sounds like someone's home," Dutch said, eyeing Brosseau.

"And it sounds like they're either watching porn or making it," I added.

Brosseau didn't even bother with the doorbell this time. Instead he knocked loudly on the door and yelled, "Detective Brosseau with the Las Vegas Police Department. Please open up!"

There was maybe a three-second delay before all noise, carnal and otherwise, abruptly stopped and all was quiet for another few seconds until a scurrying of feet and panicked voices, both male and female, echoed from inside. Brosseau shook his head and rolled his eyes and banged on the door again. "I said this is the Las Vegas PD! Open the door now!"

Footsteps dashed across a floor inside and a door slammed. Then another beat or two and the door opened up to reveal a beautiful blonde with tousled hair, thick swollen lips, and a sweaty sheen to her complexion. "Yes?" she said when she opened the door dressed in a short, pink silk robe.

Brosseau introduced himself and said, "We're here about Ricardo Delgado. We understand he lives here?"

"Yes, but Ricardo isn't here," she said, looking a little dazed, and that's when I noticed that her pupils were the size of pinpoints. Her nose looked red and raw too.

"We know," Brosseau said. "Who are you?" he asked.

"I'm his girlfriend," she said.

"Your name?" Brosseau asked. I could tell he was losing patience for the simple answers.

"Bambina Cheraz," she said.

"Do you live with Mr. Delgado?"

"Yeah," she said, but her look said she wasn't so sure. "Usually. I mean, I got my own place, but Ricardo mostly lets me crash here."

"I see," said Brosseau. "And when was the last time you saw your boyfriend?"

This got us a shrug. "I dunno," she said. "Maybe a couple of nights ago?"

Brosseau rubbed his chin thoughtfully. "You don't seem too concerned about the fact that he hasn't been home in a few days. You've heard from him?"

"Sure," she said, again sounding unsure. "I mean, he called me and said he wasn't gonna be around for a while."

"When did he call you?"

"I dunno," she said, and I noticed that her breathing was becoming rapid and she seemed close to panic. "Maybe last night?"

"Ma'am," Brosseau said, "we are currently looking into the abduction of your boyfriend and we have reason to believe he's been kidnapped. If you've received word from him, it's very important you tell us when, where, and the extent of that conversation. Otherwise, I'm going to have to take you downtown and charge you with obstruction."

"I said I didn't know!" she yelled at him. "He called me, I think, two days ago. He said he was leaving town to think or something and that he'd be back next week!"

"What phone did he call you on?" Brosseau asked.

"My cell," she said.

"I'll need to see your cell," Brosseau insisted.

Bambina sighed dramatically and stepped away from the door, which eased open while she walked over to a coffee table and picked up her purse. On the table where her purse was were small squares of tin foil, a lighter, and several Ziploc bags.

Brosseau looked at Dutch, a grin flashing onto his lips. "Sometimes they make it all too easy, don't they?"

Dutch smiled back. "They do."

Brosseau entered the residence and pulled out his

handcuffs. Bambina looked up and said, "Hey! I didn't say you could come in!"

"No, but when you opened up the door, you allowed us to take a peek inside. Drugs are clearly evident on this table, making it probable cause to come in without a warrant. Now, please turn around and put your hands behind your back."

"That's not mine!" she screamed, throwing her purse at him.

Brosseau stepped aside easily. "Ms. Cheraz," he said sternly. "We can do this the easy way, or we can do this the hard way. Which would you prefer?"

"But I'm in my house!" she said. "I'm in the privacy of my own home!"

"Actually," he said, "you're in Mr. Delgado's home, which means that unless he can testify differently, you're also trespassing."

"Ricky!" Bambina yelled as Brosseau approached her with the handcuffs. "Get out here and *deal* with these assholes!"

Brosseau and Dutch looked at each other and without hesitation Dutch pulled out his gun and pushed me into the hallway. "Stay put," he ordered, then moved into the condo. I did as I was told, but I couldn't help peeking around the corner. Brosseau had Bambina by the arm and was whipping her around as he cuffed first one wrist, then the other. Bambina was screaming her bloody head off, shouting, "Ricky! Ricky! Ricky!"

Dutch hurried through the condo and disappeared into a back hallway, his gun poised and ready for action. My heart was hammering in my chest as I grappled with the danger he could be walking into. What if Delgado had a gun of his own and didn't take to trespassers?

Suddenly, there was a crashing noise followed by shouts and what sounded like furniture being overturned and some sort of scuffle. My own scream caught in my throat as I pictured Dutch trying to wrestle Delgado to the ground and it was then that a dark blur came flying out of the back hallway headed right for the door.

Dutch was ten steps behind as he chased after the figure and I felt frozen in shock as the blur darted directly at me. "Stop!" Dutch yelled, but Delgado wasn't listening. In a lightning bolt of inspiration I pulled my head back and stuck out my leg across the threshold. I felt the impact on my shin a split second later, and it hurt something fierce and was strong enough to whip me completely around and send me to the floor of the hallway.

As I hit the deck, I heard a tremendous thud followed by an "Uhun!" and then all was quiet, except, of course, for Bambina, who was inside sobbing hysterically. I grabbed my leg and twisted into a sitting position and looked right into midnight blue eyes. "Nice moves, Edgar," Dutch said, motioning over his shoulder.

Delgado Junior was lying crumpled in a heap on the hallway floor five feet away. There was a small bloodstain on the wall where his head had hit, and he was knocked out cold. "If Candice asks," I said, "tell her I used one of those karate kicks she's been showing me."

Dutch chuckled and extended his hand down to me and helped me to my feet. I hobbled a bit when I put weight on my left leg. "You okay?" he asked, squatting to lift up the leg of my jeans.

"He cracked me in the shin," I said.

"You're going to have one hell of a bruise," Dutch said, feeling my leg and making me wince.

"I'll be fine. Maybe there's some ice in the freezer I can put on it."

Dutch eased me over to lean against the wall while he moved over to Delgado and cuffed his hands behind his back. "Hold tight," he said to me as he stood up and moved back into the condo.

I stood in the hallway and stared at the man who had

come flying out the door. He was developing a bump on the top of his forehead, but otherwise he appeared to be incredibly handsome. He had dark olive skin, and very square, almost chiseled features with a scruffy five-o'clock shadow around his chin. He was shirtless and barefoot, dressed only in jeans, and the sculpture of his body suggested he spent many hours at the gym.

But then I noticed how red his own nose was and even from five feet away I could see a fine dusting of white powder right around his nostrils. He moaned then and I hobbled across to stand over him as his eyelids fluttered and his eyes attempted to focus.

"I'd be real quiet and all cooperative-like if I were you," I suggested.

"I want my mother," he said thickly.

"I'll just bet you do," I said. "But she's busy with another detective at the moment and isn't taking visitors. But don't worry, honey. Where you're going, you'll have plenty of time to wait for her to come to you."

Dutch appeared over my shoulder and glared down at Delgado. "That hurt?" he asked, indicating the large bump forming at the top of Delgado's forehead.

"Like a bitch," Delgado said.

"Good," Dutch said as he handed me a package of frozen peas. "Maybe next time you'll freeze when I tell ya to."

An hour later we were still at the condo. Dutch had found me a chair from inside and I sat in it glumly while they processed the scene. Delgado and Bambina had been moved to separate cells at the police station. Brosseau had enough with the amount of drugs that were found in plain sight to hold them for now.

I'd had a feeling Delgado would clam right up the moment he knew he'd been caught. And he had. Other than demanding a phone call to his attorney, he hadn't uttered a word.

I could tell it was frustrating to Dutch, because by the looks of things, it appeared that Ricky Junior and his father's girlfriend very likely had something to do with Delgado's abduction. Brosseau and Dutch both felt that the scene they'd dropped in on was likely some sort of celebration. They could have been celebrating pulling off the kidnapping of Ricky's father, or just the fact that they had the place to themselves. Either way the whole thing was really suspicious.

I looked up as Dutch came out into the hallway carrying a picture frame. He handed it to me and I looked at the image. The photo was of Ricky in a sideways hug with an older version of himself. "Ricardo and Ricardo Junior?" I asked.

Dutch nodded. "Tell me what you see," he said, his voice filled with tension.

I looked back to the image. "He's still alive," I said, and I saw Dutch let out the breath he'd been holding.

"As long as he's alive, Chase might have a chance."

I dug into my purse and pulled out Chase's picture again. "He's still with us, sweetheart," I said. "Nothing's changed about his image."

"Thanks," he said warmly. "We're almost done in there, and Bob has invited us to his house for dinner. He's been going on and on about what a great cook his wife is."

"I'm game," I said. "How's your stomach feeling?"

"It can probably manage something bland," he said. "I wanted to see how you felt about it before I accepted."

"Good thinking," I said. "You guys going to question Ricky and Bambina?"

Dutch nodded again. "We'll tackle Bambina first, but we're letting her sweat it out for a few hours. Let the drugs wear off a bit and allow the paranoia to sink in. She'll be telling us anything we want to know in a few hours."

"Do you think they had anything to do with the kidnapping?"

"I do," he said, then eyed me thoughtfully. "What do you think?"

I sighed heavily. "Babe," I said, "I'm so tired right now, I don't think my radar could help you on that one way or another."

"Understood," he said, and leaned in to give me a kiss. "How's your leg?"

"Hurts."

"Can I get you some more peas?"

"Naw. Maybe just an aspirin."

"We'll nab one from Bob. He's wrapping up with them and he'll be out with us in a minute. Hold on to that picture for now, though, okay?"

"Got it," I said, tucking it into my purse, grateful that I'd brought my big bag instead of the little satchel I normally carried.

Brosseau came out into the hallway, pulling off the latex gloves he'd been wearing. "Those two really had themselves a party," he said. "We found enough coke and crack to light up more than a few of the casinos."

"So you'll hold them for the drugs while you investigate their possible connection to Chase and Delgado's abduction?"

"That's the game plan, but first I gotta eat. Did you ask her, Dutch?"

"I did," Dutch said, and I could tell he was really warming to the detective. "We're a yes."

"That's great!" Brosseau said. "My wife, Nora, is a great cook."

Dutch and I shared a look as we tried to keep from smirking. "She won't mind us dropping in on her last-minute?" I said, glancing at my watch and adding, "And at eight o'clock at night?"

"Naw!" Brosseau said. "She loves company!"

My left side felt decidedly heavy. I had a feeling Mrs.

Brosseau wasn't going to be extra thrilled to see her husband toting guests for dinner. "Can we bring anything?" I asked.

"Nah," Brosseau said, waving at the remaining patrolmen and crime-scene techs as we left the condo. "We've got four kids, so we've learned to keep the pantry full. Plus, Nora is terrific at putting odds and ends together. Twenty years ago I tasted her lasagna and that night I proposed."

We got to the elevator and I said, "You proposed because she could cook?"

"Absolutely," Brosseau said. "I mean, I loved her, but the fact that she could throw together such a fantastic dish, well, it put me over the top."

"Gee, Abby, did you hear that?" Dutch said, pumping his voice with enthusiasm. "Bob proposed because the gal he was dating could cook!"

"I heard," I said, narrowing my eyes as we got into the elevator.

Dutch turned to Brosseau and added, "I'm just trying to stop my girlfriend from poisoning me every time she goes to make a sandwich."

Bob laughed until he saw the look on my face, at which point he cleared his throat and stared at his shoes.

"Aw, come on, Edgar," Dutch said. "You have to admit, that was funny."

"You are so dead," I whispered to him. "Dead, dead, dead."

"Harsh," he said, but he was still smiling.

"Dead," I muttered again, and looked away.

Looking back, I wish I could take every single part of that retort back, because on the elevator ride down, I had no idea how right I actually was.

Chapter Four

We followed behind the detective again as he led us through some side streets back onto the highway and away from the city. Darkness had descended upon Nevada and I could see the plain desert landscape only in shadow. Traffic heading out from the city was a snap; it was the other side of the highway that carried a preponderance of cars.

When the lights from the Strip had melded into one big glob of yellow, the detective exited the highway and entered a subdivision of middle-class means. Streetlights dimly illuminated two-story homes with short lawns and very little grass. We turned right at a stop sign, drove another two blocks to another stop sign, and turned left onto a cul-de-sac at the end of which Detective Brosseau pulled into a driveway and cut the lights.

Dutch parked on the street and we got out. "Home sweet home," the detective said.

"Nice house," I said, taking in the well-tended yard absent of grass but manicured with rocks and dry mulch. Here and there a cactus stuck out and on the covered porch were two terra-cotta pots brimming with red begonias.

The door opened before we got to the front steps and a tall woman with broad shoulders and hair trimmed in a perky bob flipped on the outside light and looked out at us behind tortoiseshell glasses. "Welcome!" she said as she held the door open.

"Thank you so much," Dutch said, taking the door handle and holding it open for me.

"So kind of you to have us over," I said, passing through the entry.

She extended her hand. "I'm Nora, Bob's wife." Dutch and I both introduced ourselves. "Bob phoned me from the road and said to expect company for dinner."

In the background I could hear as well as feel the deep bass vibration coming from somewhere upstairs. In the back of the house a television was blaring and while we stood there, one small head peeked around the corner and said, "Hi, Dad!"

"Nickie!" Bob said warmly. "Come here, guy," and he held his arms out for the young boy.

"He should be in bed," Nora said. "But he likes to wait up for his pop."

From the hallway we were standing in, I could see into the kitchen. Another figure appeared in the doorway, this one a younger version of Bob but with Nora's nose and jawline. "Mom?" he said. "The timer went off."

"Our son Michael," Nora said as she turned toward him. "I'll be right there. Can you handle taking the potatoes out of the oven?"

"Duh," Michael said, and turned back to the kitchen.

"He wants to become a chef someday," she said. "Of all my kids, he's the only one interested in cooking."

"Can I interest either of you in a glass of wine?" Bob asked.

Dutch immediately shook his head and held his stomach protectively. "No, thanks, Bob. I'm going to pass."

"Oh, you poor thing!" Nora said, taking his hand and leading him into the dining room to sit at the table. "Bob told me you got food poisoning right before you came to Vegas. You sit here. I've prepared a special remedy that will help settle that stomach."

"Can I help you in the kitchen, Nora?" I asked, and nearly hit Dutch when he gave me a rather skeptical look about the suggestion.

"That would be lovely," she said. "Let the boys talk about their case. Dinner's almost ready anyway. I fed the kids hours ago, but I always like to eat with my husband."

I tagged along behind her to the kitchen and took a deep sniff. "Ohmigod!" I said. "What are you making that smells so good?"

Nora laughed. "Well, tonight I'm doing pork tenderloin with an apricot-mango compote, sweet potato soufflé, and rainbow green beans. But your boyfriend is having some homemade chicken soup and fresh-baked bread."

I sighed. "You're gonna make me look bad," I said to her.

"Honey, if I had your figure, I wouldn't need to know how to cook either."

I laughed, then asked, "What can I do to help?"

"You can sit and keep us company until the pork is done. Michael? How's that coming?"

"Another minute or two," he said as he stood over the frying pan. I couldn't get over how tall he was. He towered over his mother and she towered over me.

Nora poured two glasses of wine and set one in front of me. "Chablis okay?"

"It's fine, thank you."

"Bob tells me you're a psychic," she said.

I felt my cheeks redden. Not that it was a secret, but it just wasn't something I liked to advertise in mixed company. "For a couple of years now," I said.

"My grandmother was a professional psychic too," she said.

"Really?" I asked, my interest piqued.

"Oh, yes," she said. "She lived in Hollywood, California, and read for all the stars back in the fifties and sixties."

"That is so cool!"

"And she was the one who told me that I needed to learn how to cook, and cook well. She said that it would be an important component to meeting my Prince Charming. Can you believe I bought into that?" she said with a chuckle.

"It worked, didn't it?"

"Better than expected," she said, giving me a wink as she took out some plates and bowls.

"Pork's done," Michael said.

"Fantastic. Michael, will you go see that Nickie gets to bed while I serve dinner?"

I carried out the plates and bowls to the table while Nora brought the serving dishes of our dinner and set them in the middle of the table. In front of Dutch she set a steaming bowl of chicken soup that wafted a delicious garlicky aroma around the room and a basket of freshly baked bread. "This will cure what ails you," she said, giving him a pat on the back.

We all sat and dug into the dinner, and I have to admit, it was one of the best damned meals I've ever tasted. It was the perfect blend of sweet, sour, salty, and bitter and I ate until I couldn't eat one more bite. "That was amazing," I said with a sigh.

Nora beamed at me. "And how about you, Dutch? Are you feeling better?"

Dutch smiled kindly. "I actually am, Nora, thank you," and I could tell he was. Some color had returned to his cheeks and he seemed closer to his old self, except for the dark circles under his eyes that I knew were the result of his worry over his cousin.

Bob looked at his watch and said, "Think we've left Bambina on ice for long enough?"

"I believe we have," Dutch said. "But if we can stay and help clean up, we'd like to."

"Oh, no," Nora said. "You go work on finding your cousin. Mike and I have this."

As if on cue, Mike appeared at the table and began to gather up the dishes. We stood too and even though Nora had insisted she could handle it, both Dutch and I gathered as many plates and dishes as our arms could hold and carried them into the kitchen.

A short time later we said our good-byes and got back into our cars. "What a lovely family," I said as we pulled out of the driveway.

"They're good people," Dutch agreed. "Hey, Abs, can you take down the address? We'll send flowers to Nora tomorrow to thank her for the dinner."

"No problem," I said, squinting in the dim light to read the number on the front of the house, which luckily was posted right underneath the front light. "Two-seven-nine . . . what street is this?"

"Desert Bloom Road," he said.

After I'd jotted down the address on a gum wrapper, I laid my head back against the headrest and sighed.

"You tired?" Dutch asked.

"Very."

I heard Dutch fiddle with the clip on his belt and punch in some numbers into his cell phone. "Hey, Bob," he said. "I'd like to drop Abby off at the hotel before I meet you at the station." There was a pause, then, "Great. I'll see you there."

I opened one eye and said, "You're a great boyfriend, you know?"

"I try," he said, reaching over to squeeze my hand.

"I really gotta learn how to cook," I muttered.

*   *   *

Several hours later, I woke up coated in sweat and panting hard. I'd just had the most hideous dream and my heart was still racing. The room was dark, but I could make out shapes and my eyes immediately darted to the other side of the bed. Dutch's form was lying there and as I strained to listen, I could hear the deep sound of his breathing. "Oh, thank God," I whispered, and I reached over to lay a hand very gently on his hip. He stirred ever so slightly but went back to his deep breathing and I knew he was all right.

Still, the dream echoed in my head and I was having a hell of a time trying to quiet my nerves. I'd dreamed that I'd been attending Dutch's funeral. The pallbearers, made up of four men—Ricardo and Ricky Delgado, Dutch's cousin Chase, and his boss, Raymond Robillard—had laid his coffin into the ground and proceeded to shovel dirt over it as fast as they could.

I'd begged them to stop. I didn't want to believe that Dutch was in the coffin. "Just let me look inside!" I pleaded, trying to take Ricardo's shovel from him.

"Get back!" he'd snapped, but I wouldn't let go. And that's when I'd felt the arms of Raymond Robillard grab me from behind and his hand take hold of my chin.

"You're dead now too," he said, and fear gripped my heart like a vise. I'd seen Robillard kill before in a vision given to me by his dead victim. Dutch knew his boss was a killer and he'd been very quietly investigating him for months with the approval of Robillard's boss, but other than that, no one else in the bureau suspected the truth.

Remembering that part of the dream, I rubbed at my chin. His hands had felt so real and I shivered a little as I tried to shake it off. I got up as quietly as I could and headed to the bathroom, where I splashed cool water on my face and the back of my neck. I often had prophetic dreams, and typically they came to me in the form of a nightmare. I had the sense that this one was no different, and as I searched for the hidden meaning, I felt a real sense of cold fear settle into the pit of my stomach. Which part of the dream was I supposed to pay attention to? Robillard? Dutch's funeral? Delgado and his son lowering my boyfriend's coffin into the ground?

I wanted to sit down and contact the crew and ask them to clarify it, but I was so shaken by the images I'd seen that I hesitated. Maybe it was just a dream. Nothing important, just my anxiety during this trip acting up.

My left side said it didn't think so.

"Shit," I said.

There was a soft knock on the door. "Abs?" I heard Dutch say. "You in there?"

I opened the door. "Sorry, I didn't mean to wake you."

My sleepy-looking boyfriend grinned. "I'm not sure it was all you. Nature might have had a hand in it."

"Okay," I said, and moved aside. "It's all yours."

Dutch caught me as I tried to step past him. Lifting my chin, he looked intently at me. "What's up?"

"Bad dreams."

"Want to talk about it?"

I opened my mouth, but I couldn't form the words. Instead, to my surprise, I started to cry.

"Aw, honey," he said, pulling me into his chest. "Shhhhhh. It's okay. It was only a dream."

"Will you make me a solemn promise?" I asked him, wiping at my eyes.

"You name it," he said.

"Will you not take any chances with Robillard? I mean, if you suspect that he's on to your investigation even in the slightest, will you please let it go?"

I could feel Dutch stiffen slightly. This was the first time we'd talked about Robillard in a long time. "I'm careful, Abs," he said, but I could detect just the smallest hint of worry in his own voice. "And I've almost got him," he added. "I'm very close to getting the evidence to nail him, so don't worry, okay?"

I picked my head up and looked into his beautiful midnight blues. "I mean it, Dutch," I said, feeling another shiver. "Do not take chances. He'll kill you in a heartbeat, without thinking about it and with absolutely no remorse." Dutch opened up his mouth to say something, but I interrupted him. "And then, after he kills you, he'll come after me."

Dutch blinked and looked into my eyes earnestly. "The dream?" he asked after a moment. I nodded. Dutch blew out a sigh and pulled me into a fierce embrace. "Okay," he said. "You win. When I get back to Michigan, I'll take myself off the case."

I hugged him back fiercely and whispered, "Thank you, thank you, thank you."

Hours later as the sun came up and he and I were snuggling together, he said, "I should take you to Vegas more often."

I giggled. We'd just had a little one-on-one time—if you get my drift—and I'd been particularly . . . er . . . enthusiastic. "Must be this desert air," I said, drawing circles with my finger on his chest. "It makes me frisky."

"That settles it. We're moving here," he announced, and I laughed heartily.

"Oh, I don't think you could handle me being frisky *all* the time."

"I'm willing to take that risk," he said, grinning ear to ear.

I rolled my eyes. "So what happened at the station with that happy couple Bambina and Ricky?"

Dutch made a derisive sound. "What a couple of losers," he said. "Total waste of time. We started out with Bambina, hoping the haze would wear off and she'd be itchin' to tell us what she knew, but she's either really stupid or really good at acting stupid."

"What do you mean?"

"She insists that Delgado called her around midweek last week and said he'd be out of town for the next two weeks. She hasn't seen him in a whole week."

"Does her cell phone back that up?"

"Yes," Dutch said. "A call from a phone registered to Delgado did come in five days ago around eleven at night, but that could have been about anything. We only have her word."

"What does the son say?"

"Same story," Dutch said. "Which makes me think they got their stories straight ahead of time."

"What did the security guard say?"

"He hasn't seen Delgado since last Monday either."

"But he and Chase were abducted this past Saturday morning," I reasoned.

"Exactly," Dutch said, rubbing his eyes tiredly. "But there's no flight record of Delgado going anywhere."

"So where was he from Monday to Saturday?"

"That's the sixty-five-thousand-dollar question, Abs," Dutch said. "And, to make matters worse, we're also having a hard time finding motive for Ricky and Bambina to want to pull this thing off. By every indication we can see, Delgado's worth a butt load of money, but the son has access to a very healthy trust fund, plus he's the silent partner in most of his father's businesses. There's no job title, of course, and by everything we can see, Ricky's paid to do absolutely nothing. Without dear old Dad around to continue to bring in the dough, Junior's looking at a significant reduction in income."

"Maybe it's resentment?" I argued. "Maybe Ricky got sick of taking orders from his old man and wanted to teach him a lesson, so he hires some thugs to kidnap his dad and hold him for ransom while he hits dat thang."

Dutch picked his head up off the pillow and looked at me. " 'Hits dat thang'?" he quoted.

I narrowed my eyes back at him. "It's slang for—"

"I know what it's slang for. I just didn't think there was an eighteen-year-old rapper hidden inside my girl-friend."

"Whatevs . . . ," I said, rolling my eyes. "Back to the happy couple. My theory may be right."

"Anything's possible," Dutch said. "But Ricky doesn't strike me as the smart half of the Bambina and Ricky show."

"He's dumber than her?"

"Hard to imagine, but, yes. He peed his pants the moment Brosseau entered the interrogation room. He kept begging us not to tell his dad about 'hitting dat thang.' "

"It doesn't sound as good coming out of your mouth. Maybe you need a hand gesture," I said, curling my two middle fingers down and jamming my hand out and down.

Dutch laughed. "Yeah, *that* makes it credible."

"Have we heard anything from the dragon lady?"

"Ah, Paloma Delgado, such charm, such sincerity," he said with a mocking smile. "No, nothing new and no instructions have come in yet. And the more time we spend chasing our tails, the worse the odds are for Chase."

"So what are you going to do now?" I asked.

Dutch scratched his head. "I'm limited in my abilities to butt in here," he finally said. "The moment I start pushing my weight around and calling the shots is when things will start to go downhill fast. All I can do is sug-gest and give my opinion."

"But if it helps bring Chase home faster," I reasoned, "wouldn't you want to do everything you could, no mat-ter what the personal cost?"

"What would you have me do, Abby?" Dutch asked.

"Call in the local FBI," I said. "Let them come in, take over the jurisdiction, and you can work as a visiting agent, on loan from the Michigan bureau."

"I can't do that," Dutch said firmly.

"Why not?"

"Because it'd be a bad thing if I did. For everybody."

I lost patience and sat up to face him. "I can't believe you're not willing to risk your career over your *family,* Dutch! He's your *cousin!* You guys are like brothers! For God's sake, lay the freakin' cards on the table and use every available tool at your disposal!"

"Don't you think I know he's family, Abby?!" Dutch snapped. "Of course I want to lay everything out on the table, but there's desperate and there's smart, and right now it is best for *everybody*, including my family, if I play it smart!"

I stared at my boyfriend for several long seconds without speaking. It was getting rarer that he lost his temper with me, even though I tested his patience continually. Oh yeah, I can be a total brat when I want to. "Okay," I finally said. "You're at a better vantage point than I am to look at this situation. If you don't think it will help to call the local bureau, then I'll support that."

Dutch was breathing hard and glaring at me. The nerve I'd struck was apparently still exposed. "I'm gonna take a shower," he said, and got up out of the bed. When the bathroom door shut firmly behind him, I lay back on the bed and shook my head.

"Will I ever learn?" I muttered.

I took a shower after Dutch and when I came out, he was on the phone and rummaging around in my purse. "Can I help you?" I asked.

He looked up and his eyes were gentle again. After saying to the person on the other end, "Hold on a sec," he placed the receiver against his chest and explained, "I'm looking for the Brosseaus' address. Remember how I wanted to send the flowers?" I walked over and held out my hand. Dutch put my purse in my outstretched hand and said, "Sorry. Didn't mean to invade your space there."

"No worries. I've been through your shaving kit," I said. That won me a grin and I dug into my purse, pulling up the gum wrapper. "Two seventy-nine Desert Bloom Road," I said.

Dutch repeated the address into the phone and I tucked the gum wrapper back into my purse. He was off the phone a few minutes later and looked at me expectantly. "You ready to roll?"

"I am," I said. "Where exactly are we rolling to?"

"While you were in the shower, I got a call from Laney. She sounds bad and she wants me to stop by."

"That poor woman," I said, feeling for her.

Dutch grabbed his wallet, phone, and keys and we walked to the door. "You got your key card?" he asked.

"Sure," I said, yet my radar said I didn't. "Wait," I said, sifting through my purse. "Crap, where did I leave it?" My radar said to look in the bathroom, and sure enough, when I went there, it was on the counter under a towel.

"Found it," I said, coming back out. "Okay, *now* I'm ready."

We headed out of the hotel and into the parking garage. When we were settled and driving up the ramp to get to the Strip, Dutch said, "After we check in with Laney, I want to go back to Mrs. Delgado's place."

"The dragon lady," I mumbled.

"Be nice," he said.

"Have you *met* her?" I said. "That *is* nice."

"Abs," Dutch said, his tone telling me to chill.

"Fine, whatever," I said. Then I noticed that his brow was wet with perspiration. The AC was on at full blast and with that, I was bordering on chilly. "How're you feeling?" I said, reaching up to feel his brow.

"Not great," he admitted. "My stomach's upset again."

"And you're running a temp," I said. "Dutch, maybe you've got something more than food poisoning."

"Could be the flu," he said, then glanced at me. "You okay?"

"I'm fine. What if on the way to Delgado's we stop off at a clinic or something?"

"If it is the flu, Abs, there's nothing they can do for me. They'll just tell me to drink plenty of liquids and take it easy."

"Which isn't a bad idea. Pull over at that gas station and let's get you some Gatorade."

Dutch pulled into a Shell station and while he gassed up the car, I dodged in and got several bottles of water and two big jugs of Gatorade. We were back on the road in a jiffy and I was forcing him to sip at the Gatorade. "This tastes awful," he said. "What flavor is it?"

"Riptide Rush," I said.

Dutch shook his head and put the lid back on the Gatorade. "Maybe it's an acquired taste. Anyway, after we talk to Mrs. Delgado, we'll head back to the police station and visit with our old friends Bambina and Ricky."

"Bimbo and the Rat."

Dutch looked at me. "You live to be sarcastic, don't you?"

I smiled sweetly at him. "You gotta find the fun in life where you can."

We arrived at Laney's and Dutch parked in her driveway. We made our way to the front door, which was pulled open even before we could knock. "Thank God you're here," she said. Her cheeks were stained with tears and her eyes were red and puffy.

"What's happened?" Dutch asked as she held the door open for us.

Laney closed the door and motioned us into the living room. Hurrying over to the computer on the small desk in the corner of the room, she sat down and began typing. "I went online this morning," she explained. "The mortgage payment was due yesterday and I wanted to make sure Chase had taken care of it. And he had, but . . ." and then her breath caught and she began to sob.

Dutch moved in and squatted down next to her. Rubbing her back, he said gently, "It's all right, Laney. Tell me what's happened and we'll figure it out."

Laney pointed to the computer screen and both Dutch and I squinted at it. There were several columns on the screen and several rows were in bold red with little negative signs next to the dollar values there. "It . . . it's gone!" Laney sobbed. "All our money is gone!"

Dutch used the mouse to scroll up and down the page. The mortgage payment and a few other bills had bounced, leaving a trail of bank fees and a substantially negative balance in the account. "When was the last time you checked your balance?" Dutch asked.

"Last week," Laney moaned. "Things have been tight since the baby came, but I had that student loan I told you about come through last week for a little over ten thousand dollars. All of it's been wiped out, Dutch!"

"Have you called your bank?"

Laney nodded. "Yes, this morning. They said that a check was cashed at their drive-through the day before yesterday for the entire amount in our checking account. They were going to send me a scan of it as soon as they could."

Dutch pulled out his wallet and checked the contents. Pulling out all but a few of the bills, he handed these to Laney. "First of all," he said, "we can fix this, so don't panic."

Laney shoved the money back at Dutch. "I can't take your money, Dutch."

"The hell you can't, Laney. You and Hanna are family. I take care of my family, okay?" Laney was still leaking tears and Dutch wiped them away. "I never did get you guys a housewarming gift. Consider this it."

Laney finally took the bills. "Thank you so much," she said. "But this is a loan."

"Fine," Dutch said. "And if a fraud was committed, then the bank will insure your funds. They'll replenish the account and remove the fees."

"How long do you think that will take?"

"Day or two," Dutch said. "And in the meantime, I'm going to cover your mortgage payment so you won't have to worry about it." Laney again shook her head no, but Dutch insisted. "Don't even think about arguing this with me, because you will lose."

"He's right, Laney," I agreed. "Once his mind is made up, he doesn't back down."

"I can cut you a check as soon as they put the money back in the account, Dutch."

Dutch smiled. "Of course you can," he said. "But for now, it's one less thing you'll have to worry about."

Dutch called his bank back in Michigan and gave the wire instructions for the funds to Laney's mortgage company, including a twenty-dollar returned-check fee. After that was done, Laney called her neighbor and begged her to babysit Hanna while we went to the bank.

The three of us were escorted in to see the manager, who seemed somewhat prepared for our visit. "I thought you might drop by, Mrs. Rivers," he said to Laney.

"Mr. Thompson, this is my husband's cousin FBI agent Dutch Rivers," Laney said, introducing Dutch.

The mention of Dutch's title had a significant effect on Mr. Thompson. "I can assure you, Agent Rivers, we are working very hard to get to the bottom of this."

"The bureau would appreciate it," Dutch said, throwing his weight around for the first time since we'd landed in Vegas.

Mr. Thompson reached for a piece of paper in a file. "This is a scan of the check that was cashed," he said, handing it to Laney. "The signature matches your husband's, and the check is made out to cash. There is also a separate withdrawal slip that was included with the check in the drive-through dispenser, and that was for all but one dollar of your savings account."

Laney's mouth dropped. "This is impossible," she said.

Dutch looked pointedly at the bank manager. "Mr. Thompson, my cousin was recently abducted along with a prominent businessman on Saturday morning. If he signed this check and this deposit slip, I can assure you it was under threat of great bodily harm to either himself or his family."

Mr. Thompson turned ashen. "That's terrible," he said. Turning to his computer, he swiveled the screen around so that we could see. "And it might explain this videotape caught by our camera at the drive-through. I took the liberty of reviewing it after I received your call, Mrs. Rivers. We don't monitor these tapes unless there's a problem—otherwise I'm sure we would have contacted you."

The bank manager pressed a button and the screen populated with a very grainy picture of two men in a car. The first man appeared thin as he sat behind the wheel of the car wearing a baseball cap and large mirrored sunglasses. He had a thick mustache and wore a sweatshirt, and one of his hands was held low, out of the camera's view. The angle of his arm seemed to show that it was pointing at the other passenger.

The other passenger was clearly Chase Rivers. His blond hair was ruffled, his lip was swollen and cut, and one eye looked black-and-blue. The look on his face was lethal as he stared at the driver with menace. "Chase!" Laney yelped. "Ohmigod! He's alive!"

Dutch flipped open his cell phone and punched in some numbers. "Bob? It's Dutch," he said. "I need you and a team of techs to get down to the Bank of America on Westcliff immediately. I've got a break in the Delgado case."

Chapter Five

The bank branch shut down for the rest of the morning while a team of police descended on the building. Dutch and Bob talked privately in the corner and I knew it wasn't good. A few minutes later, Dutch walked briskly over to me and Laney and said, "We've got to go."

"What?" I asked. "Why?"

"Come on, Abby," he said, and escorted us out of the building. After piling into the car, I turned to face him and opened my mouth, but he cut me off. "Please don't ask."

I fell silent and we drove back to Laney's. "What aren't you telling me?" she asked him from the backseat as the car rolled to a stop.

Dutch turned in his seat and said, "I promise, I am doing everything I can to bring Chase back to you," he said. "I'll be in touch as soon as I hear something. But Abby and I have to go. There's something we need to do, and I don't have time to explain."

Laney blinked at him for a moment or two, the dark circles under her eyes more pronounced and the sag in her shoulders suggesting that she was on the verge of exhaustion. "Fine," she said. "I won't ask. Just please bring my husband back, Dutch."

"You have my solemn vow."

After she'd stepped out of the car and was heading up the steps of her house, I said, "She looks bad. Should I stay with her?"

"I wish I could loan you out," Dutch said as he put the car in reverse and sped down the street. "But I'm going to need that lie detector and I don't have any time to spare."

"Why are we in such a hurry?"

Dutch didn't answer me right away and just when I figured he wasn't going to at all, he said, "I think by the looks of that photograph from the bank that Chase was forced to give away the only thing that could have kept him alive."

"His money," I said, putting it all together. "Now that they've picked him clean, the kidnappers will think he's expendable."

Dutch nodded and said nothing further as he broke every speed limit between Laney's house and the Delgado mansion. When he got to the call box on the other side of the gates, he seemed to relax a little as he looked into the driveway.

Rosa let us in again and we parked next to a Volvo with a police tag. "Colby's still here," he said as we got out.

We walked to the door, where Rosa greeted us warmly. *"Buenos días,"* she said. "Senora Delgado is in the sitting room again."

We followed Rosa to the large room and found the missus sitting in the same seat, but today a woman in a pink coat and white pants sat in front of her with a manicure table and was busy filing the dragon's claws.

"Good morning," Dutch greeted her, charm and a bright smile forcing themselves onto his face.

Delgado cocked one eyebrow, but didn't look up. "What do you want?"

"Can I bring you some coffee and breakfast rolls?" Rosa asked us. I nodded while my stomach grumbled, but Dutch shook his head no. "Okay," she said. "I bring one for you." And off she went.

"Mrs. Delgado, I'd like to ask you a few questions, if I could?"

The dragon sighed. "I'm tired of questions, Detective."

I hid a smile because Dutch had never introduced himself as a detective. Delgado was only assuming he was one of the men from the local PD working the case.

"I can imagine," Dutch said. "And I'm sure we've all been asking you the same questions over and over, but there was another man who was abducted with your husband, Mrs. Delgado, and we have reason to believe his life is in the most jeopardy."

Delgado glanced at Dutch. "More than Ricardo's?" she asked.

"Much more," he said. "Your husband's bodyguard was taken in the kidnapping. He has a wife and baby at home, and he's a good man, ma'am. I know him personally."

"He's not very good at his job," she said rudely, turning her attention back to her manicure. "That's too square!" she snapped. The manicurist jumped, nodded, and hurried to correct the nail.

"Mrs. Delgado, I know you don't seem to care what happens to your husband, but what about the father of your children?"

"Why is it so important to you, Detective, that I give a damn about anyone?"

"Because we're running out of time," Dutch said earnestly. "The man who was guarding your husband has very, very little time."

"I've told you everything I know," she said. "If I knew who took Ricardo, I'd tell you." My lie detector went off and I glared hard at her. She caught the look, and for the first time, I saw her back down a little. "Fine, what do you want to know, Detective?"

"Do you think your son had anything to do with your husband's abduction?"

"Doubtful," she said. "Ricky's worshipped the ground his father walks on since he was five. He's even taken Ricardo's side in our separation."

"So there is no motive you can think of that would have your son turn on his father?"

"No," Mrs. Delgado said. Again my lie detector went off.

"Really?" I said doubtfully, giving the dragon lady the deepest glare I could muster.

Again Delgado seemed to check herself under my hard stare. She scowled at me and said, "Ever since Ricky met that *bimbo* my husband likes to slum around town with, he's been under some sort of spell. He hasn't been able to get her out of his head, and worse, the two seem to share a great love of white powder."

"Did your husband know about Ricky's involvement with Bambina?" Dutch asked.

"I'm sure he did," the dragon said easily. "There's little that Ricardo isn't aware of."

"Why didn't he put a stop to it?"

"I believe he tried," she said wearily. "I heard that Ricardo intended to put her into one of those fancy rehab facilities in Santa Fe and wash his hands of her, but he had to wait for an opening, which was weeks away."

"So," Dutch said, trying to follow her logic, "you believe that Ricky learned that his father intended to ship Bambina off to rehab, and he might have teamed up with her to get the old man out of the way?"

"No," she said coolly, blowing on the wet polish of her right hand. "I don't believe that, but you did ask if there was anything that could turn my son against his father, and the only thing that's ever come between those two was that poor excuse of a prostitute."

At that moment Rosa came back in with a small tray loaded with freshly brewed coffee and a huge syrupy breakfast roll.

"When was the last time you saw your husband, ma'am?" Dutch continued.

"It's been six weeks since I threw him out," she said.

Dutch pushed a little harder. "And you haven't seen him or heard from him since that time?"

"No." Again my lie detector went haywire, and I caught the questioning look that Rosa cast at her employer. "That will be all, Rosa," Delgado growled as her housekeeper stood there dumbly after setting down the tray.

Rosa hurried away. I nudged Dutch and he grunted uncomfortably, then said, "Did your husband ever share the details of his business practices with you?"

"What are you getting at?"

"Well, every successful businessman develops a few enemies along the way. I'm wondering if Mr. Delgado ever told you about anyone who might be an enemy or a threat to him. Maybe someone who was willing to go to the extreme such as kidnapping to extract a fortune and get him out of the way?"

"My husband had plenty of enemies," she said vaguely. "Most recently his former business partner wasn't too happy with him."

"Why is that?" Dutch asked.

"He caught my husband fucking his wife."

My eyes widened and I needed a distraction, so I picked up the plate with the roll and took a nibble. It was incredibly good. "I see," Dutch said. "What is this man's name?"

"Donovan Kelton."

"Anyone else?"

"I'll make up a list after my nails are dry. You can pick it up this evening," she said with a sigh.

Dutch put his hand on his phone as it vibrated, and pulled it up to look at the display. Clicking it back onto his belt, he said, "Thank you, ma'am. I'd appreciate it. We'll leave you to your manicure."

Pulling me by the elbow, he whispered, "We've got to go."

I quickly shoved the rest of the roll into my mouth, and Dutch gave me a sober look. "What?" I said through a mouthful of gooey dough. "It's good!"

"Come on, Edgar," he said, pulling me along. "Time's a-wasting."

We rounded the corner and bumped into the detective on guard, Colby, who was just coming out of the bathroom carrying a newspaper. "Oh!" he said when he saw us. "I didn't realize you were here. Is Bob here too?"

"No, but he should be along shortly. No word yet from the kidnappers about further instructions?"

"Nope, not a word. This is one dull assignment," he grumbled.

"Well, hang in there," Dutch said, not wanting to linger and make small talk. "We're running late, so we'll talk to you later."

As we bustled toward the front door, I noticed Rosa off in one of the other rooms dusting the furniture. I grabbed Dutch's hand and yanked him to a halt. "Wait!" I hissed. "We need to talk to her."

Dutch glanced at his watch. "Can't. We've got to go."

My radar insisted otherwise. "Dutch," I said, digging my heels in and refusing to budge. "Trust me, we need to ask her something."

Dutch's mouth pressed to a thin line. "What?"

"Come with me," I said, and hurried over to Rosa.

When she saw us coming, she stopped dusting and asked, "Did you like the roll and coffee?"

I smiled. "That has to be the best pastry I've ever had, Rosa, thank you."

The sweet maid actually blushed. "Is nothing," she said.

"Listen, I just have a quick question for you, and it's really important that you answer it truthfully, okay?"

Rosa seemed to tense. "Yes?"

"When was the last time Mrs. Delgado saw Mr. Delgado?"

Rosa fidgeted with the little Swiffer duster in her hands. "It's been six weeks or so, like the lady said," she said.

My lie detector gonged in my head. "I'm sorry, Rosa, but I don't believe you. We're trying to bring Mr. Delgado home, and if there is *anything* that you know that might be important, we really need to know about it, okay?"

Rosa looked nervously into the hallway behind us. Then she leaned in and whispered, "I could lose my job!"

"Trust me," I said. "No one will know the information came from you."

Rosa hesitated for a moment, before she shrugged her shoulders and said, "They have been seeing each other, in secret."

"Who?" Dutch asked.

"The mister and missus. He has been coming over at night and leaving in the morning."

"For how long?"

"For a little while, like, two weeks or so. They are always back and forth like a tennis ball, those two. One week they in love, the next they not so much in love anymore. Then, just when I think it working out with them, they have a terrible argument."

"Over what?"

"The lady want him to sign agreement that say if he cheat again, she get everything."

"A postnup," I said thoughtfully. "I'm assuming he didn't go for that?"

"No, not so much," Rosa said. "Anyway, he left in the middle of the night and the next morning the lady say she had enough and she file for divorce."

"When *exactly* was this argument?"

"Monday night," she said.

My boyfriend glanced again at his watch. "Abs, we *have* to go. Now."

"Thank you so much, Rosa, we really appreciate it," I said, and we boogied out the door.

Dutch hurried to the car and I jumped in after him. Without waiting for me to buckle up, he turned the ignition and drove to the gate, tapping his fingers on the steering wheel as we waited for it to open. The moment there was room for the car to fit through, he pressed on the gas. My radar whispered something in my mind and I yelled, "Go left!" as he was about to turn right.

Without questioning me, he did as I'd instructed and we zipped down the street. As we got to the end of the street, I looked in the side mirror and noticed a string of black sedans all with tinted glass pull up to the Delgado house and roll through the already-open gates. "FBI," I said, identifying the three cars followed by Bob's minivan. Turning to Dutch, I said, "Why exactly are you working so hard to avoid your own agency?"

"It's complicated," he said.

"Spill it," I insisted.

Dutch ran a hand through his hair. "I can't, babe." When I made a sound that said he was full of shit, he said, "I mean it. I really can't."

"How am I supposed to help you if you won't clue me in?"

Dutch was quiet for a long time before he finally said, "This case is a lot more complex than anyone realizes. If I told you everything I knew, I could be putting you in significant danger." And then he seemed to grow frustrated with himself and he added, "Hell, I already have put you in danger."

Pulling over to the side of the road, he stopped the car and turned to me, his eyes intense and tone serious. "Listen to me carefully, okay?"

"I'm listening," I said.

"If anything happens to me, I want you to get the hell out of here immediately. I mean, you don't wait around for anything—you just get out of Dodge and you fly to your sister's house in Boston and lay low."

"What?" I said. "Why?"

"I can't tell you. Just promise me you'll do as I say and catch the first plane out."

"Are you *kidding* me with this shit?" I snapped. "What the hell are you caught up in, Dutch?"

He didn't answer me. Instead he turned back to the wheel and put the car in drive again. "Promise me," he said after a moment.

"No." My middle name is Stubborn.

"Abby, I am not kidding around here. You either promise me or I put you on a damn plane home today!"

I glared at him. "You and what army?"

"I don't need an army," he said. "I have connections which I will use to keep you safe."

I threw up my hands and said, "Fine! I promise you, okay? But it's ridiculous!"

Dutch seemed to relax. "Thank you," he said, rubbing his side. "And by the way, the next time you need to get my attention, try kicking me in the shin or something. Your elbow is so bony I think you cracked a rib."

Dutch was always good at relieving tension. "Don't let anything happen to you," I said to him. "I don't want to deliver on that promise, you hear me?"

"I hear ya," he said, and slid his hand into mine. "I hear ya."

We drove back to the hotel and I ordered us some lunch. I wolfed down my burger, but Dutch passed on everything but a few crackers. He'd begun to look pale and drawn again, so I insisted that he go to bed and take a nap. To my surprise he didn't put up a fight and took me up on my suggestion.

Not in the mood for a nap myself, I decided to explore the hotel, so I left Dutch a note in case he woke up, and slipped out the door. When I got down to ground level, I started by touring the casino, which was dark and smoky and filled with sounds like thousands of pinball machines dinging and pinging all around.

I didn't care for the energy of the place—too many people and too much cigarette smoke—so I ventured instead near the lobby and the shops. At first I was a little intimidated by all the designer labels, but after a while I ventured into Dolce & Gabbana and Louis Vuitton and of course my favorite, Jimmy Choo. I was like a kid at the petting zoo, stroking the luxurious fabrics, cuddling with the fine leather purses, and cooing to the shoes. "Want to come home with me?" I asked one pair of beautiful snakeskin sandals. Their $450 price tag begged to differ, however, and I left them to find another home.

I meandered up and down the little mall area, window-shopping and people watching and in a haze of dreamy delirium caused by so many fantasies of what I would buy if I were really rich, when my radar gave a buzz. I glanced at my watch and noticed I'd been walking around for several hours. "Wow, time really does fly here," I said. I pulled out my cell phone and sent Dutch a text message that told him I was on my way back to the room.

I got lost a couple of times trying to find the elevator, but I finally made my way back and rode up to our floor. My radar had kicked into full gear now, and I was anxious to check on Dutch, thinking that perhaps his fever was spiking again and it was now time to insist on a visit to the doctor.

When I got to the room, I fished around for my key card and found it at the bottom of my purse. Opening the door, I was surprised at how dark the room was. "Dutch?" I said softly. No one answered.

I moved into the room and closed the door quietly. If Dutch was asleep, I didn't want to wake him. Moving to the bedroom, I glanced in and found the bed empty. My head darted to the bathroom door, but it was open and the light was off.

I walked around the suite just to be sure, but Dutch wasn't here, and then I noticed a note on the table where I'd left my own note a few hours before. I picked it up and saw that Dutch had written on the back of my note. It said:

> *Edgar,*
>   *Had to go check out a lead—your radar may be right on target. Be back for dinner. Hope you had fun downstairs. I may be buying you those Jimmy Choos after all. See you soon.*
>   *Love,*
>   *Dutch*

I smiled as I set the note down. God, I loved that man. I switched on some lights and curled up on the couch. Flipping on the television, I got comfortable and occupied myself with pay-per-view.

An hour later my stomach was rumbling and I was checking the time. It was six thirty. "Where are you, cowboy?" I wondered. I got up and pulled my cell out of my purse. I hadn't missed his call or a reply text from him—not that I was expecting one, but I was anxious to hear from him all the same.

I sent him another text, saying, *You on your way?* and set the phone on the coffee table by the couch to wait for a reply. Another half hour passed and I got up off the couch and clicked off the TV. Picking up my phone,

I dialed his cell. It rang four times and went to voice mail. "Hey, cowboy," I said. "Sorry if you're in the middle of something, but I'm hungry!" I threw in a laugh to let him know I was joking with him and then added, "Okay, so call me and let me know you're okay and when you're coming back."

I set the phone down and stared at it, willing it to ring. Nothing happened. I got up and began to pace the room again, glancing at the cell phone periodically, but another hour passed and still no word from Dutch.

I was working hard to convince myself that things were fine—just because he hadn't had a chance to call me back didn't mean anything. The man was trying to work the case to find his cousin. He might be in the middle of something really important and might have put his cell on silent.

I called down to room service and ordered dinner for both of us, chicken noodle soup for him and a club sandwich for me. The food arrived: I kept his plate covered to hold in the heat. I checked my cell again to make sure the battery was still holding its charge—it was.

I picked at the fries and twirled the phone on the tabletop. By nine p.m. I was growing frantic and I made a call to Detective Brosseau. I didn't have his cell number, so I called the local PD and they forwarded me to his voice mail. I left him an urgent message to call me, then got up to pace the room again.

At eleven p.m. I was a total wreck. I'd left Dutch two more messages, and finally I'd dialed *911 call me!* into a text message, but there was no response. And that's when it hit me. My cell phone was actually FBI regulation issue. Dutch had gotten me the phone as a Valentine's Day present and the little thing had really come in handy—in fact it had saved my life a few months back.

Being approved for use by the bureau meant that it came with all the bells and whistles, including a GPS location chip that allowed agents to link together and pinpoint one another's locations if the other's serial number was encoded into a matching phone. I knew that Dutch had linked our phones together when he'd purchased them, which meant I had the means to see exactly where he was!

I just had to figure out how to use the little gadget and I'd be able to find him. I didn't have the manual, but I didn't think it would be too hard to figure it out.

I was wrong about that. It took me over an hour, and as the clock struck midnight, I finally had a small blue dot on my screen and a little text box that read *Dutch*. Using the scroll function, I could see a red dot some distance away labeled *Abby*.

"Gotcha!" I said, grabbing my key card and my purse and heading out the door. When I reached the street level, I had to stand in line for what felt like forever in order to catch a cab, but eventually my turn came up and when I hopped into the cab, I leaned over the armrest and showed the driver my cell phone. "See this blue dot?" I said.

"Cool phone!" he said.

"Yes," I said impatiently. "I need to find that blue dot."

"The one that says *Dutch*?"

"Yes," I said. "He's my boyfriend and I'm worried about him. Can you drive me to the blue dot?"

"Come sit up front," he said kindly. "It will be easier to track it if I can check your display."

We made our way into the long line of taxis working their way slowly down the driveway of the Wynn. "Lots of traffic tonight," the driver said.

"How long do you think it will take us to make our way out of this mess?" I asked. The last thing my frazzled nerves needed to deal with was a traffic jam.

"Not long," he said. Looking at me and noticing how anxious I must appear, he said, "Don't you worry. We'll find your boyfriend."

"Thank you," I said, but my intuition was screaming that something was really wrong. I kept my focus on the blue dot at the top of my cell's display, and millimeter by millimeter our red dot crawled closer to it.

Once the driver had made his way onto the Strip, traffic did lighten up. He squinted at my cell a few times when we were stopped at a red light. "He's out off of I-Ninety-five," he said. "But he's off the road, it looks like."

I pulled my cell close and squinted at the screen again. "You're right," I said, then used the zoom option on my phone to get a closer look. Sure enough, Dutch's blue dot was just off the highway. Maybe he'd pulled over and was meeting with someone who had some information about Chase. Maybe he didn't want to interrupt the meeting and that's why he wasn't calling me back. And maybe pigs were flying these days, said my radar.

"Can we hurry?" I asked the driver.

He hit the accelerator and we raced along to the highway. "I hope I don't get a ticket," he said.

I glanced at the taxi license posted on the visor above my head. My driver's name was Ralph Sawyer. "I'll pay for your ticket, Ralph," I said. "I just have a terrible feeling my boyfriend is in trouble."

Ralph nodded and focused hard on his driving. Out on the highway there wasn't much traffic to contend with, so we moved rapidly toward Dutch's blue dot until we hit a traffic jam not a quarter mile away. "Damn it!" I swore as we came to a big pile of gridlock.

"Must be an accident or something up ahead," Ralph said, craning his neck to see around the bulk of cars. "I can see lights up there. Must be a doozy."

My knee bounced with impatience as the cars in front of us inched forward. We were being pushed to the far-right two lanes and ahead we could see half a dozen swirling red and blue lights. Whatever had happened was bad.

Trouble was, the closer we got to the fire trucks and police cars, the closer we got to Dutch's blue dot. It dawned on me slowly, even though, looking back, I should have known right away that Dutch was the focal point of all that attention up ahead. Five hundred yards from the accident I felt the world begin to swirl around me. "Oh, God," I said. "Oh, no, please, no!"

Ralph looked at me. "You all right?"

My hands began to tremble, but I managed to hold up the display of the phone. He knew the moment I turned it toward him. "Aw, man," he said with compassion. "Hold on, little lady. Let me get you up there."

Ralph edged over to the shoulder and began to blow his horn wildly. We scurried precariously along the right shoulder, nearly hitting a few cars along the way. Just before we were within shouting distance of the first fire truck, an angry patrolman stepped out onto our path and waved his flashlight at us. Ralph punched the brakes and we skidded to a stop. I jumped out of the car and ran toward the cop. "Please!" I yelled. "It's my boyfriend! I think he's here!"

"Get back in your car!" he yelled at me.

"You don't understand!" I sobbed. "My boyfriend, Dutch Rivers, didn't come back to our hotel. I've been trying to call him, and this is him!" I said, pointing to my cell phone and shoving it at him.

"Lady, I said—"

"Is there a white Lexus involved in this accident?!" I screamed. "Please, just tell me what kind of car was involved!"

The cop blinked at me—it was sinking in. I was bordering on hysterical, shaking from head to toe, and shoving my phone at him. He finally glanced at my display, noticing it was a GPS indicator, and he looked behind him over the hoods of the block of cars. "She just wants to know if her boyfriend has been injured," said Ralph from right behind me. "She means no harm."

The cop turned back to me. "Come with me," he barked.

I turned to Ralph and shoved my hand in my purse, fishing for some money to give him. "No," he said kindly, his eyes pinched with concern. "I'll wait here for a little while in case it's not your boyfriend's car and you need a ride back to your hotel or to continue looking for him. If you're not back in a half hour, then I'll head back to town. For now, you go with the policeman, and don't worry about me, okay?"

I was crying so hard I couldn't catch my breath enough to respond. Instead I just nodded and turned back to hurry up to the cop. We wound our way through the cars and as we got closer, I could see that the other side of the road dropped off into a deep ravine. My heart was hammering in my chest, and I felt dizzy and faint as I looked at a tow truck that was using a winch to pull a battered and nearly unrecognizable white Lexus up onto its ramp.

I stumbled when I saw the car. It was smashed and broken, and I didn't think anyone would have been able to survive the tumble it appeared to have taken. I sank to the ground and began to sob. Strong arms reached under me and helped me to my feet. "Come this way, ma'am," the patrolman said. "Yo! Jimmy! Get me a paramedic!"

I tried to walk a few more paces, but the nightmare that was around me was too much. My senses were overloaded and I sank to the ground again. The world closed in around me to a small pinpoint, and I could feel my chest heaving as I tried to pull in air and stay conscious. Again I felt strong arms under me, but this time I was lifted completely up off the ground and carried over to a platform. Disembodied voices filled the air and I heard snatches of conversation. ". . . says that's her boy-friend's car . . ."

". . . we're still looking for the vic . . ."

". . . found the wallet near the car . . ."

A mask was put over my face and another voice or-dered me to breathe slowly but steadily and someone held my hand. I was freezing in the cool desert air and began to shiver. A blanket was placed over my shoulders but gave me little comfort. Finally, after what felt like an eternity of agony, one of the voices around me was getting through. "Abby?" it said gently.

I willed my eyes to focus. "Bob?" I said. My voice sounded muted from the mask.

"How are you feeling?" he asked me, and I could see that his eyes were pained.

Fresh tears streamed down my cheeks. "Please," I said, pulling the mask down off my face. "Tell me where he is."

"We don't know," he said soberly. "We haven't been able to locate him."

"Over here!" someone shouted from the ravine, and a flurry of rescue-team workers hurried to the voice. Bob moved away from me and I yanked the mask up over my head and threw it behind me. The paramedic who had been tending to me yelled, "Hey, come back here!" but I ignored him and ran to the edge of the ravine.

The scene caught my breath. A guardrail had been smashed apart and the imprint of the car had been left in a single grisly descent down the ravine. Sagebrush had been torn and flattened; rocks bore the scars of metal and paint and small bits of plastic; steel and glass were strewn everywhere. To the far left of the path three firefighters crouched over something hidden by the sage. A stretcher was being carried along the top ridge over to them and there were shouts to call in a medevac helicopter.

Again my heart was racing. If a helicopter was being

called in, that meant Dutch could be alive! I raced along the ridge, cutting in and out of rescue personnel. I even dashed past Bob, who shouted at me to stop. I ignored him too and jumped over the guardrail to the side of the steep slope. Slipping and sliding, I scuttled along and behind me I could hear shouts from several men chasing after me. I didn't care.

I came closer and closer to the three firefighters, one of whom had looked up as I approached and got to his feet to intercept me. *"Dutch!"* I screamed as he caught me and pulled me back. *"Dutch!"*

"Stop!" the firefighter said as I struggled against him. "That's my boyfriend!" I pleaded. "That's my boyfriend!"

The firefighter took me by the shoulders and shook me hard. I was so stunned that I stopped fighting him. "That's not your boyfriend over there, okay, lady?" he insisted.

I looked at him blankly. What he was saying made no sense. "His name is Dutch Rivers," I said. "He's an FBI agent from Michigan."

"Lady," the fireman said gently, staring into my eyes, trying to get through to me. "That ain't no guy. That's a woman. If your boyfriend is here, we haven't found him yet."

Brosseau reached us at that moment and took over for the firefighter. "I got her," he said, wrapping a protective yet secure arm around my shoulders. I didn't speak—I couldn't—but neither did I move and Bob seemed to recognize that I couldn't be pried away until I saw it for my own eyes.

As the stretcher reached the victim and she was safely transferred onto it, then lifted from the scrub, I could see that it definitely wasn't Dutch. It was an unconscious woman with silver-blond hair, scratched and bruised and bleeding from her head. One arm was swollen and most certainly broken, and in the other hand I saw her clutching something small and black, just like I was. I lifted my cell and looked at the display. The blue dot and the red dot had almost merged and were only about ten yards apart, the distance from me to her.

I sank to the ground again and put my head in my hands. I couldn't take seeing anything more.

Chapter Six

I waited in the bay of the ambulance into the early-morning hours without speaking to anyone. I was in a sort of numb haze that surrounded me like a soft cocoon. The paramedic who waited with me in case they found Dutch alive shoved an IV into my arm and wrapped me in blankets. He tried everything he could think of to get me to agree to go to the hospital. "Ma'am, you're in shock," he said. "I'd really prefer if you allowed us to take you to the hospital."

I shook my head no.

"It's cold out here," he reasoned. "If you go to the hospital, I promise, as soon as we hear anything, I'll make sure they get word to you."

Again I shook my head no and continued to survey the rescue workers and the face of the ravine, my eyes darting around every rock, bush, and outcropping, looking for Dutch. Bob came over to sit with me after a time. He held my hand, which he gave a gentle squeeze every once in a while. "People survive these kinds of crashes all the time," he said. "If one passenger survived it, then so could Dutch."

But I knew the truth. The miracle had already been

handed off to that woman who'd been clutching his cell phone. If Dutch had been in that car, he was dead, and we both knew it. There was only one way I could tell for certain—I could ask my crew—but I couldn't bring myself to do it. I would wait to be told by the search team, and then I would wait to be shown. Proof positive would be with my own eyes—I'd accept nothing less.

But as the hours dragged on and the firefighters searched through the scrub, and a team of rescue dogs was dispatched to sniff him out, no sign of him was revealed. It was as if he'd vanished off the side of the ravine.

I shivered again in the cold morning air and thought for the umpteenth time about using my radar to find Dutch. And I wanted him found—believe me—but if my radar said he was here, I knew I'd likely find him dead, and I just hadn't been ready to face that.

While I was working up my courage, a black sedan with tinted windows pulled up near the ambulance where I was sitting. A man in a black suit got out and held the door open for another man, whose profile looked familiar.

I blinked a few times to clear my eyes and focused hard on his face. Where had I seen him before? He must have sensed someone was staring because he turned briefly in my direction and the breath caught in my throat as I realized I was looking at Raymond Robillard, Dutch's boss and the man I'd seen murder Cynthia Frost in a vision from beyond the grave she'd shared with me some months ago.

I felt Robillard's gaze settle on me. It was an icy glare, but not one of recognition. He turned away when Detective Brosseau moved toward him and introduced himself, and the two men walked along the edge of the road as Bob talked, waving his hands down the ravine and no doubt discussing the details of the accident.

I made up my mind quickly and turned my eyes to

the ravine. Squinting in the morning sunlight, I focused on projecting my intuitive radar out along the ridge and down the ravine, attempting to feel out any trace of Dutch's energy. I came up completely empty.

A tiny bubble of renewed hope made its way into my numb mind. Maybe Dutch wasn't here after all. Perhaps he hadn't even been in the car!

I had to know for sure, so I closed my eyes and called out to my crew. I felt them immediately, and I could also detect a sense of urgency coming from their energy. *Show me where Dutch is,* I said to them. *Tell me what's happened to him.*

There was a long dramatic pause—unusual for my crew—then an image formed and as it developed in my mind, my lower lip quivered and I felt fresh tears sting my eyes. I was looking at the unmistakable image of a gravestone. Carved into the surface so that they could be sure to remove all doubt was

HERE LIES DUTCH RIVERS
AT PEACE WITH OUR LADY OF SAINTS

Another line on the surface of the stone wanted to form, but I couldn't read it, nor did I want to. Instead I opened my eyes and turned to the paramedic sipping a cup of hot coffee and said, "I'd like to go to the hospital now."

I was driven away from the accident before anyone like Robillard had a chance to question me. It was the perfect getaway and allowed me a little more time to sink into that quiet detached numbness. I shivered all the way there, even though the attentive paramedic piled on the blankets. "Abby," he said gently. "You'll need to stay awake for me, okay? Your heart rate is a little slower than I'd like it to be, so try and stay awake."

I ignored him. I didn't care what the hell my heart rate was. But there was no way I could sleep right now anyway. Dutch was dead. My crew had confirmed it. And my own grandmother had suggested there was a risk that Dutch could die unless I did something to prevent it—but what had I missed? How had I let this happen?

And for that matter, how had my crew let this happen? And why, when I dug down into my broken heart, didn't *I* sense that he was dead? Why didn't that deep internal visceral feeling jibe with the imagery my crew had shown me? Because when I tried to sync up Dutch's death with that leaden heavy feeling I knew I'd feel if he'd crossed over, it wasn't there. In my gut there was a lighter feeling, one that felt hopeful.

I moved my arm and pulled up my cell phone. I had Dutch's picture loaded onto my phone, and maybe if I could really see his flat plastic image there, it would help to convince me there was nothing more for it. But when I flipped open the lid, all I got was a black screen. Sometime in the night the battery had died. Shit.

"How you doin'?" the paramedic asked.

"I'm tired," I said, letting my hand fall back to the blanket. "And I want to go home."

"Where you from?" the paramedic asked casually. I could tell he was trying to keep me talking.

I sighed. "Michigan."

"I've been there before," he said with a smile. "They get a lot of snow in the winter."

I didn't respond. He tried a few more questions but gave up when I just stared at the wall of the ambulance and refused to talk.

We pulled into the hospital bay and I was wheeled out of the cab and hurried along a corridor while the paramedic gave a woman in a white lab coat all my stats. I stared blankly to the side. It was official. I had checked out.

The woman in the lab coat introduced herself, "Hello, Abby, I'm Dr. Robinowitz."

My eyes shot up to her face. She looked tired too. "Hey," I said.

"I understand you've been having a tough night?"

I shrugged one shoulder and we came to a stop at one of the curtained bays in the emergency room. My sleeve was pulled up and a blood pressure cuff was wrapped around my arm. A nurse pumped and pumped and pumped and after a moment I could feel the throbbing in my right arm. "One twelve over sixty," she said to the doctor.

"We're going to give you a dose of glucose IV drip, okay, Abby?"

My eyes cut to her again, but otherwise I didn't move. "Is there anyone I can call for you or have check in on you?"

"No," I whispered. "I just want to lie here for a while."

Dr. Robinowitz gave my arm a pat. "I hear ya," she said. "You take all the time you need," and she left me alone.

I don't know how long I lay there. An hour? Two? Three? Long enough for the drip that went into my arm to make me feel like I had to pee, and when I couldn't take the uncomfortable feeling anymore, I rang for the nurse. She came and unhooked the IV from my arm and pointed to the end of the hall where the bathroom was.

I shuffled down that way, passing other patients. As I got to the door, I noticed that in the last bay was a woman with blond hair and a cut on her lip, and scratches on her face and arms. A large bandage covered her forehead, but she seemed to be sleeping peacefully. It took me a minute to place her, but the cast on her arm eventually clued me in. She was the woman who had been in Dutch's car holding his phone. She had to know what happened to him!

I took a step toward her bed, but then I heard voices approaching and I chickened out, ducking into the bathroom and closing the door. From the outside I could hear the voices nearing and they seemed to stop right outside my door. ". . . CT scan showed only a fairly severe concussion, no sign of internal bleeding in the brain. We've set the arm and taken a blood sample. We're still waiting on the full tox screen to come back, but we think she might have been on some sort of depressant when the accident took place."

"Did she say anything to anyone since she was brought in, Doctor?"

"She was semiconscious when she arrived, but she wasn't able to tell us her name or describe what had happened."

"How soon before she wakes up?"

"Probably a few hours," the doctor said. "We gave her a mild sedative to help her body rest and heal. I'd like to keep her quiet until at least tomorrow."

"That won't do," the other male voice said. "Wake her up, Doctor."

"Agent Robillard, I must insist that wouldn't be prudent nor in the best interest of the patient."

"Do I look like I give a shit about what's in the best interest of some bimbo car thief? I've got a kidnapped businessman, an abducted bodyguard, a felony count of forgery at one of your local banks, and a missing federal agent. That alone, Doctor, is a matter of national security! Now wake her the hell up!"

I was shaking as I listened at the door. Robillard's voice sliced the ER like a knife and I had the feeling he was well used to getting his way. Everything was quiet for a bit, but then I heard someone moan. "Can you hear me?" the doctor asked, sounding like he had moved farther away from my door. "Hello? Miss, can you hear me?"

"Wha . . . ? Where . . . ? Where am I?"

"What's your name?" Robillard barked.

"My arm hurts," said the woman. Her voice sounded garbled. "Where am I?"

"You're at the hospital," the doctor said. "Do you remember anything about what happened to you?"

"Why am I at the hospital?" the woman asked, a little more clearly. "Who are you?" she demanded, and I had the feeling she was talking to Robillard.

"Who I am is not important," he said. "It's who *you* are that's relevant here."

"I'm—I'm—I'm," she stuttered. "I don't know."

"I'll bet," Robillard scoffed. "Where is Agent Rivers?"

"Who?"

"The man whose car you stole. Where is he?"

"Car I stole?" she said. "What are you even *talking* about?!" Panic seemed to rise in her as she realized that she couldn't remember anything about who she was or what had happened.

"That's enough," the doctor said, and a moment later the woman was quiet again.

"I had more questions for her," Robillard said.

"I don't care. She's clearly suffering from trauma-induced amnesia and I will not subject her to more stress that might worsen her condition."

"I need to know where my agent is," Robillard insisted.

"And I'm telling you, right now she can't help you. The best thing to do is to let her brain recover from the concussion and hope that her memory returns."

"What do you mean, 'hope'?" Robillard said.

"In some of these cases the memory loss is permanent."

Robillard made a derisive sound. "Fabulous," he grumbled. "Fucking fabulous." There was a pause, then, "I'll send a tech team over to get her prints. Maybe we'll get lucky and she'll be in the system." His voice began to float away from the door, but his next sentence I clearly heard. "Now tell me where this other girl is, the one brought in later who says she's Rivers's girlfriend."

"I wouldn't know about her, Agent Robillard. She must be Dr. Robinowitz's patient. Let me page the doctor and send her to you."

"Fine, but move on it. We're losing time we don't have."

I opened the door a crack and looked down the hall. Robillard and the other ER doctor were walking away down the corridor. Quickly I closed the door and hurried to the toilet. I did my business, then crept out of the bathroom and inched over to the sleeping woman on the gurney.

I considered her for a long time. My radar insisted she was the key to finding out what happened to Dutch, but first I had to know who she was. My eyes darted to a small plastic cup in a plastic wrapper on the little side table beside her gurney. Quickly I pulled out the cup from its plastic sleeve and picked up her right hand while watching her face to see if she would wake up—she didn't.

As fast and as firmly as I could, I pressed her fingertips along the cup, being careful not to add my fingerprints to hers. I then boogied around to the other side of the bed, lifting her left hand and doing the same collection of her fingerprints. I then carefully reinserted the cup into the plastic sleeve and moved away from her bed.

Poking my nose around the curtain, I made sure the coast was clear and trotted to the gurney that had been assigned to me. Snatching my purse, I shoved the cup into it, then rolled down my sleeve to cover the small bit of IV tube still jutting out from my wrist and took another quick peek around the curtain to see if I could dart out without notice.

I could see the nurses' station with Robillard standing there drumming his fingers on the countertop while a nurse spoke into a phone. On the loudspeaker I heard, "Dr. Robinowitz, please come to the nurses' station. Dr. Robinowitz to the nurses' station."

I waited while my heart thumped loudly in my chest and the moment Robillard turned his back, I scurried around the curtain and headed down a side hallway. There were some double doors in front of me and I pushed through them like I knew exactly where I was going. I turned down another corridor and then another, feeling very much like a rat in a maze, when I finally located a sign that said to follow the yellow line to get to reception.

I tracked the yellow line and let out a breath of relief when I spotted the reception desk. I hurried to it and waited behind an elderly couple looking for radiology, then stepped up to the counter.

"Good morning," a lovely woman with silvery white hair and wire glasses said. "Welcome to Sunrise Hospital. How may I direct you?"

"I need to hail a cab. Can you call one for me?"

"Certainly," she said, reaching for the phone. "Where do you need to be taken?"

"Back to my hotel," I said.

I hovered at the desk while she made the call and as she hung up, she said, "They'll be about ten minutes, dear. Why don't you have a seat in our lobby? You'll be able to see through the window for the Lucky Cab driver."

"Thank you," I said gratefully, and hurried over to a chair in the corner where I was partially hidden but still had a good view to the outside. As I was watching for my cab, my radar gave a small twinge of warning and my eyes darted away from the window and scanned the lobby area. Over near the reception desk I saw a man in a black suit and a hospital security guard looking about. Quickly, I yanked up a magazine and tried to make myself as small as possible.

Over the top of the magazine I risked a quick peek

and saw that the security guard was leading the man in the suit over to the reception desk. There was a family of four asking the receptionist who'd helped me for some directions, so I figured I had less than ten seconds to think of something or my butt was cooked.

From outside I heard a honk, and to my immense relief I saw a yellow cab from the Lucky Cab Company sitting near the double doors to the hospital. I didn't think twice. I bolted.

I made it outside and yanked open the car door. "I need to get to the Wynn!" I said. "Fast!"

As I pulled the door closed, I could see the receptionist now talking with the security guard. She looked past him to me and our eyes locked. *"Drive!"* I yelled at the cabbie, and he took off like a rocket.

We pulled out of the hospital's driveway and onto a main road. I kept glancing over my shoulder to see if anyone was following us, but no one appeared to be. "How far is it to the hotel?" I asked.

The cabbie eyed me in the rearview mirror. "Not far," he said. "Five, ten minutes tops."

I sank back against the cushions. Thank God we were close. I needed to get to my room and hide out for a little while—I just wanted some time to sort everything out. I didn't know what had happened to Dutch. What lead was he pursuing last night—and what had he meant when his note had suggested that my radar was right on target? What had I been right about?

The one thing I didn't want to do was talk to Robillard. That man had some of the nastiest energy of anyone I'd ever been close to. I had felt it nearly radiating off of him as I hid in the bathroom. He was bad news and my radar said he was dangerous to me in particular and I needed to keep my distance if I could. And what was all that about Dutch's disappearance being a matter of national security? Dutch was looking for his cousin—what the hell did that have to do with national security?

The more my thoughts tumbled around inside my head, the more questions I realized I had that lacked any answers. What I really needed was just a quiet place to sit, think, sort things through, and figure out what to do next. I didn't feel I could trust the FBI, and I didn't know if that meant that I couldn't trust the local police either. Brosseau had been a lovely man and so kind to Dutch and me. But if the FBI was looking to talk to me, then I suspected Bob would hand me over without any questions; he struck me as one of those "man of duty" types.

The cab rounded the corner and I looked out the window. We were passing a strip mall and I suddenly yelled to the driver, "Whoa! Could you pull in here for a quick pit stop?"

He did and I directed him to the other end of the mall, where there was a UPS Store. I gave him some cash to hold him and told him I would be right out; then I dashed inside and was relieved to discover there was no line. "Can I help you?" a woman in a brown polo shirt asked me from behind the counter.

Digging into my purse, I pulled out the plastic cup with Jane Doe's fingerprints. "I need to overnight this to Michigan," I said.

"Absolutely, we can totally do that," she said.

Ten minutes later I was out the door again and looking for my cabdriver. He was long gone. "Bastard!" I growled, and looked around. I could see the behemoth hotels that dotted the Strip: the castle of Excalibur, the towering skyscrapers of New York–New York, and the pyramid of the Luxor Hotel and Casino. I knew that the Wynn was at the other end of the Strip. "Great," I said. "Looks like I'm hoofin' it." I began jogging down the sidewalk, trying to gauge how far I had to go. In Vegas the wide-open space hemmed in by mountains and the gigantic hotels that dot Las Vegas Boulevard throw your perception of distance way off. It wasn't long before I was breathing hard and not feeling like I'd gone very far.

I kept at it and again sent a silent thanks to Candice for pushing me every morning in the gym to keep me in shape, and finally, after jogging about two miles, I could see the Wynn only a few blocks up. I was hot and sweaty by now, so I ducked into the same Shell gas station where I'd bought Dutch his Gatorade, to pick up a bottle of water. While I was in line waiting to pay for my water, I noticed a big bin of disposable, prepaid cell phones. My eye kept lingering on the little phone in its neat plastic wrapping. As I moved up the line, my radar hummed, and almost without thinking, I grabbed one of the phones and paid for it along with my water.

Back outside I turned the phone over in my hand, wondering why my crew had suggested I needed one of these, but I couldn't come up with a reason, so I tucked it into my purse and started my jog again. About ten minutes later I'd found my way into the Wynn and went directly up to my room.

As I opened the door, I came up short, the breath catching in my throat as I stared across the room at the huge bouquet of red roses on the tabletop. Relief washed over me. "Dutch!" I called, shutting the door and rushing into the suite. "Dutch!" I said again as I surveyed the sitting room, then dashed to the bedroom. The bed had been made and the room had been tidied up, but there was no sign of my boyfriend.

I glanced again at the bouquet of flowers. There was a note propped against the bottom of the vase. I picked it up and read that it was from the hotel manager apologizing for not delivering the flowers to my room when they arrived. There was a mix-up and they were held behind the desk. He was terribly sorry and was leaving us tickets to Cirque du Soleil with his compliments.

I reached for the card that came with the beautiful long-stemmed roses. It said:

Here's lookin' at you, kid.
Remember your promise. If anything happens to
me, you know what to do.
I love you, always and forever,
Dutch

I clutched the card to my chest and felt a sob burble up to the surface. I closed my eyes tight, but felt the sting of my own tears against my lids. Then I laid my head down on my arm and cried for a long, long time.

Sometime later I'd collected myself enough to be able to think again. Moving over to my backpack, I dug around for my cell phone's charger and plugged it in. It took me several minutes, but I finally found the courage to scroll through the photos of Eggy and Tuttle to get to the single photo of my boyfriend loaded onto my cell phone.

I took a deep breath, held it, and looked at his picture. He was there smiling so handsomely in the afternoon sun of a day we'd spent at the beach off Lake St. Clair, but I wasn't looking at his photo for nostalgia's sake. I had to see if Dutch was still alive. Unfortunately, the camera on my cell phone didn't allow me to see him clearly. I couldn't tell if he appeared flat and plasticlike, the way people look to me if they're dead, or if it was just the camera.

I clicked the lid closed. I couldn't tell and I was becoming anxious about getting it right. Flipping the lid back open, I scanned through my list of saved numbers and clicked on one of them.

"Detective Johnson," I heard Dutch's best friend and former partner say.

"Milo," I whispered into the phone, my voice cracking with emotion.

"Abs?" he said. "Is that you?"

I cleared my throat. "Yes. We need your help," I said. "It's Dutch. He's missing."

"What do you mean he's missing?" Milo said, his voice immediately filling with tension.

"He left last night to go chase down a lead, and he never came back," I said. I then went on to explain all that had happened at the ravine.

"Jesus," Milo said. "And there's been no sign of him?"

Reflexively I glanced at the roses. The smell seemed to fill the room and I blinked a few times, trying hard not to lose it. "None since last night."

"Okay, so we need to contact the bureau and get them to put some men on this," he said reasonably.

"Too late," I said, and explained how the bureau was already here, and that his boss had apparently taken over the search.

"You mean Robillard?" Milo asked.

"Yes," I said.

"Shit," Milo said. "That's bad, Abby."

"So you know about him?" I said.

Milo didn't answer. Instead he said, "I can be out on a flight tonight."

"No," I said. "Thanks, Milo. I really need you here, but not yet. I need you to run some prints for me."

"What prints?"

"I sent you a package. It'll arrive by UPS overnight tomorrow before noon. Inside is a plastic cup with a woman's fingerprints on it. I need to know who she is."

"Is this the woman in Dutch's car?" Milo asked.

"Yes."

Milo paused, probably calculating just how much trouble he could get into if he butted into an FBI investigation clearly outside of his jurisdiction. "Okay," he said. "And as soon as I find out who she is, I'm flying out there."

"That would be awesome," I said. "I could really use the help."

"Hey, Abby?" Milo said, and I could tell that he was hesitating before asking his next question.

"I don't know, Milo," I said, guessing about what he wanted to know. "I can't tell if he's alive or not. I've been getting conflicting images, and I can't say for sure."

"Do you have a photograph?" Milo asked.

"On my cell, but it's too grainy and out of focus for me to tell."

"I'll bring a picture when I come out there."

"Cool," I said tiredly.

"You get some rest, and I'll see what I can dig up on my end without tipping our hand."

"Thanks, buddy. I'll talk to you later."

After I hung up with Milo, I felt so homesick I wanted to cry, but I'd done more than enough of that lately, so instead I called Dave to check up on the puppies and also to hear his voice. "How's it going?" he asked when he answered.

"Not so good," I said.

"Aw, man, that's rough, Abby. How's Dutch holding up?"

There was a lump in my throat. "Not so good."

"Well, if anyone can find his cousin, it's Dutch," Dave said warmly. "And I'm taking good care of the pups while you two do your thing out there."

"How are they?"

"Eggy keeps taking Tuttle's squeaky toys and hiding them all over the house."

I smiled for the first time in what felt like a long time. "Eggy always was a troublemaker."

"Tuttle got him back by taking his favorite pillow. Every time he gets up from his pillow, she moves in and won't move out."

"Sounds like home," I said wistfully.

Just then there was a knock at the door and a muffled

voice that said, "Miss Cooper? It's the hotel manager. Are you in?"

"Let me call you back, Dave," I said. "I think the hotel manager wants to give us some more comps for screwing up a package delivery yesterday."

"Talk to you later, and tell Dutch I said to hang in there."

"Will do," I said hoarsely, then quickly hung up and hurried to the door. When I pulled it open, I gasped. Standing in the doorway was none other than Raymond Robillard.

"Hello, Abigail," he said, holding up a little black phone identical to mine except for the scratches along the cover. "These little phones come in so handy," he said, his smile reminding me of a crocodile. "I'm Special Agent Raymond Robillard. Mind if we chat for a few minutes?"

Chapter Seven

Robillard was already moving into the room before I had a chance to register that a murderer was shoving me into a closed room with only one way out. "This isn't a good time," I said meekly.

His smile widened. "I'm sure it isn't, what with your boyfriend missing and you skipping out on your hospital bill."

My jaw dropped a fraction. I'd forgotten about giving them my insurance card. "I have insurance," I said. "I had planned to take care of that later on today."

Robillard turned and motioned to a man I hadn't noticed behind him. "This is Agent Donahue with the Las Vegas bureau. We require that you put whatever *more pressing* plans you had on your agenda on hold while we talk to you about what happened to Agent Rivers."

Agent Donahue moved into the room as well. He was a skinny man with a weak chin, protruding Adam's apple, and sunken eyes. He looked far too creepy to be an FBI agent. "We understand you were somehow assisting Agent Rivers with the investigation into his cousin's abduction?" Agent Donahue said.

"Moral support," I said. There was no way I was going to let on that Dutch was relying on my psychic abilities.

"Is that so?" Agent Robillard said. "And how much moral support did Agent Rivers need, exactly?" He looked me up and down like I was a two-bit whore and he could only guess what part of Dutch's anatomy I was morally supporting.

I didn't take the bait. For once, my thinking cap was on and I was rolling in my temper. "His cousin had just been kidnapped. If a member of your family had been abducted, wouldn't you want someone you loved nearby? Assuming, of course, you actually *had* someone nearby who actually *loved* you."

Robillard flashed his perfectly white teeth at me and moved into the room, allowing his eyes to wander. Spying the roses on the table, he moved to them and before I had a chance to intercept him, he was reading the card Dutch had left. "What promise was Agent Rivers referring to?" he asked.

"Hmm?" I said, playing dumb.

Robillard read me the line from the card. " 'If anything happens to me, you know what to do.' What would you do?"

"Call in the cavalry," I said, thinking fast. "You guys."

"And did you?" Robillard said. "Did you call the bureau?"

"Didn't have to," I said. "You guys are already here."

"I see," he said, taking a seat in the chair next to the table and flipping the card with his finger. "How long have you been seeing Agent Rivers?" he asked.

"A little over a year."

"And you two are living together, aren't you?"

"Yes."

"How much do you know about your boyfriend's business practices?"

That was an odd question coming from Dutch's boss.

I had a feeling something of a trap was being laid and I would need to walk very, very carefully. "I'm afraid I don't understand your question," I said. "I know Dutch works with the FBI, but he's pretty mum about the particulars."

"I'm not referring to his job with the bureau," Robillard said. Donahue stepped forward and handed Robillard a manila folder. Flipping it open, Robillard continued. "What do you know about Rivers Security, Inc.?"

My eyebrows knit together. I had no idea what he was talking about. "Not much," I said honestly, "other than it's a small side business Dutch started in college."

"Really?" Robillard said, his tone letting me know he didn't buy my answer. "You didn't know your boyfriend ran a security firm with net revenues last year of nearly one million dollars?"

My eyes got wide. "I had no idea his business was so successful," I said. "I mean, I believe he was even considering selling it off."

"As well he should have," Robillard said. "The bureau frowns on agents who moonlight," he said, looking at me curiously; then he took in our beautiful hotel suite. "So you didn't know your boyfriend had a successful side business, hmm?" I shook my head no. "In other words, you believed that a man who earns a little over forty-five thousand dollars a year at the bureau could afford a thousand-dollar-a-night hotel suite at the Wynn?"

I was starting to get really pissed off. "Dutch and I don't talk money," I snapped. "He has his checkbook and I have mine. I had no idea what this room cost. I just knew that he booked the room and was taking care of the payment."

"I see," Robillard said, giving me a look that said I really had to be dumb. He opened the folder back up and began to thumb through some documents. I couldn't tell for certain what he was looking at, but as the pages flipped by, I had a sneaking suspicion they were tax returns. He paused on one page and a tiny hint of a smile formed at one corner of his mouth. "What is your occupation, Miss Cooper?"

I glared hard at him. "What the hell does that have to do with finding Dutch?" I said. "Aren't you people supposed to be *looking* for him?"

Robillard's smile widened. "Perhaps, as a psychic, *you* might help *us* with that?"

I curled my hands into fists. I absolutely *hated* this man. "I demand to know what you're doing to find Dutch," I said.

Donahue made a snorting sound. He thought that was funny. "Did you know that Dutch's cousin worked for Rivers Security?" Robillard said.

I blinked rapidly a few times. "No," I said. "I had no idea."

Robillard nodded. "And what if I told you that your boyfriend had been taking large chunks of time off work recently to fly out here to Vegas and meet with his cousin?"

Dutch had been traveling a lot for work lately. Whenever he went out of town, he was pretty mum on details. "I didn't know."

"Mr. Delgado is a very wealthy man. Did you know *that*, Miss Cooper?"

"I only knew that he owned a large house and a condo here," I said. "I wasn't informed about the particulars."

"I find it curious that an exceptionally wealthy businessman is abducted along *with* his bodyguard," Robillard said. "I mean, if I were a kidnapper, I'd just shoot the bodyguard, wouldn't you, Agent Donahue?"

Donahue nodded vigorously. "That's what I'd do."

I had a sick feeling in the bottom of my stomach. Something wasn't right here. "Is there a question in there for me?" I said.

"And did you know, Miss Cooper, that Delgado hired

Chase Rivers for bodyguard duty through Rivers Security?"

Chase worked for Dutch? "No, I didn't," I said.

Robillard looked down his nose at me. He wasn't a believer. "You didn't know that Agent Rivers recently filed paperwork to obtain Mr. Delgado's tax returns through the bureau?"

I was growing impatient. "What does that have to do with anything?"

"It appears that Agent Rivers was performing a background check on Mr. Delgado prior to his abduction."

"Dutch is a thorough guy," I defended, even while my mind was reeling. "I could see him wanting to make sure his cousin wasn't guarding some crime boss or Mafia type."

Robillard snickered. "And this woman that was in Agent Rivers's car. Do you know anything about her?"

"No."

"The girlfriend is always the last to know," he said, making a *tsk*ing sound. My eyes narrowed. I really wanted to pop him one. Just then there was a knock at the door. Robillard and Donahue exchanged a look. "Expecting company?" Robillard asked.

I ignored him and went to the door. Peeking through the little peephole, I saw Bob Brosseau standing in the hallway. "Bob!" I said when I'd hauled the door open. "Great to see you. Won't you come in?"

"Hi, Abby. I just wanted to check and see how you were—" He caught himself when he noticed Robillard and Donahue in the room. "Oh," he said. "I didn't realize you were here."

"We were just catching up with Miss Cooper, Bob," Robillard said lazily. I could tell by Bob's stiff stature that he didn't much care for the assistant special agent in charge. Turning back to me, Robillard leaned forward with his elbows on the table and placed his hands in a steeple. "Here's what I think happened," he said softly,

DEATH PERCEPTION   **121**

his tone suggesting he had it all figured out. "I think that Delgado contacted our boy Dutch and signed a contract for protection. Rivers enlists the help of his trusty cousin to watch over Delgado while he does a background check into the Delgado family assets. When that report suggests that Delgado's worth a mint, Rivers and his cousin concoct a plan to kidnap Delgado and hold him for ransom.

"Naturally Rivers doesn't want either himself or his cousin implicated, so he lies to me on the phone at the airport, suggesting that he's taking his girlfriend to Lake Tahoe for the week while conducting a little fake investigation of his own out here in Vegas, where it appears his cousin has been abducted along with Delgado, and works to throw the investigating local PD off the track. But when things get sticky—that is, when the Las Vegas bureau finally gets called in—Agent Rivers knows he's in trouble and he leaves his wallet and his cell phone in his rental car along with the keys, hoping someone will come along and steal it, and maybe he cuts the brake lines too, ensuring that whoever nabs the car will end up crashing it. Maybe it will take a while to identify the body, and by that time, Rivers and his cousin will be long gone with Delgado's money."

I was aware that my jaw had dropped about midway through Robillard's absurd accounting of what might have happened to Dutch. "That is *ridiculous!*" I shouted, and turned to Bob to back me up, only his look suggested that he wasn't about to do that.

Instead he shrugged his shoulders. "Abby, I talked to Dutch while you were in with Nora the other night. I told him that I thought we should bring in the Feds. He talked me out of it; in fact he *insisted* that I not call them unless it was absolutely necessary."

I took a deep breath, but I felt dizzy from lack of sleep and all that had happened in such a short period of time. "There is no way Dutch had anything to do with Delgado's kidnapping!" I said. "He came out here one hundred percent convinced that Delgado and Chase had been abducted by unknown kidnappers. He's one of the good guys, Agent Robillard. Which I suppose someone like *you* wouldn't recognize. I guess I'm just wasting my time trying to talk you out of your illusions."

Robillard's eyebrow arched. "Someone like me wouldn't recognize one of the good guys? Why is that exactly?"

I glared hard at him. I was seething at his absurd implications about Dutch. "No reason," I said lightly, rubbing my arms as if I were cold. "Is anyone else here feeling a bit of a *frost*?" I was pinning Robillard with my eyes and still rubbing my arms. "It's *murderously* frosty in here, wouldn't you say, Agent Robillard? It's especially *frosty* around my *neck*."

Robillard's eyebrow lowered and joined its twin in an evil glare. "What did you say?"

"You heard me," I said quietly, my eyes never leaving his. Donahue and Brosseau were looking at us, probably fully aware that something had happened below their radar, but unable to figure out what.

"I'm not cold," Brosseau said into the very still silence that followed.

Robillard got up from the table, his eyes never leaving mine. He got my meaning, and then some. "Don't leave town, Miss Cooper," he said with an icy coldness.

"My boyfriend is missing," I snapped. "Until I find out what happened to him, I'm not going anywhere, but I do have some people that I could complain to about it being *frosty* in here. I mean, some people who could actually *do* something about it."

"Call the front desk," Brosseau said. "They can send up someone if you're uncomfortable."

Robillard smiled wickedly, but there was no mirth in his eyes. "I doubt that, Miss Cooper. I doubt that very much."

"Yes, but do you really want to take that chance,

Agent Robillard? I mean, I'm not as naive and trusting as, say, some of your former coworkers at the CIA."

Donahue turned to Robillard. "Am I missing something here, Ray?"

Robillard picked my cell phone up off the table, which was still connected to the charger in the wall. Flipping open the phone, he began clicking through the menu items. "She's made two phone calls since this morning," he said, pulling the charger out of the wall and handing all of it over to Donahue. "Find out what they talked about."

"Hey!" I yelled, and grabbed for the phone. "That's mine!"

Donahue held it out of reach. "This phone is registered to Agent Rivers," Robillard snapped. "We're confiscating it as evidence."

I could feel the heat rise in my cheeks. "Get out of this room," I said evenly. "I mean it, I want you out of here now!"

Robillard regarded me as if I were a pesky fly. "Like I said, don't plan on going anywhere, Miss Cooper. It's a dangerous city out there. I wouldn't want anything happening to you."

"Yeah, like I might fall and break my neck, right, Robillard?"

He smiled again evilly. "Exactly like that, Miss Cooper. A neck like yours could snap quite easily if you're not very, very careful."

"I'd worry less about me and more about finding Dutch, Mr. Agent in Charge," I said, using finger quotes around his title to show him what little respect I held for him. There was no way I was backing down to this son of a bitch.

Robillard actually laughed and then motioned to a confused-looking Donahue, who was scratching his head at our exchange, and the two left the room.

Bob waited until they left before he said, "What was that about?"

I turned to face him. "Bob," I said, "you have got to believe me when I tell you Dutch Rivers is as straight an arrow as they shoot. He didn't have anything to do with Delgado's abduction."

"I know you believe that," he said gently. "But you have to give Robillard a little credit. It is suspicious that Dutch has a personal connection to Delgado."

"I won't be giving Robillard the smallest ounce of anything," I snapped. "That's your bad guy, Bob!"

Brosseau pushed a hand through his thick gray hair. "Abby," he said gently, "right now I don't know what to believe. I will say this, though: If Rivers is bad, then you could be in some serious trouble. You might want to think about retaining a lawyer."

I could feel that icy trickle of fear winding its way along my spine. It suddenly dawned on me how alone and vulnerable I really was. I was far from home and friends who believed in Dutch, and out here in this city I was completely out of my element. Bob was right; I was in trouble. "Thanks," I said at last. "I'll consider it."

Bob gave me a nod and turned to leave. "Call me if you hear anything, okay?" he said, and I could tell he had no agenda behind that statement. He just wanted to help.

"I will," I said, and waved good-bye.

When he'd gone, I went into the bedroom and lay down on the bed feeling weary beyond belief. My head felt full of cobwebs. I knew I needed a plan, but I was having trouble forming one. I closed my eyes and before I knew it, I was asleep.

"Hey there, sweethot," Dutch said. He was leaning against the wall of a big room with white marble walls and small doors up and down the length of it.

"Where have you been?" I asked him, relief flooding my senses.

"Right here," he said, and pointed to one of the little doors. "I've been waiting for you to find me."

I walked over to the door he was pointing to. It was about two feet tall by two and a half feet wide. On the door was written DUTCH RIVERS.

I turned back to Dutch for an explanation, but he'd disappeared. Curious, I pulled the door open, and without warning, something big and heavy came sliding out at me. I jumped back as the thing came to a stop and that's when I realized that what had slid out was a coffin.

"No, no, no!" I said, placing a trembling hand on the coffin. "Please! Dutch, please don't be in here!" I wanted to walk away without lifting the lid, but I felt compelled—I had to know if he was alive or dead.

Gritting my teeth, I grabbed the handle and began to lift the lid. I saw a hand with hair on the knuckles, then the TAG Heuer watch I'd given him for Valentine's Day, then his favorite blue shirt, and finally I saw his pale and still face with eyes that were lifeless and staring. I screamed and sank back from the coffin, and that's when I realized I was sitting straight up in bed, sweaty and panting.

There was a loud knock on the door to the room. I placed a hand over my heart, shaken and upset. The knock came again and I heard my name called through the door. I went to the door and opened it. Standing in the hallway was a tall man in a dark suit wearing sunglasses. "I heard a scream," he said.

"I'm sorry," I said, wondering if he was a VIP here at the hotel. "I was having a bad dream."

He nodded and turned away, walking away from the floor about four feet before stopping and leaning against the wall. It was then that I noticed the slight bulge at his waist and I realized the FBI wanted to make sure I didn't go anywhere after all. "Am I under arrest?" I asked.

"No," he said, without looking at me. "We just want to keep an eye on you."

"I see," I said, totally irritated. "Well, as long as my tax dollars are hard at work!" And with that, I slammed the door. I went back inside and sat down on the couch rubbing my eyes tiredly. That dream had been awful and the fact that it was the second dream in a row that I'd had with Dutch playing a corpse had me really worried. My crew was trying to tell me something, but maybe I just didn't want to hear it.

I got up and headed into the shower. I still didn't know what I was going to do, but maybe a nice hot shower would help clear things up. Thirty minutes later when I'd emerged from the bathroom, I had a small plan forming. But first, I needed to disappear from the FBI's most watched list.

Gathering some extra clothes and stuffing them into my backpack, I grabbed my purse, Dutch's note, and one rose from the vase, which I placed in the paperback I'd been reading, and headed out of the room. "I'm going to get something to eat," I said to my guard.

He didn't say a word, but followed behind me about ten paces. I waited with some other guests at the elevator and when it came, we all piled on. We went down a floor and more guests got on. Two more floors, and yet another group of people. We were pretty well squished in, so at the next floor a large party let our elevator go by, opting to wait for the next car down. I could feel the FBI guy edging closer to me. He was obviously on guard in case it looked like I might bolt.

I worked hard to look like I was still shell-shocked about Dutch's disappearance and when we made it to the ground floor, I could feel the agent hounding me relax just a little bit. People began piling out of the car and there was a flurry of motion as hotel guests waiting to get on tried to make room for those of us getting off. While I waited for my turn, I dug around in my purse and pulled out a small map of the hotel that I'd found in our room. Pretending to gaze at it while I shuffled forward off the elevator, I managed to edge myself next to the side of the car as a woman with a stroller started getting on.

I continued to look distracted and got off the elevator, which was still taking on passengers, and I could see the agent watching me closely as his big hulky frame was pushed by the rush of people. I could see the elevator doors beginning to close right behind me and I lifted my leg as if I was about to take a step forward when I whirled and jumped through the doors as they closed.

I heard the FBI guy behind me shout, but he was blocked by a large Asian family and he couldn't get close enough to stop the elevator before the doors closed and we were shooting upward. "Sorry," I said to the woman with the stroller I was leaning up against. "Forgot something in my room."

At the very first opportunity I fled the elevator, which let me out on the fourth floor. I bolted down the hallway, running to the east side of the building, glancing over my shoulder every chance I got. When I was sure that FBI guy wasn't behind me, I slowed and caught my breath. I didn't quite know how I was going to get out of the Wynn, and I had to assume that my guard had already alerted the troops, who would be swarming the exits of the hotel to prevent me from getting away. What I needed was a safe place to hide out for a little while and lie low without risk of being discovered. I turned my radar to ON and asked for help.

I got a tug to my right and it felt like I needed to walk down a side corridor. I rounded a corner and began walking, looking for the sign my crew wanted to show me. I passed one of the hotel's cleaning women, who was tossing some sheets into the bin of her cart. My radar dinged as I passed her, and an idea entered my mind. I walked to a door just to the left of the cart, checked the radar, which sent me an affirmative, and took out my key card. I swiped it through the pad and the red light went on. "Shit!" I swore, then looked up apologetically at the cleaning woman. "Sorry," I said. "When I get tipsy, I swear a lot." I wobbled for emphasis and bobbed my head like I was three sheets to the wind.

"S'okay," she said, hiding a smile.

I went back to the key pad and swiped again. "Stupid door!" I said, and gave it a little kick.

"It no work for you?" she asked, trying to be helpful.

"Could be me," I said, waving the card in the air, "or it could be that I dropped this thing in the toilet and had to fish it out before it flushed. Say, can you get this thing to work?"

The cleaning woman's face looked repulsed by my story. She came over to me and looked down at the key card, inspecting it to make sure it was issued by the Wynn. I tried to hand it to her, but she shook her head and used her own key card to open the door. "Well, thank you very much," I said, teetering into the room. "S'very kind of you. I'ma gonna lay down now." I burped a little into my hand. "Or maybe I'll jus' go throw up instead."

With that, I entered the room and pretended to wobble until I heard the door shut behind me. The room was freshly cleaned. There was a suitcase on the dresser next to the television and some toiletries—both his and hers—in the bathroom. I checked the clock on the nightstand; it was noon.

With any luck the occupants wouldn't be coming back up here anytime soon, and if they did—well, I'd deal with that when and if it happened. For now, I was safe and free of the FBI and their prowling eyes.

I took my backpack off my shoulders and dug around for my purse. Hauling it out of the backpack, I rummaged around until I pulled up the small disposable cell phone. It was encased in a thick coating of plastic and I looked around for something to open it with. Nothing sharp enough to cut the plastic came into view. I wandered into the bathroom, where the toiletries littered the countertop. I rummaged around in the man's valise, thumbing through toothpaste, mouthwash, shaving cream, a bottle of prescription Viagra (*quelle surprise*), and, at the bottom of the leather case, a gold wedding ring.

"Scumball," I muttered as I moved over to the woman's makeup case. I hit pay dirt there when I finally found a pair of cuticle scissors among all her wrinkle creams and diet pills. Using the tiny scissors, I was able to slowly and painstakingly cut out the phone.

When it was free, I loaded the two AAA batteries that came in the package and pressed the on button, then waited for a signal. "Yahoo," I said softly when one showed up on the screen. Punching in a ten-digit number I was quite thankful I remembered, I waited impatiently through the first three rings until to my utter relief I heard a woman's voice say, "Candice Fusco."

"Oh, thank God!" I said into the phone.

"Abby?" she said. "Is that you?"

"It is, girl."

"This isn't your number," she said, and I imagined her looking at her caller ID display. "It says 'Las Vegas caller.'"

"Yes, I'm in Vegas, but there's no time to explain," I said. "I'm in trouble."

There was a slight pause, then, "Is it safe to talk where you are?"

"Not really."

"On a scale from one to ten, how bad is the trouble you're in?"

"Eleven," I said even as I heard ringing in the background.

"I'm just guessing here, but does the fact that my office phone is ringing with an ID registered to the Federal Bureau of Investigation have anything to do with the kind of trouble you're in?" she asked.

I groaned. "Yes."

The ringing stopped and there was a clicking of keys in the background as I waited for her to say something. After a moment she said, "My flight gets in at midnight your time. Can you meet me at the JetBlue baggage claim?"

"They might be looking for me at the airport," I said. My paranoia was beginning to get the better of my imagination.

"Meet me in front of the fountains at the Bellagio, unless you think you'll be spotted."

"Okay, that's good. Nice and crowded and poorly lit. I'll find you at, what, twelve thirty?"

"I'll be there," she said. "And, Abby?"

"Yeah?"

"This kind of trouble usually takes some cash to get out of. How much do you have on you?"

"How much do I need?"

"Ten, maybe twenty grand," she said, and I felt my insides go weak.

"I'll make a phone call to Boston," I said, referring to my too-wealthy-for-words sister, Cat.

"Tell your sis I said hi," she said. "And lay low until I get there."

"Candice?" I said.

"Yes, I know, Abby," she said, and I could feel the humor in her voice. "You owe me."

"I really do," I said.

We clicked off and I hugged the phone. Candice was one of those friends that if you ever got to a point that you had to murder someone, you could not only count on her to keep your secret; you could count on her to help you hide the body.

When I had collected myself, I punched in ten more numbers, hoping I had remembered them correctly. The other line rang three times and was finally picked up. "Catherine Cooper-Masters," said my sister in her crisp business voice.

"Cat?" I said, and my voice wavered.

"Abby?" she answered. I could hear the alarm in her voice. "What's happened?"

"I'm in trouble," I said.

"You're *pregnant*?" she squealed.

I smacked my forehead. Why was it never easy with Cat? "No! I am *not* pregnant!"

"Then what kind of trouble are you in?"

"The expensive kind," I said.

"How much do you need?"

"Fifteen to twenty thousand dollars."

There was a long pause, then, "I see that this call is coming in from Vegas."

"Yes," I said. "That's where I am."

Cat sighed dramatically. "Abby, don't you know that gambling never pays?"

I smacked my forehead again. "Cat, listen to me carefully—," I began just as I heard another phone ringing in the background.

"Oh, my business line is ringing. Can you hold on for a second?"

"No, Cat, wait!" but it was too late. She'd already put me on hold.

I waited some anxious moments when she finally came back on the line and said, "Abby! That's the FBI on the other line! They want to know if I've heard from you."

"Please tell me you told them you hadn't," I said.

"No, I told them to hold because I was on the other line."

"Cat! Go back to them and tell them you haven't heard from me!"

"Okay, okay!" she said, and put me back on hold. I waited again for a few agonizing seconds when she returned back to me with, "What the hell is going on out there?"

By this time all the stress was catching up with me. Tears were welling in my eyes and I was having trouble holding my emotions in check. "Dutch is missing," I said hoarsely. "His car was found early this morning all smashed up at the bottom of a ravine, but he wasn't in it. He's vanished off the face of the earth! And his boss from the FBI thinks that Dutch and his cousin might have taken part in the kidnapping of a local business-man, and that's why Dutch has vanished. The FBI came to my hotel room accusing me of being involved in this big conspiracy and I had to escape one of their goons!"

"Ohmigod, Abby!" she said after I'd blubbered through my speech. "I really wish you'd said you just needed to pay off some gambling debts."

I let out a sob. "I'm scared, Cat!" I said. "I can't feel Dutch's energy. My crew keeps showing me his grave site when I ask them where he is. I don't know if he's alive or dead. I don't know if his cousin is alive or dead. I don't know who I can trust out here, and there's no way I can get home or find Dutch without some help!"

"Tell me what to do," she said. "I can wire you some money to your bank account. How about that?"

"No!" I said. "If the FBI is calling you, then that means they know I might try to contact you for help. They'll be watching my bank accounts and credit cards to try and track me down."

"Fine," she said, and I could hear the take-charge tone in her voice. "I know exactly what to do. I'm send-ing a courier on a plane out to Vegas immediately. They will have your cash in hand. Can you meet them at the airport once I confirm the flight?"

"Can't you just send it Western Union?"

"Don't be silly, Abby!" she said. "If they're watching your bank accounts, they'll certainly watch any wire transfers, especially Western Union!"

"Oh, right," I said, rubbing my temple. I had a wicked headache. "Okay, then, send the courier."

"Perfect, can you meet them at the airport?"

"Uh, no, I can't. But Candice is heading out here. Her flight gets in at midnight. I can call her and tell her to wait for your courier. She can bring me the money."

"Perfect. Give me Candice's number. I'll book the courier's flight and give Candice the information."

I blew out a breath. "Thanks, Cat. And I'll pay you back when this all blows over, I promise."

"Don't even think about it, Abby. You're family. We stick together, okay?"

I gave her Candice's phone number and thanked her again before hanging up. It felt good to have people like Cat and Candice on my side.

I put my new cell phone back in my purse and thought about what I should do. Obviously I couldn't hide out here until tonight. Who knew when the couple who was staying in this room would be back?

As if on cue I suddenly heard voices just outside the door. "Oh, shit!" I hissed, and ran around the room in a circle, looking for a place to hide. I pulled up the bedspread, but the bed went all the way to the carpet. I jumped up and looked around the room again, in a state of total panic. Just before the door opened, I made a quick decision and bolted for the closet.

Chapter Eight

I squished myself as far back into the closet as I could get and held very, very still, barely daring to breathe, while my heart thudded against my chest. Out in the room I could hear a man and a woman come through the door with much giggling and laughter. "Red, you are *so* naughty!" said the woman.

"I know you like it naughty, Mama," said the man.

Ewwwwww! I thought.

There was more giggling and something that sounded like the quick removal of clothing. I held in a groan.

"I want you so bad!" the woman said breathlessly.

"Mama," he growled. "Go ahead and take me."

This was followed by what can best be described as a series of groans, grunts, the occasional "Oooh!" or "Ahh-ha!" and the rapid creaking of bedsprings.

I closed my eyes and rammed my fingers in my ears, but nothing helped. "Oh, yeah, big Red!" the woman squealed. "Mama likes it like that!"

"She does, does she?" he said with a groan. "Well, does Mama like it when I do *this*?"

Mama shrieked, leaving little doubt that she definitely liked it when big Red did that. "Oh, baby, oh baby, oh baby, *oh baby!*" she yelled. "Give it to me! Give it to Mama!"

Now, I'm a bit of a prude by nature, and if I wasn't already squeamish at the thought of watching—or, in this case, hearing—other people having sex, then this little lovemaking session was definitely forcing me to consider the nunnery. Getting a rather ballsy—pardon my pun—idea, I dug into my backpack and managed to find the small digital camera I'd stuck in there almost as an afterthought.

The bed continued its rocking horse squeaking and I edged to the door of the closet. "Oh, Mama!" Red said. "You make me so hard!"

I paused and put a hand to my mouth. Red was making me throw up a little. Easing open the door, I stuck my hand out holding the camera and snapped a picture. The creaking stopped abruptly, but a gasp echoed in the room. "What the—?!" I heard them both say, and I stuck my head out of the closet.

Unfortunately, Red was a little late pulling up the covers, and I caught a glimpse of his milky white bum and his portly round belly, not to mention little Red, before he managed to pull up the bedsheet. "Gah!" I said, squeezing my eyes shut while I snapped the shutter again. "For God's sake, Red! Put that thing away!"

"Who are you!" he demanded, and I lifted a lid. Red, who seemingly got his name from the smattering of red thinning hair sticking out at odd angles along his liver-spotted scalp, had pulled up the covers and his "date" was now smunched underneath him. She was looking at me with wide, horrified eyes.

"I'm the PI your wife hired to make sure you weren't giving it to someone else, out here in Vegas."

"The PI?!" he nearly shouted. "Oh, shit! Kate's gonna kill me!"

I nodded. "She will," I said, making a *tsk*ing sound and edging out of the closet. "I've met her and she doesn't put up with shit like this, Red. You should have known better."

"I'll pay you!" he said desperately. "Name your price! Whatever Kate paid you, I'll double it!"

"Hey!" Mama said. "I thought you were getting a divorce!"

"All in good time, Ivory," he said, and wiggled away from her. "Come on, Miss PI! Can't we be reasonable here?"

I'm not a big fan of blackmail, but someone needed to teach Red a lesson. "How much you got on you?" I asked, leaning against the wall.

Red grabbed for his pants at the edge of the bed and pulled out his wallet. "I've got about a thousand on me," he said.

I arched an eyebrow.

"Two thousand!" he said, and pulled out another wad of bills. My other eyebrow rose skeptically. *"Fine!"* he snapped, and pulled at his pants again, lifting out an *enormous* wad of cash from his rear pocket. "Ten thousand," he growled. "That's all the spare cash I've got!"

I tapped my lip thoughtfully and looked at my camera. "Here's how we're going to play this, Red," I said. "I'll take that two thousand from your wallet, and the ten thousand from your back pocket will be used to buy your wife a gigantic bauble. And none of that fake stuff, I'm talking about something that would pass an appraisal."

Red let out the breath he'd been holding and moved to hand me the two thousand dollars. "Thank you," he gushed.

"Don't get up!" I said. "I'll come to you." Moving forward, I took his money and eyed Mama. She was a busty, full-figured girl and—dare I say it?—not very attractive. She was also about twenty years younger than Red, which still put her in the forty-to-fifty-year-old age range. "And you," I said, glaring down at her as she clutched the bedsheet. "Ivory, is it?"

She nodded, emitting a tiny squeak and pulling up the covers tight to her chin.

"What's your last name?" I demanded.

"Quinton," she said in a high, squeaky voice.

I resisted the urge to smile. People tended to give up their personal information when they were lying naked next to a guy caught cheating on his wife. "Yes, Ivory Quinton, you need to get a life and stop being such a ho."

Ivory nodded. "I will!" she said. "I swear. No more married guys!" Despite her bobbing head, my left side felt heavy—my sign for not likely. Ah well, once a ho, always a ho, I guess.

As I was leaving, I said, "I'll be calling your wife in a few days with an update, Red. Unless she's willing to gush about the brand-new diamond bracelet or ring or necklace that her dear husband just purchased for her, I'm sending her the pictures."

Red nodded furiously. "I'm going straight to Tiffany's!" he promised. "I swear!"

I left the room, pocketing the cash and feeling pretty good about having just taught a cheating slimeball a valuable lesson. Still, I felt bad for Kate. I could only hope the new bauble that Red guiltily presented her with set off some of her own internal alarm bells and got her into an attorney's office.

I hurried down the hallway and made my way to the elevators. It had been about two hours since I'd ditched the FBI goon who'd been guarding me. And that was hopefully long enough for the Feds to think I'd managed to leave the building.

I waited for an elevator anxiously and one finally arrived loaded down with people. I edged into the car and we made the short trip to the lobby. I stayed put until everyone else had gotten off, and kept peering around at the faces in the lobby, afraid a Fed might still be stationed there.

No one who looked like FBI was in the lobby, so I moved out of the area and scanned for the nearest exit. There was one off to the left, but as I made a first pass by the doors, I noticed a man in a dark suit and sunglasses making a point of watching every guest who exited the hotel. "Shit," I muttered, and made my way over to the casino.

The casino was smoky and crowded with tourists sitting in front of computerized games of poker, blackjack, and keno. I eyed the room, and to my horror saw Raymond Robillard not thirty yards away. "Eeek!" I squeaked, and dashed out of the casino, my eyes darting here and there, looking for a place to hide. My radar pinged and I felt a little nudge to turn to my right. Immediately I saw a small curtained room that looked like maybe it was a coat check, so I wasted no time dashing over and ducking behind the curtain.

"Welcome," said a young woman about my age with dark brown hair, a head scarf, and large gold hoop earrings.

"Er . . . hey," I said as I scanned the small room we were in. She was seated at a card table covered with a blue cloth decorated with silver stars. In the center of the table was a deck of tarot cards, and to the right a small sign on the wall said, KNOW YOUR FUTURE NOW! $45.00 FOR A 30-MINUTE SESSION, $75 FOR A 60-MINUTE SESSION.

"You're a psychic?" I said, then realized I'd said that as a question.

"Yes," she said, giving me a funny look. "Didn't you see the big neon sign outside the curtain?"

I flashed her a smile. (Did I mention that my crew has a gigantic sense of humor?) "Nope. Must've missed the sign. Listen," I said, thinking fast, "would you mind telling me when your shift ends?"

She gave me another curious look, but then her eyes moved to the clock on the wall. "I'm supposed to be here until two, but if you want an hour session, I can stay an extra half hour."

I reached into my back pocket and pulled out two hundred dollars. "Or," I suggested, "you could take this money and go home early."

"Huh?" she said.

"I was hoping I could pay for your time and your uniform."

"You want my uniform?"

"Yes. We're about the same size. I could trade you a clean pair of jeans and a shirt for your skirt and head scarf—oh, and those earrings!"

"You want to impersonate me?" she said, and I could tell she was starting to get freaked-out.

"Not really. But I'm here with my boyfriend, and we like to play practical jokes on each other. I thought it might be cool if I showed up in our room dressed like you and read his palm. I mean, we've been together for a while and we're trying to invent new ways to spice things up a bit."

"Why not just get some massage oil and some edible underwear?"

" 'Cuz we've been there and done that," I lied, feeling my cheeks flush. "Come on! *Please?*"

She wavered for a few seconds, so I pulled out another hundred. "Fine," she said, taking the money. "But I don't want your clothes. I've got my street clothes in my duffel bag."

"Awesome!"

She took off her head scarf and handed it to me along with the hoop earrings. "There's a ladies' room right next door. Come on and I'll change and give you the skirt and the blouse."

I followed her into the ladies' room, scanning the area for any FBI agents before ducking into the powder room. While psychic chick changed, I ran a comb through my long brown hair and French-braided it into a ponytail that reached nearly to my waist. I then put on the head scarf and the earrings, giving my reflection a nod of approval and thinking I made for a passable Gypsy.

My accomplice came out after a few minutes and handed me the skirt and the blouse. "I'm a size four," she said. "Hope those fit."

"They should," I said gratefully. "And thanks again!"

"Good luck with your boyfriend," she said, and left the ladies' room.

I darted into the stall and hauled off my jeans and my shirt, changing into the flowing ankle-length velvet black skirt and white puffy shirt with an embroidered vest. To my immense relief, "Corina" had forgotten to take her name tag, which was still pinned to the embroidered vest.

When I was finished changing, I headed out and back into the main section of the hotel. As I was scanning the floor, I noticed a bellhop moving toward the lobby area. "Excuse me!" I said to him.

He stopped and took in my outfit. "Hey," he said.

I gave him a big toothy smile and said, "This is my first day here, and I'm a bit lost. Can you remind me where the employee exit is from here?"

"Sure. It's down that hallway all the way to the end, where you're going to turn left, then straight ahead and through a set of white doors marked Employees Only. Don't forget to punch out before you leave—otherwise, they'll dock your pay a half hour."

"I won't, thanks!" I said as I hurried along in the direction he pointed. I kept my eyes straight ahead as I focused on making myself appear like just another Wynn Resorts employee. When I rounded a corner and located the hallway leading to the double doors, my heart lurched into my throat when I noticed the big beefy guy in a black suit and sunglasses looking this way and that.

Luckily, I was right behind a group of cocktail waitresses who were giggling and gossiping about the guests they had waited on. I moved to the very edge of their group and plastered a big ol' grin on my face, hoping to appear like one of the crowd.

It seemed to work because the suit at the door let us pass without a second look. I followed the girls through the double doors and into a narrow corridor with a room off to my left that appeared to be an employee lounge, and a door at the end with a big neon sign that read EXIT.

The troop of cocktail waitresses bustled into the employee lounge and I kept moving, going through the exit door without looking back. I squinted in the bright sunlight of the afternoon and felt the heat rising off the pavement and soaking into my skin. I dug around in my backpack again and came up with my sunglasses, and once I could see clearly, I glanced around at my surroundings.

It appeared I was standing on a landing with stairs leading down to a medium-sized parking lot at the rear of the building. I couldn't see much from this vantage point except the mountains in the distance, but off to my left I could just make out the Las Vegas Convention Center. I headed down the steps and turned toward my right, crossing the lot and making it out onto Spring Mountain Road. I headed west and made it to Las Vegas Boulevard without much trouble. From here I had to decide what to do.

I stood on the corner for a few minutes trying to figure out where I should go next. I knew that I needed to lie low until Candice arrived, but where did one lie low in a ridiculous Gypsy outfit in the middle of the Las Vegas Strip?

I heard a honk to my right that caused me to jump about a foot. "Need a lift?" a cabbie said, and I realized he'd pulled over and was addressing me.

"Sure," I said without hesitation.

I got into the cab and he asked, "Where to?"

I looked at him blankly for a few seconds. Then an idea occurred to me. "Hold on," I said, fishing through my purse. Coming up with a gum wrapper, I said, "Two seventy-nine Desert Bloom Road."

The cabbie punched the address into his dashboard GPS device and we were on our way.

I got out of the cab and stared up at the Brosseau residence. "That'll be twenty-five fifty," the cabbie reminded me.

"Oh, yeah," I said, turning back to him and pulling out some money. "Keep the change."

The cabbie pulled away and I went up the walkway, wondering if I'd made the right decision. The door opened before I'd made it to the top step, and Nora stood in the doorway looking at me curiously. "Can I help you?" she said.

"Nora," I said. "It's me, Abby Cooper."

Nora blinked and her eyes widened. "Ohmigod, Abby!" she exclaimed. "I didn't recognize you! Come in, come in!"

I walked through her door and was engulfed in the smell of something so good my mouth watered. "Whoa, what is that smell?"

Nora closed the door and pointed toward the kitchen. "Five-cheese macaroni. Have you eaten?"

My stomach gave a loud embarrassing gurgle. "Not since the last time you fed me," I admitted.

We came into the kitchen and Nora pulled a chair out for me at the breakfast bar. I took a seat and she bustled about, getting down a plate and a large spoon. Then she dug out a huge portion of mac and cheese, added a bratwurst link, and handed the plate to me. "God, that smells good," I said, taking the plate gratefully.

"Bob and I have been really worried about you," she said as I unfolded my napkin and placed it in my lap.

My fork hovered above my plate. "Then you know what's going on?" I said.

She smiled kindly at me and came around to sit at the breakfast bar next to me. "Bob's a talker," she said. "He never could resist filling me in on all the grisly details. He's a kind man at heart, and sometimes his job really gets to him. He doesn't hold it in like most cops."

"He's lucky to have you," I said, blowing on some of the macaroni.

"How are you holding up?"

"Not good," I admitted, my fork again hesitating in midair. "Did Bob fill you in on the FBI's latest theory?" Nora nodded while motioning to me to try the food. I popped the fork into my mouth and moaned. "Ohmigod," I said. "I think I've died and gone to heaven."

Nora smiled. "I make it with sweetened condensed milk, five kinds of cheese, and half a dozen eggs. It gives it extra texture and just the right amount of sweetness."

I gobbled down several forkfuls of the delicious-tasting stuff before we talked further. "I can't believe Dutch's own boss thinks he had anything to do with this!" she said after a bit. "He seems like such a good man."

"Trust me," I said. "He is. He's the best man I know, in fact. But it's complicated."

"What do you mean?"

"Despite appearances, Raymond Robillard isn't one of the good guys."

"Bob doesn't trust him either," Nora said. "He thinks Robillard may have some ulterior motive."

I wiped my mouth and sat back in the chair. It felt good just to relax after such an intense night and day. "Oh, he's full of ulterior motives. And one of those involves pinning some fabricated crime on Dutch, and probably on me too."

"Why you?"

I gave her a sideways glance. "Because, like an idiot, I've now revealed that I know too much."

"About what?"

"About a murder that took place almost thirty years ago."

"Robillard was involved in a murder?"

I didn't answer her. This was getting sticky and the last thing I wanted was for Nora to be caught in the middle. "It's better if you don't know all the details," I said. "In fact, coming here probably wasn't a good idea."

Nora scowled. "Don't be ridiculous," she said. "You've been through hell and it sounds like you're in some serious trouble. Where else would you go all alone out here in Sin City?"

I felt my shoulders relax. "You are a good egg, Nora, you know that?"

"So Bob keeps telling me."

"Speaking about things Bob might tell you, has he mentioned this woman they found at the accident with Dutch's car?"

"Jane Doe?" Nora said. "No, Bob hasn't told me much."

Something about the way she said that made my radar "ting" like she was holding back something. "Dish," I said, making a waving motion with my hand.

Nora's eyes sparkled. "Before Nickie was born, I used to work the swing shift at the hospital—I was a nurse there for sixteen years, and that's how I met Bob, in fact."

"You're a nurse?"

"Comes in handy when you've got four kids, let me tell you."

"Can you help me with this?" I asked, pulling up one

sleeve to reveal the small IV needle still stuck in my arm.

"Oh, my," Nora said, and she got up to grab some paper towels and some antiseptic from under the sink. "You shouldn't be walking around with that." Coming back around, she placed one of the paper towels over the little plastic tube sticking out of my arm and gave a gentle but firm tug.

"Ouch," I said, but in a moment the pain was gone. "Thanks, that's better."

Nora dabbed some antiseptic on the area and covered it with a Band-Aid before taking her seat again. "Now, as I was saying about the hospital, I still have coffee twice a week with my best friend, Trina, who took my job as shift supervisor when I left. I was at the hospital this morning, in fact. I think I just missed you when you made your getaway."

"I'm totally going to settle my bill!" I said, realizing she must think I was horrid for dashing out before I could offer up my insurance card.

"Give me your insurance information after you eat and I'll call it in for you," she said kindly.

"No sweat," I said, still feeling guilty. "But will Trina let on that you know where I am?"

"Trina and I go way back. She'll keep her mouth shut if I ask her to."

"Terrific. I'd hate to have anyone trace me back to you."

Nora laughed. "Oh, please, I can handle myself. Besides, between the two of us, Bob's always the good guy. Any trouble I get in is just to help keep us balanced. So, as I was saying, this morning when I had my coffee with Trina, the accident was all she could talk about and she gave me the lowdown on our Jane Doe."

"Which is . . . ?" I said, anxious to coax it out of her.

"Jane has no idea who she is or how she got into that

car crash. She's got a whopper of a concussion, and her left radius is broken, but other than that, she's fine. The FBI has been questioning her all day, and she finally told them to go stuff it. Trina said they've posted an FBI agent outside her door and they're basically holding her at the hospital until her memory improves enough to identify herself."

"Do you believe she doesn't remember?"

Nora picked at the place mat on the countertop. "I know from all my experience that it's far more common than people think."

"How soon before she gets her memory back?"

"Hard to say. Could be tomorrow or it could be never. Each reaction to head trauma is different."

"She's the key to finding Dutch," I said. "I can feel it."

"If I hear anything more, I'll let you know," she said, then switched topics. "Have you thought about what you're going to do from here?"

"My main priority is finding out what happened to Dutch," I said. "I'm hoping there's a way to retrace his steps somehow and locate him before anyone else does. If the FBI is convinced that he's gone bad, there won't be a lot of opportunity once they get their hands on him to clear his name. That means I've got to get to him first, and if the FBI has me under surveillance, I'm thinking that might hamper things a bit."

"Looks like you've managed to duck away from their radar so far," she said with a laugh. "Bob told me he got a furious call from Robillard a few hours ago. Extra agents have even been called in!"

I felt the blood leave my face. "Extra agents?" I asked meekly.

"Oh, Abby, don't worry about it. They would *never* think to check here. And your secret is safe with me. I won't even tell Bob, because that man cannot keep his mouth shut."

"When does he come home?" I asked, glancing nervously at the clock. "I have a friend coming in to help me look for Dutch, but her plane doesn't get in till midnight."

"Then you're fine to stay here until then. It's Bob's poker night and since he's been all but cut out of the Delgado case now that the FBI's taken over, he'll be with his buddies until after midnight."

"Awesome," I said, looking down at my plate, which barely had a scrap of food left. "Wow, I must have been hungry," I said.

Nora took my dish and got up. "The greatest compliment you can give a chef is to ask for seconds," she said. I was starting to like this woman more and more.

Nora dropped me at the fountains right outside the Bellagio Hotel at eleven thirty. I was back in my regular duds, but she'd lent me one of Michael's baseball caps, which I'd pulled down low to hide my face as much as possible.

I watched the fountain show with a thick crowd of people and tapped my foot nervously, keeping beat to the music. Around twelve thirty I began scanning the crowds, anxious for Candice to show up.

Nora had put me to bed in a basement guest room out of sight from the kids, so I'd managed to sleep most of the afternoon, and now I was keyed up and wide-awake. I'd had another horrible dream about Dutch and the cemetery, and I could feel that I was running out of time. Deep down, in spite of the pictures my crew kept showing me, I just felt that he was still alive. Maybe it was my own wishful thinking in spite of the facts that were presenting themselves to me, but something deep within my radar said that Dutch was still breathing, but that he was in some *serious* trouble.

I found a bench to sit on and wrapped my jacket around me tightly. It was so odd that a place so hot in the middle of the day could turn so chilly when the sun set. I watched as the fountains shot water high in the air during the carefully orchestrated show and just as the finale kicked in, I felt someone tap my shoulder. It was so unexpected that I think I jumped a foot and stood up off the bench. Turning on my tapper, I almost fell over when my sister, Cat, waved her hand and shot me a big cheesy grin. "Hey there, cap girl!" she said brightly.

"What the . . . ? How the . . . ?" I sputtered. "Cat! What are you *doing* here!" I realized too late that I'd been a little loud, and people near us were openly staring.

Cat waved at them as sweetly as she'd waved at me, and put a finger to her lips. "Shhhh!" she said. "Do you really want to call so much attention right now, Abby?"

I lowered my voice to a hissy whisper. "What are you doing here?!" I demanded.

"You didn't think I would send anyone else to deliver twenty thousand dollars in cash to you, did you?"

"Ohmigod! I am living a freaking nightmare!" I hissed again. "You *cannot* be here, Catherine! You have got to get right back on that plane and head home!"

"No way," she said stubbornly. "If you're in trouble, you'll need me."

I sputtered and glared at her and paced back and forth a few times. This was all I needed. My completely in-the-way sister showing up at the absolute worst time imaginable. "Cat," I said firmly. "I mean it. I'm in some deep shit here. I've got the Feds after me, and they are not playing around. I don't know what's happened to Dutch, but I have a feeling it isn't good, and the last thing I need is to be worried about keeping you safe."

"Oh, please," Cat said with a flip of her hand. "When did you get to be such a drama queen?"

I growled at her, *literally* growled at my sister, and I probably would have grabbed her by the shoulders and shaken her silly if someone hadn't placed a firm hand on my own shoulder. "Give it up," Candice said in my ear. "I've already tried every argument under the sun with her. She refuses to hand over the cash if we don't let her stay."

I whipped around and faced Candice. "Thank God you're here!" I said, throwing my arms around her neck.

"Well, that's nice," Cat snapped. "I'm your own sister and you go giving Candice a hug?"

I let go of Candice and rounded on Cat. "I asked Candice to come," I said. "I asked you for money."

"Yes," said my sister, beginning to work herself into a big ol' huff. "And not just a little bit of money, but a *lot* of cash, Abby."

"I said I'd pay you back," I argued weakly. "Cat, come on! Do you really want the kind of trouble that I could be in? Think of your family!"

"Abby," she said reasonably, "*you* are my family. Besides, I've got the best lawyers in the world on retainer. It's about time they proved their worth."

I stared at her for several seconds, realizing that if the tables were turned, I'd want to be there for my sister, and by "be there" I meant physically. "Come here," I said, and pulled her into a fierce hug. "You drive me crazy," I muttered into her hair.

"Likewise," she said back.

Candice cleared her throat. "I hate to break up this Hallmark moment, but, ladies, we need to boogie."

"Right," I said, letting go of my sister. "Where are we headed?"

"Somewhere far away from the Strip," Candice said. "Come on, my car's parked about three blocks from here."

We hoofed it over to Candice's rental and piled in. I rode shotgun and Cat nabbed the back. "I'm just going to take a little catnap," she said, tongue in cheek. "Wake me when we get to the hotel."

Candice pulled out and we made our way along the

heavy evening traffic of the Strip. As we inched forward, I began to notice a whole lotta Elvises, Chers, and Celine Dions. "What gives?" I asked, spotting a Siegfried and Roy combo, each holding a stuffed tiger.

"It's Halloween," Candice said. "People get dressed up as their favorite Vegas celebrity every year."

"It's only the twenty-first," I said, doing the math on the date in my head. "Halloween's not until late next week."

"People start dressing up the moment October breaks," Candice said. "Folks around here love to party and dress up. It's what makes Vegas, Vegas."

"You come here a lot or you just heard about it on the Net?"

"I used to live here," she admitted, hiding a grin.

"No way!"

"For sure," she said. "I lived here as a little kid until I was about twelve, then I came back here from Michigan and went to school at the University of Nevada."

"You were a student out here in Vegas?" I said. "Must have been hard to study with all this distraction."

"I was too busy working as a showgirl to get distracted," she said with a hint of pride.

"You were a showgirl too?"

"Yep, for five whole months until the stress of exams got to me and I got fired for being five pounds overweight. That's when I went to work for a local PI, and that is the story of how I got into this biz."

"Wow!" I said, looking at my partner in a whole new light. "You have led quite the life, you know that?"

"And all that was before I joined the marines," she said, giving me a wink.

"They make movies about people like you," I said seriously.

She laughed. "Trust me, it hasn't been all glamour."

"So you really do know your way around here," I said.

"Yep," she replied, but her look was guarded.

We finally made it off the Strip and Candice took I-15 heading toward Utah. "There's a motel out here nicely tucked away from the city. Used to be a good place to scout cheating husbands back in the day, and I'd expect not much has changed and it's still a good place to scout stuff like that."

"Oh, you don't have to venture off the Strip to find cheating husbands," I said, remembering Red and Ivory. "Trust me on that one."

Candice glanced at me. "Sounds like there's a story there," she said.

"And a picture show," I said. "Remind me to tell you about it later."

"Will do. Now that we can actually talk, fill me in on all the details. What's going on that has you running from the Feds?"

For the rest of our journey out to the motel I talked about everything that had happened from the time Dutch's mom had called.

"And here I thought you and Dutch had run off to Vegas to get married," Candice said, trying to make light when she heard my voice cracking as I talked about how Dutch was missing.

"That would be quite the shocker," I said.

"Not really," Candice said. "I totally see you two walking the aisle."

"I'd settle for bringing him home," I said honestly.

"What does your crew have to say about all this?"

I shifted in my seat and took my time answering. "They've been relatively quiet." I know I should have told her what I'd been shown, but a part of me couldn't bear to speak about the scenes of Dutch's funeral. I was afraid that saying it out loud might make it come true.

"Really?" she asked. She could sense that I was holding back.

Up ahead I could see a pink neon sign glowing in the darkness of the desert that read MOTEL. "Looks like they've got a vacancy," I said, pointing to the sign.

"They've always got a vacancy, Abs," she said.

We parked and I woke Cat up from her curled-up position in the backseat. "Huh?" she said when I shook her arm.

"We're here."

"Oh, right," she said, and got out of the car.

The motel was laid out in a big U, with the office at the front, sporting the vacancy sign. The place was low maintenance and obviously in poor repair. "Gah!" Cat said. "Where *are* we?"

"Someplace safe," Candice reassured her. "And from what I remember, they may not take care of the outside, but they do clean the rooms thoroughly."

Cat scowled. "Why don't I just pay for a decent hotel?" she said. "There's got to be something better than this!"

"Our objective isn't comfort, Catherine," Candice said sternly. "It's keeping your sister safe while we figure all this out. Remember?"

Something about that exchange made me think Candice had laid down some ground rules with Cat before meeting me at the water fountains. "Okay," Cat said reluctantly. "But this is *way* below my standards, Candice."

"Noted. Now let's go inside and book a room."

We headed inside and met a sleepy-eyed man with a high forehead, mussy brown hair, and no chin to speak of. "Need a room?" he asked.

"We do," Candice said.

"Three?" he asked hopefully.

Candice smiled. "One with double beds and a rolla-way cot, if you please."

"Fine," he said, and shoved a form at Candice. I pulled out some money and peeled off a few twenties.

"I thought you didn't have any money," Cat said to me.

"I managed to get some," I whispered to her. She gave me a confused look and I said, "I'll explain later."

"That'll be two hundred a night," the clerk said.

"Excuse me?" I said, my eyes widening. He had to be joking, two hundred a night for this dump?

"I'm assuming you don't want me to remember you three if anyone comes looking?" he said. "My memory comes and goes, you know. Sometimes it's really clear and sometimes it's a little foggy."

I began to sputter at him, but Candice gave me a warning look and said, "That's fine. We're happy to pay."

I shrugged my shoulders and handed him enough money for two nights. He pocketed it and gave us a worn, orange room key. We trooped out of the office, got our bags from the car, and walked over to our room, which was just down from the office. "I am beat," Cat complained. "Are we going to flip for the beds?"

"I'll take the cot," I said quickly. I knew Candice would have taken it without complaint just to prove she was tough. "I got a lot of sleep earlier and I'm pretty well rested."

"Thanks, Abby," my sister said. "Let's just hope the sheets are clean."

We got into the room and set our bags on the bed. The desk clerk came by a few minutes later with the cot and I began to unfold it as Cat put on her pajamas and got ready for bed. "Thank God I brought my silk pj's," she said. "I can't bear the thought of anything else touching my skin." Did I mention my sister isn't just high maintenance? Her kind requires an oxygen mask.

Candice had changed into a pair of yoga pants and a tank top. She was sitting at the small table in the room with her laptop. "Abs," she said, "get changed and then

come over here and we'll see if we can't put some kind
of plan together."

"Awesome," I said, and turned to move into the bathroom when the quiet of our room was broken by a loud,
hammering knock.

"LVPD!" we heard a gruff male voice announce.
"Open up in the name of the law!"

Chapter Nine

All three of us froze. There was a heartbeat or two of silence; then the pounding started up again. "LVPD!" shouted the knocker. "Open up *now*!"

Candice was the first to move. She jumped to her feet, rushed over to me, and pushed me into the bathroom. Before closing the door, she said, "Do not make a sound and do not come out until I call for you."

I hustled over to the tub and pulled the curtain closed, squatting down and trying to make myself as small as possible. I could hear muffled voices from the room: Cat's high and squeaky voice of panic, Candice's more calm and collected, and a male's, low and full of authority.

Then the tones changed. Candice's seemed to grow angry and loud, while the cop's seemed to become calm and soothing. I imagined that he already had Candice in cuffs, Cat was probably going along willingly, and any moment the bathroom door would be kicked in and I'd be pulled gruffly from the tub.

My heart pounded against my chest as I waited for the inevitable, but the voices outside in the room continued and no one burst through my door. Finally, there was a gentle knock, and to my surprise, I heard Cat call, "Abs?" I peeled back the curtain as she opened up the bathroom door. "You can come out now," she said.

"Did the cop leave?" I asked, confused as to why she wasn't in handcuffs.

Cat chuckled. "No, that wasn't a cop. Just Candice's ex-husband playing a prank."

My eyes widened. "Her ex-*husband*?" I said. "Candice was married?"

Cat nodded. "Apparently. He's also a PI and he was out here doing surveillance when he saw us drive up. He said he couldn't resist pulling a practical joke on Candice."

I got out of the tub and followed Cat back out into the room. Sitting on the corner of the bed was a tall, lanky, great-looking guy with a square jaw and beautiful cheekbones. He wore a white T-shirt, a black leather jacket, and worn jeans. He reminded me a lot of James Dean. "Ah, the fugitive emerges," he said as I came out into the room.

"Lenny," Candice warned.

"Oh, I'm only joking, Candy, shit. Lighten up, would ya?"

Candice glared at him and you could sense the history wafting from the pair. My radar told me their relationship had been based on a whole lotta physical attraction and was pulled apart by that same passion. "Abby," Candice said stiffly, "this is Lenny Fusco, my ex."

"Hey," I said when Lenny shot out his hand.

"Glad to meet you," he offered, giving me the once-over. "So, who you running from?"

"That's it!" Candice said, and got to her feet. "You!" she announced, pointing to Lenny. "With me, outside, now!"

Lenny got up and muttered to Cat and me out of the corner of his mouth, "She was like that when we were married too."

"I said now, Lenny!" Candice warned as she held open the door and motioned with her hand for him to exit.

He grinned at us like he was completely unperturbed by Candice's mounting temper and sauntered out of the room. Candice grabbed her coat and exited after him, closing the door firmly behind her.

"Charming guy," Cat said.

"I can't wait to hear about that love story," I said.

"She's an interesting woman," Cat added.

"Something tells me we haven't even cracked the surface," I agreed.

Cat stretched and yawned and regarded me with droopy eyes. "I'm beat."

"Go to bed," I said. "And thanks for coming to my rescue, Cat."

She gave me a big squeeze and hurried off to her bed, where she put in earplugs, donned a sleeping mask, and was snoring softly in less than five minutes. I had to admire my sister's ability to fall asleep fast, but then, looking at the clock on the nightstand, I realized it was four thirty a.m. Eastern time. No wonder she was tired.

Meanwhile, I pulled out a pad of paper and a pencil from my backpack. While I waited for Candice to come back, I figured I could work out my radar and try to get a bead on Dutch. I sat with the paper in my lap and closed my eyes. When I felt calm and centered, I called out to my crew.

People often ask me what it feels like to interact with your spirit guides. The best that I can describe is that it feels like a warm blanket that gets thrown over your shoulders and a very fuzzy feeling of the presence of other entities around you.

It isn't, however, an overly descriptive encounter. I don't really know what my crew looks like. Through years of interaction I've been able to identify them by the energy they emit; for example, my main guide, who is the speaker for the rest of the group, someone named Samuel, has a sort of protective energy that is patient and kind, even when I'm throwing a hissy fit in his direction.

The problem is, the language of intuition is less than clear. It's mostly made up of pictures, threads of thought, songs, pop-culture references, and a hodge-podge of emotions. And sometimes—okay, make that most times—what I'm shown doesn't easily translate into English.

As a professional psychic, I'm a decent translator, but sometimes there isn't a good frame of reference for what I'm being shown, either because it hasn't occurred yet or because my client refuses to cooperate. Think of it like I get to stare into a murky pond and describe what I'm seeing, "I see seaweed and maybe some logs," but if my client won't think about how seaweed and logs relate to his or her life, it can make for a frustrating session.

Case in point, the week before Dutch and I came to Vegas, I'd had a session with a client and the image I saw was a large tree. On the tree branches were what looked like name tags. *Easy enough,* I thought, and asked my client if she had been researching her family tree.

"No," she said.

"Has anyone else been researching your family tree, then? Maybe a sister?"

"I'm an only child."

"Cousin? Aunt? Some other relative?"

"No, absolutely not," she insisted. "No one has been researching our family tree."

I went back to my crew and asked for more info. They showed me one branch on which dangled several name tags, and one of those name tags got an X through it and was ripped off the tree. My translation? "I get the feeling like someone connected to you may actually be researching their family tree, and there's been an error of some kind. Maybe who they thought was their uncle isn't really their uncle. They keep showing me that a mistake has been made."

"That makes no sense to me," she insisted, causing me endless frustration. Finally, at the end of the session when I turned it over to my client to ask me questions, she *actually* said to me, "The whole reason I came here was to ask you if you knew if I was adopted. I keep looking at my birth certificate and it doesn't add up— the seal doesn't seem real—and I can't find a record of my birth from the city records, and whenever I asked my mother about it before she passed, she clammed up and refused to talk about it."

I know. . . . I know. . . . There are days when I realize I'm not charging enough. So while I was anxious to try to use my radar in any way possible to locate Dutch, I also realized that because intuition is *always* open to interpretation, I could get that interpretation wrong and send us on a wild-goose chase.

The way to limit any misinterpretations was to ask the right questions. *Samuel,* I thought, *show me what happened to Dutch.*

I felt a slight thump on the back of my head and goose bumps immediately rose along my arms. Dutch had been hit hard across the back of the head.

Show me where he is right now, I asked.

My mind's eye filled with the same scene I'd seen earlier. Dutch's gravestone, *Here lies Dutch Rivers. . . .* My heart skipped a beat. *Is he dead?* I asked, holding my breath.

My left side felt thick and heavy, and I let out the breath . . . but sucked it right back in when my right side began to feel the teensiest bit of lightness. My lower lip trembled. Dutch wasn't dead, but he was definitely dying. *Please, Samuel,* I begged. *Help me find him!*

I was shown a sketch pad. I opened my eyes and looked down. In my lap was the pad of paper. I held my pencil over the pad and waited for my mind to fill with an image. I saw a large tree, very much like the one I'd seen for my client the week before complete with the name tags on the branches. I made a rough sketch of the mental image and waited for more information. In my mind's eye the tree began to change. It turned from something like an oak tree to a palm tree and the name tags shifted off the branches of the oak tree onto the coconuts of the palm tree.

I sighed heavily. This was making no sense. *Draw . . .* came into my mind. Samuel wanted me to draw the image. I flipped the page of my pad of paper and drew the image of the palm tree. At the root of the palm tree in my mind's eye was a large rock. I penciled this in, but I kept feeling it was wrong. I closed my eyes and focused on bringing the rock closer. And that's when Dutch's gravestone entered my thoughts. I felt tears sting my eyes. "I don't understand," I whispered. "Samuel, are you telling me that I won't be able to find Dutch until it's too late?"

"Hey, there," Candice said, coming through the door, and my eyes snapped open. "Who you talking to?" she asked when she saw that Cat was fast asleep.

"No one," I said, and wiped my eyes.

"You okay, Abs?" she said, looking at me critically.

"We need to find him, Candice," I said, and more tears spilled down my cheeks. "My crew is insisting that we have very little time."

Candice's mouth pressed into a thin line. "I promise you, I will do everything I can to help."

I swallowed hard. "Thank you," I said.

"Come on," she said, motioning me over to the small table. "Fill me in on everything and we'll form a game plan."

Candice and I talked until the sun began to rise. She had dark purple circles under her eyes by the time I called it quits and insisted that we both get a little shut-eye. I woke up a few bleary hours later to Candice shaking me gently. "Hey," she said. "Abs, wake up."

"Wha's up?" I mumbled.

"Where's your sister?"

"Wha . . . ?" I said, blinking at her.

"Cat," Candice said in a tone that meant business. "She's not here."

I sat bolt upright and looked around the room. "Where'd she go?" I said, now fully awake.

"I don't know. She's gone and the car's gone. I'm thinking she took it to run an errand or something."

I threw the covers back and got stiffly out of bed. "I didn't hear her leave," I said. "Is there a note?"

As if on cue, the door to the room opened and in pranced my sister, carrying two big bags that smelled like heaven. "Morning, ladies!" she said brightly. "I thought you might like some breakfast."

Candice gave me a look that suggested I needed to lay some more ground rules with my older sister. I returned her look with a shrug of my shoulders. You didn't so much control Cat as just pray a lot that she didn't get into too much mischief. "Catherine," Candice said, turning to help her with the bags. "We appreciate the food, but next time, please let one of us know where you're going."

"I was only gone for a bit," Cat said, giving Candice a wounded look. No one could pout like my sister.

"Yes, but Abby and I were worried. We're not on vacation here, remember?"

"Oh, fine," Cat said, handing me one of the bags. "I promise to leave a note next time."

"No," Candice insisted, looking Cat dead in the eyes. "You'll ask me if you can go, and I will probably say no. If Abby and I needed to make a quick getaway, we'd be hard-pressed without a car."

That hit home with Cat. "Oh, God!" she said. "I didn't even think of that!"

"Which is why we need to discuss where each of us goes from now on."

"Got it," said Cat with a smart salute.

I hid a smile. Candice had her hands full with that one. "Thanks for the food," I said, trying to make peace.

"I found this kitschy little diner about five miles from here."

"Moe's?" Candice asked.

"Yes," Cat said.

"They make the best pancakes on the planet," Candice said fondly.

Cat pulled the bag I was looking into out of my hands and handed it over to Candice. "Then dig in!"

We ate breakfast, which was in fact delicious, and talked about our next move. "This is going to be tricky," Candice explained. "If Robillard is intent on finding Abby, then he'll already know we've come into town and that we're helping her hide. That means we won't be able to move around without extreme caution. It also means we won't have the luxury of being able to interview people out in the open. In other words, this can't be the open investigation that I'd normally conduct, so to get to the bottom of things, we'll have to work covertly, off the record and under the radar."

"Where do we start?" Cat asked as she dived into her scrambled eggs.

Candice reached for her own notepad and flipped to a diagram in the back. "We start at the top, with Abby's first impression about the kidnapper, or is it kidnappers?" she asked, looking at me.

I checked the radar. "Kidnappers, plural," I said. In my head I saw the number two. "There were two of them."

Candice wrote that down. "Good. Now, your impression was to start with family, right?" I nodded. "So we need to do background checks on the son, Ricky, and the mother and the daughter, along with some extended family."

"They're all in Spain," I said. "Ricardo is from Spain and according to his wife, he's got a couple of sisters who still live there." My radar chimed in again, and I saw that image of the oak tree in my head, with an emphasis on the lower branches. "My feeling is this is closer to home—immediate-family scenario."

"Cool. Now, we'll also want to look at Delgado's business associates."

"Why?" Cat asked.

"Because one of my theories is that Ricky got tired of being in his old man's shadow. He starts banging Ricardo's girlfriend and maybe he thinks he's a player and can take over for dear old Dad. Abby, didn't you say that Delgado's wife suggested that Ricardo was having an affair with his partner's wife?"

"Yeah, but I'd be cautious about that info," I warned. "Paloma Delgado strikes me as someone who calculates everything she says and does. I don't trust her."

"Noted," Candice said, scribbling a few more notes.

"Can I ask a question?" Cat said.

"Sure," Candice and I answered in unison.

"Why did I need to bring twenty thousand dollars to this party?"

The corner of Candice's mouth twitched up. "We're in Vegas, baby. Nothing here is free, and that includes intel."

"We have to pay to get the information we want?" I clarified.

Candice pushed her container of half-eaten pancakes away. "We will. See, there are two types of people in Vegas. Those who want to be noticed, and those who definitely don't. You can float it either way here, but it's expensive. That's why we need the cash."

"How are we going to get this information?" Cat wanted to know. "I mean, who are we going to pay?"

"I've got a friend in town that I used to work with. He's the best because he's quiet about it. But he's pricey. If I'm going to cut through the bullshit and find out what we're really dealing with ahead of the Feds, I'm going to have to pay him some large coin."

I looked at my sister and reached out to squeeze her arm. "Thanks again for offering to put up the money, Cat."

She gave my hand a pat. "Of course!" she said. "I'd only spend it on shoes anyway."

"What about Jane Doe at the hospital?" I said. "How do we find out about her?"

Candice looked over her notes and sighed. "I haven't figured that out yet, Abs. Unless you can get me some fingerprints, I'm not sure how I'm going to dig into discovering who she might be and what her connection to Dutch is."

"Ohmigod!" I said. "I *totally* can help with that!" Excitedly I reached for my backpack and yanked out my cell phone. Punching in some numbers, I waited with my knee bouncing away until I heard the line picked up. "Johnson," I heard Milo say.

"Milo!" I said into the phone, never happier to hear his voice. "It's Abby."

"Hi, honey," he said, and immediately I caught that his voice sounded tense.

"What's the matter?" I whispered.

"Oh, nothing. I'm just here with some friends of Dutch's and we're in a little meeting." There was a muffling sound and I heard Milo say, "It's my wife. I'll be off in a sec."

My heart skipped a beat. Milo was talking to the FBI. "Don't tell them it's me," I pleaded.

"No worries, honey. Listen, I've got to go talk to these folks. Can I call you back?"

"Yes, but I'm at a different number."

"You're at the hair salon and the car's acting up?

Okay, what's that number, Noelle, and I'll call the tow truck as soon as I wrap up here."

I gave Milo my new cell number and he said, "Terrific. You sit tight and I'll get back to you in about an hour."

I hung up with Milo and noticed for the first time that Candice and Cat were both staring at me intently. "Trouble?" Candice asked.

"Could be," I said, putting the cell away. "That was Milo. By his tone I get the impression that he's currently chatting it up with the FBI."

Candice frowned. "They're everywhere on this, aren't they?"

"Looks like it."

She gave me a direct look. "Why is Dutch's boss so quick to believe he's part of the kidnapping?"

I hesitated. Candice didn't know about Robillard's past. I'd been discreetly quiet about that for fear that there were some things she was better off not knowing. But then I realized that if Robillard caught up to us, he was the type to assume that as her partner I'd naturally filled her in on all the grisly details; therefore, at least if I actually told her, she'd be prepared. "A couple of months ago, when you and I were working the Bruce Lutz case, I tuned in on one of Dutch's really old cold cases. About thirty years ago a CIA agent named Cynthia Frost was murdered. Her neck was snapped by a killer who left her dead while her six-year-old daughter slept upstairs. I met Cynthia's daughter and offered her a session with me and Theresa."

"Ohmigod, you're talking about Bree," Candice guessed, referring to the young woman whom I'd briefly worked with while I was doing an undercover stint at a mortgage company.

"Yep," I said. "Her mom was CIA."

"So how does Robillard figure into this exactly?" Cat asked, very confused.

"Robillard is also ex-CIA. When Theresa, Bree, and

I all sat down together, Bree's dead mother, Cynthia, shared a vision of her murder with me. The guy I saw kill her was unknown to me, but I told Dutch I could work with a sketch artist to help identify him. Dutch was pretty surprised when he realized the man in the sketch was Robillard."

"Why isn't Robillard in jail?"

"Proof," I said simply. "Dutch went to his boss's boss—the special agent in charge, or SAC, for all of Michigan—and told him what he suspected. He's been working discreetly on the SAC's orders ever since to try and find something to connect Robillard to Cynthia's murder."

"Why did he murder Cynthia?" Cat asked.

"She had something on him."

"Do you know what?"

"No," I said. "But there were several connections. . . ." My voice faded as I remembered something key.

"What?" Cat and Candice both said when they saw my alarm.

"One of those connections was to Vegas," I whispered. Chills ran up and down my spine.

"You think Robillard suspected Dutch was on to him, and now that your man is missing, Robillard's trying to ruin his credibility."

My mouth fell open. "Oh, God," I said as I realized how Robillard could use his influence in the investigation any way he wanted. "He's not working to find Dutch at all!"

"Probably not," Candice said. "If I were him, I'd be pointing everyone in the opposite direction while making it look like I was tracking down leads."

Then I realized that I'd tipped my hand to Robillard about what I knew regarding Cynthia's murder. "I'm in deep shit," I said.

Candice gave me a sharp look. "Please don't tell me you told Robillard what you'd seen?"

"I might have alluded to it," I said weakly.

Candice's shoulders fell. "Shit," she whispered. "No wonder he's trying to hunt you down. Abby, you're in some serious danger here."

Cat's face had turned pale. "He wouldn't try to hurt her, would he?"

Candice didn't answer her, which was almost as good as saying, "Uh . . . yup!" Instead, she got up from the table and said, "Come on, we've gotta roll."

We left the motel and headed back toward town, skirting the Strip as we stuck to the northwest section of town and cruised along some streets and alleyways that looked mostly industrial.

Candice parked in a dirt lot outside of a rusty-looking warehouse with razor-wire-topped fencing skirting the building's border. We all got out of the car and walked to the gate, which was secured by a chain and a lock. Candice stood in front of the gate and looked up to the top of one pole where a small security camera was perched. Taking off her sunglasses, she stared into the camera and said, "Hiya, Freddy."

Nothing happened for several seconds. "Maybe he's not home," Cat suggested.

"Oh, he's home," Candice said as she continued to stare into the camera. "He's just deciding whether or not it's worth his time to come out and play is all."

The seconds continued to click by and still there was no sign that we were addressing anyone through the camera. Behind me I heard Cat sigh. "Oh, this is ridiculous," she said. Cat's never been big on patience and she's learned to get her way by flashing her money around. "Here," she said, thrusting a big wad of cash up toward the camera. "If you're in there, we're paying."

Immediately a large garage door attached to the building began to creak open. "Nice trick," Candice said over her shoulder.

Cat smirked. "I've found it to be quite effective over the years," she said.

After the door had clanged to a stop, a small portly man with apparently bad knees hobbled out from the dimness of the garage. It took him quite a while to work his way over to us as he bobbled from side to side, but eventually he arrived at the gate huffing and puffing.

"Long time no see, Fred," Candice said.

With a voice gritty as sandpaper and about as warm, he said, "I thought we'd seen the last of your candy-ass."

That made Candice laugh. "Yeah, well, you can take the showgirl out of Vegas, but you can't quite take the Vegas out of the showgirl."

I studied Fred as he fiddled with the chain and the lock. He looked really familiar, but I was having trouble placing him until Cat whispered with a giggle in my ear, "I wonder if Ethel is here too?" and then it dawned on me that this guy could have been the identical twin to Lucy and Ricky Ricardo's neighbor Fred Mertz.

"You might as well come in," he said after he undid the chain and pulled at the gate.

Cat and I followed behind Candice as she walked toward the garage. Behind us I could hear Fred locking back up. "Aren't we going to wait for him?" I asked, casting a glance over my shoulder.

"Nah," she said. "He'll catch up."

We made our way into the warehouse and Candice led us straight over to a spiral staircase. We walked up the stairs, stepped through a door, and found ourselves inside a beautifully renovated loft. "Whoa," I said as we came through the door into the area. Bamboo flooring covered the entire floor of the modern-looking loft, which was decorated like an upscale New York apartment with crisp linen fabrics, modern furniture, and a large open floor plan. One section was curtained off, but through the fabric you could see a king-sized poster bed. The kitchen had stainless steel countertops and appliances with glass-center cabinets and really cool track lighting. "This is gorgeous," I said with a whistle.

"Fred's got taste," Candice agreed.

"And money," Cat added. "I know some of these designers—they don't come cheap."

We waited for Fred to make his way back to us, which seemed a long time, but eventually he came through a door at the opposite end of the loft, which I realized held a cargo elevator.

Waving to us from across the huge room, he motioned for us to sit in the seating area. "Lemme get a pad," he said as he waddled over to a desk that was covered in computer screens—one of which held a camera's view of the front gate.

We took our seats and Candice motioned to her chest, indicating that she would do the talking. Cat and I nodded—we'd be quiet and let her handle things. "So, what brings you by, Candy?" Fred said as he took a seat and whipped out some reading glasses.

"We need some intel," Candice said, pulling a notepad out of her purse.

"Names?"

"First set is Ricardo Delgado and his estranged wife, Paloma. Their son, Ricky, daughter, Bethany, and any other immediate family members you can locate."

"Easy enough," Fred said as he scribbled.

"Next we'll need any dirt you have on Bambina Cheraz."

"Got it," he said.

"And Delgado's business partner, Donovan Kelton, especially if you can find a connection to Ricky or Bambina."

"Anyone else?"

Candice hesitated and shot me a look that said she wasn't sure about something. I cocked my head to the side curiously, when she seemed to make a decision and said, "Yeah. I need you to look into Rivers Security. I need to know if they've got a clean reputation in town or not."

I could feel myself sit up straighter and I was about to protest, but Candice held her hand up in a small stopping motion, and gave me a cautionary look. With effort I settled back into my chair, but I was pretty hot under the collar.

"That it?" Fred asked, apparently not noticing our exchange.

"One more," Candice said, looking back to her notes. "Raymond Robillard. He's FBI, but he used to be CIA. See if he's got a connection to anyone local."

Fred shook his head back and forth. "That's going to cost you," he said. "You know how the Feds feel about me poking around in their records."

"We have cash, Fred," Candice said.

"Fine, but I want the money up front this time," he insisted.

"What?" Candice snapped. "No way, Fred. Our deal has always been half now, half later."

"Times have changed, Candy," he said. "And I know this Delgado guy. He's got a nasty rap for pissing people off by ripping them off. There's word that he's got some family connections."

"Family?" Cat asked, then caught herself and apologized for speaking. "Sorry, Candice, I'm not here. Forget I said anything."

"It's fine, Cat," Candice said. "He means Delgado could have friends in the Mafia."

"I'm too old to be sticking my neck out like this, Candy," Fred insisted. "You want the scoop, you gotta put up the dough."

"How much?" she asked.

"Ten grand," Fred said.

Candice was on her feet, with her fists balled. "Do you think just 'cuz I've been away for a while I've lost some brain cells, Fred?!" she yelled. "Do you think I'm now open to being *ripped off*?"

"I ain't rippin' you off," Fred growled. "Prices have gone up everywhere! You ever heard of inflation?"

"Oh, don't give me that inflation bullshit!" Candice roared. I glanced at Cat. She looked as alarmed as I felt by Candice's reaction. "You're not the only guy in town that can give me what I want, you know."

"Fine," Fred said, leaning back against the sofa cushion. "Go find someone else. This is an ugly job, and I'd rather not take it."

Candice glowered at him for several long seconds. Finally she said, "Five grand, Freddy."

"Nope," he said smugly. "The full ten or nothin'."

"Seven," she said.

"Ten."

"Eight fifty and that is our absolute final offer."

Fred scratched his chin and smiled up at her. I got the feeling he found her outburst quite amusing. "Fine," he said after a moment. "I suppose for old time's sake I can let you rob me on this job."

Candice leveled a look at him that clearly stated she was the one getting robbed, then motioned to Cat. "Pay the man, Cat."

Cat glanced at me, unsure about the deal, but I nodded to her encouragingly and she took out her wad of money. She counted out eighty-five hundreds and handed them to Fred.

He took them and recounted the money, which didn't seem to sit too well with my sister. "It's all there," she snapped, insulted by his double count. Fred ignored her and kept counting. I put my hand on her arm to settle her down, but she gave a loud "Humph" anyway.

"I need a number," Fred said when he finished counting.

Candice looked at her notes and gave Fred my disposable-cell number. "Call us on that line when you have something solid."

"Will do," he said, and we got up to leave. "Might as well ride down with me," he said, motioning over to the freight elevator.

On the ride down Candice asked, "Is Wyatt still in town?"

"He is," Fred said, eyeing her critically. "You in trouble, Candy?"

"No, not yet anyway," she said. "But these two could use someone with his talents. Do you know how I can get in touch with Wyatt?"

"I can have him call you," Fred said.

"Awesome," Candice said. "Thanks, Fred."

We got back into Candice's rental and my phone rang. "Hello?" I said.

"Abby?" said a male voice barely above a whisper. "It's Milo."

"Oh, thank God!" I said. "Listen, Milo—"

"Hold on," Milo said, cutting me off. "Let me do the talking, okay?"

"Okay," I said, shocked by his abruptness.

"What did Dutch tell you about his investigation into Robillard?"

"Not much," I admitted. "I mean, I knew he was looking into Robillard's past, trying to find a link between him and this woman who was murdered—"

"Cynthia Frost," Milo interrupted.

"So he filled you in too?"

"Briefly. He said that you'd had a vision and that it was clear to him that his boss had been responsible for the death of a CIA agent. He said that he'd been given the green light from the higher-ups to conduct a very quiet investigation, and the trail led to Vegas. That's why he brought me in on the loop, as a matter of fact— Dutch wanted to use our security company as a front to help him dig around in Robillard's past. He said he was going to use his cousin to help gather some intel and see what came to the surface."

"It seems something pretty bad must have popped up," I said. "But I wonder why Dutch had to use Chase. I mean, wasn't there an agent here in Vegas that could have helped uncover something?"

"That's where it gets extra sticky," Milo said. "Early on, Dutch discovered that Robillard and the head of the Vegas bureau were college roommates and are still good friends. They even took a vacation together last year, from what Dutch had been able to uncover."

"I knew that Donahue guy was too creepy for words."

"It gets worse," said Milo, and his voice sounded really tired.

"What's happened?" I asked, sensing that it got worse for Milo in particular.

"I've been suspended," he said.

"What?" I gasped. "Why?"

Milo sighed. "Robillard's people came in here this morning and pretty much spent two hours grilling me about Dutch and our security company. They claim Dutch has been using his federal access to illegally get financial information on the company's clients. They're also claiming that he's been extorting money from our clients for months."

"That's ridiculous!" I shouted. "Milo, that is absolutely not true!"

"Abby, will you let me talk?" Milo hissed, and I worked to rein it in and let him speak. When I didn't say anything, he continued. "I know it's bullshit," Milo said, "but the company has been recording a tidy profit for the past year and a half. We can account for all of the money, but the FBI is currently convinced Dutch and anyone associated with him is on the wrong side of the law. And that includes me and you."

"Oh, I'm aware of what the FBI thinks about me, Milo," I said. "But tell me how this got you suspended?"

"Robillard made a call to my boss while I was sitting in with the other agents. He's convinced my lieutenant that they have enough preliminary evidence to suspect I've been assisting Dutch with these supposed extortions. My lieutenant had no choice but to suspend me with pay until the federal investigation reaches a conclusion."

I rubbed my forehead and closed my eyes. "This just keeps getting worse and worse," I said.

"Tell me about it," Milo said. "Anyway, I'm about to head over to my attorney's and get some advice. In the meantime, I was able to get that cup you sent me to the crime tech before things turned ugly for me. We ran the prints through CODIS."

"And?" I asked, hoping we'd have a lead on who our Jane Doe was.

"We got bubkes," Milo said. "She's not in the database."

"Crap," I said. "Somehow I knew this wasn't going to be easy."

"It gets a little worse," Milo said. "With this hanging over my head, I can't make it out to Vegas and help you look for Dutch. The Feds pretty much told me to stay put or else."

"Well, I wish you were here, Milo, but at least I'm not alone on this."

"Don't tell me. Candice flew out there and is helping you skirt the law."

I smiled; Milo knew us too well. "Yep, and Cat's here too."

There was a wheezy sound on the other end that I knew was Milo's laugh. "Got your hands full there, don't you, Abby?"

"Desperate times call for desperate measures," I said. "The Feds aren't playing fair, so they've left me no choice but to call in the big guns."

"The Feds are also *really* interested in finding you," he whispered seriously. "So do me a favor—don't contact me unless it is an absolute emergency. I wouldn't put it past these guys to start tapping phones and listening in on my private conversations."

"Right," I said, looking around the area for any suspicious-looking black sedans. "On that note, maybe I should let you go."

"Be safe, Abs," Milo said. "And tell Candice that in return for putting her license at risk to help us find Dutch, any favor she needs from the Royal Oak PD, she's got it."

That comment got a smile out of me. Candice and Milo hadn't exactly been best buds ever since they'd had themselves a little stare-down a few months back. "Will do, my friend. And thank you."

I hung up with Milo and filled Cat and Candice in on the details of Milo's suspension. "Robillard's a hardass," Candice said. "I'm really going to enjoy putting that son of a bitch behind bars."

"Where are we going now?" Cat asked from the backseat.

Before Candice could answer, my phone rang again. I answered it and heard another male ask, "Candy?"

I handed the phone over to Candice. "It's for you," I said.

She took the phone and talked briefly to the caller, ending with, "Great, we'll see you at the motel."

"Who was that?" I asked when she gave me back the phone.

"Wyatt," she said. "He's a forgery specialist."

"Why are we meeting a forgery specialist?" Cat asked.

"Because we need a specialist to forge up some ID for you two."

Cat and I exchanged a look. "Why do we need fake IDs, exactly?" I asked.

"Because this thing could get really bad, Abs. As in, we might all need to move to Kansas before it's over."

Cat laughed, thinking Candice was making light, but

the chill up my spine and Candice's set face suggested that she wasn't kidding.

We drove along in silence for a while and I stared blankly out the side window, thinking of Dutch and praying I'd find him before time ran out. "Aw, shit!" Candice said suddenly.

I snapped to attention and looked out the windshield, but I couldn't see what was causing Candice to look so alarmed. "What is it?"

"Up ahead," she said. "The car in front of us."

"What about it?" Cat asked from the backseat.

"Look at the tag," Candice said. "It's got federal plates. That's the FBI, ladies."

"No way!" I said, and ducked down low in my seat.

Candice slowed subtly until she was passed by another car, putting us safely behind another vehicle. "Please do not tell me that they're headed where I think they are," she said out loud.

But they were. We followed at a safe distance until the exit for our motel, and sure enough the black sedan with the federal plates pulled off and turned right at the bottom of the exit—which only had one thing in that direction, the Desert Springs Motel. Candice passed the exit and kept right on truckin'. "We are so screwed," she said.

My right side felt light and airy—my sign for *You bet your tuchus.*

Chapter Ten

The tension inside our car was palpable. Candice wore a look that could freeze lava. "I am going to kill that asshole," she kept muttering. I glanced behind me to Cat, who seemed equally confused about who exactly "that asshole" was.

For a long time no one but Candice spoke, and her conversation was definitely one-sided. "Of all the snarky, low-down, bullshit things to do!" she said, and slammed her hand on the steering wheel. "He's dead," she said, nodding her head vigorously as if agreeing with the conclusion. "D-E-A-D—*dead*!"

"Er . . . Candice?" I asked meekly.

"I'm gonna kill him. And I'm gonna kill him slow," she continued.

"Yoo-hoo?" I said, waving my hand at her. "Sanity to Candice. Do you copy?"

But it was no use. She wouldn't do anything other than curl herself forward, hovering menacingly over the steering wheel, as she wove in and out of traffic at ever increasing speeds.

Cat sat back in her seat and closed her eyes while she whispered under her breath. It appeared she was praying and I thought that might be a great idea. I closed my eyes too, but pretty much all that was going through my head was *"AHHHHHHHHH!"*

The car swerved sharply and I opened my eyes. Candice was exiting off the freeway, which was a relief until I noticed that she hadn't decreased her speed very much. A few turns later I was starting to get carsick, and rolled down my window for some fresh air. "Candice!" I heard Cat yell from the backseat. "Look out!"

My eyes flashed forward and I noticed that we barely missed an eighteen-wheeler. "Please!" I said to her. "I'm begging you to slow down!" But she wasn't listening. Nope, Uma was intent on killing Bill.

Finally, just when I thought I might really lose my cookies, Candice squealed into a ratty-looking trailer park and zoomed to the end of the street, coming to a screeching halt in front of a blue and white trailer that had most definitely seen better days.

Before I could even unbuckle my seat belt, Candice was out of the car and marching toward the front door. *"Lenny!"* she yelled loud enough to wake the dead.

The front door opened and Candice's ex strolled out onto the front step, beer in hand and wearing a big fat grin. "Honey," he said cordially. "You didn't think I'd let a prime money-making opportunity like that pass me by, did you? I mean, the Feds pay so much more than the local PD for a good bit of intel."

In a move that stunned me with both its speed and ferocity, Candice grabbed Lenny by his shirt collar and yanked him forward while lifting one knee. Lenny bent double and let go of his beer as he got out a muffled, "Umph!"

Candice let go of him and stepped back. "Even when we were married, you were a snaky son of a bitch!" she yelled at him, right before she brought her elbow down into the middle of his back.

"Oh, I've seen that move," Cat said from the back-seat. "The boys watch WWF wrestling every Saturday morning."

"Do you think we should stop her?" I asked, watching Candice walk around Lenny and give him a solid kick in the ass.

"You're kidding me, right?" Cat asked seriously.

I looked back at Candice and Lenny, who seemed to have recovered his senses enough to turn around, lie on his back, and try to fend off Candice by sticking his legs up in the air at her. "Yeah," I said, realizing a Sherman tank might not be able to fend off my partner. "Better to let her tire herself out."

About the time Candice was kicking Lenny's butt to the curb, the front door to the trailer opened, and quick as a flash, a woman of about Candice's height but with jet-black hair came up behind her and held a mean-looking knife under her chin. "Uh-oh," Cat said. "Looks like Lenny's got reinforcements."

"Why, hello, Michelle," Candice said coolly, holding her hands up in the air and not moving a muscle. "It's been a while. Last time I saw you, you were riding my husband."

"It has been a while," said Michelle smoothly. "And I see you've gotten heavier with age."

Candice laughed. "Muscle weighs more than fat, but I wouldn't expect someone of your body mass index to know that."

The brunette, who was quite striking, took hold of Candice's hair and gave a tug back, exposing Candice's throat to the knife. "It all bleeds the same, Candy," Michelle said.

Lenny got to his feet and said, "Hold her, babe. I'm going in to call the Feds."

"Time for a rescue," I said to Cat, and quickly pushed myself across the car to the driver's seat. Starting the engine, I put the car in neutral, then gunned the engine. "Let her go!" I said two seconds before I punched the gas and the car shot forward.

Lenny dived out of the way, pulling Michelle with him, and Candice spun in the other direction. I wheeled the car in a tight turn and skidded across the dirt, stopping only long enough for Candice to open the car door and throw herself inside. *"Drive!"* she yelled, and I hit the gas.

Once we got back onto a main road, Candice said, "We're gonna have to dump this car," she said. "But first, we've got to warn Wyatt."

"Ohmigod!" I said. "He's on his way to the motel!"

"I know," Candice said gravely. "Abby, pull over here and let me drive."

We switched seats and got back on the highway. This time Candice was watching her speed and watching for cops. "Why did Lenny turn us over to the Feds?" Cat asked.

Candice glanced at my sister in the rearview mirror. " 'Cuz he sorta owed me one," she admitted.

"There's a history here," Cat said to me. "Spill it, Candice," she insisted.

Candice rubbed her neck and I saw a small red nick where the knife had pressed against her throat. "Like I said," she began, "after I got fired as a showgirl, I needed a gig. Lenny was hiring, so I went to work for him, working the night surveillance shift."

"Lenny was the PI you worked for?" I asked.

Candice nodded. "Yep. And I was young and stupid. He seduced me, and I fell for it. I even married the asshole," she said with a mirthless laugh. "And I ignored every sign I told the wives whose cases I worked not to shrug off. The late nights, the unexplained phone calls at all hours, the hang-ups I got whenever I answered the phone, his sudden interest in getting into shape. All of it I tossed off as coincidence. But one night the guy I was running surveillance on got pulled over and arrested for DUI. That freed up my evening and I went home to find that black-haired *thing* back there humping my husband."

"What did you do?" Cat asked.

The corner of Candice's mouth lifted. "I called one of the bookies Lenny owed a big wad of cash to, and tipped him off. See, Lenny and I used to move around a lot, mostly because he liked to gamble, but he sucked at it."

"What'd the bookie do when you told him where to find Lenny?" I asked.

"Lenny spent a few weeks in the hospital. I hear he's going to need a hip replacement one of these days."

"Ouch," I said.

Candice shrugged. "Trust me, Abby, that slimeball had it coming. His affair wasn't the only thing I ignored. Lenny was an opportunist in the worst way. He didn't mind breaking the law if it suited his purposes, and the reason he needed me in the first place was because his license had been suspended so many times that the state had him on probation. In other words, if he got caught running surveillance in a restricted area or private property, he'd lose his license. If I got caught, I'd get a fine and a warning."

"Let me guess," I said. "Lenny never told you what would happen if you got caught."

"Bingo," Candice said as she pulled off the highway, and headed back to the warehouse district. We arrived in front of Fred's not long afterward, and he let the garage up before we'd even gotten out of our car.

After he'd let us in again, Candice apologized for bothering him twice in one day, and then explained about Lenny calling the Feds on us. "Shit, Candy!" Fred said. "You put Wyatt in the middle of a Fed raid?"

"I swear to God, Fred, I never meant to put Wyatt in

a jam!'' Candice insisted. "It was only luck that got us behind them on the way to the motel. Otherwise, I'd be in the back of a cop car right now.''

Fred waddled over to a phone at his desk, and after looking up a number, he jammed it into the phone and waited. "Wyatt?'' he said as we all looked at him anxiously.

I knew immediately that something was wrong, because Fred's pink complexion turned ghostly pale before he slammed down the phone. "Shit, shit, shit!'' he said.

"What?'' Candice said.

"Who the hell is Abigail Cooper?'' Fred demanded.

Cat and Candice looked at me with wide eyes. "That would be me,'' I said weakly.

"That was the FBI, some guy named Robillard. He says he knows where you are and he's coming to get you. You can expect the same fate as someone named Cynthia.''

I felt my own blood leave my face, and before I could even react, Candice was in motion. "What can I grab?'' she asked Fred.

"My computers!'' Fred said as he turned to his desk and began unplugging things as quickly as his shaking fingers would let him.

"Get to your car, Fred!'' Candice said. "Take the freight elevator and go! We'll be right behind you!''

Fred nodded and waddled in the direction of the freight elevator, breathing heavily. "Oh, God,'' Cat said as she saw him shuffling. "I'll help you get to your car, Fred!'' she said.

I went to Candice's side as she grabbed the three laptops on the desk, handing one to me, and we were about to go when Fred said, "My book! Candy, grab that black book on the counter! And my notepad, grab that too!''

Candice handed the black book to me and she took the notepad and we dashed to the door and the spiral staircase. "Hurry!" Candice said. "Abby, we've got to move!"

I urged my feet to keep pace with my rapidly pounding heart as we charged down the stairs and through the garage. Fred was in his car with Cat at the wheel, his breathing labored and his complexion still very pale. "Herc's the key!" Cat said, handing the key to the lock on the front gate to me.

"Follow us!" Candice ordered, and she and I ran full tilt toward the gate. It took me three tries to get the key into the lock; I was shaking so hard. In the distance I could hear sirens. "Take a deep breath," Candice coaxed as my fingers overshot the lock for the second time. I inhaled and held my breath as I willed the key into the little hole. The lock came undone and I unhooked it from the chain. Behind us I could hear the creaking of the metal garage door as it ground down to close up the building. Candice and I opened the gate wide to let Cat and Fred through. Candice piled the computers into the backseat of Fred's car and then she and I dashed to our rental car.

The sirens were definitely closer as Candice started up the car. "Abby!" she said to me before I could click my seat belt. "Rechain the gate!"

"What?!" I said, my eyes wide with fright. "Why?"

"Because it will slow them down!" she insisted, and backed the car up to the edge of the gate. "Come on, do it!"

I jumped out of the car and ran to close the gate. I wound the chain around the two metal doors several times while I panted with the effort. "Come on!" Candice called as I notched the lock through the loops of the chain and clicked it closed.

The sirens sounded far too close for my comfort as I dived back into Candice's car and she hit the gas. Behind us I heard Fred's car squeal after us and we zoomed down the street, taking a right turn, then a quick left, then another right so fast that I kept tilting wildly in my seat. "Jesus!" I exclaimed as I tried to brace myself with my feet and my hand on the dash.

"She's keeping pace!" Candice said as she glanced in the rearview mirror. I looked behind me. Cat's face was pulled taut by the strain of focusing on keeping up with Candice, while Fred was leaning far back in his seat and appeared to be gasping for breath.

As I looked at him, my radar started sounding the alarm. "Candice," I said to her. "Fred needs to go to the hospital!"

Her eyes cut to mine as she raced down a long stretch of pavement, putting distance between us and the sirens. "What?" she said, and glanced again in the rearview.

"I mean it!" I said. "Something's wrong with him. We need to get him to the emergency room!"

Candice's jaw clenched. "Okay." She put on her blinker before pulling over to the side. "We can't risk driving in this thing any longer anyway," she said. "If I know Lenny, he's given the make and model over to the Feds anyway."

Candice and I hurried to pull our personal items out of the car and dash back to Cat, who was idling behind us. She got out as Candice approached the driver's side and said, "Fred's having trouble breathing. I think we need to take him to the emergency room!"

"That's the plan, Cat," Candice said as she hopped into the front seat while Cat and I moved the computers over and got into the back. "How you doin', old man?" Candice asked as she put the car into drive and peeled away from the curb.

"Candy . . . you . . . got . . . to listen . . . to me," Fred said, panting like he'd just come off the track.

"Not now, Fred," Candice said sternly. "Your job is to sit there and try and calm down while I get you to the hospital."

Fred shook his head no and reached out to lay a hand

on her shoulder. When Candice glanced at him, Fred took a deep breath and said, "I'm serious. You have . . . to find . . . Jabba."

"Okay," Candice said calmly. "We'll find Jabba. Did you want him to come to the hospital?"

Again Fred shook his head no. "Jabba's the one . . . who can . . . help you . . . get your intel."

Candice gave Fred a funny look. "You mean all these years you've been dealing in information, you weren't the one pulling it?"

Fred leaned back against the seat and worked to take air in and let it out for a few seconds before he answered her. "I used to do . . . all the legwork," he said. "Then I met . . . Jabba . . . and he got me . . . intel no one else could."

"How?" Candice asked.

"Hacker," Fred said. "The best . . . there is."

"How do we find him?"

Fred closed his eyes and took a few more breaths. "He's in . . . the black . . . book. Take my laptop . . . to him . . . for safekeeping. He'll get you what you need."

Fred's black book—the one we'd taken off his desktop—was next to me on the backseat. I opened it and flipped through the pages to the Js. Midway down the page was the word *Jabba* plus a phone number and address. I held up the book so that Candice could see it in the rearview mirror.

She glanced at me, saw the book, and gave a nod into the mirror. "Thanks, Fred, I owe you one."

Candice dropped Cat and me off in front of a drugstore just before she got to the hospital with Fred. If things got sticky when she took Fred in, she didn't want Cat and me to get caught. We waited anxiously for her for over an hour, and when she finally came back, she looked tired and worn down.

Cat and I jumped back into Fred's car and I handed her the chips and soda I'd bought for her in the drugstore. "Thanks," she said absently.

"How is he?" I asked.

"He's having a pretty bad asthma attack, but the doctors are getting him to calm down and they'll keep him overnight because Fred's also got a heart condition and diabetes."

"Yeah," I said. "I was picking up that ticker problem pretty strong."

"Are we going to Jabba's now?" Cat wanted to know.

"Yes, but first we'll need to ditch Fred's car."

I glanced behind us, suddenly alarmed. "You think they'll know we took it?"

"Remember that camera on the outside of the fence?" Candice said. "My guess is that they'll be looking at the feed from our escape, and once they find my rental, they'll put two and two together."

"How will we get around?" Cat asked.

"I know a guy," Candice said.

"Of course you do," I said lightly.

Candice smirked. "And he owns a used-car lot. We can get a cheap car with no questions asked and no pesky paper trail."

"What are we going to do with this car?" I asked.

"I told Fred I'd park it at the mall. Like everything else here in Vegas, it's twenty-four hours and we can leave it there without anyone becoming suspicious. Plus, the car lot's only a few blocks from there."

It seemed like it took forever to park Fred's car and make our way out of the gigantic parking lot and walk the several blocks to the used-car lot. We each carried a laptop and with every step they seemed to grow heavier and heavier.

When we arrived at Lucky Seven Motors, I'll admit, I wasn't feeling so lucky. "This place is a dump," Cat whispered.

We walked into the lot and scanned the cars. Candice headed right over to a worn and weary Chrysler K-car.

"Wow," I said as Cat and I joined her to inspect the car. "I haven't seen one of these since the eighties."

Candice peered through the window and checked out the odometer. "I had one of these when I lived in Vegas," she said. "That was a great car," she added fondly.

"They don't make 'em like that one anymore," said a male voice with a heavy Southern accent behind us.

We turned around and saw that a tall, lanky man with a pencil-thin mustache and a sharply pointed nose had come to help us. "Candy?" he said when he saw Candice. "Oh, my God! Is that really you?"

"Fats?" she said, her jaw dropping as she took in the man's appearance. "I can't believe it! Where did the rest of you go?"

Fats smiled and tucked his thumbs into the top of his pants, pulling out his waistband before letting it snap back. "It's the new me," he said.

"You must have lost, like . . . two hundred pounds!" Candice exclaimed.

"Closer to three," he said proudly. "I got me that LAP-BAND and it worked purty good."

"Whoa," she said, standing back to take a good look. "I cannot believe it's you! Your new nickname should be Skinny!"

Fats puffed his thin chest up and beamed at her. "What brings y'all by?" he asked, getting to the point.

Candice flashed him her most winning smile. "We need a car," she said. "Cheap."

"I can help you with that," Fats said. "And that model K's a good start."

"How much?" Candice asked.

"For you?" Fats said. "A thousand."

"What?" Candice roared, her fists balling up and her eyes bugging out. "Are you kidding me with this bullshit, Fats? I thought we were tight!"

"Prices have gone up, honey," Fats said, completely unfazed by her outburst. "Chalk it up to inflation."

"Oh, that's a load of crap, Fats!" Candice said. "And you know it!"

I glanced at Cat and the look we shared meant that we were both beginning to think this outrageous form of haggling was the way things were done in Vegas. "I'll give you a hundred bucks for it," Candice said.

Fats made a derisive sound. "One thousand dollars, Candy. And that includes all the paperwork you'll need not to flag anyone if you should get pulled over. And I've seen you drive, child. You are one red flashing light away from a good speeding ticket, if you ask me."

"Five hundred," Candice said.

"Seven fifty," he countered.

Candice stomped the ground and clenched her fists some more. "Six twenty-five and that's our *final* offer, Fats."

Fats pulled at his mustache for a while as he thought about it, his eyes roving to the K-car, then back to Candice, then over to us. Finally, he broke out into a big old grin and said, "Well, since you were so nice about calling me skinny and all, I suppose I can take a hit on a car this one time."

Candice extended her hand and the two shook on it.

"I'm glad that's settled," Cat said. "Abby, hand me my purse so I can pay the man."

I looked at Cat blankly. "I don't have your purse," I said.

The color drained from Cat's face. "You didn't get it out of the rental?" she asked in a high-pitched voice.

"Oh, shit!" Candice said. "You left your purse in the rental?"

"Yes!" Cat squealed. "I left it behind when we went into Fred's and I thought Abby grabbed it before we took him to the hospital!"

"We've got to go back and get it!" I said desperately.

Candice looked at Fats. "Say, Fats," she said, "can we

borrow this car for about a half an hour? We'll bring the money to you. We just have to go get it."

Fats laughed like she'd just told him the funniest joke. "Apparently, Fats isn't into loaning out his cars," Cat mumbled.

"Fine!" I said, and dug into my backpack, where I pulled out the wad of bills that Red had given me. I counted off six hundred dollars and change, then handed that to Fats. "Can we have the keys, please? We're in a hurry."

We drove out of the lot with our model K coughing and sputtering while I was having second thoughts about forking over six hundred dollars for something so smelly. "Can we roll down the windows?" Cat said from the backseat. "It's like something died back here!"

Candice tried running the air, and there was more sputtering and coughing, but nothing even remotely close to cool air wafted out of the vents. Candice lowered the windows and we did our best to lean toward the open air and try not to breathe through our noses.

It didn't take long to thread our way back through the warehouse district—avoiding the street Fred lived on—and over to where we'd left the rental. I felt like weeping as we pulled up to the curb where we'd left the car and there was no sign of it. "Shit," Candice said. "They've already taken it."

"All my ID was in that purse!" Cat wailed from the backseat. "I won't be able to get any more money without my ID!"

Candice pulled away from the curb and back through the dizzying array of streets, glancing in the rearview mirror often to make sure we weren't being followed. "How much cash do you have left?" she asked me.

"About a thousand," I said.

"I've got about the same," she said. "Come on, let's

go see this Jabba character and see how much he charges. With any luck he'll only want two grand."

"Five thousand," said a porky young man with curly black hair covering most of his head and arms.

"What?!" Candice hollered, and so began the negotiations. I looked around while the two of them argued money.

Jabba lived in the basement of his mother's one-story ranch. The house upstairs was a testament to cows. There were cows on the welcome mat, cartoon cows on the throw rugs. Cow figurines on the mantel, cows on the wallpaper in the kitchen. Cows on the magnets on the fridge, and a cowbell in the center of the kitchen table.

Down in the basement, however, we entered a galaxy far, far away. Jabba was no different from the stereotypical young hacker. His walls were covered with posters of the *Star Wars* trilogies. A Han Solo figurine perched atop his computer, and hanging from the low ceiling on fishing wire were Federation Battleships and Death Stars.

Now I understood the "Jabba" reference, and looking at the slothlike youth, it was easy to see the comparison.

"Two thousand, Jabba, and that's our *final* offer!" Candice yelled, pulling my attention back to the haggling.

"I don't argue over price, Miss Fusco. My price is my price, and that price is five thousand dollars. You don't want to pay it, then go somewhere else."

"Fine," Candice said. "We'll pay you fifteen hundred to get started, and bring you the rest later."

Jabba considered that for a few seconds. Shrugging his shoulders, he said, "Okay. Give me the list again of everyone you need dirt on."

Candice handed him the list and he surveyed it. "Hmmm," he said. "Some of this stuff may be tricky, but I'm always up for a challenge." I noticed the twinkle in his eye as he looked at our list.

"Just don't get caught," Candice said.

"Never do," Jabba said with a sly grin. "I'll call you when I've put your packet together."

"How long will it take?" I asked.

"Not long. Maybe a day, or two at the most."

Candice gave him her cell number and we left Jabba to his hacking. We got back in the smelly K-car and Cat exclaimed, "It smells worse!" as she pinched her nose. "God Almighty, something bad happened in this car."

"Hopefully we won't need it for long," Candice said as she backed out of the driveway.

"Where are we going now?" I asked.

"How much money do you have in your bank account?" she asked me.

"Enough to cover what we owe Jabba," I said. "But weren't we trying to avoid the banks and their cameras?"

"I know a guy," she said. "He's got an ATM that will let you withraw any amount from your account with no limit."

"No cameras?"

"Nope," she said.

"Will I need to change my PIN number?"

"Immediately afterward," Candice said with a small grin.

"Fabulous," I said woodenly.

Candice drove us a few miles over to a street lined with pawnshops and adult bookstores. "Quaint," Cat said from the backseat.

We parked the K-car at the curb outside Buckey's Pawn and Lotto and headed inside. "Candy!" said a little old man about four feet tall with huge Coke-bottle glasses, black pants, a white grimy T-shirt, and suspenders.

"Hey, Buckey," Candice said smoothly. "We need to use your ATM."

Buckey smiled, revealing two sets of gums and no

teeth. "Ish right over there," he said with a toothless lisp as he pointed to an ATM in the corner of the shop.

We approached the machine with caution. Candice stepped in front of me and looked at the side of the machine, whispering, "Just like I thought. Abs, you'll be able to withdraw as much as you need from this puppy. It's got a gadget that will override any preset limit, but I would suggest you withdraw *all* of the cash in your account, because it will also grab your PIN number and make a withdrawal of its own after we leave."

"Comforting," I said with a grimace as I moved in and pulled out my ATM card. Swiping the card, I punched in my number and waited while the electronic readout suggested it verified the PIN.

After several seconds Cat asked, "What's taking so long?"

Candice's face was registering concern too. "I'm not liking this," she said as the display continued to show the hourglass with no signs of verifying my PIN.

Alarm bells were going off in my head when suddenly the machine displayed a message that said, *Unable to verify, please reenter your PIN.*"

I moved my finger over to the keypad, but Candice caught my hand. I looked up at her and she shook her head no. "Let's roll," she said quietly and calmly, but I could hear the urgency there too.

"How's it coming?" Buckey said from his perch behind the counter.

"Great, Buckey," she said as she hustled us toward the door.

"I've got a special on watches today," Buckey called to us.

"We're good, thanks!" Candice said, and we shot out the door.

When we were back in the K-car and Candice had zoomed away down the street, Cat asked, "Why did we leave before getting the money?"

"I think the FBI's put a trace on Abby's account. I've heard of the technique where they encode the account with a tag that keeps asking you to enter or validate your information while setting off an alarm at the FBI. While you're busy reentering your PIN number over and over, they're sending the posse to your location to nab your ass."

"Clever," Cat said.

"Very," Candice replied. "I figure they'll be at Buckey's in under two minutes."

"So we're totally screwed," I said grumpily.

"Oh, I don't know about that," Candice replied. "I think there's still a way to come up with some dough."

"How are we going to come up with three thousand five hundred dollars when we've got no access to bank accounts and Cat's fresh out of money?" I asked.

Candice shot me a grin. "How's that old radar working these days?"

My brows knit together. "Fine, I guess."

"Ever try your hand at using it to beat the odds?" she asked.

"Oh, that's brilliant!" Cat chirped nasally from the backseat. "Abby! We can just win the money!"

"*That's* your big plan?!" I gasped. "Candice, I've never done something like that!"

"Whoa, didn't you once tell me about a strip-poker game you played with the Royal Oak PD that cost every cop there everything but his underwear?"

I blinked furiously at her. "Yeah, but that was for fun. This is different!" I said, feeling the pressure.

"You're right, Abby—this is different," she said soberly. "The difference is that unless we come up with some serious coin fast, we can't move forward with our search for Dutch. It's not like I can go around and interview people, because of this little pesky business about being *wanted by the law*. That leaves us little recourse if we want to chase down leads here, girl, and unless you can come up with a better idea, your radar is the only thing that will move our chess piece forward."

My right side felt light and airy and my crew gave me a small mental nudge. "Okay," I said reluctantly. "I'll try."

"Great," Candice said as the K-car coughed and sputtered while we idled at a light. "We'll need to go back to the Strip, and that means we'll also need to go incognito."

"Like with disguises?" Cat said cheerfully.

Candice glanced at her in the rearview mirror. "Exactly," she said. "And I know just the place."

"Oh, Abby, this could be fun!" Cat said, and I remembered how she always loved to play dress-up as a little girl.

Cat changed her tune about an hour later as she came out of the dressing room dressed in a black bouffant wig and a short cocktail dress. "I look ridiculous," she said, observing her petite frame in the mirror.

I stepped out from behind the curtain dressed head to toe in rhinestones, a black puffy wig, thick round sunglasses, and a belt buckle as big as Iowa. "Sorry, the title for ridiculous has already been taken."

Candice giggled from behind her own curtain. And when she stepped out, I realized I might have spoken too soon. "My dahlings," she said, casting her hands wide to show off the electric blue cape studded with its own series of rhinestones and feathers, a white puffy shirt with elaborate collar and cuffs, and in her hand a plastic candelabra. "To my piano!" she said.

"I should have gone with Liberace," Cat said, eyeing Candice. "Priscilla seems so dull next to him."

"There's not much available in your size," I said, reminding her of that fact. My sister is tiny, like, five-feet-nothing, and she weighs less than a hundred pounds.

"Prince," Cat said, already taking off her wig. "He's

small. I'll bet there's something in my size back in his section," and with that she was off.

Candice and I waited while Cat traded Priscilla for Prince, and I had to admit, as she spun around in the mirror and did a little, "Who-ah-whoo!" she did a pretty good impression.

"Can we get this show on the road?" I said, impatient to get this thing over with.

We paid for our costume rental, which took up half of the rest of our available funds, and made our way back to the Strip.

By now it was full dark out and the traffic along Las Vegas Boulevard had slowed to a crawl. "Where do you think we should start?" Candice asked me.

I sighed as my insides felt like jelly. We had to turn $250 into close to $4,000 and we didn't have a lot of time to do it. Jabba had already called to tell us that the intel was ready for pickup as soon as we had the money.

I closed my eyes and tried to settle my nerves. Calling out to the crew, I thought, *Gang, I really need your help here. Please assist with this however you can. Tell me where to go, please.*

My mind's eye filled with a desert scene. *Great. I'm already in the desert. Where to after that?* I said to them as I thought that my crew might be a *little* slow on the uptake. From the desert in my mind rose a sphinx, and then around the sphinx a glass pyramid formed, encasing the great statue and pointing me in the right direction. My eyes flashed open. They hadn't been slow at all; I'd just misunderstood—as usual. "We start at the Luxor," I said confidently.

Candice flashed me a grin and pushed up her Liberace wig, which was slightly too big for her head. "We're there," she said, and wove through traffic in the direction of the big black pyramid.

We parked the K-car and hurried into the casino. "I feel so tall!" Cat said as we went through the doors.

"Prince really has something with this platform-shoe thing."

"Whoa," I said, coming up short as I walked into the gigantic space with a ceiling that seemed to touch the sky. "This is cool!"

We all twirled in a circle and stared up. The Luxor is built in the shape of an enormous pyramid and the rooms line the walls of the structure. Inside such a wide-open space it felt like we were tiny—even Cat shrunk back down to size.

In the center of the massive structure was the casino, and it resembled every other casino I'd seen so far with lots of pinball-sounding *ding*s and electric neon lights and dim lighting. The air was also filled with smoke and the chatter of hundreds of people. "Where should we go now?" Cat asked as we stood at the edge of the casino and looked around at all the neon lights.

I waited for my radar to direct me, but with all the other sensory input surrounding me, it was hard to feel the subtlety of my intuition. "I'm not sure," I said. "Let's walk around and see if I feel pulled in any direction."

We entered the casino and began to roam around. About half the patrons we saw were dressed as their favorite Vegas celebrity. I saw dozens of Elvises, and about an equal number of Chers, Celine Dions, Siegfried & Roys, and of course Liberaces. Cat was lucky—there weren't a whole lotta Princes.

"You feeling anything calling out to you?" Candice said as we cruised the rows of slot machines.

I shook my head no. "Nothing," I said, then paused in front of one machine. "This one feels good," I said, sitting down and shoving in a five-dollar bill. Candice stood to my side and looked down at me skeptically, but she didn't say anything.

I read the directions and selected the highest odds. Then I pressed the button and the little wheels began to turn inside the machine. Suddenly an eruption of noise sounded from the machine. "Whoo-hoo!" I said. "We won!"

Candice looked at the display. "We won a hundred dollars," she said. "That's great, Abs. Now can you do that thirty-four more times?"

I moved my finger over the button but hesitated. My radar said the good luck had run out on this machine. I cashed out and took the paper receipt with our winnings as I got up off the stool. "Come on," I said. "We'll need to find more machines like this one."

A very long time later, when Cat was now complaining about her aching feet, we were up a thousand dollars, bringing our grand cash total to about twelve hundred dollars. The winnings had come slowly, here a hit, there a hit, but my radar also failed me several times. It was just too hard to focus in this type of atmosphere.

By eleven forty-five I was exhausted and I had a headache and I realized I'd had little more to eat that day than breakfast and a bag of chips. "This is no use," I finally said. "Candice, I can't do this anymore."

"Okay, Abs," she said easily. "We tried. Maybe Jabba will give us a partial delivery for the twelve hundred dollars."

Feeling dejected, tired, and hungry, we began making our way out of the casino. Over the loudspeaker a woman's breathy voice said, "The lucky-sphinx jackpot drawing will be in fifteen minutes! You still have time to purchase your ticket to win! Don't miss it, folks! Come on over and get in on the fun!"

I paused as my radar went *ding!* inside my head and again my crew flashed me the image they had before of the sphinx being encased in the pyramid of glass. "Stop!" I said to Cat and Candice as they walked on ahead.

They both turned to look at me curiously. "What's up?"

"We need to get a raffle ticket," I said excitedly. "Where do they sell them?"

"At the other end," Candice said. "But they're, like, five hundred dollars a pop, Abs."

"Then we'll buy two," I said.

We hurried over to the counter where a line of people waited to purchase tickets for the raffle drawing. "What's being given away?" Cat wondered while we inched forward.

"I'm not sure," Candice said, trying to see over the crowd of people gathering for the drawing. "I think it's a car or something."

"Ooo!" Cat squealed. "Does that mean we could lose the K-car?"

Candice smiled. "Probably not. We'd have to trade it in for some quick cash and pay Jabba."

"If there's money left over, can we buy another less-smelly car?" Cat asked.

"Maybe," Candice said with a giggle.

It was our turn at the counter and I shoved one thousand dollars of our hard-earned winnings through the window. "Two tickets, please," I said as my heart thudded in my chest. If this didn't work, I had no idea what we were going to do.

The woman behind the glass tore off two tickets and handed them to me. "Good luck," she said.

After purchasing the tickets, we moved over to the gathering crowd and waited the last few minutes until midnight for the drawing. "I'm so nervous I could pee!" said Cat. "No, wait. That's really my bladder calling. I'll be back in a flash," she said, and zipped off to the ladies' room.

"How're you holding up?" Candice asked, eyeing me critically.

"God, I hope I'm right," I said as I gripped the two tickets in my now-sweaty fingers.

"Even if we don't win, Abby, we'll figure something out, okay?"

I gave her a short nod, but all my focus and concentration went to the small stage in front of a black curtain that hid the grand prize. "Hello, folks!" said a busty brunette as she got up on stage and waved at the crowd. There was a small bit of applause, and a gentleman joined her holding a large fishbowl partially filled with little gray tickets. "Welcome to the Luxor Hotel and Casino!" she said. "Tonight's grand-prize winner will be walking away with quite a catch!" With that, the black curtain dropped and two beautifully shiny Mini Coopers glistened in the spotlight. A grin began to form on my lips. "Mini Coopers," I said. "My crew has one hell of a sense of humor."

"What do you mean?" Candice asked.

"When the Mini Cooper first came on the market, Cat wanted to buy us one each. She said it would be cute to drive around in a car named after us."

"Really?" Candice said, her focus going back to the cars. "That's freaky!"

"Not for me," I said, and let out a long breath. "We're going to win them, Candice," I added confidently, knowing it in my heart.

"Coopers!" I heard Cat squeal from behind me. "Ohmigod! Abby, remember how I wanted to buy us one each?"

"I do," I said with a smile.

"And they're even the colors we wanted. One blue, one red. I get the red one!" she said quickly like she was calling shotgun.

"And to go with your matching Mini Coopers, we're also giving away a little cash!" said the announcer. "Tonight's cash jackpot will be twenty thousand dollars!"

Candice draped an arm over my shoulders. "You are freaking amazing," she whispered, shaking her head in admiration.

"It's the crew," I said happily as the announcer
reached into the fishbowl and pulled out the ticket. As
she called off the numbers, my smile broadened and I
knew for certain even before she called off the last digit
on my second ticket that it was really true—we'd actually won the jackpot. Cat began to jump up and down
with happiness, hugging me, hugging Candice, hugging
people next to us. . . . She was a Princely bundle of joy.

"Come on, ladies," I said after the last digit was
called. "Let's go claim our prize."

It was a good thing we had Candice along, because
the prize people wanted to see a valid ID before they
would sign off on the paperwork. Candice placed a hand
on my arm and said, "I know you left your wallet back
in the car. Why don't you let me give them the ID?"

I nodded absently as I realized with the FBI looking
for me, my claiming a huge raffle drawing might send
off smoke signals. Candice handed over a Las Vegas ID
with her picture, and the man filling out the paperwork
said, "Thank you, Miss Dubois."

Candice winked at me. "Oh, please," she said to the
man, "Call me Samantha."

I looked sharply at Candice when I realized that the
older sister she'd lost in a car accident was named Samantha. Candice's eyes told me to keep a lid on it for
now, however, so I didn't comment.

The man filling in the paperwork handed her back her
ID and said, "We place a twelve-hour hold on the delivery of all our raffle prizes."

"What?" yelled Cat, balling her fists and getting hot
under the collar in a fabulous impression of Candice
at her negotiating best. "That's insane! We need our
prizes tonight!"

The prize representative blanched in the face of such
fury. "I'm so sorry, ma'am, but those are the rules."

"Rules, schmules!" Cat hollered. "This is ridiculous!"

Another man dressed in a beautiful sleek black suit

and metallic lavender tie hurried over to us and spoke into the prize guy's ear. Prize guy turned pink, gave a nod to the man who walked away, and said to Cat, "As a consolation it would be our honor to add a three-day voucher to the Luxor Hotel and Casino, including meals and a day at the spa."

Cat eyed him critically. "What kind of accommodations does that include?" she said. "I only stay in the best rooms available."

"Of course," said the man, scribbling on a pad of paper. "Take this to the lobby, ladies, and we'll put you in the best suite available."

"Man," I said as we turned and walked away toward the lobby. "You two really know how to strike a deal."

"Great job," Candice said to Cat.

"By the way," I said, curious about Candice's ID, "when did you steal your sister's identity?"

Candice's face reddened a little. "I know," she said quickly, "it's a pretty lame thing to do, but when I was in school out here, I got some speeding tickets and I couldn't afford the insurance, and my mother had given me Sam's birth certificate because she knew we were close, so I used it to get a license."

"How is it even still valid?" I asked.

"I've kept it up," she admitted.

"You've kept up your fake Nevada's driver's license?" Cat said.

Candice nodded. "Sam was killed out here," she said. "I know it sounds crazy, but it makes me feel more connected to her to carry it around and keep it up. By having her as my alias, it makes me feel like I still have a sister, and trust me, she's the one with the spotless driving record and perfect credit. My cell is even in her name."

"That's cool that you want to feel close to your sister, Candice," I offered, knowing Candice probably felt embarrassed about having to admit that she'd stolen her sister's identity. "And now I know how the Feds haven't been able to track us through you."

"I like to think it's my sister's way of helping me stay out of trouble," Candice added, and I noticed she was still a little embarrassed by the pink in her cheeks.

"If you died, I'd totally take your ID," Cat said earnestly.

I smiled. "That's okay, honey," I said, giving her shoulders a gentle squeeze. "I don't think using my name would get you very far these days."

We checked into a suite with two double beds in one room and a gorgeous king-sized bed in the other. "Now, this is what I'm talking about!" I said as I rolled around on the king bed.

"Let's order some food!" Cat said, coming into the room carrying a menu.

Candice eyed her watch. "We need to get these costumes back, ladies," she reminded us. We'd rented them for only six hours.

"Oh, pah!" said Cat. "So we don't return these ridiculous outfits. What are they going to do, report us to the costume police?"

"That's exactly what they'll do," Candice said. "These things are actually worth a fortune. Come on, we'll return these and come back here before one, I promise."

With a tired sigh I pushed off the bed and we made our way out of the room and downstairs. "It's probably a good idea anyway," Cat said. "They have our clothes, after all."

I'd forgotten that the costume company liked to keep your clothes until you returned with theirs. As I was the only one with a change of clothes because mine were in my backpack, while Candice and Cat had unfortunately left their things back at the motel, I could see how Candice was anxious to get back to the rental company.

Things did not go smoothly, however, because when we got to our car, it refused to start. "It's like it knows that we've dumped it," Cat said from the backseat as Candice tried again to get the engine to turn over.

"Stupid Fats!" Candice yelled as she pounded on the dashboard. "I should have known better than to trust that guy!"

"We still have about two hundred and fifty dollars," I said, referring to the leftover cash I had after I'd purchased the raffle tickets. "Maybe we should get a cab?"

"Public transportation will be cheaper," Candice said. "I'm thinking that until we claim our prize money and the cars, we should try to be as frugal as possible."

Candice led us to a bus stop and Cat sat down on the bench with a groan. "Oh, my aching feet!" she said.

"How late do the buses run?" I asked as I stood next to Candice, who was studying the bus route posted on the side of the building that was the bus stop.

"Till two," Candice said, glancing at her watch. "We'll have enough time if we hustle."

Two African-American men came down the street, wearing big long chains, lots of gold, baggy pants, and baseball caps turned to the side, and sat down next to Cat on the bench.

Cat eyed them, apparently fascinated. One of the men caught her staring and turned to look at her. She smiled, held up two fingers in a peace sign, and said, "Word."

The young man nudged his buddy and laughed. "Waz up, baby Prince?" he said.

"Ain't no thing," she said. "Nice bling," she added, referring to the gold around his neck.

"Yeah, you know it," he said, hooking a thumb through his necklace. "What brings you to Vegas?"

"Just hangin' with my homies," she said, pointing to us.

"Abby," Candice whispered. "Can you do something about her?"

"Yo homies?" said the man, and he nudged his partner again and began laughing in earnest.

"Yes," said Cat in all seriousness. "You know, they're shizzel and fizzle and all dat."

"Cat!" I said, casting a warning glance her way. The last thing we needed was to start offending total strangers.

"What?" she said innocently. "I'm just talking to these dogs."

"Who you callin' dogs?" said the other man as he suddenly stopped laughing.

"Oh, I'm sorry," Cat said. "I've heard Randy from *American Idol* say that a lot. Isn't that what you all call each other? You know, like that rapper man, what's his name . . . Snoopy Dog?"

"Cat!" Candice and I said together.

Behind us we heard the roar of an engine and the smell of exhaust filled our nostrils. The bus had arrived. Cat got up, still smiling at the two young men, who were shaking their heads and laughing at her.

I reached over and pulled her tight to me, offering the two men an apology. "I'm so sorry," I said. "She left her medication at home."

"No thing, lady," the young man said, still laughing with his buddy at my socially challenged sister.

"What did I say?" Cat said as we got on the bus.

I hadn't let go of her arm since we allowed the two men on the bus ahead of us. "You need to stop watching MTV," I said to her as we took our seats.

"I was just trying to make some conversation, sheesh."

We arrived at the costume-rental place—which like everything else here in Vegas seemed to be open twenty-four hours—and hurried to change into our street clothes.

Candice and I teased Cat in the dressing room between us while we changed. "Yo, dawg," I called to Candice.

"Word," Candice replied.

"Ha-ha," Cat said mirthlessly. "Very funny, you two.

Here I am trying to blend in, which is more than I can say for the two of you!"

Candice and I continued to giggle and we stepped out of the curtained area around the same time. "Oh, come on, Cat," I coaxed to her curtain. "We're just playin'." Candice laughed again and squeezed my arm.

Cat yanked back the curtain with one hand while holding her Prince costume in the other. She was back to looking like her old self except for the thin penciled-in mustache on her upper lip—which of course made Candice and me howl.

Cat glared at us and opened her mouth as if to tell us both off when her eyes suddenly widened and the color drained from her face. I instantly realized that a cold chill was starting to creep up my spine, and behind me I could hear a man's voice saying, ". . . from the FBI. We're conducting a search looking for a person of interest named Abby Cooper. This is her photo. Can you tell me if you've seen her or perhaps rented out a costume to her recently?"

"Oh, shit!" I mouthed, and looked at Candice, who was glancing over her shoulder at what I assumed were two FBI agents.

Candice tossed her costume into the dressing room and did the same with Cat's and mine. "Back door *now*!" she hissed, and shoved us toward a door with a sign that said, FIRE EXIT ONLY! ALARM WILL SOUND IF DOOR IS OPENED!

Candice ignored the sign and pushed the door open, when a god-awful racket sounded in the store as the fire alarm went off. *"Run!"* she yelled, and we bolted out the door and ran for all we were worth down the street.

Chapter Eleven

"Hey, stop!" someone shouted over the noise of the alarm as the three of us dashed down the store's back alley and rounded a corner as fast as we could.

Candice was in the lead and I was close on her heels, and my speedy sister was pumping her tiny legs something fierce to keep up. We ran down the street and Candice turned left into another alleyway. I followed and heard Cat bringing up the rear. At the end of the alley Candice put on the brakes and turned to us. "We've got to split up!" she ordered. "Meet back at our room at the hotel. If you're caught, call your attorney, keep quiet, and do *not* under any circumstances give away the location of our hotel room!"

Cat and I nodded and Candice bolted across the street. I grabbed Cat's arm before she could run away and shoved two twenties into it. "Get back to the hotel safe and don't talk to strangers!" I insisted. She gave me a quick nod and we both ran in opposite directions.

I ran down the street and ducked into another alley. At the end of that street I came out onto a busy four-lane road where, to my relief, a bus had just pulled up to a stop on the opposite side of the road. I had to dart in and out of traffic but managed to make it across and hurried onto the bus, paying the fare and taking a seat quickly. Out of the tinted window I could see two winded-looking FBI agents staring hard at the bus I'd just hopped aboard, but there was a wall of cars zooming down the street that prevented them from crossing.

As my heart pounded, the bus finally pulled away from the stop and I watched them looking at the bus until they faded from view. At the very next stop I got off the bus and ran down the street in the direction of a small casino off the Strip. Edging closer to it, I noticed a taxi pull up to the curb and let out a patron. "Yo!" I called to the taxi before the patron shut the door. "Hold that cab!"

The taxi let me off at the Wynn. I knew it was risky to be so close to where Dutch and I had been staying, but I had a sneaking suspicion that my image had been sent to every cab company in town, and if my cabbie remembered picking me up and decided to tip off the FBI, I wanted to make sure he told them I was a long way from the Luxor.

The problem with my plan was that I was a *long* way from the Luxor, located at the opposite end of the Strip. It seemed to take forever to half jog, half walk all the way back there, especially since I was working my way at odd angles in case any black sedans with tinted windows were cruising the Strip in search of me. Thinking about the photo the FBI agents were passing around, I made a quick detour into the New York–New York Hotel and Casino and bought an "I ♥ NY" black sweatshirt and a Yankees ball cap, then made my way to the restroom, where I braided my hair and tucked it under the ball cap before continuing on my way back to the Luxor.

When I was dog-tired and sore and so hungry I'd eat my own cooking, I pushed through the front doors and trotted to the elevators. The doors opened and I stepped in with another couple, who got off ahead of me. I leaned against the back of the car and closed my eyes, wondering if Cat and Candice had made it back before me.

When I got to the room, I gave a soft knock before sliding my key card into the slot. I entered an empty hotel suite and my heart sank. The clock on the wall read two a.m. It had taken me over an hour to get back. Where could the other girls be?

I paced the floor in front of the door for twenty minutes before hearing a soft click at the lock and the handle turned. Candice stepped inside and quickly shut the door behind her. "Thank God you're here," she said to me.

I went to hug her, then stepped back, my nose scrunching up. "Jesus!" I exclaimed. "*What* is that smell?"

Candice scowled. "Dumpster," she said. "I happened to round the corner just as you were making your getaway on the bus, and the Feds caught sight of me and gave chase. I ended up running down a dead end and had to dive into a Dumpster to avoid them."

"Gah!" I said, putting my hand to my nose. "You smell worse than the K-car! Go take a shower, will you?"

"Gladly," she said, and began heading in that direction. "Is Cat here?" she asked over her shoulder.

"No," I said, and started pacing again. "And I'm worried."

Candice paused at the door to the bathroom. "Don't worry until dawn. If she's not back by then, we'll go looking for her."

"Thanks," I said gratefully.

Candice showered and wrapped herself in one of the terry-cloth robes provided with the room while she rinsed out her only change of clothes in the tub. "Here,"

I said, handing her a fresh shirt. "It's clean, and I'd give you my jeans, but your legs are too long. I doubt they'd fit."

"This is great, thanks," she said. "Any word from Cat?"

"No, and it's nearly three!"

"Abby," she said calmly, "don't worry until it's light out, okay? For now, just keep it together. Cat's come through in the past. I'm sure she's just trying to work her way back here and it's taking her a little longer."

I went back out and paced in front of the door. By three thirty I was going out of my mind. "She should have been back by now," I grumbled. Candice was on the sofa propped up with some pillows, working hard to keep her eyes open. "We'll go look for her the moment my jeans aren't soaking wet," she said. "And we can be sure the Feds have given up the chase."

Just then there was some noise outside our door and a knock. Candice sat bolt upright and we both stared uneasily at the door. "Who is it?" Candice said after a moment.

"Spencer and Willis!" came a muffled reply. "We got somethin' that belongs to y'all."

Candice walked quickly to the door and peered into the peephole. "I don't believe it!" she said, and stepped back to pull on the handle. As the door swung open, I could see why, because I didn't believe it either. "Waz up?" said my sister, wearing a crooked ball cap and a thick gold chain as she dangled limply between the two men from the bus stop.

"Yo, she's had some a dat jungle juice," said one of them.

"*What* did you give her?" I demanded, taking my sister from them and working hard to hold her upright.

"We didn' give her nothin'. She ordered it herself, yo," said the guy on the right. "Willis was drinkin' his drink and the Catwoman here said she thought that looked good, so she be flaggin' down the bartender before we could stop her, no?"

"What was in that drink?" Candice said, reaching out to help with Cat.

"I dunno," said Willis. "But dey call it da bomb for a reason-like, you know what I'm sayin'?"

"Da bomb!" Cat said, swinging her arm up like she was swigging a beer.

"How did you all end up together exactly?" Candice asked.

"Yo, we was in this bar and suddenly the Catwoman here, formerly known as Baby Prince, bust in and was all like, 'You gotta help me hide!' and so Spencer and me, we helped her lay low till things outside chilled out."

"My sister hid out in a bar with you guys?" I said.

"Yeah, but it was cool. Yo, she said she was head of some big marketing firm and that she could help us launch our own label, but that ain't for real, right?"

"I'm Catherine Master-Coopers," Cat slurred. "Head of a multimillion-dollar marketing empire. You two stick with me, and I'll make you richer than Pee-diddley!"

"Yo," said Spencer. "Can you give her our cards so when she ain't so drunk, she can call us, like, and we can talk and stuff?"

"Er . . . ," I said, taking the card and noticing that Spencer and Willis really *did* design clothing. "Sure, I'll give it to her."

"Thanks again for bringing her back here," Candice said while I took off the ball cap and the thick gold chain and handed them back to Willis.

"Ain't no thing," he replied, and then the boys took their leave and we moved Cat into the bedroom and laid her on the bed. "They were such nice young men," slurred Cat.

"Okay, Cat," I said, removing her shoes and pulling the comforter up around her. "Nighty-night."

"Ga'night," she said, and in a moment her eyes were closed and she was breathing deeply.

"Well, Abby," Candice said as she stared at my sister, "I can tell you one thing."

"What's that?"

"If we make it out of this, Cat's little adventure on the wild side will be one of those 'What happens here, stays here' scenarios."

"Tommy would so flip," I said, referring to her husband with a giggle.

"That's why you hold it over her head and only *threaten* to tell on her when you need her to stop doing something annoying."

"So I should whip that one out all the time?" I said with a laugh.

"Pretty much," Candice agreed. "Okay, let's hit the hay. We can sleep until noon, collect our prize money and the cars, and make it to Jabba's to pick up our intel."

As it turned out, we slept until around eleven a.m. and I got the first good night's sleep in what seemed like a very long time. "Take a shower," Candice said when I wandered into the sitting room.

"Cat's still asleep," I said.

"I know. We won't wake her until we have to. I've got a feeling that drink she had last night is going to leave a few shock waves in the way of a hangover."

I took a ridiculously long shower and came out feeling pretty good. Candice had ordered us a huge breakfast of eggs, toast, waffles, pancakes, fruit plates, etc., etc. "Jeez, Candice," I said when I saw the banquet. "Did you order the whole menu?"

Candice beamed from her place at the table, where she was making pretty good headway into a Spanish omelet. "I did," she said. "Hey, it's on the house. We might as well eat up while it's free."

"Owwwwwwwwwwwwwwwwwww . . . ," came a long low moan from my sister, who was just now shuffling out of the bedroom, holding her head with both hands.

"Hey, Catwoman," I said cheerfully. "You not feelin' it this mornin'?"

Cat looked at me through slitted eyes. "Oh, I'm feeling it," she said.

"Eat something," Candice offered. "It'll make you feel better."

Cat wandered over to the table and plopped down in a chair. "I feel awful," she said.

"Serves you right," I scolded. "You had us worried sick last night."

"How did I get back here?" she asked as she took a sip of the coffee Candice had poured for her.

"Your homies brought you back," I said, winking at Candice.

"Oh, yeah," she said. "Willis and Spencer. They were a riot! At least I think they were a riot. I couldn't understand a lot of what they were saying. And after a few sips of something called a bomb, I don't think I remember much else."

"You're just lucky they took care of you," I said. "You could have ended up in real trouble, Cat."

"Oh, please," Cat said, waving her hand dismissively. "I was fine."

"You ever pull a stunt like that again, and I will post the pictures I took on the Internet," I said.

Cat froze and only her eyes darted up to meet mine. *"What* pictures?"

"The ones I took when Willis and Spencer dropped you off. I don't think Tommy would like to hear about all the fun you had here in Vegas."

Candice hid a smile and raised the newspaper she was reading. "You took pictures?" Cat said hoarsely.

I hadn't, but Cat didn't know that. "Yep," I said.

"And unless you follow Candice's directions to the letter, I'm sending them to Tommy."

Cat scowled at me. "Oh, please, how bad could they be?"

"Bad," Candice said from behind the paper. "Really bad."

Cat grew even paler. "I think I need a shower," she said after a moment, and she shuffled off to the bathroom.

"Okay," Candice said as I sat down to some food, "I'm off to sign for our prizes. Then we'll need to boogie over to Jabba's."

"I'll make sure Cat's ready," I said.

I ate far more than I should have before Cat appeared with wet hair dressed in a terry-cloth robe. "I'm getting too old to drink," she said as she came over to the table and picked at some pancakes. "And I don't have any change of clothes or makeup with me," she complained.

"After we pick up the info from Jabba, we can stop at the mall and get us all some new digs."

Eyeing me in my last pair of fresh clothes with a look of envy, she said, "Do you happen to have any facial cream at least?"

I dug into my backpack and began pulling out items—dirty clothes, notebook, appointment book, picture frame, cell phone, wrapper from some crackers I'd had on the plane. "Who's this?" Cat asked, and I looked up to see that she was holding the picture frame I'd gotten from Delgado's condo.

"The guy who was kidnapped," I said, coming up with the face cream.

"He's handsome, don't you think?" Cat said, swiveling the picture around to let me see.

And that's when the world seemed to stop and I felt an icy coldness run through my veins. As I stared at

Delgado's photo, something terrible began happening. His three-dimensional image was changing before my very eyes and quickly becoming flat and plasticlike. "Oh, no!" I said breathlessly as I grabbed the frame. "No, no, no, no, *no!*"

"What is it?" Cat asked, her voice filled with alarm. "What's happening?"

Goose bumps lined my arms as I gripped the picture. Delgado's fingers, hands, and torso had all transformed, his neck and chin were next, and then the flatness of his appearance made it to his eyes, and in my head I heard something like a *pop!*

"Abby!" Cat said. "Please, tell me what's happened!"

I looked up at her, haunted by what I'd just seen. "Someone just killed Ricardo Delgado!"

We filled Candice in when she arrived with a fistful of money and two sets of car keys. "Are you sure?" she asked me, her eyes full of concern.

I closed my own eyes, feeling the emotion of watching someone spiritually fade away. "Yes," I whispered. "He's gone."

"What about Chase?" Cat asked. "Is there any way for you to tune in and see what's happened to him?"

I remembered the other photo in the backpack, the one that Laney had given me off her fridge. Frantically I dug around in my backpack and when my fingers hit on it, I didn't pull it out right away. I wasn't sure how I would react if Chase's image was also flat in appearance. All my hope for Dutch had been hanging on a theory that he'd discovered who'd kidnapped Delgado, and was also being held captive. If Chase was dead, that would likely mean Dutch was too. "It's okay," Candice said, obviously reading my body language. "You can look at it, Abs. You can do it."

I took a deep breath and pulled out the photo, giving it a quick glance before closing my eyes.

"Oh, no," Cat said sadly. "Oh, Abby, I'm so sorry!"

"No," I said hoarsely, opening my eyes to look at my sister. "He's not dead, Cat. Chase Rivers is alive."

Candice heaved a sigh of relief. "Thank God," she said, then got straight to business. "Okay, ladies, it's pretty obvious we're running out of time here. This is the game plan: First, we take both cars over to the Las Vegas Hilton and leave one there."

"Why?" Cat asked.

"Because if we get spotted while we're in one car, we can dump it, make our way back to the Hilton by bus, taxi, or monorail, and still have a car to drive."

"Good thinking," I said.

"Next we're heading to Jabba's. What he gives us will determine our next move. Either way, we're done with the Luxor, so grab everything you came in here with 'cuz we're not coming back."

Cat sighed as she looked around at our cushy digs. "So sad to let the other two days on our voucher go to waste."

"We can't risk it," Candice said. "We already know the Feds are handing out flyers. All we need is for one observant hotel guest to notice how familiar we look and we're trapped."

"Let's roll," I said, pulling on my Yankees ball cap and some dark sunglasses, as I felt a renewed sense of urgency. I didn't know what had happened to Delgado, but my radar hinted that he'd died violently and as quickly as his image had faded from his photograph.

Candice and I cruised to the Hilton with Cat following close behind in her red Mini. "Obey all traffic signals and speed limits," Candice had warned. "The last thing we need is for one of us to get pulled over."

After dropping the red Mini at the Hilton, we backtracked along Las Vegas Boulevard to the highway, then drove to Jabba's house. We rang the bell and his mother answered. "We're here to see Jabba," Candice said when she answered the door.

Jabba's mother looked a great deal like her son, with the same curly black hair, puffy red cheeks, and black-framed glasses. "He's in the basement," she said. "Come right in."

We made our way down the stairs and found Jabba at his desk playing a video game. "I was wondering when you guys were going to come by," he said, firing off a series of lasers at the enemy warship.

"We got hung up," Candice said, reaching into her purse and coming up with a wad of dough. "There you go," she said. While Jabba counted the money, Candice asked, "Have you heard from Fred?"

"Yeah, he came by last night. He grabbed his computers and he left town."

"He left town?" Candice said. "Do you know where he went? He owes us our money back."

Jabba looked at her as if she'd just said something stupid. "Good luck with that," he said. "Fred's heading to Costa Rica. He's officially retired."

Candice looked at me and Cat as if to say, "Sorry."

"It's fine," Cat said. "We got our money back last night, Candice, plus two cars. It's fine."

"It's all here," Jabba said, then reached to the shelf above his computer and handed us a thick envelope. "Some of that stuff I'd already researched, so I just made a copy of what I'd dug up."

"What do you mean?" I asked as my radar hummed.

"A guy came to me the other night and asked me to pull some intel on one of the names on the list."

"What guy?" I said, my heart beginning to race.

Jabba looked at me squarely. "He didn't give me his name, and I wouldn't tell you if he did."

"That's fine," Candice said. "I can respect that. But can you at least tell us what he looked like?" Jabba considered that for a moment, so Candice added, "Her boyfriend's gone missing, and we think he's in danger. We're trying to find him and anything you can tell us might really help locate him."

With a sigh Jabba said, "I dunno, he was kinda tall and he had blond hair."

My heart thumped harder in my chest. "Dutch," I said breathlessly. "Jabba, when did he stop by?"

Jabba shrugged. "Two or three nights ago?" he said as if it was a question. "I can't remember."

Candice and I shared a look. "What intel was he after?" she asked, but as she did, an alarm sounded on Jabba's computer.

"Warning!" it said. "Warning, Will Robinson! Intruder! Intruder alert!"

"Oh, *shit*!" Jabba said, whirling around to his computer screen, where his fingers began to click furiously on the keyboard.

"What's happening?" Cat said.

"No, no, no, no, no!" Jabba growled. "That's not *possible*!"

Jabba's computer continued to bleep and whistle. Candice peered over his shoulder. "Someone's breached your firewall," she said.

"Tell me something I don't know!" Jabba snapped as sweat broke out onto his forehead. "Goddamn it!" he yelled at the screen as his fingers continued to blaze across the keypad.

"Come on," Candice said to us. "We need to go—*now*!"

Before we could even turn to leave, Jabba jumped up and yanked the plug out of the wall. He was breathing hard and running his hands through his hair. "Yeah, that's a good idea!" he said, and he began to hurry around the room grabbing notebooks and a few *Star Wars* figurines and shoving them into a duffel.

As we headed for the stairs, we heard him shout, "Ma? *Maaaaaaaaa*!"

She opened the door as we reached the top stair. "Yes, dear?" she said as we hurried past her.

"We gotta go!" he said. *"Right now!"*

"Oh, my," she said as I looked back before we walked out. Her face was pale and frightened as she hurried around grabbing up as many cows as she could hold.

"Abby!" Candice said, and I whipped my head back around. "Let's go!"

We bolted out the door and Candice already had the engine turned over and was gunning the gas before I had a chance to strap on the seat belt. "What was that all about?" Cat asked from the backseat.

"From what I could tell it looked like a federal hacker got into Jabba's system," Candice explained. "They'll trace it back to his house within a half hour if they're any good."

"Jesus!" I said as I stared in the passenger side mirror. "I'm starting to feel like no matter where we go or who we talk to, we're barely one step ahead of the Feds."

"At least we've been ahead," Candice said. "But you're right, this Robillard guy is relentless."

"What do we do now?" Cat said.

"We go someplace where a guy like Robillard would never think to look for us. We need to hide in plain sight and sort through this intel, then come up with a game plan." Candice said.

"Where's that?"

"You'll see," she said with a smirk. "I promise, it won't be boring."

"You weren't kidding," I said as we pulled up to one of the most unique-looking buildings I'd ever seen. Reflective glass, black-and-white piano keys, a pink neon piano, and white wavy walls with painted sheet music formed the entrance to the Liberace Museum.

"I've always wanted to come here," Cat said over my

shoulder. "Sort of an indulgence into tacky, wouldn't you say?"

"I met Liberace when I was little," Candice confessed as she pulled into a parking slot.

"You did?" Cat and I said in unison.

Candice smiled, her eyes taking on a distant cast. "My dad played in his orchestra," she said. "My sister and I used to hang around backstage. One night before his show, he took us to his dressing room and let us try on his jewelry and his capes. I'll always have a soft spot for him."

"You are hands down the most interesting person I know," I said.

Candice's smile widened. "Then you need to get out more."

We paid the admission of twelve dollars and fifty cents per adult and entered the foyer of the museum. Paintings and photographs of the pianist were everywhere. "Come on," Candice said. "We can go to the cafeteria and get something to drink while we look this stuff over."

We followed behind her as we wove through the tourists and exhibits, but Cat kept getting distracted. "Would you look at that?" she said, stopping in front of an elaborate and downright gorgeous fuchsia, pink, and peach turkey-feather cape.

"We're not here to sightsee," I reminded her.

After getting a round of Cokes, we sat down at an empty table and Candice pulled out a thick stack of paper from the envelope Jabba had given us. "He's thorough," I commented.

"Apparently," Candice said as she flipped through the pages. "Let's break this down into three piles," she said. "Abby, do you still have that notebook?"

I dug around in my backpack and came up with the pad of paper, which I handed to her. She began to flip the pages back to get to a blank page when she stopped on my drawing of the oak tree. "What's this?" she said.

I looked at the pad and shrugged my shoulders. "I have no idea. When I was trying to have my crew direct me to where Dutch was, I kept getting that tree, but it morphed into this one," I said, turning the page to the palm tree.

"And what's this?" Candice asked.

I could feel myself growing anxious as I saw her point to the rough gravestone at the base of the tree. "A gravestone," I said quietly.

"Whose?"

I looked her in the eyes. "Dutch's."

"Oh, Abby," Cat said, and she squeezed my arm. "Did they tell you he'd been killed?"

I could feel the tears welling in my eyes. The image on that page was so disturbing that I refused to look at it again. "Not exactly," I said. "But I have this terrible feeling that if we don't find him soon, he'll die."

"Then let's get to it," Candice said, and pulled off three sheets of paper while I passed out pens. "Take notes on anything you might think is important so that we can summarize for the whole group when we've gone through the material."

An hour later we were ready to each give a summary of the material we'd skimmed through. Cat went first. "I had Ricardo Delgado and his family," she began as she squinted at the notes she'd jotted on her paper. "I'll start with the kids; Bethany Delgado is the youngest at twenty-two. She's been in rehab twice, both times for prescription-pill addiction, and has been jailed once at the tender age of eighteen for possession. In the past two years it looks like she's gotten her act together. She's currently attending the Las Vegas beauty school and her graduation date is set for this spring.

"Moving on to Ricky Delgado," Cat continued, the

corners of her lips pulling down in a frown. "This kid's a major troublemaker. He's got a line of arrests from assault on an ex-girlfriend to possession of narcotics with intent to deliver, to three DUIs."

"Model son," I mumbled. Candice smirked and Cat nodded.

"Now, the wife is an interesting woman. In the eighties she was a backup singer for Bette Midler and had mild success with a CD she released in Japan. She and Ricardo were married in nineteen eighty-two and they've been legally separated three times."

"Some couples never learn," I said.

"Well, it looks like this time around Paloma Delgado might have. She filed for divorce a week ago. Ricardo's attorneys have yet to respond."

"What about Ricardo?" Candice asked.

Cat's eyebrows danced. "He's the juicy part of the report," Cat said, turning her paper over to get to the notes on the back. "Ricardo Delgado was born in Spain, and given a special political-asylum visa that has been renewed every six years since nineteen eighty."

"Huh?" I said. "Why hasn't he just applied for citizenship through his wife or his kids?"

"Oh, he's applied," said Cat. "And he's been denied every single year, again, since nineteen eighty." I opened my mouth to ask another question, but Cat held up her hand. "Hold on," Cat said, "I'm getting there. It seems that when Ricardo was in Spain, he had close ties with a certain member of the Spanish Mafia. Delgado became an informant to the CIA, and it was the CIA who offered to help him get asylum when a contract was put on his life because of some missing mob money. It appears the CIA has been willing to offer him sanctuary in this country for his cooperation, but they're unwilling to allow him citizenship."

I gasped. "Delgado was an informant to the CIA?!"

"He was," Cat said. "And guess who his handler was?"

"Raymond Robillard," I said putting two and two together.

"Wrong," said Cat smugly. "It was Donovan Kelton."

Candice looked through her notes. "You spoiled my surprise," she said. "I had the summary on Kelton."

I blinked several times, trying to piece the jigsaw together. "So Delgado's business partner was also CIA?"

"Ex-CIA," said Candice. "He resigned abruptly from the agency in nineteen seventy-seven, when he failed a lie detector test regarding what he knew about Delgado, and the CIA began monitoring his personal bank accounts. It appears that the CIA was suspicious about the amount of money Delgado stole before he was granted asylum in the U.S. The implied sense in these reports is that Delgado may have revealed the real sum to Kelton at some point, who may have hidden that figure from his superiors. Oh, and it gets even better," she said, her eyes twinkling with the bit of juicy news she had to tell us. "Kelton has made a freaking fortune being Delgado's business partner. He's got gobs of money and his real estate holdings are quite substantial."

My radar hummed again. "So, how does Robillard figure into this, then?" I asked. "I mean, there has to be a connection between Robillard and Delgado."

"I've got Robillard," said Candice, pulling out her notes. "But on paper there's no direct link that I can find between him and Delgado or Kelton, or even Frost for that matter."

"So tell us what you have," I said.

"Raymond Robillard began working for the CIA in nineteen seventy-five. He was deployed to Brussels for three years before coming back to the States in nineteen—"

"Whoa!" Cat said, interrupting Candice as she dug through her notes. "Did you say Brussels? As in Belgium?"

"Yes," Candice said.

"Delgado lived there for a year, nineteen seventy-six to nineteen seventy-seven, right before his asylum was granted and he came here. In fact, that's where Kelton was based out of for the first two years he worked with Delgado."

"That's it," I said. "That's the connection. They had to have met in Brussels right before Kelton got in hot water."

"So, what?" Candice said. "Delgado and Robillard meet, and hatch some plan to hide the mob money that we're assuming Delgado stole? Then Frost finds out about it later?"

"It works," I said. "At least, geographically. And Kelton could have been in on it too, which would explain why he and Delgado have been tight all these years. They'd each have something to lose if the other talked."

"It's a little sketchy for me," Candice said.

I sat back in my chair and looked at them as a memory came back to me. I remembered sitting with Dutch right after I'd worked with a sketch artist to draw the profile of the man who'd killed Cynthia Frost and I'd told him that there were was a link to Vegas and to Thailand. "There's a connection between all three," I said firmly. Delgado, Kelton, and Robillard. I can just *feel* it!"

"If there is," said Candice, "then it would explain what Robillard is really doing out here and why he's so intent on destroying Dutch's reputation. He'd have to know that Dutch suspected a link between Kelton, Delgado, and Robillard, and that Dutch was investigating him using his security company as a cover."

"You said Kelton and Delgado were in business together?" I asked Candice.

"Real estate development," she confirmed. "Both Delgado and Kelton have funded buildings all over Vegas."

"Delgado owns property everywhere," Cat said, going back to her notes. "He's got property in Nevada, Texas, New York, and Arkansas."

"Arkansas?" I said. "That's an odd place to invest in. What's he developing, pig farms?"

"Diamonds," Cat said.

I blinked. "There are diamonds in Arkansas?"

"According to this there are. Delgado owns a diamond mine in Murfreesboro, Arkansas."

For some reason my radar hummed extra loud at that and my head filled with the oak-tree image again, which morphed into a palm tree.

"What?" Candice said as I sat and stared off into space.

"I don't know," I said. "But there's something about that diamond mine. Does Kelton have an interest in it?"

Candice shook her head. "His partnership with Delgado seems local."

I rubbed my forehead and closed my eyes, frustrated at all the questions and my seemingly wacky radar. "Paloma Delgado said that Ricardo was sleeping with Kelton's wife," I said, trying a different angle. "Maybe Kelton found out, staged the kidnapping, and murdered Delgado?"

"Could explain why Robillard is trying to throw the scent in the direction of Dutch," Candice said. "To keep his old CIA buddy out of the ring of suspicion."

I sighed heavily. That conclusion just didn't feel right. "So we're no closer to figuring out who kidnapped Delgado and why, or where they're being held or where Dutch is."

"What did your notes say?" Cat asked gently.

I picked up my paper. "I had Rivers Security," I said, looking down at my notes. I'd discovered a lot about my boyfriend and his business dealings; some of it surprised the hell out of me. "Rivers Security was established in nineteen ninety-two in Ann Arbor, Michigan, with a small office and one employee. . . ."

"Dutch," Cat said.

I nodded. "Yep. It looks like he ran security detail for some of Motown's celebrities like Aretha Franklin and Bob Seger as well as bigwigs like Lee Iacocca and the Ford family. Those connections led him to open up a branch in Southern California with five employees and they run security for the likes of Leo DiCaprio, Keanu Reeves, and Goldie Hawn."

Candice whistled. "Dutch has connections."

"Apparently," I said.

"He never told you about this stuff?" Cat asked me.

"Nope," I said. "He's kept his security business on the down-low, but then, that's Dutch. He's been trained to keep his mouth shut, which is why he made a great detective and a good agent."

"What else?" Candice said.

"The Vegas branch isn't the newest division of Rivers Security," I said with a frown. "It looks like Dutch has just secured a license to open up a division in Dubai."

"The new Vegas," said Cat. "A playground for the world's most wealthy. My company is also looking at a few marketing plans for some retailers there. It's amazing how much money a tiny little country in the center of the Middle East can attract."

"Yeah, well, I had no idea about any of this," I said, whipping my notes on the tabletop.

"Do you think that Dutch was purposely keeping it from you?" Candice asked.

I blew out a sigh. "No," I admitted. "I think that like everyone else, with Dutch, I'm on a need-to-know basis."

Candice and Cat exchanged a look. "The bright side is that Dutch is rich!" Cat said suddenly, breaking the heavy mood. "You should marry him immediately."

That got a laugh out of all three of us, until I said, "First, I've got to find him, Cat. Then I'll worry about our relationship."

"What I don't get," Candice said thoughtfully, "is why, if Dutch was making such good coin in the security business, would he continue to work a day job making, what, forty grand at best?"

"Forty-five," I said. "And the truth is that Dutch actually likes his job. I think that the security business was just that—his security. He could count on the extra income when it came time to retire and it allowed him to live comfortably. He isn't flashy about his money, and he could subcontract out the detail to guards in L.A. and here without a lot of headache or time spent. I think at most he devoted fifteen hours a week to the security business. And Milo was a partner too, so between them they ran it really well."

The three of us fell silent as we thought about all that we'd learned. It was Cat who finally broke the moody silence. "Now what?" she asked us.

I turned my hands up in an "I have no idea" motion, but Candice had an idea. "Here's what I'm thinking," she said. "What we need is to get back to basics. We know we can't go near certain people, like Mrs. Delgado and Ricky, but we might be able to get close to one of the other suspects—at least indirectly."

"Kelton?" I said, taking a wild guess.

"Yes, but not the mister. I want to talk to the missus, and dig around in her relationship with Delgado a little."

"You want to interview Mrs. Kelton?" Cat said, her expression letting Candice know exactly how dumb she thought the idea was. "Don't you think that might be a little like walking into the lion's den?"

"Not really," Candice said. "If we're right about there being some sort of a relationship between Kelton and Robillard via Delgado, then Robillard will be working double time to keep the focus off Kelton and on Dutch and Chase. My guess is that's the one place we won't find a single FBI agent."

"Pretty big risk," I said.

Candice flashed a confident grin. "It beats sitting here and doing nothing," she said reasonably.

I nodded. "Okay, I'm in."

Cat looked at us both as if we'd grown three heads. "You two are crazy," she said. "It's way too risky!"

"It's the only way we're going to prove our theory about the link between Delgado and Kelton," said Candice. "And if you don't want to commit, you don't have to. We need to keep the car out of sight anyway. While Abby and I talk to the missus, you can drive around the block and keep out of sight."

"And just how do you know that Mrs. Kelton will even talk to you?" Cat said, still working to talk us out of the crazy plan. "I mean, how do you know she won't just call the police or Robillard the moment you introduce yourselves?"

"Leave it to me," Candice said as she started to gather the papers on the table back into one pile.

"A time to worry," Cat muttered.

My right side felt light and airy, my sign for *No kidding*.

Chapter Twelve

On the way to the Kelton residence, Candice stopped at a small shop just off the Strip called Foxy's Spy Shop. "What are we getting in here?" I asked as we walked through the door.

"Badges," she said quietly. "But let me do the talking, okay?"

"Sure," I said.

Cat was back in the car fiddling with the radio and keeping cool with strict instructions to call my cell phone if any black sedans with tinted windows came within fifty feet of the shop.

"As I live and breathe," said a beautiful black woman with short-cropped hair, big brown eyes, and red glossy lips when we entered. "Candy Fusco, is that you?"

"Hey, Foxy," Candice said with a wave.

"Get your butt over here, girl, and give me some sugar!" demanded Foxy as she came out from behind the counter where she'd been sitting.

Candice walked to Foxy and got hugged hard enough to crack a rib. "What's it been? Ten years?"

"Eleven," said Candice.

"You still with that son of a bitch Lenny?"

"Nah, I dumped his ass years ago."

"So you're single now?" said Foxy, and I noticed a spark of interest in her eyes.

"Not exactly," said Candice delicately. "And I'm still attracted to men, I'm afraid."

Foxy looked disappointed and she wiped a hair out of Candice's eye. "One night with me, baby, and I could make you forget about men for good."

"Foxy," Candice said seriously, "if I leaned that way, I swear, you'd be the one for me."

Foxy puffed her chest up at the compliment and seemed satisfied. "And who's this vision?" she said, turning to me.

"That's my business partner, Abby Cooper. Abby, meet Foxy."

"Lovely to make your acquaintance," I said formally as I extended my hand.

"The pleasure is all mine," said Foxy, eyeing me up and down. "Mmmmhmm!" she said. "You bitches are gorgeous, you know that?"

I could feel myself blushing. "Er . . . thank you," I said.

"And I bet she's straight too?" she said to Candice.

" 'Fraid so," said Candice.

"She into a little experimentation?" she asked coyly.

Candice laughed. "Oh, I doubt it, Foxy, but glad to see you're still on the prowl."

"Foxy's always on the prowl," she said in a voice that ended with a purr. "So what can Foxy do for you today if not to offer you the delight of her body?"

I hid a snicker and gazed around the shop at all the spy equipment lining the shelves. "We need to do a little detective work," said Candice. "Of the *official* variety, if you get my drift."

"Local or federal?" Foxy asked, picking right up on the hint.

"Federal."

"That's gotten expensive, Candy," Foxy said pensively. "The fines for impersonating someone of that nature are pretty stiff these days."

"We're aware," Candice said casually. "And we've got the coin, so tell us how much."

"One for each?" she said, pointing to both of us.

"Please."

"Come on back." She waved and moved off toward a curtained area. "We'll have you set up in about twenty minutes."

Closer to an hour later we were back in the car. "*What* took you so long?" Cat said. "I was beginning to worry."

"Foxy likes to flirt," I said, feeling another blush hit my cheeks.

"Yeah, but her work is good," Candice said, flashing Cat her new badge.

" 'FBI, Agent Katrina Barlow,' " Cat read aloud.

"Look at mine!" I said excitedly, and I fished out my own badge from my backpack. "Agent Melanie Milton. Oooo, I like the double Ms."

Candice pulled out from the parking space and moseyed into traffic. Noting the time, which read three fifteen, she said, "We'll have to hurry. We still need to hit the mall before we can knock on Kelton's door."

"Why are we going to the mall?" I asked.

"You ever seen two FBI agents on duty in jeans and wrinkled shirts?"

"Good point."

"I love the mall!" Cat said. "I get to pick out your outfits!"

I groaned. "Cat, we can't be trying on clothes all day. We'll need to grab the first blazer-and-slack combo that fits and move on."

Cat clapped her hands happily. "I am the *queen* of power shopping. Trust me, I can have you in and out of there in ten minutes."

I was doubtful, but true to her word, Cat did have us out the door in nine minutes flat. "That was amazing," I said as I looked down at my new gray tweed blazer and matching pants.

"Told you so," Cat said happily from the backseat as she dug through a bag of clothes she'd nabbed for us while Candice and I had quickly changed into our suits. Once she'd had our sizes, she went on a shopping spree that resembled something out of a cartoon featuring the Tasmanian devil. "I got you each two extra changes of clothes. Oh, and nightshirts for everybody. There's no way I want to sleep in these things again."

Candice concentrated on traffic and I noticed that she kept glancing at the clock on the dashboard. "Why are we so pressed?" I asked.

"I want to get to Kelton's before the end of the work-day," she explained. "My guess is that the missus is more likely to be home alone between three and five than any other time."

"How are we going to make sure that mister won't be home?" I said.

Candice glanced my way. "We're going to have to wing it, unless that radar of yours can give us a heads-up."

"Worth a shot," I said. "I'll try and tune in as we get close."

Candice drove past the Keltons' residence and we all craned our necks trying to get a look through the gate to see how many cars—if any—were parked in the drive-way. "Lexus SUV in the front," I said. "No sign of any other vehicle."

"What's your gut say?" Candice asked me.

I focused. "It says we're good to go, but we'll need to hustle."

Candice pulled over at the end of the block and Cat got into the driver's seat. "Head over a couple of blocks," Candice told her, "and don't come back this way until I call you."

"What if you don't call me?" Cat asked, her eyes showing her worry.

"Then get the hell out of Dodge, Cat," Candice said simply. "Drive this puppy straight back to Massachusetts."

Cat gulped and pulled away, while Candice and I walked toward the Keltons' residence. "So, I'm assuming you're gonna want to do all the talking again," I said, clipping my fake FBI badge to my waist band like Candice.

"Yep," she said. "You just nod a lot and keep that radar on."

"Got it."

We stopped at the gate and noticed it wasn't latched. Candice pushed it open and we went through, all casual-like. "Let's hope this works," Candice whispered as we walked up the steps and rang the doorbell.

"Coming!" we heard someone call from the interior. Then the clicking of high heels on a wood floor approached the door and stopped. There was a pregnant pause as I imagined Mrs. Kelton peeking at us through the spy hole; then the door was opened and a beautiful, tall woman looking to be in her late thirties or early forties with gray eyes and an impossibly perfect face asked, "Yes?"

"Mrs. Kelton?" Candice asked.

"Yes, that's me," she said, and I noticed her eyes darted to the shiny badge at Candice's waist.

"FBI agents Barlow and Milton," Candice said as she pulled her badge from her waist and held it up for Mrs. Kelton to inspect. Mrs. Kelton took a quick glance and stepped back into the foyer. "Yes, Agent Robillard called just a little while ago and said he'd be stopping by after six, but I expected him in person."

Candice looked at me before frowning at Mrs. Kelton.

"I'm sorry, ma'am, but Agent Robillard had to chase down a new lead. He asked us if we'd like to interview you, but he never mentioned a time. If this is bad, we can come back later."

"No, no," Mrs. Kelton said. "You're already here. Come on in."

"Thank you, ma'am, we appreciate it," Candice said, and stepped into the front hallway.

Mrs. Kelton shut the door after I entered, and waved us into the interior. We had to step over some luggage in the front hallway as we followed after Mrs. Kelton. Over her shoulder she said, "I just got back from visiting my sister in Reno and was getting ready to pour a glass of wine. I don't suppose you ladies would care for one?"

"We aren't allowed to drink on duty, ma'am," Candice said as she breezed through the hallway after Mrs. Kelton. I really had to hand it to my partner—she projected confidence in both her voice and her walk.

We entered a Spanish-style kitchen with green distressed cabinets, bright yellow tiled countertops, and terra-cotta floors. "Please have a seat," she said, pointing to the two barstools at the island.

Candice and I took a seat and waited to speak until Mrs. Kelton pulled the cork from the bottle of white wine and poured it into a glass. "I'm assuming you spoke with Agent Robillard at length?" Candice said as she pulled out her notepad.

"No," said Mrs. Kelton. "He was actually quite brief. He asked to speak to my husband and I gave him Donovan's cell number, but with the time difference, it's going to be a few more hours before he turns his phone on."

"Time difference?" Candice asked.

"Yes," Mrs. Kelton said, coming over to the other side of the island to sip her wine. "Donovan's in Thailand."

Candice and I nodded as if we'd just remembered hearing that. "And how long exactly has your husband been out of town?"

"About two weeks," she said. "He left on the eighth and won't be back until the fifth of November."

"I see," said Candice, jotting that down. "And what is he attending to in Thailand?"

Mrs. Kelton blushed slightly and tried to cover it by taking a long sip of her wine. "Business," she said, stroking her neck with her other hand. "He has several businesses over there."

"What kind of business?" Candice asked.

Again, Mrs. Kelton blushed. She ran a hand through her frosted-blond hair and said, "To be honest, Agent Barlow, I'm not sure. My husband and I don't often discuss his business dealings."

My lie detector went haywire. "How long have you two been married again?" Candice asked, flipping through her notepad as if she already had that answer somewhere.

"Twelve years," she said.

"Does he travel often to Thailand?" Candice probed.

"Yes," she said. "At least once a month."

"And his business partner, Ricardo Delgado. Does he travel with your husband on occasion?"

At the mention of Delgado's name, Mrs. Kelton turned away from us and moved to the sink, where she rearranged the two plates that were placed there. "No," she said. "My husband and Mr. Delgado dissolved their business relationship a few weeks ago. But even before that, they were only partners on a few of their development projects."

"I see," Candice said. "And how well do you know Mr. Delgado?" Candice said.

"We're acquaintances," she said brusquely. "Excuse me, Agent Barlow, but what exactly is going on here? I mean, Agent Robillard was very light on the details. Can you please tell me what this is about?"

Candice looked right into Mrs. Kelton's eyes. "Mr.

Delgado has been kidnapped, ma'am, and we have reason to suspect he may have been murdered.''

Mrs. Kelton's face drained of color and her knees seemed to give out a little as she reached for the countertop behind her. "Oh, God," she said. "Oh, no!"

Candice waited and watched Mrs. Kelton as tears began to stream down her cheeks and she looked anywhere but at us. It was a long minute before Candice spoke again. "You seem incredibly upset for a woman who was only the acquaintance of Mr. Delgado."

"Of course I'm upset!" she snapped. Then she seemed to catch herself, adding, "Donovan will be devastated."

"But you just said that they had ended their business relationship," Candice probed. "Why would he care if they're no longer partners?"

Mrs. Kelton looked at Candice sharply. "She told you, didn't she?" she said, her lower lip quivering.

"Yes," I said, and gave Candice a look that said I could take over for a minute. "Mrs. Delgado intimated that you and Mr. Delgado had been quite close. She suspected that's why her husband might have been kidnapped. Perhaps your husband's trip out of the country provided him with a nice alibi and he made arrangements of some kind to have Mr. Delgado taken care of?"

Mrs. Kelton shook her head vigorously. "Donovan can be a son of a bitch," she confessed. "But he wouldn't have cared about Ricardo and me."

Candice gave her a curious look. "Why is that exactly?"

Mrs. Kelton dabbed at her eyes. "Because Donovan doesn't find me attractive," she said bluntly. "I'm not his type."

My jaw dropped. This woman could have held her own in any beauty pageant. How could a man not find her attractive? "I find that hard to believe," I said, only then realizing my lie detector hadn't gone off when she'd made the suggestion.

"Oh, trust me," she said with a laugh that held no mirth, "Donovan isn't into me. In fact, he's not really into women. He's more of a young man's man, and by that, I mean very young."

A sick coil of alarm settled into my stomach. "How young exactly?" Candice asked pointedly.

"Let's just say it would only be legal in Thailand," Mrs. Kelton said. "I'm decoration," she added. "I'm here to keep up appearances."

"Why would you stay with someone like that?" I asked, amazed that anyone would tolerate something so horrible in a partner.

Mrs. Kelton's face reddened and she gave me a hard look. "I have a high school education, Agent Milton. My husband proposed to me when I was eighteen and fresh off the beauty pageant tour. I was just a naive teenager back then, and I'd never had a real job in my life. Look around you—do you think I'd be able to *get* a job that would afford me to live like this with that for a background?"

"My apologies, ma'am," I said, ducking my chin. "I meant no disrespect."

Candice tapped her pen against her lip thoughtfully. "When was the last time you saw Mr. Delgado, Mrs. Kelton?"

"Last week," she said sadly, and the tears seemed to return. "He had to go out of town for a few days, but he was going to call when he got back in."

"Do you remember where he was going, specifically?"

"No," she said. "But he was always flying somewhere in that plane of his. He had a hard time staying still."

Again my radar hummed in my head. "Mrs. Kelton," I said delicately. "We have interviewed another woman who claims that she was Mr. Delgado's girlfriend. Did you know about her?"

Mrs. Kelton laughed, but there was little mirth in the

sound. "You mean Bambina?" she scoffed, then shook her head. "Ricardo liked to have a cover too, I suppose. Bambina was nothing to him except an ego boost. He liked to show her off on the golf course, but their relationship certainly wasn't serious."

"And yours was?" Candice asked.

Mrs. Kelton's face reddened again and she stroked her cheek. "I'd like to think so," she said quietly. "Besides, the last I heard, Ricky Junior had taken an interest in Bambina."

"Who told you that?" I said.

"Ricardo," she said. "Who else?"

"He knew his girlfriend was cheating on him with his son?" Candice said. "Didn't that upset him?"

Mrs. Kelton shook her head. "Obviously not," she said. "I think he even felt relieved."

"So why was Mrs. Delgado so furious about your affair with her husband, and not so upset with his affair with Bambina?" Candice said.

"Probably because Ricardo always came back to her after he got through playing with the bimbos. But I'm different," she said. "He was willing to leave her for good for me."

"He told you that?" I said.

"Yes, just last week, in fact. And I believed him, especially when I heard that his wife was filing for divorce. Ricardo said that he was going out of town to tie up some loose ends, and when he got back, he was going to have his attorney move forward with the divorce."

"When was the last time you talked to Mr. Delgado?" I asked.

"It would have been last Wednesday," she said. "Whatever date that was."

Candice and I shared a look. Delgado had been kidnapped either late Friday or early Saturday morning. "And you hadn't heard from him since last Wednesday?" Candice asked.

"No," Mrs. Kelton said. "Not a word."

Candice got up from her seat and I got up too. "Thank you for your time, Mrs. Kelton. We appreciate it, especially Agent Robillard."

"Why especially Agent Robillard?" she said as we walked out of the kitchen toward the front door.

"Because of his friendship with your husband, of course," Candice said casually. "Agent Robillard says they go way back to their days in the CIA."

Mrs. Kelton looked surprised. "Agent Robillard is ex-CIA?" she said.

"You didn't know?" I asked, watching her intently over my shoulder.

"No," she said, and my lie detector said she was telling the truth. "But then, Donovan doesn't talk much about those days. He says that some memories are better left in the past."

We arrived at the front door and Mrs. Kelton opened it for us. Before we took our leave, Candice said, "Again, we appreciate your honesty and cooperation, ma'am. Oh, and one more thing: We're obviously holding back the details of this case to the press, and we've been getting a few reports of eager journalists trying to impersonate FBI agents to get information. That's actually the lead that Agent Robillard is tracking right now. It seems that someone is even going as far as trying to impersonate him. If anyone comes to your door pretending to be the FBI, or Agent Robillard, do not answer the door unless they give you the password."

"Password?"

"Yes, Agent Robillard said that anyone coming to your door should say the name *Cynthia Frost*. If they fail to say the password, then they're an impostor. If that happens, simply call the police and tell them that someone impersonating the FBI is trespassing. They'll know what to do."

"Oh, my," said Mrs. Kelton. "Do you really think they'll come here?"

"I'm afraid we suspect a leak in our office, ma'am. Someone's got ahold of our list of interviewees and has been making the rounds. So far, they've been one step ahead, but with your help, we finally might be able to catch the bastard."

"I'll do what I can," Mrs. Kelton said. "And one more thing, Agent Barlow. Do you really think Ricardo is dead?"

Candice looked at me and I gave a small nod. "Unfortunately, ma'am, we have some solid evidence that may in fact be the case."

Mrs. Kelton's eyes watered again. "Oh, Ricardo," she whispered.

I reached up and put my hand on her arm. "We're very sorry, Mrs. Kelton."

She nodded and we left the house.

"That was interesting," said Candice as she and I walked out of the gate and down the street where we could already see Cat parked at the bottom of a hill. "I thought I told her to hide out a couple of blocks over," Candice said when she saw the blue Mini.

"And when have you known Cat to listen to details?" I asked. "Should we call her?"

"Nah, let's walk and talk this out."

"Good," I said. "We now know that Kelton didn't appear to have motive for kidnapping Delgado, and the fact that he's out of the country makes it seem like he isn't even aware that Delgado's been abducted."

"What does your radar say about that theory?"

I swirled the idea in my head and came back with an affirmative. "Kelton didn't kidnap Delgado," I said. "Someone else did."

"And how interesting that Delgado was really going

to leave his wife. I wonder what loose end he had to fly out of town for."

My radar hummed. "I don't know, but we keep hearing about this supposed trip out of town, and yet we know he was at the strip club on Friday. Maybe we need to look into his flight plan and see where the hell he went?"

"Good idea," Candice said. "And as it happens, I know a guy who can give us that info."

"Of course you do," I laughed.

"What?" Candice said. "So I know some people. Is that a crime?"

"With the types of people you claim to know? Oh, I think it may be, yes."

Candice rolled her eyes. "Whatever. But, speaking of knowing people, what about Robillard and Kelton?" Candice said. "Do you really think they knew each other?"

"My gut says yes, but it's proving it that's going to be difficult." And then an idea hit me and I grabbed Candice's arm and stopped her. "There is one person who might know," I said.

"Who?"

"I don't know his name," I admitted.

"That's helpful," she said.

I shook my head. "No, I mean I don't know his name *yet*, but I may know how to find out."

"Who are you talking about?" she said, growing impatient.

"Raymond Robillard is the ASAC, or the assistant special agent in charge," I explained. "And the guy above him, the SAC, used to be Robillard's boss at the CIA before bringing the both of them over to the FBI."

"Is this the guy that told Dutch to investigate Robillard quietly?"

"Yes!" I said. "We've got to get in touch with him."

"So let me ask you," she said, "if the SAC has known

all along that Dutch was digging into Robillard's past, why the hell did he send Robillard to investigate what happened to Dutch?"

That stumped me. "I'm not sure," I admitted. "But I'm sure there's a logical explanation."

Candice looked at me skeptically as we reached the car. "How'd it go?" Cat asked, getting out of the car so Candice could drive.

"It went," Candice said tiredly. "How about we find a safe place for the night and get some takeout?"

"Works for me," I said. "Besides, I've got some calls to make."

Candice wasn't taking any chances at being spotted close to the city, so we ended up renting a cabin near Lake Mead about thirty miles southeast of Las Vegas. "How do you know about this place?" Cat asked as we pulled up to a stop in front of our cabin, which was one of twelve spread out over about a half mile of land with a distant view of the lake.

"Came here on my honeymoon," she said.

Cat and I both looked skeptically at the cabin. "I see Lenny spared no expense," Cat said.

"You saw his trailer," Candice said as she got out of the car and stretched. "He never was the big spender he thought he was unless it came to placing a bet."

"At least the pizza smells good," I said as I got out holding the box that had kept my lap warm for the last ten miles.

"Some of the best in town," Candice assured me. "You won't be disappointed."

We entered the cabin, which admittedly was far nicer on the inside than I'd expected, comprising a small sitting area, a galley kitchen, two separate bedrooms, and a pullout sleeper sofa, which I offered to take. We ate our pizza at the kitchen table and told Cat what had happened at Mrs. Kelton's. "That's horrible!" she exclaimed when we told her about Donovan's sexual preferences.

"Yep," I said. "He's a sick bastard. Seems like he and Robillard ought to know each other if they're members of the sick-bastard club."

"How were you going to find out the name of this SAC again?" Candice asked me.

Cat looked confused, so I filled her in on my plan to contact Robillard's boss. "I just need to get into my e-mail," I said. "I remember a couple of months ago Dutch sent me some directions to a restaurant I was going to meet him at, and he mentioned that he might be late because he was meeting with so-and-so, the SAC."

"You have no memory for names," Cat said with a *tsk*. "Me? I remember my kindergarten teacher and all of my classmates."

That made me laugh. "It's true, I barely remember kindergarten."

We finished dinner and Candice loaned me her laptop. I hopped online and logged into my e-mail, sorting through my folders until I found one that I thought could be the one I was looking for. I gasped when I opened it.

"What?" Cat said, peering over my shoulder. "Oh, look, that's a cute picture of the two of you."

My eyes watered. The file I'd opened had been sent from Dutch. He'd taken me for a long ride on his motorcycle out to the beach along Lake St. Clair and we'd watched the sun set together. The photo was taken from the digital camera his mother had sent him on his birthday and it showed the two of us smiling in the lens while Dutch held it at arm's length. "He's alive," I said, and sucked in a sob. "Oh, thank God!"

Candice came over to also peer over my shoulder. "We'll find him, Abs," she reassured me. "I promise."

I nodded and clicked the file closed. After watching Delgado fade away, I felt a bit scared to linger over photographs. A few minutes later I found the e-mail I'd been looking for. "Special Agent in Charge Bill Gaston," I said. "All we need to do is call the FBI and ask to speak to him."

Candice looked at her watch. "It's nine p.m. Eastern time," she said. "Maybe it'd be better to wait until tomorrow morning, first thing?"

I jotted down the name on a piece of paper. "Good idea," I said, then reopened the file with Dutch's photo for one more quick peek.

"Save that to the desktop," Candice advised.

"Why?" I said, glancing at her over my shoulder.

"Because I think you'll need to reassure yourself from time to time, Abs," she said gently.

"You're a good friend, Candice."

"Back atcha, girlfriend."

Before we all turned in, Candice made a call to her "guy" about Delgado's flight plan. It was a short conversation and she filled us in after she hung up with him. "Delgado didn't go anywhere," she said.

"What?" I said. "But Mrs. Kelton said he'd gone somewhere to tie up some loose ends."

Candice shook her head. "No flight plan was filed," she reported. "My buddy said the last time Delgado's plane put in a flight plan was three weeks ago. He flew to New York and back."

"That would explain why everyone was surprised when it turned out Delgado and Chase were in town the night he was kidnapped," Cat said. "Didn't you tell me that Laney thought Chase was going out of town?"

"Yes," I said, scratching my head as my radar said it didn't jibe with the report from Candice's source.

"They could have driven somewhere," Candice offered. "Maybe they drove out of town?"

"What for?" I asked.

"Maybe they drove to L.A.?"

I shook my head. "Something doesn't fit here, ladies," I said.

"What?" Cat asked.

"I wish I knew."

We talked for a while after that and came up with possible theories for Delgado's whereabouts leading up to his kidnapping. I didn't know where he and Chase had gone, but I was certain that wherever their trip had taken them was integral to why they'd been abducted.

That night I slept fitfully. My mind felt full of information, like a million tiny pieces of a giant jigsaw puzzle that needed to be sorted through to find out how everything interlaced and connected. At the end of that puzzle was my boyfriend, but I kept feeling like I was missing something obvious. Like I had the answer, but I just didn't know which pieces held the answer and how it could connect me to Dutch.

At some point I must have fallen asleep, because the next thing I knew, I was staring at a huge oak tree. The branches of the tree were thick with green fluffy leaves and on each leaf was written a name in black ink. I went to the tree and pulled one of the lower branches toward me. Just then, my deceased grandmother stepped out from behind the tree. "Hello, Abby-gabby," she said.

"Grams!" I shouted, and flew into her arms. "Ohmigod! I'm so glad to see you!"

"I'll bet," she said with a knowing look in her eye. "I see you've found your way to the tree."

"Yeah," I said, holding the branch up for her to see. "What's with all the names on the leaves?"

"That's what we've been trying to show you, dear," she said, and turned one of the leaves toward me. The name read *Dutch Rivers*.

"I don't get it," I said.

Grams pulled another branch toward me. She turned up the bottom leaf on that branch and I read *Hanna Rivers*.

"Oh!" I said as her meaning dawned on me. "This is Dutch's family tree!"

"Yes," she said. "And at the roots of this tree you'll find Dutch."

"Huh?" I said.

"Step back, and I'll show you," she instructed. I did and the mighty oak morphed into a giant palm tree with large coconuts. "You might want to step a little farther back," she said.

When I did, one of the coconuts dropped to the ground and burrowed under the grass. Immediately a stone popped through the surface and began to grow. When it was about two and a half feet tall, it flattened out and turned partially oval. My heart began to beat rapidly. I'd seen this scene before. "Don't," I said, wanting to turn away, but my eyes were fixed on the tombstone in front of me. Writing began to appear on the stone. HERE LIES DUTCH RIVERS AT PEACE WITH OUR LADY Of SAINTS. . . .

"Stop!" I shouted, and looked to my grandmother for help, but she had vanished. In her place was Dutch the way I'd never seen him before. He looked thin, incredibly pale, and nearly translucent—like a ghost.

"Abby!" he said, holding his side. "You've got to help me!"

I rushed to him, but he disappeared like vapor on the wind. I stood in his place and felt chilled to the bone, his voice echoing in my head. "Follow the coconuts . . . ," he said. "You'll find me there, but you'll have to hurry!"

"Dutch!" I yelled. "Dutch, come back! Please! Tell me where you are! Dutch! *Dutch*!"

"Abby!" my sister said into my ear, and my eyes snapped open. "Abby, are you all right?"

It took me a full minute to comprehend that I'd been having a very vivid dream, and to come to terms with where I was and why Cat was shaking me. "Are you okay, Abs?" Candice asked when I continued to look blankly at the two of them.

"Yeah," I said, pulling my knees up to my chest. "Just a really intense dream."

"Want to talk about it?" Cat said.

I ran my hand through my hair. It was damp with sweat. "It's the same one I've been having, and it still doesn't make sense." I proceeded to fill them in on the details.

"I miss Grams," Cat said with a sigh.

"Me too," I said. Our maternal grandmother had always been more of a mother figure to us than our own mother.

"Follow the coconuts?" Candice said, puzzling over the meaning of the dream.

"I know," I said. "It's crazy. But I keep feeling like all I have to do is put it into context and I'll have all I need to find Dutch."

"Is there some tree out here that maybe Chase and Laney planted in honor of Hanna?" Cat asked.

"Not that I know of," I said.

"That makes sense," said Candice. "You know, since we've become so earth conscious, people are planting trees for any special occasion."

"Maybe we could call Laney and find out?" Cat offered.

I was already reaching for my cell phone when Candice caught my arm. "Whoa there," she said.

"What? You think it's too early?"

Candice glanced at the clock radio on the table. "Yes, five a.m. may be a bit early for a phone call, but more importantly, my guess is that our friendly Feds are running taps on Laney's phone line."

"Just the same," I said, sitting back again. "I don't know Laney's number anyway."

"Well, it's eight a.m. back East," Cat said reasonably. "Should we call Agent Gaston?"

I looked to Candice. "Still a bit early for that," she said. "Better give it a half hour. Since we're up, let's get something to eat. I know this great twenty-four-hour diner not far from here and we can call Gaston from the pay phone there."

"Why the pay phone there?" I asked. "Why not from my cell?"

"Because we're not sure that Gaston will be on our side," Candice said. "For all we know, he could completely believe Robillard and think Dutch is an agent gone bad."

"Good point."

"We'll eat, then make the call and boogie on out of there. It'll be hard for the Feds to find us from that place. It's a common truck stop, ten miles north of here, and there are plenty of seedy motels along the route to keep them preoccupied if they managed to trace the call and came looking for us."

We got dressed and loaded up the car. We had every intention of returning that night, but Candice's point was that we'd been surprised by the Feds before—best to take everything we'd need with us in case they managed to track us back to the cabin.

I wasn't really hungry when we arrived at the diner, my stress level over finding Dutch intense since I'd seen his awful condition in my dream. Somehow, I had a feeling he was in pain and suffering greatly, and that took away any appetite I might have had.

I waited for Candice and Cat to finish their breakfast, then said, "Okay. I'm going to make the call. Do you know where the pay phone is?"

"It's in the back by the restrooms," Candice said. "We'll pay the bill and wait for you here."

"Cool," I said, and headed toward the pay phone. I fished around in my backpack for loose change and pumped in a bunch of quarters. Dialing the main number for Dutch's office—which I knew by heart—I was rewarded with a receptionist who said, "Federal Bureau of Investigation, Troy, Michigan. How may I direct your call?"

"I need to speak with Special Agent in Charge Bill Gaston," I said. "And it's kind of important."

"Special Agent Gaston is at a summit in Germany. May I redirect your call to the assistant special agent in charge, Agent Robillard?"

"No!" I said, then quickly lowered my voice. "I mean, that won't be necessary. I really needed to try and reach Agent Gaston. Do you know if he checks his voice mail?"

"He does," she said. "But I'm not sure how often. Would you like me to put you through to it?"

"Please," I said. Then I heard some background hold music followed by a confident male voice that told me I had reached the voice mail of Special Agent in Charge Bill Gaston, who was out of the office until October 29. If I liked, I could leave him a message, or contact the assistant special agent in charge, Ray Robillard, at extension 262.

When the beep finally sounded, I said, "Hi, Agent Gaston, my name is Abigail Cooper and I'm Dutch Rivers's girlfriend. I don't know what you've heard from Agent Robillard, but Dutch is in serious trouble. I think he might be gravely injured and I also believe that Agent Robillard is doing everything in his power not to find Dutch and to discredit him in the process. I also believe that there is a connection between Ricardo Delgado, Agent Robillard, and Donovan Kelton, and I believe somewhere in that triangle is the secret to why Cynthia Frost was murdered."

At this point I hesitated as I thought about how to have Gaston contact me so that I could talk to him about Dutch and Robillard and not on a traceable phone. No idea came to me, so I decided to put my trust in the man that Dutch had also trusted and I said, "I'm in Las Vegas. Robillard is searching for me, and I believe when he finds me, he will kill me. I *really* need to talk to you, Agent Gaston. Please call me at the following number. . . ." I left him my disposable cell phone number and hung up the phone, only then realizing how slick with sweat my palm was and how shaky I felt.

I trudged back to the table and sat down. "How'd it go?" Candice asked.

"He's at a summit in Germany until next week. I got voice mail."

"Did you leave a message?"

"Yes."

Candice looked at me critically, and I could tell she knew I'd given my cell number to Gaston. "Kind of risky to have him call you back, ya know."

"I know, but what else are we going to do?"

"That's a good question," my sister said. "What *are* we going to do next? I mean, we're sort of at a road-block here. We can't walk around freely and interview the people we need to. What's our next move?"

Candice took a long sip of her coffee and tapped her fingers on the table. Finally, she met our eyes and said, "You're right. We can't interview the people we need to, so how do you two ladies feel about kidnapping a witness?"

Chapter Thirteen

Cat gasped. "How do we feel about *kidnapping* a witness?" she hissed in a breathy whisper.

"I think Cat tends to frown on it," I said.

"Candice," Cat said. "You can't be serious!"

"Oh, I'm serious," she said calmly.

I held up my hand and said, "Whoa there. So far all we've done is a little impersonating of federal agents, which we both know is hard to prove and probably only a misdemeanor. This is serious shit, Candice."

"Not necessarily," Candice said. Then she pushed her breakfast plate to the side and leaned in. "The key to finding a missing person is to talk to the person that saw them last. And the person that we think saw Dutch last is sitting in a hospital room, probably scared out of her mind and being held against her will. My guess is there's one lowly guard on her, who's likely not even a Fed. They probably have the hospital security posted outside her door. If we can get her out of that hospital, she may be the key to finding Dutch. What if we were able to get into her room, and asked her if she wanted us to help her get out of there?"

"It wouldn't be kidnapping," Cat said with a note of

optimism. "I'm sure my lawyer could get us off if she agreed to come with us of her own free will."

"Are you both *crazy*?" I said. "May I remind you that Jane Doe doesn't remember anything about the night she went off the road?"

"She doesn't have to," Candice said. "She just needs to be in the same room with you while you turn on that radar and give her a reading."

My mouth dropped open and I stared at Candice for a full minute. "That won't work!" I said.

"Why not?"

"Because, Candice, when I do a reading with someone, I need them to help me with the information. If Jane isn't able to confirm what I'm seeing, then the calibration will be off and nothing much will make sense!"

"Have you ever had a session with a client who refused to help you?" Candice said, her face the perfect reflection of reason and good sense.

I sneered at her. "Of course I have, and you damn well know it. I complain about it to you every time it happens."

"Then how is this any different?"

"Abby," Cat said, tugging at my sleeve. "I really think Candice may be on to something here. I mean, what if all Jane needed to bring her memory back was a few recognizable clues to who she is and where she's from? I mean, maybe all she needs is a hint about who she is, and her full memory will come back!"

"This is ludicrous," I said. "It's risky, it's breaking the law, and it could mean that you two end up in prison for helping me."

"You're worth it," Cat said, squeezing my arm. "You're my sister, and I love Dutch like a brother. Candice, I'm in!"

Candice shrugged her shoulders at me. "Looks like we're both okay with it, Abs. Besides, it's the only thing we haven't tried, and judging by that dream of yours, we're running out of time. I recommend we try everything we can while we still feel we have time."

I slumped down in my seat, my heart feeling the pressure of being stuck between a rock and a hard place. "Fine," I said after a moment. "But, Candice, please come up with a plan that doesn't land us in federal prison, okay?"

Candice smiled. "I've managed to avoid it so far, Abs. Maybe the lucky streak will continue."

Several hours later we had a plan, but it was a bit sketchy and it involved someone I really didn't want to include. "Ask her," Cat said for the third time. "Abby, if she says no, then we tried, and if she says yes, then she should fully understand the risks."

"I hate this," I said as I pulled out my phone and looked at the display. "Ah, crap," I said. "The battery died."

"Do you have the charger?"

"Doesn't come with one," I said. "You just get another AAA battery and you're good to go. Candice, can I borrow your cell?"

Candice handed me her phone and I punched in the number I'd jotted down in my notepad. "Hello, Brosseau residence," said Nora.

"Hi, Nora, it's me, Abby Cooper."

"Abby!" she said. "Ohmigod! Are you okay?"

"I'm fine," I reassured her. "But, listen, there's something that I need to trust you with."

"Absolutely," she said. "What's up?"

I explained to her that we were desperate and running out of options and that the only way we knew of to find out what had happened to Dutch the night he went missing was to spend some time with Jane Doe so that I could give her a reading. "That sounds like a pretty good plan to me," she said. "And who knows? Maybe something you say will trigger her memory."

"That's what my sister thinks," I said. "The tricky thing is, as I know you're aware, I don't see how we're going to get to spend any quality time with Jane at the hospital. The FBI might actually frown on her having visitors."

Nora snorted a laugh. "Those guys are all full of themselves," she said. "From what my friend Trina's been telling me, that poor woman's civil rights are being abused."

"Really?" I said.

"Yeah. Trina said that Robillard took Jane to one of the hospital conference rooms and interrogated her for three hours. When she came out, there was a red mark on her cheek and Trina swears Robillard hit Jane."

"No way!"

"Way," said Nora. "As far as anyone can tell, they haven't charged her with anything, but they won't let her leave the hospital. They've got poor Charlie guarding her room."

"Who's Charlie?"

"One of the security guards. He's a sweet guy, about two months away from retiring, and they're making him stand there next to her room for eight hours a day."

"Sounds like everyone's getting a raw deal," I commented.

"So let's do something about it," Nora said. "What we need is to get Jane out of her room. That hospital is a maze—a patient could get lost anywhere."

"I'm open to ideas," I said.

"Well, since she's pregnant, we could—"

"I'm sorry, *what*?"

"Oh, maybe I forgot to mention that. According to Trina, she's about two months along."

My radar was humming, and my mind filled with coconuts. I shook my head. I couldn't focus on the plan if my radar kept sending me signals that made no sense. "It's amazing her baby survived the crash," I said.

"It is indeed," Nora agreed. "But that gives us an excuse to run some tests and get Jane out of that room."

"Won't Charlie need to follow her?"

"Yep, but he'll only go as far as the waiting room in obstetrics. Charlie's a little old-fashioned when it comes to a woman's anatomy. He won't be itching to stick too close to her once the elevator opens on the third floor. If you bring some street clothes for Jane, maybe a hat and some sunglasses, we can give her a good disguise out of Charlie's view."

"How do we get Jane out of there without taking her back by Charlie?"

"We'll need a distraction," Nora said.

My eyes wandered to Cat as an idea hit me. "Leave that to me."

"Great. I'll call Trina and make sure she's on board."

"Do you think she'll be okay with this?"

"Oh, if I know Trina, I know that she will definitely be okay with this. She was absolutely livid when Jane was slapped around by that bastard Robillard. Plus, she's got a soft spot for pregnant women."

"Will anyone get in trouble?"

Nora sighed. "Charlie might get reprimanded, but as I said, he's two months away from retirement. The very worst that could happen would be that they'd have him take retirement early, and trust me, that's not going to bother Charlie one bit."

"Trina won't get in trouble?"

Nora laughed. "That place couldn't run without her. They'll ask her what happened. She'll say that she went to answer a page and when she turned around, Jane was gone. It's not her job to police the patients, after all."

"Nora, I so owe you for this," I said.

"Don't sweat it, Abby. This is the most fun I've had in years!"

* * *

Several hours later we arrived at the hospital. We wanted to blend in as much as possible, so Candice had come up with the brilliant idea to stop at a medical-supply company and purchase a set of nursing scrubs for me, and a white lab coat and stethoscope for her. Cat was the only one of us going as a civilian, but we'd found a terrific way of disguising her. She had a round little pillow secured under a baggy shirt and she looked about five months along. "I think I still remember how to wad-dle," she said as she patted her belly.

"Just don't overdo it," I advised.

"Oh, please," she said with a wave. "I took theater in college. I can totally pull this off!"

Nora met us at the front and handed us two hospital badges. "I've had those for years," she said as we snapped them to our shirts.

"The hospital never asked for these back?" I said, flipping the badge over so that the back faced out and hid Nora's picture.

She laughed. "We're not as big on security as you would think," she said. "Those will be good enough to have you go anywhere in the hospital. Now, Trina will be escorting Jane to obstetrics and she'll tell Charlie that she'll sit with Jane through the gyno exam—"

"There's going to be an exam?" Cat asked.

Nora grinned. "No, no exam, just an empty room for Jane to sit in while you guys talk to her and see if you can convince her to leave with you."

"What if she doesn't want to go with us?" Cat asked me.

I looked sternly at Candice, who was about to answer, so I cut in with, "We leave her there. And that's not open for discussion, Candice. I will not have you guys convicted of kidnapping. Either Jane comes with us will-ingly, or we leave her there."

Candice shrugged her shoulders, giving in. "Okay, Abs," she agreed.

Nora listened to our discussion closely and when we'd

come to an agreement, she continued with, "Trina and Jane will be in room three fifteen at exactly two thirty. I'm going to have Trina paged at two thirty-five. You'll have fifteen minutes to convince Jane to leave with you and exit the hospital. Trina will walk back into the room at exactly two fifty, and when she discovers Jane missing, she's going to alert the staff."

"She'll be covered that way," I said. "No one will suspect she had anything to do with this."

"Exactly."

"Awesome. We've parked in the lower level of the parking garage, so all we have to do is make our way back there."

"You'll want to take the west-end elevator," said Nora. "You'll have to pass through the waiting area, so your distraction for Charlie better be good."

"It will be," I said, eyeing Cat.

"Piece of cake," she said, waving her hand easily. "Leave it to me."

"Do you have the street clothes for Jane?" Nora asked.

I held up the small white garbage bag. "I thought it would look a little suspicious if I was carrying a purse or a duffel bag," I said.

"It would. Garbage bag works," said Nora. "I used to clean out a lot of trash when I was a nurse."

Candice glanced at her watch. "We'd better roll," she said.

Nora gave us each a hug and said, "I'll call you around three to see how it went, okay?"

"You've got my number," Candice said. "And thanks, Nora, this plan is great."

Nora beamed and we walked into the hospital and made our way to the elevators. We were alone in the car and Candice pressed three. "I'll admit, I'm really nervous," I said.

Candice gave me a pat on the shoulder. "It's good to be nervous. Keeps you thinking."

The doors opened at the second floor, and in walked a nurse with purple scrubs and a security guard who looked tired and grouchy as he pushed a woman I recognized in a wheelchair. Jane sat stiffly in the chair as the man who must have been Charlie wheeled her around to face the doors. "Where am I going again?" she asked.

"Obstetrics," the nurse, who I assumed was Trina, answered. "They want to do another ultrasound and make sure the baby is still doing well."

Jane put her hand over her stomach. "I hope it's a boy," she said. "And I hope he looks like his father."

"You remember the father?" Trina asked as the doors closed.

"No. That's why I'm hoping he looks like him. Maybe after the baby's born, I'll be able to remember his dad."

Trina looked at her sadly and the elevator doors opened again, revealing the third floor. We waited for Trina, Charlie, and Jane to get off before we stepped off ourselves. "This way," Candice whispered, pulling us away from them and down the hall.

"Why aren't we following them?" Cat asked.

"We have to wait five minutes so Trina can leave Jane alone in the room," Candice explained. "And in the meantime, I'd rather not have Charlie get a really good description of us while we stand around waiting for the time to pass."

We ducked into the ladies' room and paced the floor until two thirty-five. "Time to move," Candice said. "Cat, do you remember what to do?"

Cat gave a firm nod. "I do," she said. "I'm waiting exactly ten minutes and then it's showtime!"

I looked skeptically at Candice. "A time to worry."

Cat was undaunted. "You wait—you'll see. I should have gone into show business. I'm a natural."

"Okay, Meg Ryan," Candice said. "I'll make sure to send you a little gold statue if you pull this off. In the meantime, stay here for a minute or two after Abby and I leave. Give us time to go into Jane's room."

"Got it," Cat said, and we boogied out of the ladies' room.

Just as Nora had predicted, Charlie was sitting in the waiting area just outside a set of double doors, reading a magazine. I followed right behind Candice, carrying my little trash bag, and tried to look casual.

With all her confidence, Candice could have easily passed for a doctor. She pushed through the double doors like she owned the place and I was close on her heels. We made it down the corridor and counted off the room numbers, stopping just outside of room 315. "Fingers crossed," whispered Candice. Then she opened the door and we stepped inside.

Jane was sitting on the edge of the examination table. Her thin legs were poking out of the hospital gown and her pale skin was turning pink in the coolness of the air-conditioned room. "Good afternoon," Candice said, pulling up the small stool on rollers and taking a seat.

"Hey," said Jane. "Is this going to take long? I wanna get back to my room and watch my soap opera."

Candice regarded her with steely gray eyes and a long pause. "What if you missed your show today?" she asked Jane softly.

"This is going to take a while?" Jane asked, and I could tell she was starting to feel a little uncomfortable under Candice's scrutiny.

"Only if you say yes," Candice said.

"Huh?" Jane said. "Say yes to what?"

Candice looked to me and I leaned against the wall and said, "Jane, we're not here to examine you. We're here to offer you an alternative to being cooped up in a hospital room against your free will."

Jane blinked at me for several seconds before saying, "I don't understand."

"We're not employees here," Candice said. "I'm not a doctor, and she's not a nurse. We're here to help you leave, if you want to."

Jane crossed her arms protectively and seemed to lean away from us. "Why would you help me?" she asked nervously.

"Because we need your help," I said simply. "The car you had the accident in was my boyfriend's. You were holding his cell phone when the paramedics found you. I know you don't remember what happened that night, Jane, but I believe that you hold the key to finding him. I think he's in terrible danger, and I don't believe he has long to live." As I finished my sentence, my voice shook with emotion and my eyes began to water. I swallowed hard and worked to compose myself.

"Abby is a psychic," Candice said, realizing that I couldn't continue. "She's one of the best I've ever met, and we think that by using her abilities, we might be able to help you get your memory back."

Jane seemed to take this in stride, which said a lot for her. "How would that work?" she asked. "I mean, would she read my palm or something?"

I smiled. "Not exactly. The way I work is to focus on your energy, and by that, I mean that I will be homing in on what most people think of as an aura. It's the area around us that surrounds us like the branches on a Christmas tree. And it's by concentrating on those branches that I'm able to describe the events that have affected and will affect you, a bit like describing the ornaments on your particular tree."

"How will I know if you're right?" she said.

I sighed. "That's the tricky part," I admitted. "Without a memory of who you are and how these events relate to you, it will be a difficult session. But Candice and I were hoping that with enough clues brought out during the session, it might trigger something memorable for you. It might even be the key to unlocking all of your memories and finding out who you are and how you ended up in my boyfriend's car."

"And if I can remember that, you think you'll be able to find your boyfriend," she said.

"Yes."

Jane was quiet for a few seconds as she thought about what we were suggesting. I noticed Candice glancing at her watch, and the thin line her mouth settled into told me we had very little time. "What would I have to do?" Jane said.

"We won't be able to hold the session here," I said. "There are too many eyes and ears around, and I don't think the FBI is interested in my psychic impressions right now. We'd have to sneak you out of the hospital, and, Jane, we'd have to go now or not at all."

Jane looked down at her gown. "I don't have any street clothes," she said.

I held up the white garbage bag. "We brought you some new ones. I had to guess at your size, but I figured some medium-sized sweatpants and hoodie would fit?"

Jane smiled and reached for the bag. "They'll be fine." She changed immediately and we put her gown in the garbage bag to take with us. When the alert went out, I wanted to make sure the description fit a woman in a hospital gown.

"Here," I said, pulling up the hood. "Tuck your hair up so that it hides as much of it as possible."

As she did that, Candice went to the door and opened it a crack. Peering out, she hesitated, then opened it wide and waved us forward. "Stick close to us, Jane, and try to act casual."

We walked down the corridor and in the direction of the double doors. Off to the left of us I could see the back of Trina, as she faced away from us and talked on the phone. To the right lay my sister on the ground sipping some water and fanning herself while Charlie hovered over her along with another nurse who was taking her pulse. "Oh, I'm just so dizzy!" she said when she saw us approaching. "Charlie!" she said, grabbing his shirt and pulling him close to her. "Stay with me, won't you? Oh, why is everything going so dark?!"

"I'm right here, Belinda," he said, patting nervously at the hand clutching his shirt.

We scooted by the little scene and hurried to the elevators, which opened almost immediately, thank God. Jane got in first and hid in the corner, Candice and I stepped in front of her to block her from the hallway, and Candice pushed hard on the CLOSE DOOR button. As the doors were closing, we heard Cat say, "Oh, my goodness! I suddenly feel *so* much better!"

The elevator could not move fast enough for my thudding heart. Sweat broke out along my hairline and I struggled not to fidget nervously. The doors opened up to the lobby and we hustled out and down the corridor and turned left. Candice had scoped out the hospital before we met Nora, so our route was direct and quick.

At the end of the corridor we took yet another left, walked about halfway down, and pushed open a door that said STAIRS TO LOWER-LEVEL PARKING.

Candice went first down the stairs, then Jane, then me, my ears pricked for the sound of an alarm, or pounding feet or someone giving chase behind us.

We made it to the bottom of the stairwell without incident and pushed open the double doors to the nearly empty bottom level of the hospital's five-level underground parking garage. Candice had felt the fewer witnesses to our departure, the better.

Our car was parked about fifty yards away, between a pylon and the corner of the parking garage, a tight fit even for the Mini, and it was parked butt to the wall so that if we needed to, we could bolt out of the space without having to back up.

Candice hit the automatic locks and she got into the driver's side, while I got into the front passenger seat and Jane got into the back behind me. Candice started the engine and glanced at her watch. "She'd better be on time," she said.

I glanced at my own watch. "She's still got two minutes," I said nervously. "She'll make it."

My foot tapped on the floor of the car and I craned my neck to watch the door to the garage, waiting for Cat to push through. But the seconds continued to tick on and still there was no sign of my sister.

"Shit!" Candice swore as time ran out. "Abby, I can wait sixty more seconds. Then we'll have to assume something's gone wrong."

I didn't say anything. I just stared hard at that door and prayed for the sight of my sister.

My heart sank when Candice said, "Time's up. We'll have to go to plan B."

Pulling out of the space, Candice pumped the gas and we drove to the ramp that led to the surface. Just then, Candice's cell bleeped.

She looked at the caller ID. "It's from inside the hospital," she said, handing the phone to me so that she could focus on the garage's tight turns.

"Hello?" I asked tentatively.

"I got stuck!" Cat said, almost in a panic. "It was the nurse—she wouldn't let go of my hand!"

"Where are you?"

"I'm in some corner of the hospital, and I have no idea where I am. I think the alarm went out on Jane, 'cuz there are people running around like crazy!"

"What floor are you on?"

"The fifth," she said. "I just jumped into the first available elevator and it took me up instead of down."

"Stay put, Cat, and call me back in exactly two minutes, okay?"

"Okay," she said, and I could hear the fear in her
voice.

I quickly relayed to Candice what had happened. "We
can't go back for her, Abby," Candice said. "If we get
caught with Jane, we're toast."

"I have an idea," I said, thinking quickly. I pushed
the redial number and after two anxious rings I heard
Nora say, "How'd it go?"

"We got separated from Cat," I said. "We're about
to get out of the parking garage, but we can't risk going
back for her!"

"Is she still inside the hospital?"

"Yes. She's stuck somewhere on the fifth floor."

"Can you call her back?"

"She's going to call me in less than a minute."

"Tell her to make her way down to the basement.
That's where the laundry is and there's this little tiny
parking lot that nobody ever uses. Have her meet me in
that parking lot and I'll pick her up. Then call me and
let me know where you want me to drop her off."

I thanked Nora and closed the phone, waiting the last
twenty seconds for the phone to ring. By this time we
had pulled up to the garage entrance and were stuck
waiting behind two other cars in line. "Come on," Candice muttered. "Move!"

Her phone rang and I answered it quickly. I gave Cat
a quick set of instructions and told her to hustle. "I'll
find it," she promised, and hung up.

We inched forward to our turn and Candice whipped
her arm out the window holding a five-dollar bill.
"We're in a bit of a hurry," she said to the man who
took her money and punched some keys on the register
to give her change.

Just then my radar gave me a loud jolt and I turned

my head to look out my window. At that exact moment a black sedan right next to us was rolling down its tinted window and Raymond Robillard was reaching to take the ticket the mechanical box had pushed out. Our eyes met and I felt my blood run cold as I realized who I was looking at. *"Shit!"* I yelled, tugging on Candice's arm.

Robillard's jaw fell open and he blinked, right before he began yelling. Candice gunned the engine just as the arm on the gate swung up, and she punched the gas. We shot forward and raced away from the gate. Behind us I heard the squealing of tires and I turned my head to look. Robillard's car was backing up when suddenly there was a loud crunching sound. He'd hit the car behind him.

"Go! Go! *Goooooo!"* I begged Candice, whose face was set and firm with determination.

"I'm moving as fast as I can, Abs!" she yelled back.

We bolted out onto the street, narrowly missing an oncoming car. "Hey!" Jane yelled from the backseat. "Pregnant lady in the back here!"

"Pregnant lady better buckle up and hold on tight!" Candice shouted as she made a right turn tight enough for two of our tires to leave the ground.

I kept looking back for Robillard as we zipped down a busy four-lane road, weaving in and out of traffic. We got stuck at a red light and I watched Candice stare into the rearview mirror hard. "You son of a bitch!" she said, and I turned my head again to look behind us.

In the distance we could see Robillard, doing his best to catch up to us. Our light turned green and Candice came close to driving into the car in front of us. "Go!" she screamed at the driver. "Move your ass!"

We finally got enough room to zip around him and wove in and out of the traffic around us, nearly clipping a few vehicles in the process. Robillard was several car lengths behind us, stuck in the congestion himself, but he wasn't letting us get away so easily.

Candice came to another intersection as the light turned yellow. "Hang on!" she shouted as the cars in front of us began to brake. Pulling hard on the wheel, she took us onto the sidewalk and lead footed the accelerator, turning the car sharply to the left at the last second before we hit a utility pole, and we narrowly missed getting creamed by oncoming traffic.

"You're going to kill us!" Jane squealed.

"Would you rather I stopped and let you out so Robillard could give you a lift?" Candice snapped. That shut Jane up. She sat back in her seat and gripped the door handle for support.

Candice's phone rang again and I answered it. "I've got your sister," Nora said. I relayed this to Candice.

"Where are they exactly?" Candice asked, glancing in the rearview mirror again and making a face.

I could tell that Robillard was after us again. I hit the speakerphone and asked Nora where she was. "We're a block west of Charleston."

Candice pulled on the steering wheel and we took another sharp right turn. Craning her neck to look off to her left in the direction of a gas station, she suddenly smiled. "Nora!" she shouted. "I need you to hurry as fast as you can to the corner of East Bonneville and Main! There's a gas station there with a small car wash. I need you to pull up to the wash, put some quarters in, but *do not* enter it until I tell you to, okay?"

"Um . . . ," Nora said, sounding a little unsure as to why she was being instructed to pull up to a car wash. "Okay," she finally agreed.

"Good, stay on the phone with me and tell me when you're there, okay?"

We made a few more sharp turns, and my attention was now glued to the passenger side mirror, waiting to spot Robillard, who always seemed to be about a half mile behind us.

Finally Nora said, "Okay, I'm at the gas station."

"Great," Candice said. "Do you see anyone in line for the wash?"

"No."

"Good! Pull up to the box—it takes both coins and bills. I'll pay you back—just please ring up the Super Deluxe wash, okay?"

"I'm almost there," Nora said.

"Candice!" I said as I noticed Robillard beginning to gain on us. It had been a little bit since we'd made a turn, and the street we were zipping down didn't have as much traffic. "Robillard's gaining!"

"It's eight dollars," Nora said.

"Here!" I heard Cat say. "I've got a ten!"

"Damn," Nora said. "It spit the money back out."

"You put it in the wrong way," Cat said. "See? It's supposed to face that way."

"Candice!" I said, my eyes glued to the side mirror. "He's coming up fast!"

"Nora, I really need you to order up that wash!" Candice said as she made another sharp turn and we were suddenly zipping down a narrow back alley.

"Okay, it took my money," Nora said. "Which button is the Super Deluxe?"

Robillard was three car lengths behind and closing in on us. "The green button, I think," said Cat. At the end of the alley was the entrance to what looked like a parking lot, but the view was blocked by a building on the left and beyond that a street. The alley was slick with water and our car slid ever so slightly even while Robillard continued to gain.

"He's right on our tail!" I shouted at Candice.

And at that moment, Candice did something that astonished me. She actually slowed down.

"It says we can enter the wash," Nora said from the speakerphone.

"Nora!" Candice shouted as I pulled my feet up to brace against the dashboard and pushed back into my seat as far as I could while I watched Robillard close the gap between us. "I need you to put your car in reverse and hit the gas on my mark! Are you ready?"

"I'm ready!"

Robillard's grille was ten feet away from our rear bumper.

"Three!" Candice shouted.

The black sedan was five feet away.

"Two!"

"He's going to ram us!" Jane screamed.

"One!" Candice shouted. To the left of us just as we passed the building and light hit our car, I heard a squealing of tires while simultaneously Candice pulled on the steering wheel and our car rocketed forward and left.

Before I knew what was happening, we were airborne, landing with a hard thud in a dark enclosure as our windshield filled with water. Candice didn't slow down. With her foot still firmly pressing the gas, she corrected the wheel and raced out of the wash just as a huge spinning brush came at us and knocked the top of the car.

Behind us, there was a roar from an engine, and my eyes darted to the side mirror, where I had a clear view of Robillard's car rocketing after us while he attempted to chase us through the wash. However, his large sedan hit the entrance at a disastrous angle and my jaw fell open when he ended up bashing his auto against the side wall of the wash, creating a tremendous crashing sound. Like a ball in a pinball machine, he bounced off that wall and into the other. Then the momentum caused him to swerve sideways with much grating and squealing metal until the sedan came to an abrupt stop as it wedged itself between the big blue roller brush and the sides of the car wash. As we accelerated away from the scene, I could see soap foam, car parts, and pieces of broken washer brush everywhere.

"Nora!" Candice said as we made another sharp right and zipped down the street. "Get the hell out of there!"

"Where should I go?" she asked, her voice pumped full of adrenaline.

"Ohmigod, did you guys *see* that? His car is completely wrecked!" Cat said.

I noticed a small grin on Candice's face. "Head to the parking lot of the Las Vegas Hilton. We'll meet you there."

Chapter Fourteen

We exchanged our blue Mini for the red one and met Cat and Nora at the front of the Hilton. "That was some stunt you pulled," Nora said with a big grin on her face. "I almost wish I could have stuck around to take a photo of Robillard's face after he got out of the car!"

"I bet he's a big foamy mess," Cat said with a giggle.

"How did you even know to do that?" I asked her with admiration. "I mean, did you just figure that out on the fly?"

Candice laughed, all the tension from earlier leaving her. "No, I'm not *that* fast on my feet. It was actually a stunt Lenny told me he pulled to get away from a bookie once. To be honest, I'm not even sure how *he* figured it out, but at least the story came in handy."

Nora laughed too. "That sure as hell beats the PTA bake sale I was supposed to attend!"

I glanced at my watch. It was nearly four p.m. "Your kids will be missing you," I said. "You better get home before we get you into any more trouble."

"My mom's in for the weekend," Nora said calmly with a wave of her hand. "I told her I might be out at the sale until after dark. This is a lot more fun. Can I hang with you guys?"

I looked at Candice, unsure.

"I have two dozen fresh-baked Devil's Own Brownies," Nora said, holding up a big plate full of chocolate gooeyness.

That made up everyone's mind. "Of course you can hang with us," Candice said. "We're heading back to the cabin. It's better if we lay low for a while anyway. I mean, I know they'll be looking for a blue Mini Cooper, but a red one with three women might flag someone too."

"Then you'd better make it two women," Nora said. "I've got room in my minivan. Why doesn't Jane ride with me?"

"Gladly!" said Jane, and she jumped into Nora's car behind Cat, slamming the door.

"Some people don't like the way I drive," Candice said with a shrug of her shoulders.

On the way to the cabin we stopped for a few groceries (Nora was like a woman on a mission, racing up and down the aisles, piling up our basket), and I hunted down a package of AAAs for my disposable cell phone. "Has that thing been off this whole time?" Candice asked as we got back on the road and she noticed me putting in a new set of batteries.

"Yes," I said. "Remember? I had to borrow yours this morning."

"And which number did you give Gaston to call?"

"Oh, crap!" I said, realizing my disposable cell didn't come with voice mail. "Well, hopefully if he called before, he'll try again later."

"Let's hope so," she said as we pulled off onto the road to the cabin. We made our way along slowly, with Candice keeping close watch in her rearview mirror for any signs of trouble. No one, however, had followed us or even passed us as we got to the cabin, and I felt myself relaxing for the first time in what felt like all day.

After we'd unloaded the car and unlocked the cabin, I changed out of my nursing uniform back into my Yankees cap and black sweatshirt, and when I came out into the sitting area, I noticed that everyone had found a comfortable place to sit down. Everyone, that is, except for Nora. The woman must have come with her own set of batteries, because while everyone else had collapsed on any old seating surface, Nora went straight to the small galley kitchen and began unloading the bags and fishing through the cabinets for cookware.

"I'll have us a good hearty meal in no time," she sang.

"Can I come live with you after this is all over?" I joked as I took a seat on the couch next to Candice, who nodded in agreement. She and I were cut from the same undomesticated cloth where breakfast was a cup of coffee, lunch came in a to-go container, and dinner was anything that came ready to eat after being zapped in the microwave.

Cat got up to help Nora, and Candice and I focused on Jane, who sat looking scared and timid on a chair by the window. "How're you doing?" I asked her.

"Better now that I'm outta that friggin' hospital," she said. "Thanks for taking such a risk to break me out."

I rolled my head and cracked my neck. "Like I said, we need your help too."

"So how does this work?" she asked curiously.

I took a deep breath and got up off the sofa, moving to the kitchen table. As I took my seat, I waved her over and Candice came as well, carrying a notepad and pen to take notes.

"First, I'll need to get centered and focused," I said. "That may take just a few seconds, so I'm going to close my eyes and do my thing, and then I'll begin the reading, okay?"

"Okay," said Jane, and I could tell she was nervous.

I closed my eyes and took several deep breaths, pulling out my abdomen and filling my lungs with air, then letting it out slowly. Immediately I felt calmer. I quickly ran through my chakras, then pictured a glass dome encircling everyone in the cabin. On the surface of that dome I pictured the glass turning gold and extremely reflective—this is a protection technique that I always employ before the start of any reading to keep out any negative or lower energies that might like to influence the reading.

After that, I called in my crew and I felt them enter my space. *Help me along here, guys,* I said, then opened my eyes and told Jane I was ready to begin. "I realize you won't be able to confirm any of the information I come up with, Jane, but as I give you my impressions, please let me know if anything sounds or feels familiar, okay?"

"Absolutely," she promised.

I looked at the table and asked for anything my crew wanted to give to me. "The very first reference I'm getting is the state of Florida," I said. "Do you have any idea if you might be from there or have lived there in the past?"

Jane actually gasped. "When I was in the shower this morning, I noticed this!" she said, pulling up her pants leg to reveal a small tattoo near her anklebone of the state of Florida.

I smiled. This might work after all. "That's terrific," I said. "Okay, so the next thing that I'm getting is this reference to a diamond ring, and there's something really shiny about it—which makes me think that it might be new."

"Shiny means new?" Jane asked.

"Yes," I said with a smile. "My crew will often give new things, like a new car, a shiny quality to let me know it's new to the owner."

Jane looked at her fingers; she wore no jewelry. "I

don't remember any diamond ring being given to me," she said. "But I'm pregnant, so maybe I was engaged or newly married?"

"Maybe," I said, but somehow that didn't fit with the energy I was picking up from her. "Now I'm getting a tall man with blond hair around you," I said. "Do you have any kind of recollection over who the father might be?"

Jane's face scrunched up and I could tell she was trying to think very hard. "Maybe?" she said. "I mean, sort of in the back of my mind, I think that fits?"

"Don't force it," I advised. "If it doesn't make sense, then it's okay, we'll keep going. All right, now I'm seeing a stage. I feel like I want to get up and dance—do you know if you liked to dance at all?"

"I love to dance!" Jane said in a burst of emotion. "Ohmigod! I know that I love to dance! See? It's working!"

Cat had come over to stand behind Candice and watch the session. "Good job, Abs," she said encouragingly.

"And with this dancing thing," I said, moving quickly to the next series of impressions, "I keep seeing money associated with this. It feels to me like you may actually be a professional. Someone who gets paid to dance."

"Maybe I'm famous!" Jane said.

I smiled. "Unfortunately," I said, "that would be a different set of symbols, so while I don't think you're actually famous, I do believe that you're paid well for what you do." The stage in my mind's eye began to fill with fog and I sat back as I tried to figure that one out. "That's weird," I said, focusing on the imagery.

"What?" Jane asked.

"I can't tell if this is just a metaphor or something about the show you might be in, but my crew is filling the stage where you dance with fog."

"Oh!" said Cat. "I'll bet it's got to do with Cirque du Soleil! They use a lot of fog in their shows."

"Wow," said Jane. "That would be so cool if I worked at Cirque! Abby, keep going!" she said.

"Now I'm getting a school bell," I said. "Jane, do you remember if you were in school?"

Jane's eyebrows furrowed together. "Not really," she said.

My mind filled with a few more images. "There's something to do with health care here, like maybe you were going to school for something in the health-care field."

"Oh!" Jane said, perking up. "That kinda makes sense!" We all looked at her eagerly, so she explained. "See, this morning they were taking some blood from me for some tests and the nurse who was drawing the blood must have been new at it because she couldn't find a vein to save her life, so I ended up taking the syringe and doing it myself."

"You drew your own blood?" Cat said, completely fascinated.

"Yeah," Jane said with a laugh. "How freaky is that?"

My radar was still humming and the images weren't stopping because we were having a conversation, so I interrupted with, "Now I'm getting something about a trip or a vacation. . . ." I tried to feel out the series of impressions I was getting. "There's this feeling of you having taken a trip and I feel like I'm being pulled backward, which to me means that it's in the past. Do you have any kind of memory of taking a trip somewhere?"

"No," Jane said, her face scrunching up again as she tried to recall anything that could confirm that for me.

"That's okay," I said, trying not to put too much pressure on her. "Anyway, getting back to this trip, there's this feeling that it was quick, like you went somewhere and you came right back, and again they're giving me this impression of a diamond ring or some piece of jewelry being given to you. Also—there's this blond-haired guy again connected to this, which tells me that maybe your boyfriend swept you off your feet and took you somewhere to propose."

Even as I said that, I knew it was off slightly, but I couldn't figure out which part felt wrong. The whole of it made sense to me, but my crew was indicating that I hadn't gotten it quite right. "How romantic," Nora said over her shoulder as she stirred something delicious-smelling from the stove.

"Oh! I wish I could remember!" Jane said, balling her hands into fists and rubbing her eyes like a child.

"It'll come if you don't try to force it," Candice advised. "Trust me, Jane, if you push yourself too much, none of it will come back."

When Jane had calmed down again, I continued. "Okay, now they're giving me the impressions of the car accident and something else, like I'm being pulled backward again and there's this feeling like firecrackers or something loud. . . ." My voice trailed off as my mind filled with an image that haunted me. Death Valley.

"Abs?" Cat said, and I realized I'd fallen silent.

I shook my head as if to clear the image still fluttering through my mind. Suddenly, I got up and moved over to where Candice had set down her belongings. "What'cha after?" she asked as I poked through her things.

I pulled up her laptop and brought it back to the table. Pulling it open, I punched the power button and waited anxiously while the screen loaded. "What's happening?" Jane asked.

I didn't answer her. Instead I clicked on a folder and the screen filled with the picture of Dutch and me. Whipping it around, I showed Jane the image. "Do you recognize him?!" I demanded.

Jane's eyes became large round orbs at the sudden change in my demeanor. "I . . . I . . . I . . . ," she stammered as she focused on the picture.

"That's my boyfriend," I snapped. "Do you know him?"

Jane gulped and Cat put a gentle hand on my shoulder, but I pulled away from her. *"Tell me!"* I yelled.

"He does sort of look familiar," she said, sitting back in her chair and crossing her arms uncomfortably.

I pushed out of my chair again and hurried over to my backpack. Shuffling around, I pulled out the picture of Delgado. Pointing to it, I said, "How about *him*?"

Jane squinted at the framed photo. "Maybe I've seen him before?" she said, almost as a question.

I threw the photo into the backpack. "Come on," I said to Candice, my voice filled with a steely edge. "There's someplace we need to take you."

We left Cat and Nora at the cabin. Neither was anxious to ride along with the happy psychic. "I'll have dinner ready for you when you get back," Nora promised. Then she leaned in to whisper to me, "And go easy on her, Abby. She may be involved or she may just have been caught up in something that was beyond her control."

Candice drove—Nora had also loaned us her minivan—and I directed her back toward Las Vegas. It took us only about twenty minutes to get there and I had Candice pull around to the back of the building I pointed out. "Around there," I said, trying not to stare at the giant green cat sitting on the castle turret.

"This looks so familiar," Jane said in a breathy voice from the backseat. "God, I swear I've been here before!"

We pulled into the back of the alley and parked down from the strip club where Delgado had been kidnapped. The crime-scene tape had been removed by now and we got out of the van and looked up and down the length of the alley.

Jane was looking like she'd just seen a ghost, and Candice and I both knew that something must be registering just by the way she began to walk down the alley with purpose, like she knew exactly where she was going.

We followed quietly behind her until she was about two blocks from the club. She stood outside a door with a small window and inside the door was a lit stairwell. Jane reached for the door, but it was locked tight. She stepped back and looked up to the second-story window to the right of the stairs. "I live here," she whispered.

Candice grabbed my arm and gave me a look that said, "Whoa!" I nodded and we waited another moment while Jane worked it out. Finally she moved over to a beat-up garbage can and turned it over on its side. Under the can was one of those magnetized hide-a-keys. She pulled the small metal box off the can and slid the top open, revealing a key. This she inserted into the keyhole of the door and turned it. The door clicked open.

We followed her through and up the stairs to the second floor, and stood outside a door. Jane tried to open that one too, but it was also locked. She looked at the key in her palm, inserted it into the keyhole, and turned, and the door unlocked.

Before Jane could enter, Candice had her hand on her shoulder. "Wait," she whispered to Jane. "Let me check it out first."

Jane stepped aside and Candice eased herself close to the door. Very carefully she opened it a crack and looked into the interior. I was behind Candice and I could tell a light was on inside that hadn't been visible from the window below.

Candice opened the door another inch and a tiny creak sounded from the hinges. She moved it open another crack and scanned the interior of the room just beyond the door. Finally, she opened it far enough to wedge herself through, and Jane and I waited anxiously for Candice to come back to the opening and give us the all clear.

Finally, Candice came back to the door and pulled it all the way open. "It's clear," she said. "No one's here."

We moved into the room and I took in the interior. A large living room opened up to a small galley kitchen, much like the one back at the cabin, and what must have been a bedroom and a bath just down a small hallway.

There was a desk against one wall with a leather chair and a laptop computer sat closed on the desk. My radar hummed and I gave the desk a closer look, and that's when I noticed it. "Oh, God!" I said, dashing to the leather chair where a jacket hung loosely around it.

"What?" Candice asked.

I held up the jacket, my eyes filling with tears. "It's Dutch's," I said.

Candice looked at Jane. "Where is he?" she demanded.

"I don't know!" Jane said, and I could tell she meant it. "I don't even know how I know I live here!"

Candice scowled at her and moved over to me. Taking the jacket out of my stunned hands, she went through the pockets and pulled out Dutch's FBI badge. She gave this to me and I clutched it like it was a talisman.

I left Candice to investigate the computer as I walked farther into the apartment. Jane, meanwhile, was watching both of us like a caged animal. "I swear I don't remember anything else," she said as I passed her on the way to the bedroom.

"I know," I said flatly.

I went into the bedroom and flipped on the light. The bed had been slept in and judging by the way the sheets on the queen bed had been tossed around, I knew a man had occupied it last. I moved to the bed and sat down, staring around the room. A pair of men's jeans lay on the floor, and I reached down to pick them up. I checked the size. They were the same size Dutch wore.

Jane came into the doorway and looked at me with a

guilty expression. "That guy on the computer," she said carefully. "I swear I know him."

My eyes found hers. "How well?"

Jane fidgeted with her shirt. "Really well," she admitted.

It was beginning to add up. All Dutch's quick trips out of town starting from about four months ago. His insistence that if anything should happen to him, I go to Boston and forget about our life together. The secrets, the lies, the deceptions.

I got up off the bed and moved past Jane back to the hallway. Flipping on the bathroom light, I opened the medicine cabinet. Dutch's brand of hair gel and his shaving cream were neatly stored on the shelves there. I closed my eyes and I swore I could even smell his aftershave.

"Abby?" Candice called from the living room.

I shut the medicine cabinet and left the bathroom. "What?" I asked as I went to her at the desk.

"This is Dutch's computer," she said.

"I know."

"You do?" she asked, turning to me.

"Yes," I said. My voice sounded flat and distant in my own ears.

"Well, most of the stuff on it has been erased," she said. "But I did find this in the drawer," she added, pulling out Dutch's passport.

"His wallet was found at the accident," I said. "So he held on to this to allow him to travel with ID."

"That's what it looks like," Candice said soberly.

"We should go," I said. I wanted to get the hell out of the apartment. A million thoughts were flying around inside my head and the foremost of them was the fact that in Jane's energy was a tall blond man who had recently given her a diamond and gotten her pregnant.

"Should we take this stuff with us?" Candice said, pointing to the computer and the jacket.

"No," I said. "Leave it. Let's just go."

Candice ignored me and picked up the jacket and the computer. I gave her a dark look, but she wasn't taking it. "There's more to this story, Abby. I just know it."

Jane followed us out into the hallway. "Hey," she said as we looked at her. "Is it all right if I come back with you guys? I mean, I still don't know who I am, and you were doing so great about helping me figure it out."

"The guy who's been living here can probably identify you," I snapped. I wasn't trying to be rude, but I was feeling a mountain of hurt at the moment.

Jane flinched at the ice in my voice. "I don't remember him," she said. "What if he beats me up or forces me to turn tricks or something?"

Candice actually cracked a smile. "It's fine, Jane," she said. I gave her another dark look, which she ignored as much as the first. "Again, there's more to the story," she insisted.

I sighed heavily and turned away and we left the building, making our way back to the minivan. As we were about to get in, a guy came out of the back and looked at Jane. "Misty?" he said. "Is that you?"

Jane looked at him briefly, shook her head, and jumped into the van.

"Yo! Misty!" he called again as Candice started up the engine. "Where you been, babe? The guys have all been asking about you!"

Candice was in the front passenger seat with the computer. She'd suggested that I drive back to the cabin. "Hit it," she told me when everyone was seated.

I pulled out of the alley with the guy still calling for Misty. From the backseat we could hear Jane begin to cry. "What's the matter, Jane?" Candice said.

"I'm a stripper," she said. "I don't work for Cirque. I'm nothing but a cheap stripper named Misty."

Candice shot me a look and mouthed, "Fog," and I

suddenly realized what my crew had been trying to tell me. I shook my head and focused on driving.

We drove for most of the way in relative silence, other than Candice clicking on the computer keyboard and Jane—Misty—sniffling in the back, but about five miles from the cabin my radar gave a ting and I happened to glance at Candice. She was staring at the computer screen with such a look of contempt that I asked, "What?"

She jumped, startled by the question and the fact that I'd caught her finding something she obviously didn't like. "Nothing," she said, and slapped the lid of the laptop closed.

I turned my eyes back to the road. "You might as well tell me," I said. "I'll figure it out eventually anyway."

Candice gave an audible sigh. "A lot of the hard drive has been erased," she said. "What remains are the recent Internet Explorer searches, and I was able to track a few of those."

"What was Dutch researching?" I asked, feeling like a lead weight had settled into my stomach.

Candice swirled her fingertip on the top of the computer. After a long moment she said, "The last two searches were to the Bank of Las Vegas and JetBlue airlines. I couldn't track the Bank of Las Vegas search beyond their home page, but the JetBlue search revealed that he was looking into booking a trip to Dubai via the Tijuana Airport."

That news flash hit me like a punch in the gut. "Did he book the flight?" I asked.

"Not that I could tell," Candice said. "But the departure date he plugged in was for the day after tomorrow."

"Gives him time to drive to Tijuana," I said, suddenly feeling extremely tired.

"There's more," Candice said.

"Dish."

"He was looking at the price for two adults."

"He's expecting company," I said, and my eyes veered to the rearview mirror, where the reflection held Jane sitting with her knees pulled up and tears dribbling down her cheeks while she gazed forlornly out the window.

When we got back to the cabin, Nora and Cat were just finishing up dinner, which, even though I wasn't at all hungry, still made my mouth water. "Nora has news from the Las Vegas PD front!" Cat said as we entered.

"Awesome," Candice said. "We do too, but you guys go first."

Nora got up from the table and pointed to the chairs around it. "Sit down and I'll get your plates ready while I fill you in," she instructed. We each took a seat and she bustled about the kitchen and filled us in. "I spoke to Bob about ten minutes ago—he wanted to know how the bake sale was going. Anyway, I told you, Abby, that he tells me everything, and apparently Robillard is fine, but his car is totaled and the car wash had something like fifty thousand dollars' worth of damages to it!"

"I hope that comes directly out of the bastard's pocket," I said moodily.

"Not likely," Candice said.

"But that's not the biggest news," Nora continued as she brought our plates to the table and set them down. "The instructions finally came in from the kidnappers of Mr. Delgado."

Candice glanced at me. "Did Bob give you any of the details?"

"Yes, he said . . ." Nora's voice trailed off as her eyes fell on Jane and she seemed to catch herself.

"What?" Jane asked when all eyes turned instinctively to her.

Nora came round and set a plate in front of her. "The kidnapper wants two million dollars and . . . you."

"Me?" Jane gasped. "What do you mean, they want *me*?"

Nora leaned against the kitchen counter. "The instructions are that two million dollars are to be hand delivered to the Jane Doe being held prisoner at the hospital, and direct her to be escorted across the U.S. border into Mexico. Apparently, the kidnappers don't realize you've escaped. They also said that if you're followed, Delgado's a dead guy."

"Too late," Candice snorted, and Nora and Jane looked at her.

"Delgado's already dead," I said. "He died yesterday around noon, in fact."

Nora gasped. "No!" she said. "Oh, those bastards!"

"Bastard," Candice said. "We believe there's only one guy pulling the strings."

I pushed the food around on my plate and I could feel Cat's eyes pinned to me. "Abby?" she said. "What's happened?"

I felt a huge lump in my throat and I found it hard to swallow. Candice recognized that I was on the verge of losing it, so she said, "Abby thinks that Dutch might be behind this entire thing."

A collective gasp went on at the table. "Robillard was *right*?"

And suddenly, my left side felt thick and heavy. Hearing the theory out loud was all I needed to understand that things were definitely not as they seemed. "No," I found myself saying. "It's not Dutch. It's someone who really wants to make it look like Dutch."

"Who?" Candice asked.

"I don't know," I said, and my gut filled with a sense of dread. "But if we don't find Dutch soon, I know in my heart of hearts he's going to die."

"Abby," Candice said. "You've got to try and focus on his location. Ask your crew for any kind of clue! Maybe we can piece it together like we did for Jane."

I closed my eyes and concentrated. Reaching out to my crew, I begged them to tell me where Dutch was.

My mind's eye filled with the image of an oak tree with name tags that suddenly morphed into a palm tree. I opened my eyes and got up from the table and began to pace, scratching my head in frustration. "I can't make any damn sense of this!" I said.

"Sense of what?" Cat said gently.

I looked up and saw the faces of three dear friends and one genuinely concerned stranger. "It's that stupid oak tree and palm tree thing," I said, and a name tag floated into my mind along with the distinct name of *Hanna*.

"That's the stuff you drew on the notepad, right?" Candice said as she got up from the table and hurried over to the pad of paper.

"Yeah," I said, even while I heard Chase's daughter's name over and over in my head like a drumbeat. "Now all I keep hearing is the name Hanna," I said, my frustration growing by the second.

"Hadn't we decided on the theory that a tree might have been planted in Hanna's name?"

"We've got to find out," said Cat. "Abby, we've got to ask Laney if she and Chase planted a tree in Hanna's name. Maybe they planted it at a park or something, and that's where Dutch is, being held captive, tied to that very tree!"

Ridiculous as it sounded, something about what Cat said rang true in my mind. "How can we talk to Laney?" I said desperately. "Robillard's going to have his bozos watching her like a hawk and, Candice, you said they'll have her phone lines tapped! They'll spot any one of us a mile away if we try and get to her."

"Not *every* one of us," Nora sang with a distinct twinkle in her eye. Then she reached over and picked up one of the plates of brownies and said, "Hello, Mrs. Rivers, I'm your neighbor down the street, Susan Hoffman. I heard about your husband and thought you might need a little company tonight. My friends tell me I'm a very good listener."

Candice broke into a big grin. "Nora," she said, "if I ever come back to Vegas and put up a shingle, I'm *so* hiring you for a sidekick!"

Half an hour later we were all in Nora's van with Candice at the wheel parked at the curb one block over from Laney and Chase's house. Nora stood on the street with her plate full of brownies, and my cell phone. "Do you remember the address?" Candice asked.

"I do," Nora said.

"Okay," said Candice. "Now, just cut through that yard like we talked about and make sure you come down the driveway on the other side. If the Feds in that sedan parked across the street from Laney's notice you, they'll think you're coming out of your house."

"Got it," Nora said, and I could tell she was anxious to be on her way.

"Whatever you do," Candice said, "don't make eye contact with the guys in the sedan. It makes them uncomfortable, and if they get uncomfortable, they start getting curious." We had driven down Laney's street a few moments before, and sure enough a black sedan with tinted windows was parked across the street from Laney's house.

"Roger," Nora said, and saluted.

"Call us the moment you move Laney into the kitchen, and make sure the television is on," said Candice. "That way, if the Feds have any listening devices, all they'll hear is the TV."

"Candice," I said gently. "We've been through this. Let her get on with it!"

"Good luck," Candice said.

Nora hurried down the driveway just to our right with her plate of brownies. Candice edged the minivan forward so that we could watch her cut through one yard and into another, quickly hurrying down the driveway lest she be spotted by the homeowners. Once she'd made it to the street beyond, we boogied to the lot of a grocery store, where we wouldn't look so suspicious.

As we found a parking spot, Candice's phone rang and she hit the speaker button. "Hello?" we heard Laney's voice say. "Abby, are you there?"

"I'm here, Laney," I said, feeling a flood of relief hit me. "How are you holding up?"

"Not good," she said. "I'm worried sick about our boys."

"I know, but they're both still alive, if that's any consolation." Before getting in the minivan, I had checked both the photo of Chase and Dutch's computerized image. Chase's photo was fine, but to my horror, Dutch's image seemed to be fading ever so slightly from a three-dimensional image into a slightly more plastic and flat appearance.

"Oh, thank God!" Laney said, emotion clear in her voice. "Dutch came by the night before the accident," she added. Someone had obviously filled her in on Jane's crashing Dutch's car.

"He did?" I said.

"Yes. He stopped by around eight and asked if he could look at my bank records again to make sure the bank was good on their word about removing their fees."

My radar hummed, and I knew that Dutch had had some kind of ulterior motive with this request of his cousin's wife. "How long did he stay?" I asked.

"About an hour," she said. "He looked at my records online, we talked for a little while, then he said he had to check something out, and he was gone."

"Do you know where he went?" I asked.

"No."

"What was he asking you about?"

"Mostly about Chase and me, how we were doing as a couple."

"I don't get it," I said. "What'd he mean by that?"

There was an audible sigh through the phone and Laney didn't speak for a few moments until she said, "I know Dutch didn't share this with you, but about two months ago Chase and I separated."

Candice, Cat, and I stared at one another, completely stunned. "You're kidding," I said.

"It was only for about two weeks or so, but with Hanna and our money worries we weren't getting along at all. One night Chase called me and said he needed some time to think, that he didn't know if he could handle being a father with all this responsibility. I was desperate, and I called Dutch, who flew out immediately and talked some sense into Chase. He hired him to head his security company out here and that gave us some real, steady income for the first time in a long time. Dutch even told Chase that he had a special assignment for him, and I think that gave my husband a real sense of importance. Chase was able to quit working two jobs and he came home and we got on with our lives."

"And since then things have been good between you?" I asked, sensing that there was still a little more to it.

"Honestly?" she said. "No. It's been hard, Abby. Chase is different, and I can't really tell you how or why, but since he's been back, he's been keeping more to himself, and he's not as engaged with Hanna as he was when she was first born."

"Ask her about the tree," Cat encouraged.

"Say, Laney," I said, getting back to why we'd come, "I realize this is a crazy question, but did you and Chase maybe plant a tree in Hanna's name when she was born?"

"No," Laney said. "We didn't. But it's funny you should ask me that, Abby."

"Why's that?"

"Because Dutch asked me pretty much the same thing, but he asked me if Chase had done anything crazy or out of character when Hanna was born. The only thing I could think of was that the day after she was born, Chase told me he'd purchased three cemetery plots."

I stared with confusion at the cell phone. "He what?"

"I know, crazy, huh?"

"And morbid," I said as Candice and Cat both nodded.

"I thought so too, but you have to know Chase. He was working two jobs to help with all our expenses and his second job was as a night watchman at this cemetery. He was fascinated by the place—apparently lots of famous Las Vegas people are buried there. Anyway, he said he got this amazing deal on three plots right next to each other. The cemetery cut him a discount because he'd been doing such a good job at reducing the juvenile vandalism there.

"Anyway, I was furious. I mean, we had just made a deposit on the house and our expenses were really tight with all my school loans and credit cards and the new baby, but Chase has never been good with money, and his reasoning was that it was an expression of love to our daughter. He told me that this way our daughter would be with us forever, from the cradle to the grave."

As Laney talked, my whole body began to tingle. "What's the name of the cemetery?" I demanded.

Laney hesitated before answering, obviously taken aback by my tone. "I . . . I don't remember," she said. "I mean, I'm sure he told me, but I was pretty distracted with school and the baby, not to mention that I was so pissed off that he'd squandered our money like that. I told him I didn't want to hear another word about it, especially when he told me we couldn't get our money back. Neither one of us has brought it up again since then because of all the other tension between us."

"Did he leave any literature about the cemetery around the house? Is there a file or something where you think you might be able to find it?"

"Um . . . ," Laney said. "I'm not sure."

Candice had already reached for her laptop and she was furiously clicking away on the keys. "Was it the Palm Meadows Mortuaries?"

My mind filled with an explosion of imagery. The oak tree morphing into the palm tree and the gravestone emerging up from the ground. "Ohmigod!" Laney said. "I think that's it!"

"Laney!" Candice commanded as she slipped her laptop back into her bag and handed it to Jane, who tucked it next to her. "Tell Nora to get back to the van *now*!"

We zipped out of the grocery-store parking lot and sped back over to Laney's neighborhood. Nora met us in the driveway of the house where we'd dropped her off, puffing and huffing as if she'd been running. We opened the door and Cat helped her in. "We gotta get outta here!" she said. "I was barely down the street before I heard those agents in the sedan run up to Laney's house and start pounding on the door!"

You didn't have to tell Candice twice; she pushed hard on the gas and we sped away as fast as the minivan could go. "Everyone, buckle up!" she ordered.

I pulled the seat belt across and lost the cell phone I'd been holding. "Shit," I said when it slipped under the seat.

"I got it," Jane said.

"It's Candice's," I explained when she tried to hand it back. "Can you put it in her bag with her laptop?"

"Sure," Jane said as Candice pulled hard on the steering wheel and we all swerved to the left.

Ugh! Jane, Cat, and Nora chorused from the backseat as they mashed into one another.

"Sorry!" Candice said. "But here comes another one!" and she pulled the wheel to the right this time.

"I'm moving to the back row," Jane said, and squeezed over the second row to the third row when Candice straightened out the van.

We got onto the highway and wove in and out of traffic. "He's at the cemetery," I said anxiously.

"That's where I'm heading," Candice said.

"Start with family," I said, shaking my head like I really should have known.

"What?" asked Candice, swerving to avoid a collision with a pickup truck.

"When Dutch and I first got to the strip club where Delgado had been abducted, my crew said to start with family."

"And you naturally assumed it was Delgado's family."

"Yeah," I said. "I never did pick up that maybe Chase was behind it all along."

I glanced behind me in the van. My sister and Nora had their eyes pinned to the windshield, and their hands gripped the sides of the van. Jane sat in the very back, her head down, trying to make herself as small as possible.

I turned back to Candice. "You're terrifying the passengers," I said as we swerved again, narrowly missing an eighteen-wheeler.

"Well, I can focus better if no one's talking to me," Candice said with the barest hint of a grin. "Besides, we're almost there."

Candice took the next exit driving sixty miles per hour; the posted speed limit was thirty. She ignored the hint and I felt the minivan's right wheels lift a little off the ground as she made the turn around the exit ramp. "We're going to tip over!" Nora yelled, but Candice regained control and we leveled off on our four tires again.

"The cemetery is up ahead," Candice advised.

"Thank God!" Cat said behind me. "Abby, you drive us after we find Dutch, okay?"

Candice got us to the Palm Meadows parking lot, and the moment the car was put in park, three doors opened and four people leaped out as if the van were on fire. Candice was the last to get out, looking at us quizzically. "Oh, it wasn't *that* bad," she said when she saw our faces.

"Candice," said Cat, "I believe I speak for everyone when I tell you that it really was."

"Come on," I said, moving to the large iron gate that guarded the entrance. I tugged at it and checked my watch. It was well after seven p.m. and the gate was locked tight. "We'll have to go up and over."

"I'm in," said Candice, and the two of us looked at the other three behind us.

"I'm pregnant," said Jane. "I don't think I can get over that thing."

Nora looked at us skeptically. "There's no way," she said as her gaze drifted to the ten-foot fence.

"I'll stay with them," Cat said. "You two will be faster on your own. Call us the moment you find Dutch."

Nora handed me my cell and I tucked it into my back pocket. Candice cupped her hand and edged over to the fence, where she bent down on one knee and braced herself. "I'm going to get Abby to the top of the fence. Then I'll need some help from you guys to go up behind her."

I stepped into Candice's cupped hands and felt myself lifted in the air. "You're lucky you're light," she groaned as I stretched my arms up and gripped the metal railing.

I swung my legs up and wrapped them around the top bar, then pulled up my torso, shimmied over to the other side of the fence, where I swung down, and let go, landing hard on the ground on the other side.

Nora moved over to help Candice. "I'm a little heavier than Abby," she admitted.

"I threw shot put in college," Nora said. "I think I can handle your skinny butt," and with that, Candice was lifted high in the air with relative ease.

She followed my technique and dropped to the ground beside me, wiping her hands. "Again, Nora, anytime you want a job as a sidekick, you're hired."

Nora smiled from the other side of the fence. "Be careful," she advised.

Candice and I turned and headed into the cemetery. There were no lights, but we could still see well enough to vaguely make out shapes. Candice reached into her bag and came up with a flashlight. Clicking it on, she said, "Which direction?"

My radar gave me a tug to the right. "This way," I said, and we trotted forward, skipping around tombstones and flowers. "Over here," I said as we crested a small hill and I moved even farther to the right, my internal compass pulling me forward.

We came to an intersection toward the heart of the cemetery and I gazed around. I had stopped feeling that pulling sensation and I was aware that something was right in front of me, but I couldn't see what. Finally, my eyes fell on a huge oak tree at the top of another small hill and beside that was a white marble mausoleum. I stepped forward onto the road that led there and my foot kicked at a coconut from one of the many palm trees also on the grounds.

I bent to pick it up, remembering my grandmother's advice. "Follow the coconuts," she'd said. My eyes strayed to the ground again and I could just make out what looked like a line of coconuts leading up the hill to the tomb under the oak tree.

"He's in there!" I said, and dashed forward. "Dutch!" I called. "Dutch!"

Candice was right behind me and we hurried to the structure at the top of the hill. As we approached, I could see in the glint of Candice's flashlight the lettering over the metal doors that marked the tomb's entrance. OUR LADY OF SAINTS WATCHES OVER US was carved into the marble wall.

We got to the double doors and I yanked at the handle. It was locked. Inside I swore I heard a moan. *"Dutch!"* I yelled as I pounded on the door. "We're coming!"

"Abby," Candice said, "stand back!"

I did as she instructed and she reached into her duffel bag and pulled out a small tool kit. Handing me the flashlight, she said, "Hold the beam so that I can see the lock."

I did as she instructed and she inserted a key that was in her kit. I was completely puzzled, especially when she took out a small hammer. "Let's hope this works," she said. She put her ear to the key and moved it in and out a little until she was satisfied with its position; then she hit the key with the hammer hard just once and tried turning the key. Amazingly, it turned.

"Key blocking," she said. "Some of the old locks have flat-headed tumblers and this works. The newer ones have rounded tumblers and this doesn't work at all. We got lucky—this is an old lock."

Turning the key more, she pulled at the door and it opened. I dashed around her into the room, the beam of the flashlight darting around the musty and slightly decaying room. "Abs," came a hoarse whisper and my light whipped around and lit on Dutch, but I nearly dropped it when I saw him in the harsh glare of the beam.

"Oh, God!" I said, and ran to him. He was slick with sweat and burning up, his skin several degrees hotter than mine.

He groaned in pain and I noticed his right hand clutching his abdomen. "Something's . . . wrong . . . ," he panted.

"Shit!" I said as I felt Candice crouch at my side. "He's hurt!"

Candice pulled the light from my hand and scanned Dutch. There was no blood, but it was clear he was in agony and fevered. "I think it's his appendix," she said.

Dutch moaned again. "Gotta . . . get me . . . out of . . . here," he said. "It's Chase. . . . He's the one."

"I know," I said, feeling hot tears slide down my cheeks. "I know all about it, Dutch."

Candice was rummaging around in her bag. "Where's my damn phone?" she growled. "It's missing!"

"What?" I said, distracted by the terrible shape Dutch was in. "I've got mine," I said, and quickly reached into my pocket and pulled out my phone. At that exact moment it rang and I jumped. Reflexively I answered it. "Hello?!" I nearly shouted.

"Abigail Cooper?" said a male voice that had a small degree of familiarity.

"Yes, I can't talk right now. I have to call an ambulance!"

"It's Agent Gaston," he said quickly. "What's happened?"

"It's Dutch!" I yelled into the phone. "He's in bad shape! He needs an ambulance!"

"Where are you?"

"I'm at the Palm Meadows Cemetery at a tomb in the middle of the graveyard!"

"Stay put," Gaston ordered. "I'll send help immediately!"

Dutch moaned again and Candice, who was still rummaging around in her bag, pulled something out and handed it to me. "Here," she said as she gave me a bottled water. "See if you can get him to drink."

I tried getting some water to go past Dutch's lips, but he was shivering so hard much of it just spilled down his front. "Shit!" I said, easing him back against the wall.

"Help should be here soon," Candice said, but we were both alarmed by how bad Dutch looked.

That's when I thought of something and I flipped the lid of my cell back open and punched in some digits. The line on the other end rang and rang, then went to voice mail. "Shit!" I swore, and suddenly I had an image of Jane in the backseat of the minivan with her head bent. On a hunch I punched in some other digits and to my surprise the line was picked up by Jane.

"Hello," she said, answering Candice's phone. "Jane!" I said when she answered. "What are you doing with Candice's phone?"

"I had a text to send," she said easily.

A slow creepy feeling traveled its way up my spine, but I ignored it and focused on what I needed. "Put Nora on the phone," I demanded. "We've found Dutch and he's in terrible shape! He needs medical help, and he needs help now."

"Stay put," she said. "We'll be there in a minute."

A second later the line was cut and I realized that Candice had suddenly stood up and was listening intently to the noises outside. I was so confused that it took me a moment to realize there were voices in the graveyard. "I think help's arrived," Candice said hopefully.

My left side didn't agree and my anxious mind began to put two and two together. "Son of a bitch!" I swore as it all clicked into place. "She fucking texted him!"

"Who?" Candice asked, thoroughly confused.

"She had your phone!" I said as I remembered telling her to put the phone into Candice's bag after I'd dropped it. "She remembers everything, Candice! She sent a text to Chase! I think he might even be *here*!"

Candice stared at me for a full three beats before she said, "We've got to go!" Grabbing Dutch under the arm, she said, "Take his other side. Maybe there's a place we can hide until the ambulance arrives."

Candice and I labored to pick Dutch up off the ground.

He moaned loudly and hot tears stung my eyes. "Come on, babe," I said to him. "We're going to get you out of here."

We were almost to the mausoleum's door when voices outside became very loud. An argument was taking place just beyond the door and Candice and I stopped to listen. "How could you do that?" I heard my sister say. "How could you just *leave* him when he's your own cousin!"

"I told you to shut it!" said an angry male voice that sounded eerily like Dutch's.

"I will *not* shut it!" my sister retorted. "You abandon your wife and baby, and you leave your cousin in some tomb? What kind of monster are—?!" Cat never finished her sentence.

All we heard was a loud slap and a gasp followed quickly by Jane's voice. "Chase!" she said. "Don't do that!"

Candice motioned to me. "Set him down," she whispered, and we did. She then moved toward the door, clicking off the flashlight, and we waited silently in total darkness. I stood near Dutch, with my heart pounding and my fists balled. We heard the door creak loudly on its rusted hinges and in the tiny bit of light we could see a figure enter. There was a shuffling noise from where Candice had been standing, and in the next instant a loud scream echoed off the four walls of the tomb.

The mausoleum was suddenly illuminated by two bulbs hanging from the ceiling and to my astonishment I could see Candice gripping Nora in a choke hold. Nora was shouting to be let go as Chase stood behind them with a gun, his finger still on the light switch.

"Thought you might try something like that," he said as he shoved the gun squarely into Candice's back.

Candice had by this time let go of Nora, who was rubbing her neck and looking angrily at Chase. "I'm the mother of four!" she yelled at him. "How *dare* you make me go first through that door!"

"I'm sorry," Candice whispered to her.

"It's not your fault," Nora said, stepping back as more people came into the now-crowded room.

My sister came in, followed by a wide-eyed Jane. "Chase," she begged. "Don't hurt them. They were nice to me."

He glanced at her. "As long as they're willing to cooperate, baby, no one gets hurt."

I looked pointedly at Dutch. "Except your own flesh and blood, right, pal?"

Chase glanced at me. "You must be Abby," he said. "I've heard all about you."

"Fuck you," I snarled.

Chase pulled his gun out from Candice's back and pointed it at me. "You'll find I'm not as nice as my cousin," he said in a warning tone.

"Oh, well then," I said, feeling the heat of an anger so deep fill me up completely, "let me rephrase. *Fuck you!*"

Chase's face hardened to a granite look that was eerily similar to Dutch's. His finger curled around the trigger as we stared each other down. "Don't!" came a throaty whisper. "Chase . . . don't do . . . it."

Chase glanced at his cousin and scoffed. "You'd thank me in time," he said, but pulled his finger off the trigger.

I glanced at Jane, who had her hand on his arm and was shivering in fear. "Baby, please!" she said. "Please don't hurt them!"

I realized suddenly that in the odd lighting of the tomb her jawline matched a photo I'd seen before. "You were with Chase in the car at the bank," I said. "It was the mustache that threw me. It was thick enough to make us all believe you were just a skinny guy."

She glanced at me in surprise, then gave me a small nod.

I then turned my attention back to Chase and his cut lip and bruised eye. "No makeup needed for that look, though," I said. "I'm guessing you got that from Delgado?"

Chase gave me a mirthless smile. "He put up one hell of a fight getting into the trunk of Misty's car," he said.

"And I'm sure he gave up an even bigger fight when it came to his diamonds," Candice said.

"Five million in stones," Chase said. "Kind of tough to ignore that kind of temptation, if you know what I mean."

"So you killed him," I said, shaking my head and trying to let it sink in that someone so bad could be related to someone so good.

"It was an accident," Chase said, and waved his pistol at the wall, where we all suddenly noticed a huge rust-colored stain. "He jumped me when I came in here to bring some aspirin to Dutch. We fought and my gun went off. All I wanted was the stones and Misty. I just wanted a chance for a clean slate and a new life without always having to live up to my cousin. I mean, do you know how hard it's been all these years? Dutch is like some kind of hero in my family, Mr. Goody-goody. Hell, even my wife worships him."

"He saved your *ass* from debt collectors and all kinds of financial trouble!" I yelled at him. "He gave you a chance to be a man, Chase, not a no-good loser!"

"There's just no saving some people," Chase said sarcastically. "I could never live up to my good old cousin Dutch. Everyone would always look at me as being second-best. So, one day, I decided that if I couldn't be the best good guy, maybe I'd be the best bad guy."

"But what about your wife? Your baby?" Cat said. "How could you just leave them?"

"Trust me," he said. "They're better off without me."

"Make no mistake about it," Candice said to him in a deadly calm voice. "If anything happens to Dutch while you two are off making your getaway, I will hunt you to the ends of the earth, and I will kill both of you without a second thought."

My heart welled with emotion to have a friend like Candice in my corner. "And I'll keep her well funded for as long as that takes," said Cat, rubbing the red mark on her cheek. "Count your breaths, Chase Rivers. They are definitely numbered."

Chase regarded us moodily. "I'll send an ambulance once we're up in the air," he said. "He can hang in there another couple of hours."

"No, he can't," Nora said, bending down to Dutch and feeling his brow. "He's septic. I'd give him maybe an hour, but it might already be too late."

My heart seemed to stop and I knew that Nora was telling the truth. "You've killed him!" I screamed at Chase. "You fucking bastard! He's your own flesh and blood!"

"It's his own fault!" Chase roared back at me. "If he'd just left it alone, none of this would have happened!"

I did something then that I've never done before. I lost my sanity. When they talk about crimes of passion, where all cognitive thought leaves you and some animal instinct takes over, I know exactly what they're talking about. I flew at Chase. His eyes became large round orbs registering his shock and he moved to point his gun at me, but he didn't get off a shot before I slammed into him and pulled him into my knee, just like I'd seen Candice do.

He doubled over and I grabbed a fistful of his hair, slamming his nose into the hard marble floor. *"You bastard!"* I shrieked. *"You . . . stupid . . . fucking . . . piece of shit . . . bastard!"*

I could feel something hit my back, and sharp nails scratched at my back. "Let him go!" Jane yelled, but I wasn't even close to finishing the pummeling Chase deserved.

I stood up and slammed my elbow back hard. It hit Jane in the chest and she let go of me. Then I started kicking Chase with all the strength I could muster. "I hate you!" I kept shouting. "I hate you, you bastard!"

He was rolling around on the ground, trying to get away from me, but I followed him and kicked and kicked and kicked. I was panting hard, but I kept going . . . until a shot rang out just over my head. Then everybody froze.

Chapter Fifteen

"Ah," said an oily male voice. "Dinner *and* a show. You just have to love Vegas." I knew without looking up that Robillard had finally tracked us down, and I also knew that meant we were all as dead as the bodies laid to rest around us. In the distance I could also hear the sounds of sirens, and I realized with a leaden feeling that I'd heard them faintly when I was kicking Chase and hadn't been aware until just this second that they had seemed to come close to the cemetery, but were now moving away into the distance.

"Oh, don't let me stop you," Robillard said when I finally looked up at him. "Continue on, Miss Cooper. It will help with my alibi when I tell my colleagues that I walked in on a scene of total carnage. I'm thinking of making it look like the end of *Hamlet,* you know, how *everybody* dies?"

"Go to hell," I said, my chest heaving as I stepped away from Chase, who was curled up in a fetal position holding his nose, which was bleeding through his hands.

Robillard smiled evilly. "Spoilsport," he said, then seemed to notice that we were all listening to the distant sound of sirens. "Ah yes," he said. "The cavalry. They were initially directed to the cemetery, but on their way here another call came in. Apparently you and your merry band have been spotted half a mile south, in the parking lot of a Wal-Mart."

"Oh, no," my sister said, and a quick glance told me she'd begun to cry.

Robillard ignored her. "What I want to know before I kill you, Miss Cooper, is how you knew about Cynthia."

"She told me," I said, enjoying the look of surprise on his face. My satisfaction, however, was short-lived as that look was replaced quickly by skepticism. "Don't believe me?" I asked coolly.

"Don't tell me," he said. "You had some vision where she came to you in a dream and gave you all the gory details," he said, and the oil sound in his throat became extra slick.

"Not quite," I said, still cool and calm, hoping that by keeping him talking, I might give Candice time to try one of her famous karate-chop moves. "It wasn't a dream, but Cynthia did show me her entire murder scene. How you and she met at her house late one night and sat in the kitchen at the table. You were wearing this light blue suit, and a thin black knit tie with a gold tie clip. I remember you were also wearing a wedding ring, but that's a thing of the past now too, huh?" I said, pointing to his left ring finger.

I had Robillard's full attention, and I could tell by the flick of his eyes that he had barely resisted the urge to glance at his own hand.

I continued. "There were big sunflowers on the wallpaper, and her dishwasher was on in the background along with the television. I remember hearing the music to *The Tonight Show,* so it must have been right around eleven thirty at night, right? You and she sat at a table and she said, 'It's all there, Ray,' and that's when you pounded the table with your fist. She asked you to keep it down because her daughter was upstairs sleeping, and that's when you struck. You got to your feet, almost casually, pulled her from the chair, twisted her around, and snapped her neck. You killed her in about three seconds flat. Then you grabbed that folder and left."

"Fascinating," he said, and pointed his gun at Candice, who had made the tiniest movement forward in his direction. "Careful, Miss Fusco. I promise you I'm a very good shot."

My heart sank. Robillard knew whom to keep his eye on. That didn't stop me from trying to distract him, however. "What I want to know, Ray, is, what did she have on you?"

Robillard's smile broadened. "Now, now," he said. "Some things are better left in the past."

"Stolen mob money," Dutch croaked. "She knew you'd helped Delgado hide the money he took from his Mafia boss back in Spain."

Robillard's eyes roved over to Dutch. "Agent Rivers, I underestimated you," he said. "Yes, we split the money. I met Delgado in Brussels at a restaurant. Can you imagine what a coincidence that was? Here he was, informant to the CIA, being handled by some young, barely out-of-training agent—Kelton—and he and I meet casually at a restaurant. We struck up a friendship, and he explained that he was having some difficulty with his handler. His faith in the CIA to get him safely out of the country and into the U.S. did not run deep, and while he liked Kelton, he didn't feel he had the pull at the agency that was necessary to get Delgado to safety.

"I agreed to privately mentor Kelton. We saw each other in the Belgium office on occasion, but I was working mostly with a KGB informant at the time, so our relationship appeared to everyone else to be quite informal. We'd have lunch and I'd give him advice about how to wind Delgado through the system and help him get settled in the U.S.

"It was at one of these lunches one afternoon that

Kelton revealed that he not only knew the exact amount that Delgado had stolen but where the money was hidden. He'd kept this information private, until he'd had a chance to run an idea of his by me."

"The plot thickens," Candice said with a snort.

Robillard regarded her with his cobralike eyes. "And so it does," he said. "Kelton suggested that the three of us do some creative financing. He explained that the agency had never really known how much money Delgado had stolen. He was very evasive when it came to facts and figures, and he'd told three different agents three different amounts over the months that he'd been an informant.

"What can I say? The idea of ten million dollars split three ways in the late seventies was very attractive and I succumbed to the temptation. We devised a plan to report the lowest figure that Delgado had given as the actual amount he'd stolen, and sock the rest of the money away for ourselves. I know that the higher-ups at the agency always suspected there might be more, but they could never actually confirm the amount. So, the three of us agreed to turn most of it over to the agency, and we very quietly secured some funds for our own individual retirement plans.

"Everything went smoothly until I received a call from the accounting department. Kelton had been the subject of some intense scrutiny as the money trail began to wind its way back to him. He was Delgado's handler, after all, and the agency was suspicious of the amount that had been turned over, as the Spanish mob boss in custody continued to insist Delgado had stolen more than he'd turned over to our agency. Kelton was given a lie detector test, which he didn't quite pass, and he resigned rather than put up with being further scrutinized.

"He and Delgado remained close, keeping each other's secrets, and neither of them ever gave me up, but that could be because I had some insurance on that end."

"You know about Kelton's sexual preferences," I said with a distasteful scowl.

"Yes, and I also had influence with certain higher-ranking members of the immigration panel who renewed Delgado's visa every six years. One word from me, and Delgado could have been flown immediately back to Spain."

"Where he'd be assassinated before he even got off the tarmac," Candice said.

"Precisely."

"Which doesn't explain how Cynthia figures into this," I said.

"Ah, yes. That droll-looking toad of a woman. She was a nothing at the agency, a joke really. The only one who ever took her seriously was Gaston, claiming she was a *genius* when it came to numbers, so the agency kept her on. Mostly she worked audits on old files, just to make sure things were on the up-and-up. And some-how she tracked the money down to the very Belgian bank we each had our accounts in. She believed I was her ticket to being respected, you see. She figured if she brought me in, she'd no longer be a joke. But we all know who got the last laugh there," and Robillard made me queasy with the derisive laugh he had at what he believed was a fond memory.

"Once she was taken care of," he continued, "we moved the money to a more secure Swiss-bank-account location, and the three of us were able to breathe easily. Then, in a stroke of genius and to make sure no one ever tracked us to the money again, I kept the investiga-tion of Cynthia's murder going, blowing smoke where I needed to or pulling the case away from eager beavers who were in danger of discovering things they shouldn't. And for nearly thirty years no real leads were ever turned up, until, of course, I discovered that our rising star here, Agent Rivers, was doing some digging into the lives of my dear friends out here in Vegas. Speaking of which, where is my old chum Ricardo?"

"He's dead," Dutch said, and his fevered face turned menacingly to his cousin. "He tried to escape and Chase shot him."

"It was an accident," Chase said, still on his hands and knees.

"Well then," Robillard said, "all I'll need is those diamonds, Mr. Rivers, and we can get on with it."

Chase looked up at Robillard, his face a bloody mess. "What diamonds?" he said, but it was obvious he knew.

"I discovered that a plane matching Delgado's description had landed at a small Arkansas airport," Delgado said. "No flight plan had been filed, which is the pilot's responsibility, and since you were the pilot, I can only assume you didn't want anyone looking into Ricardo's trip to visit his diamond mine."

Chase didn't say anything; he just glared at Robillard. Robillard sighed. "I see you don't think I'm serious," he said, and aimed his gun at Jane. Not even a second later a shot rang out. She yelped once, clutched her heart, then dropped to the floor.

All of us were so stunned that no one moved for several seconds. Robillard then aimed the gun directly at Chase. "The diamonds, please?"

Chase was shaking and didn't seem to be able to take his eyes off of Jane. "Why?" he began to sob. "She was pregnant!"

"I'm going to count to three," Robillard said. "And if I get to three, you will lose the ability to father another bastard. One . . ."

"Jane!" Chase wailed at her still and bleeding form.

"Two . . . ," Robillard said.

Chase's shaking hand reached into his coat pocket and pulled out a fist-sized black velvet bag. "Here!" he shouted, holding it out to him.

Robillard smiled. "Three," he said, and pulled the trigger again.

Chase fell straight back and Dutch shouted, *"Nooooo!"*

Robillard moved over to Chase and picked up the bag, tucking it into his suit pocket. He looked at Dutch's anguished and shocked face for a long moment before he said, "For digging into things that don't concern you, you'll be the last to go." Then he swiveled slightly and aimed the gun at me.

I took an involuntary step back and put up my hands defensively. "Stop!" I said, my worst fear unfolding in front of me. "Don't!"

"This is for the car wash," he said with a sick and twisted smile, and the gun fired.

I sank to my knees and grabbed my chest and it was a moment before I realized I was face level with Robillard, who had also sunk to his knees and was grabbing his own chest. The difference was, it was his chest that was bleeding.

Stunned, I looked around and saw Nora holding a gun with smoke still curling from the tip. "That was for Jane!" she said. "And this is for Cynthia, you rotten piece of garbage," she added before pulling the trigger again and making a round hole dead center in Robillard's forehead.

Robillard's head snapped back and he fell to the marble slab with a sick, dull thud.

Several hours later I sat with Candice and Cat in the lobby of the emergency room, wrapped in a blanket and sipping at some coffee. "It's been hours," Cat said, getting up to pace the floor again. "You would think that we would have heard *something* by now!"

"Here comes Nora," Candice said, pointing down the hallway.

"Jane's out of surgery," Nora said. "They think she's got a pretty good chance."

"What about her baby?" Cat asked.

Nora smiled ruefully. "That kid is holding on tight," she

said. "Jane is still pregnant, but it's too soon to tell what effect the drugs and anesthesia will have on the fetus. Still, it's a really good sign that she hasn't miscarried."

"And Dutch?" I asked, anxious for more good news.

"He's still in the OR," Nora said. "But that's normal," she added when she saw my worried expression. "A ruptured appendix can take a long time to clean out. We got really lucky just getting him here in time. Another half hour and he wouldn't have made it."

"Can I join this party?" Bob Brosseau asked, coming up behind his wife and carrying two cups of steaming coffee.

"How'd it go with Laney?" I asked. Bob had been tasked with delivering the news about Chase.

"She's a tough one," Brosseau said. "She said she'd been waiting for us to show up, because she felt Chase had died suddenly right around eight o'clock, which was almost the exact time that Robillard killed him, right?"

"It was," I said sadly. "After I know Dutch is okay, I'll head over to her house."

"Does she know everything?" Cat asked.

"She does now," he said. "A social worker is staying with her until Chase's mom and aunt can arrive. I mean, it's not bad enough to learn that your husband's been killed, but to find out he's a kidnapping murderer who tried to steal his cousin's identity and bolt out of the country, well, that's tough."

"Imagine how poor Dutch is going to feel," I said. "He loved Chase like a brother and trusted him to help look for evidence against Robillard when Chase does the double cross."

"Have you found Delgado's body?" Candice asked.

Brosseau nodded. "It was in a shallow grave not far from the mausoleum."

"That was one hell of a good hiding place," Cat said. "I mean, who the hell would ever have thought to look in there?"

"He chose it well," Brosseau said. "The mausoleum belongs to the Hurston family. They've been a prominent family here in Vegas for almost seventy-five years, and the last time they buried someone was in the sixties. I called the family and they said they haven't even been out there for ten years."

"I've never heard of a tomb with electricity before," Cat added.

"Allows the family members to visit day or night," Brosseau said. "I'm sure Chase replaced the bulbs in there once he decided to use it to hide Delgado."

"Do we know how Robillard eventually tracked us down?" I asked. "I mean, how did he even find us?"

"Your cell phone," Brosseau said. "His guys confiscated Wyatt's phone and found a number that was registered to a disposable cell. They assumed that's the phone you were using and all he had to do was wait for you to use it one more time and get a hit off a tower to help triangulate your position."

"And I used it to talk to Laney and then to Gaston."

Bob nodded. "Once he saw that you were on your cell, he was on his way over to intercept you when the police scanner announced a call for an ambulance to the cemetery. He figured you were calling for help, and made sure to redirect the troops."

"He almost got away with it," Candice said, then looked gratefully at Nora.

"He did," Bob said, also beaming proudly at his wife. "How're you doing?" he asked her.

"I'm fine," she said, and the way she said it I could tell she'd reassured him several times. "Really, Bob. I don't feel bad about killing Robillard. He would have murdered all of us if I hadn't done something."

"Where did the gun come from?" I asked, still curious about that.

"Chase dropped it when you were punching his lights out. I spotted it about five seconds before Robillard shot Chase," said Nora.

"Well, I'm grateful," I said to her. Nora made a sound that said it was nothing.

"Excuse me," said someone off to our right, and we all looked up to see a man in a dark suit standing nearby. "Miss Cooper?" he said, holding a cell phone out to me.

"Yes?"

"Special Agent in Charge Gaston would like to speak with you."

I took the phone from him and got up from the group to talk to Gaston. "Hello?" I said wearily.

"Good morning, Abigail," Gaston said. "Is there any word on our boy?"

"He's still in surgery, sir," I said.

"Well, I'm sure he'll pull through. Dutch is as tough an agent as ever I've had the honor of working for me, you know."

My eyes misted a little. "I do know, sir."

"And you? How are you holding up?"

"I'm okay," I said. "Just worried about Dutch."

"When you get word that he's come out of surgery, my men will take you to any hotel you'd like and put you and your friends up until Agent Rivers has made a full recovery."

"Thank you, sir."

"I'm leaving the summit early and heading back to Michigan to take care of any loose ends around Robillard. I'd like to personally thank you, again, for your involvement in this, Miss Cooper. I know it came at great personal risk."

"I'm just glad we don't have to worry about him ever again," I said.

"There's one more thing I'd like to ask of you, if I may?"

"Yes, sir?" I said.

"There's a case we're working here in Michigan. It involves the disappearance of some kids from college and we think we may have another serial killer on our hands.

I understand you're very gifted in the sixth-sense department."

I smiled. "It's come in handy in the past," I said.

"I'd like to invite you officially to take a look at the evidence and get your impressions. I'll clear it with Dutch, of course, to make sure that he's on board, but what would you say to helping us out on this one?"

"It would be my honor, sir," I said. Just then there was a tap on my shoulder and I turned to see Nora wearing a huge smile on her face.

"Dutch is out of surgery!" she whispered. "He came through it fine, and the surgeon says he thinks Dutch's chances are excellent!"

I felt all the tension leave me and I almost sank to the floor with relief. "Oh, thank God!" I said, and filled Gaston in.

"That's wonderful," Gaston said kindly. "Go be with your boyfriend, Miss Cooper. You and I can chat later."

Dutch spent a week in the hospital and his family put off Chase's funeral for a few days to allow him to attend. It was an awfully sad affair, given the details that had come out about Chase's double life. I worried the most about Laney, but she turned out to be a woman to reckon with.

Misty officially changed her name to Jane but not before she was sent to prison for three years for her role in the kidnapping of Delgado. She narrowly escaped a murder charge, as, under Nevada law, if during the commitment of a felony (like kidnapping) a person is murdered, all accomplices can then be charged with that murder, regardless of who actually pulled the trigger. So even though Jane wasn't with Chase when Delgado was killed, she still could have been charged.

The DA was talked out of the charges, in fact, by none other than the dragon lady herself, Mrs. Delgado, who was afraid that all the sordid details of her husband's extracurricular activities would come out in the trial, along with the fact that Jane cooperated fully in giving up the details relating to the kidnapping of Delgado, Dutch and even an attempt to kidnap me.

Jane revealed that a few months earlier, right after Chase left Laney, Dutch found his cousin and Jane together, shacking up in Jane's small apartment. With a whole lot of effort, including a job offer and promises of financial support, Dutch convinced his cousin to go back home to his wife. And Chase did go home, but he wasn't willing to give up Jane, so when he discovered she was pregnant, everything changed.

It was Dutch, in fact, who had given him the perfect opportunity to escape his stressful life when he asked Chase to help investigate Delgado and Chase learned of the diamond mine. He hatched the kidnapping plan soon afterward, pushing Jane to help him by withdrawing a few pints of his own blood and storing them in the fridge to use at the scene of the kidnapping so that everyone would think he'd also been abducted and likely killed.

But Chase got greedy, and he got sloppy. He knew his wife had just received some cash in the form of the student loan, and Chase figured it was enough money to see them out of the country to a place where he could safely fence the diamonds.

Dutch admitted later that he caught on when he saw the photo of Jane with her fake mustache and a beaten up but otherwise physically sound Chase—something just seemed fabricated about the photo and it pushed him to look a little deeper.

Meanwhile, Chase had Delgado hidden in the mausoleum, and he intended to wait just long enough for the heat to die down before releasing Delgado so that he and Jane could slip out of the country, but a suspicious Dutch showed up at the apartment and nearly ruined all of Chase's plans. The two fought, and Chase gave Dutch one sound blow to the back of the head, which took Dutch out of the struggle quickly. He and Jane moved

Dutch to the cemetery, then a panicked Chase ordered Jane to drive Dutch's car back to the Strip and find me by using Dutch's cell phone with its built-in GPS. His instructions were for her to locate me and appear frantic. She was to explain that Dutch had been wounded, and offer to take me to him. Chase was aware of my inboard lie detector, and it seems he was careful to word it so that I wouldn't be overly suspicious.

Chase wanted me out of the way, because he was convinced that I had been the one to send Dutch after him, and he wanted me and my intuition safely locked up until he could make his getaway.

Jane reported that when she was driving on her way to the Wynn, she was trying to turn off the ring tone because I kept calling and that's when she lost control of the car and crashed into the ravine.

Dutch said that's when Chase really came unglued. He didn't want to leave without Jane, and he suspected that the FBI was already aware he might have gone over to the dark side, so he began to take on Dutch's persona, gathering the same hair products and aftershave to try to become his cousin as much as possible, and the two definitely looked close enough in appearance for Chase to pull it off. He also intended to use Dutch's passport and badge to make his way to Dubai, where he and Jane and their child could live off the diamond money for the rest of their lives.

But we all know it didn't quite work out that way for Chase, who, ironically, was buried in the very same plot he'd purchased for himself when his daughter was born, although Laney admitted she probably wouldn't be taking the slot next to him when her turn for burial came up.

And in an even more surprising twist, it was Laney who offered to raise Jane's son until she was out of prison. Laney reasoned that she couldn't bear to watch little Chad (the name Jane chose for her son) end up in foster care, where he might very well follow in the criminal footsteps of his father. Jane eventually agreed, and Laney made sure to take Jane's son for regular visits to the prison.

Candice, Cat, and I returned home with new cars and new friends. Nora still keeps in touch with us, and has not given up coaxing me into the kitchen with her "very easy to follow" recipes. Uh-huh . . . tell *that* to the fire department.

As for Dutch, he was quick to recover in body, but his conscience has suffered a deeper wound. He's been working hard to forgive his cousin, and he worked even harder to forgive himself. His reasoning was that if he'd never enlisted his cousin's help to spy on Delgado and get the evidence he needed against Robillard, Chase wouldn't have been tempted.

I'm trying to be his voice of reason with that one. I mean, we all take responsibility for our own actions, and Chase was an adult who made really poor choices. In time, I'm sure Dutch will see it that way too.

In the meantime, he and I have a bad guy to catch . . . but that's another story.

Read on for a sneak peek at
Victoria Laurie's next Psychic Eye Mystery,

DOOM WITH A VIEW

Coming from Obsidian in September 2009

I entered the grungy-looking house with Candice close on my heels. Our FBI escort, the assistant special agent in charge, Brice Harrison, came along a minute later, after he'd wrapped up his cell phone call out on the porch.

The interior was a surprise given the house's rough exterior. The wallpaper was from an earlier era but had a sunny print that still held some glow, the carpets were worn but well cleaned, and pictures and paintings on the walls had been hung with care.

We entered through the breezeway into the living room. The sofa was upholstered with faded roses, and pink throw pillows trimmed in gold were neatly placed at each end. A crucifix hung on the wall above the sofa and a long outdated copy of *House & Garden* magazine lay on one side table; the other held a cute yellow lamp and a porcelain angel. Near a window was a wing chair, and next to that a small table with knitting needles and yarn.

I moved into the kitchen and surveyed that too. It was small, with rather outdated appliances, but spotless and clean. "Are you getting anything?" Candice whispered.

The volume on my radar was dialed up to high, but

nothing about this space had so far signaled an alarm. My mouth pulled down into a frown. Surely if something violent had happened here, I'd know it, wouldn't I? "Not yet," I answered, and drifted out into the dining room.

Four chairs sat demurely around an oval dining room table covered with a crisp white tablecloth. I ran my hand over the fabric; it was soft cotton. I glanced at the walls, which were covered in wallpaper with a more formal print than in the living room. I glanced around some more, not sure what I was really looking for.

"I'm guessing the bedrooms are down that hallway," Candice said, motioning to the opposite side of the dining room, where there was a doorway that led to the back of the house.

I nodded and noticed that Harrison was leaning against the kitchen doorjamb. "Getting any hits yet?" he asked with a smug smile I badly wanted to remove.

"Give me a minute," I said, even while I was feeling the pressure. Since Candice and I had arrived in D.C., I'd done a really lousy job of converting the skeptics at the bureau. I moved quickly down the hall, out of Harrison's view, and into the first bedroom on the right. Dim light trickled in through the peacock blue curtains at the window. A full-sized bed with a white handmade quilt dotted with blue squares was the focal point of the room. To the side of the bed was a simple nightstand, and on that was a Bible.

I walked into the room and closed my eyes, willing myself to pick up on anything that might give me a clue about what had happened here. Nothing but soft, warm energy enveloped me. "Shit," I said under my breath.

"Nothing?" Candice asked, her tone now worried.

"I don't know what it is!" I said quietly. "Maybe I'm so nervous out here that I'm blocked or something, but I keep coming up with zilch."

"Let's try another bedroom," she suggested.

We moved a bit farther down the hall, passing the bathroom on the right, and went into the second bedroom, which was obviously the master. The moment we turned the corner into the room we both sucked in a breath, and Candice reflexively grabbed my arm tightly. "Holy mother of God!" she gasped.

I was so horrified by the scene that I couldn't even breathe. The mattress had been fully exposed—no sheets or bedspread remained on it—but on its surface were giant rust-colored stains so dark that they had to go all the way through. The headboard and wall above the bed were dotted with thousands of red dots and wretched-looking splatters. A broken lamp lay with shards of porcelain all about the nightstand, and more droplets were clustered around the beige carpet near the bed.

I glanced toward the ceiling and was repulsed to see that blood had even been spattered up there, freckling the overhead light fixture with small rust dots.

"Jesus!" I finally managed, and stepped out of the room, taking in big gulps of air.

"Not a pretty scene, is it?" said Harrison, who had joined us in the hallway.

"What the freak *happened* in there?" I exclaimed as I looked at Candice, who was starkly pale and looking as queasy as I felt.

"You're supposed to tell me," said Harrison, reminding me of our deal. I had one last chance to prove myself to this guy, and that was to tell him about the death that had occurred in this house.

I took a few more deep breaths and looked at Candice for moral support. "It's okay, Abs. You can do it," she said. Good old Candice, a true supportive friend if ever there was one.

I swallowed hard and tried my best to suck it up, but for the record, the last thing on earth I wanted to do was tune in on what horrible fate had befallen the person who lived here, and by the surroundings I was guessing it was a sweet old lady who'd done nothing to deserve the violence that had so obviously been unleashed here.

Finally I pushed away from the wall I was leaning against and moved back toward the doorway of the bedroom. My eyes didn't linger on the blood spatter about the room; instead I closed my eyes and inhaled deeply, doing my level best to try to center my energy so that I could utilize my radar. I called out to my crew and asked, *What's happened here*?

I then braced myself for the visions I was certain would flood my mind, but instead I was quite surprised when all I saw was a stage. *I don't understand,* I said to my crew. *I need to know what happened in this room!* Again, a stage filled the vision of my mind's eye, but off to one side I noticed some stagehands working on scenery, as if they were getting the set ready for a play.

I squeezed my eyes shut and concentrated as hard as I could. *I don't understand!* I mentally shouted at my crew. *I don't get what a stage and set decoration has to do with anything! I need to see the murder here! Show me what happened!*

Suddenly, the image in my brain changed, and I had the distinct feeling I needed to go back to the kitchen. I snapped my eyes open and turned around to head back through to the kitchen, bumping into Harrison in my hurry to get there. "Sorry," I called as I practically ran there.

I could hear Candice's footfalls behind me as I reached the doorway to the kitchen and looked around, waiting for a sign from my crew. I got one when I felt a tug on my energy over to the sink. I moved there and looked around. Nothing near the sink called my attention even though my eyes darted back and forth, searching for the thing on which my crew wanted me to focus. *Outside,* I heard in my head, and I immediately looked up and out the little window above the sink. The house directly behind the one I was in seemed to glow with urgent energy.

My mind's eye filled with the image of a chalk outline, and a gravestone that read RIP. "We're in the wrong house," I said breathlessly. "The murder didn't happen here!"

"What?" Candice and Harrison said together.

I whipped around and stared angrily at Harrison. I knew he knew the truth of it. "That's a staged crime scene," I said, yanking my head in the direction of the master bedroom. "The woman who lived here died of natural causes. There was no murder."

Harrison's smug expression immediately turned to one of shock, but was quickly replaced with a cop's faceless expression. "That's correct," he admitted. "No one was murdered here."

"You are a total asshole!" Candice shouted at him, her hands balling into fists.

"The real murder took place over there," I said, pointing to the house behind us.

Harrison's cop face was quickly replaced with one of triumph. "Wrong," he said, the smug smile returning to his lips. "There was no murder. This house belonged to the widow of the former head of the FBI. She left this place to the bureau when she passed away quietly in her sleep a few months back, and we've been using it as a staging ground to train agents ever since."

Candice's face was full of rage. "You mean you purposely brought us to a fake crime scene just to throw her off?"

"It beats having her get to a crime scene staged by a murderer out in the real world and pumping us full of false info," Harrison snarled back, the friction between him and Candice heating up again.

"You have got to be kidding me," said Candice, her temper flaring again. "That is total bullshit, Agent Harrison, and you know it!"

I was about to add to Candice's comment and tell Harrison where he and his little FBI buddies could all stuff it when my radar insisted that I turn around and look at the house behind us again. I did and kept seeing a chalk outline. "Something happened there," I said again. "Something bad went down in that house right behind us. And it happened recently."

"Nothing happened there," Harrison said, glancing with annoyance at the house I was pointing to. "I told you, *this* is the staged crime scene."

I looked at Candice. "Come on," I said to her. "Let's check it out."

Without another word Candice and I walked over to the back door, which led to the backyard.

"Hey!" Harrison called. "You can't go trespassing around out there!"

Candice and I ignored him and walked through the door, Candice making sure to slam it behind her. "You're sure someone was murdered over here?" she asked me as we trudged our way through the leaves on our way to the other house.

"I'm positive *something* happened," I said. "I mean, I don't expect to find a dead body, but I want to get close enough to make sure the energy I'm picking up is right."

Behind us we heard Harrison yank open the door and begin to chase after us. "I'm serious!" he said. "That's private property!"

I flipped him the bird and kept walking. I didn't care if he was Dutch's new boss; he'd finally pushed me over the edge. When I got close to the house I quickly jogged over to the back door and rapped loudly three times.

Candice stood next to me and rubbed her hands as the cold wind blew around us. Meanwhile Harrison had come up and attempted to grab me by the arm. It was the wrong move in Candice's opinion, 'cuz the next thing

I knew Harrison was twisted around with his nose against the wall of the house and his right arm pulled up at an odd and painful angle behind him.

"Ach!" he shouted, and tried to twist out of the lock she had him in. But Candice merely pulled up harder on his arm while pushing hard into his back.

"Move a muscle and I'll break it, Agent Harrison," she said menacingly.

"You're assaulting a federal officer!" he shouted at her. "I can put you away for good on just that!"

My attention had left the door and I was now staring slack-jawed at my partner, who had apparently lost her sanity. "Candice," I said in a low, even tone. "Really, honey . . . that's not necessary."

"Knock again, Abby," she said with a strange calm. "And if no one answers, head around the house and look in all the windows. Let's make sure before we get hauled off to jail."

I gave another three raps to the door and called, "Hello?" but no one answered. I then cupped my hands and peered through the window of the door. There was a sheer curtain over it, but I could just make out the shapes inside.

After a moment I stood back and gave Candice a sober look. "Let him go," I said tiredly. Candice hesitated for a few seconds. "I'm serious," I said. "Let him go."

Candice gave one more small tug on Harrison's arm but finally released him, and he wasted no time in whipping around and grabbing Candice roughly by the shoulder and slamming her into the side of the house, where he cuffed her hands behind her back. "You are under arrest," he snapped, then looked at me as if he was weighing whether to call in reinforcements.

"Go ahead," I said, for once giving him a smug smile. "Call in the cavalry. Oh, and while you're at it, you'll need to call the coroner too. There's a dead guy on the floor in there. By the looks of it, he's been dead at least a week."

Harrison stared at me for a full minute, no doubt trying to decide if I was bluffing. Finally, he pulled Candice along the wall toward the door and ordered me to sit down on the ground with my hands on my head.

I humored him by sitting down and lacing my fingertips above my head, but I continued to smirk at him.

After I was sitting all nice and quiet-like, Harrison edged over to the window and peered in. I watched with great satisfaction when his head whipped back as if he'd been slapped. "Shit!" he said, and yanked the cell phone from his waistband. "Bentsen?" he barked into the phone. "It's Harrison. I need a team of techs, agents, and the coroner to meet me at the back of the staging house, pronto!"

Candice, who was still pressed up against the side of the house, squirmed her head far enough to give me a big, gorgeous smile. "Way to go, Abs," she said. "Way to go."

Penguin Group (USA) Online

What will you be reading tomorrow?

Tom Clancy, Patricia Cornwell, W.E.B. Griffin,
Nora Roberts, William Gibson, Robin Cook,
Brian Jacques, Catherine Coulter, Stephen King,
Dean Koontz, Ken Follett, Clive Cussler,
Eric Jerome Dickey, John Sandford,
Terry McMillan, Sue Monk Kidd, Amy Tan,
John Berendt…

You'll find them all at
penguin.com

*Read excerpts and newsletters,
find tour schedules and reading group guides,
and enter contests.*

Subscribe to Penguin Group (USA) newsletters
and get an exclusive inside look
at exciting new titles and the authors you love
long before everyone else does.

PENGUIN GROUP (USA)
us.penguingroup.com